MW00912756

Born in September 19(
South Wales with only
boy, she found employ
education and early writing. *The Pea-Pickers*, based on those early
years, was published in 1943. Her second published novel
appeared in 1954. The rest of her novels, all unpublished, are
held in the Mitchell Library of the State Library of New South
Wales. Eve Langley spent seven years in a psychiatric hospital
and later changed her name to Oscar Wilde.

IMPRINT CLASSICS

THE PEA-PICKERS

EVE LANGLEY

*Introduced by
Lucy Frost*

An imprint of HarperCollins*Publishers*

AN ANGUS & ROBERTSON BOOK
An imprint of HarperCollinsPublishers

*First published in Australia
by Angus & Robertson Publishers in 1942
Reprinted 1943, 1958, 1966, 1976, 1984, 1989
This Imprint Classics edition published in 1991 by
CollinsAngus&Robertson Publishers Pty Limited (ACN 009 913 517)
A division of HarperCollinsPublishers (Australia) Pty Limited
Unit 4, Eden Park, 31 Waterloo Road, North Ryde
NSW 2113, Australia*

*William Collins Publishers Ltd
31 View Road, Glenfield, Auckland 10, New Zealand*

*Angus & Robertson (UK)
77-85 Fulham Palace Road, London W6 8JB, United Kingdom*

National Library of Australia
Cataloguing-in-Publication data:

Langley, Eve, 1908–1974.
  The Pea-pickers

  ISBN 0 207 17172 6

  I. Title.

A823.2

Cover: Minos of the Shades, *(detail)* 1952
by Jean Bellette b. 1909 Australian
oil on canvas, 59.4 x 74.6 cm
Purchased 1952
Courtesy: National Gallery of Victoria, Melbourne
Printed in Australia by Griffin Press Limited, Netley, South Australia.

5 4 3 2 1
95 94 93 92 91

INTRODUCTION

When *The Pea-Pickers* was published half a century ago (1942), it was praised as a celebration of Australia, a joyful book, expansive, marked by the vigour of a youthful narrator wandering the byways of a young nation.[1] In recent years it has been read as autobiography, sometimes by critics who discard 'Steve' altogether and write 'Eve' for the narrative voice, as if nothing stood between the character and her creator. Given the horrors of Eve Langley's life, this approach casts quite a different slant on the book.[2]

While all texts alter in the reading, *The Pea-Pickers*, with its meandering plot and picaresque heroine,[3] seems particularly elusive. Like a kaleidoscope, the novel's configurations form and reform. In my reading, I am looking for Steve. Later, I shall return to Eve Langley.

Steve is an intriguing character. There is no one else quite like her in Australian fiction. Never satisfied, always reaching beyond the moment for the ideal and eternity, she swaggers through her world with bravado uncharacteristic of women. From the first she is determined to construct the self she wants, regardless of what other people think. She even does her own naming. Before she is 'Steve' she is without identity, the undifferentiated 'I'. The name she chooses comes laden with stories: 'the comic literature of the Australian bush has always had a Steve in it and, of course, we had always loved Steve Hart in that bushranging song that Mia sang to us now and again.' The literature of the bush was, as this mother and her daughters knew well, a male preserve: to enter its discourse as subject, a female must take on (in both senses) 'maleness'. This happens when 'I' becomes 'Steve'.

Cutting across boundaries set up to exclude female from male in a culture with rigid gender separation, Steve begins in high spirits the journey which shapes the narrative. Power seems hers for the taking. She renames her sister/companion, transforming June into 'Blue', and arranges their jobs as apple packers for Mr Nils Desperandum. Together the sisters fashion clothes to suit themselves. At the end of the twentieth century no one would think twice about their garb — khaki overalls for working, tailored trousers with silk shirts and ties for swanning about — but the novel is set in the late 1920s when dresses belonged to women and pants to men. Women in pants could be charged with impersonating men — as if clothes were currency, and their crime, fraud.

Steve and Blue will learn this when, seeking work in northern Victoria, they are questioned by the police. The girls are outraged and chagrined. They are not, they insist, impersonators denying their femaleness. Their quarrel is with clothes as ontology.

Clothes are never neutral. They position the wearer in society. The more stringent the dress code, the less space for individual manoeuvre. Steve, hemmed in by assumptions about femininity, pushes against the barriers. She is nineteen when the novel starts, an age for turning from somebody's daughter to someone else's wife. She says no to this socially constructed scenario, and instead sets out to be an adventuring heroine, in charge of her own life and telling her own story. Literally and figuratively, she is the subject of sentences with active verbs.

But not always. The *cri de coeur* heard again and again is couched in passive form: 'When will my two great desires, to be loved and to be famous, be satisfied?' These desires are a drain on autonomy. To be loved requires a lover; to be famous, an audience.

Although tension between the desire for autonomy and for love is common to narratives of many a romantic novel, *The Pea-Pickers* gives the theme strange twists. Steve's longing to be loved is not as simple as it first seems. On the surface, all is orthodox: here is a woman who wants the love of a man.

The prose, though never directly, questions this. To begin with, Steve's descriptions of the men she loves makes me as a reader wonder how I can be expected to believe they are sufficiently attractive to arouse heterosexual ardour. Never are they written as erotic. Sixteen-year-old Kelly Wilson is introduced as a grotesque: 'a short, bow-legged youth with a great head of golden brown hair, two narrow blue eyes that roved from side to side, a hooked white nose, and a flat red mouth with two white teeth in it.' He sits across the room, 'staring at me with fixed hypnotic eyes,' and under this gaze, 'Down I fell, in love.'

The playing out of this love reveals more about Steve's sexuality than she either can or will admit. As she moves toward the first kiss (representing in the text initiation into sexual contact), she flails about, abruptly switching tone and topic. Steve is intensely anxious. She and Blue have gone to the local races on Easter Monday at the invitation of Kelly's mother. For hours they picnic and do tomboy things, like swinging on gum-trees. Suddenly Steve — oppressed by 'misery' for no specific reason — goes off on her own, lies down on the ground, and studies the sky. There she sees a cloud 'shaped into the face of an Egyptian woman . . . the mutilated lips trembling into dissolution'. Kelly's kiss, when it comes, is likened to 'a blow from a hairbrush'. Though this may not be mutilation, it is scarcely alluring. Steve is led immediately to thoughts of an old man who cannot leave the bottle once he begins to drink. She then imagines consequences rather nearer the bone:

> And with youth, by the time the feelings of passion have gone, we are under the coverlets, wedded, bedded, with little interminable gongs called 'offspring' that will not run down until they are jammed with bread and milk.

Steve walks home with Kelly, kissing, as 'our blood mounted'.

Afraid of desire, I tried to remember some saying of a great man. Tolstoi. 'Women are like dogs. They have no soul,' he said. 'They have,' I cried to heaven.

Steve is determined to prove she has a soul (and is not a dog):

There was the cold but happy ideal of the virgin in my mind, forever, a joy and a torment to me, and I laughed as we parted, saying, 'We conquered . . . we conquered. Hands and heart go pure to bed.'

This is all very high-minded, but is it not also the rationalisation of sexual distaste? Steve's image of the cloud as a woman with mutilated lips is telling (and from that cloud, after the kiss, 'a few hot drops fell'). She has not enjoyed Kelly's actual kiss, even though he aroused desire.

The pattern of Steve's response to men has been set in this episode, and never changes. A man who wishes to touch her threatens defilement. Her admirers are represented as aesthetically unappealing (like Charles Wallaby) or racially inferior ('I felt that to be loved by an ex-camel-train driver from the East was an abasing thing').

The one seeming exception is Macca, whom Steve certainly desires. But even here, she opts for the transcendental. She divides Macca into body and soul. His body (like Kelly's) is an occasion for comedy. He is freckled, pigeon-toed, and during the one night she invites him to sleep in her bed ('decorously'), his 'calm animal sound maddened me'. She strikes him sharply and sends him grumbling away.

Macca snoring is flawed, and Steve wants perfection: 'I shall work on him, and make him more complete in body, mind and soul than the gods.' This is a tall order. To fill it, Steve casts herself into the role of ultimate subject, of creator. The material with which she works is language. As poet, she will refashion the world and its people.

Macca is entranced for a while. Steve's words do cast a spell over him. But in the end her vision (associated throughout the novel with the moon — high, pure, cold) loses its appeal. Earthbound, bodybound, Macca learns to dance the Charleston, and spends his evenings with less articulate girls. When Steve and Blue come back to Metung in the spring, Macca stays up at Black Mountain, sweet on a cattleman's daughter. Men inevitably disappoint Steve. They refuse to be de-sexed, and she will have them no other way.

The bodies from which Steve takes pleasure belong to women. Asleep in the hut with Blue, she delights in her sister as she will in no man, although the love of men is a convenient cover here for a touching that is taboo:

> We were in love . . . And, as we snored side by side in dreams, we toyed with each other's hands in joyful bliss. When we awoke, we recognised each other with a grunt of disgust and jumped over to the other side of the bed.

There is no future in this relationship, however, and ultimately Steve insists that Blue return to town to marry a man who has no presence in the text at all, not even a name. Blue would rather stay with her sister:

> 'If you would only adventure with me, all over the world, and be my mate, I'd never marry, and I'd be as happy as the day's long,' said poor Blue . . .

> As we lay in bed, Blue talked over the old days in the alps, and tried to persuade me to take her as my mate, forever. But I was anxious to be alone, so that I could win Macca's love back; and I fended her off by telling her that she would be happier married.

Steve's explanation to Blue is disingenuous. Her sister has nothing to do with retrieving Macca. The motive provided by the narrative remains unacknowledged on the surface of the prose. Steve's interest has shifted from her sister to another woman.

Just before this conversation with Blue, Steve pays a visit to the woman she calls the Black Serpent. She goes there impulsively, stopping in the middle of pea-picking — the only time in the novel she walks away from work:

> I put down my tin of peas, and walked out of the paddock down to the hut. There I dressed myself in breeches, pressed by Karta's iron, silk shirt and blue tie. I took my gun, and walked with a firm tread and swinging hips out on to the open road which burnt white and deep in the morning sun.

Guns were carried by Kelly and Macca when they were wooing Steve: 'This is how the bush courted.' Steve (who has become a collector of guns) now positions herself as a male in the courting ritual.

In contrast to the grotesque and comic men, the Black Serpent is physically alluring. The first time she met Steve,

> she took my hand in her own sensuous clinging one and pressed it warmly, while she smiled, catching her lower lip delicately with her teeth, and her breasts swayed as she moved towards the bedroom taking us in to talk for a moment.

Happy, fertile, exuding sexuality, she is at ease with her body and its desires. She always kisses Steve (whom she calls 'Stess' using 'Tess' to obliterate the boy's name she hates) full on the mouth. These kisses — unlike Kelly's blow from a hairbrush — are welcome.

And that is Steve's problem. To admit the attraction seems wicked — or so the Biblical references suggest. Allusions to the story of a serpent tempting Eve to eat of forbidden fruit recur throughout the novel. St/eve sits hulling strawberries with Macca and the Black Serpent, who smiles 'with a writhing of ripe mature lips over her teeth'. That evening on the lake shore, Steve and Macca perform a symbolic marriage ceremony, exchanging vows of eternal love. Sex has nothing to do with this. Although Steve claims she 'longed for his touch, his kiss', she keeps to the ethereal: 'his love is too pure for that.' They spend the night together in the hut, 'innocent and undesirous', while above them 'the black serpent and its mate sang in the rigging and writhed joyfully'.

Eventually the 'purity' will drive Macca away. Steve, agonised and unconsolable, turns to the Black Serpent for comfort. That seems straightforward enough, one woman lamenting to another the loss of her man. The prose, however, shifts attention from Macca to the woman whose presence stirs the senses:

> 'Hello Stessa!' she called to me, and kissed me with frank lips on the mouth. She flung her large arm around my shoulders, and we walked into the house that I loved.

Inside, the women talk in the code of those whose cryptic interchange is sexually charged, and dangerous. They are interrupted:

> Her little son came in . . . She kissed the little boy and nursed him tenderly, richly. I was jealous. Perhaps she guessed this, for she kept him by her and kissed him many times. At last, I could bear it no longer. I wished to be alone with her, and talk freely of no one but Macca.

Macca acts as a socially (heterosexually) acceptable shield. He is irrelevant to the jealousy Steve feels while the Black Serpent caresses her little boy, who is himself a decoy, used by his mother to arouse another woman.

Or so Steve suspects, although she never allows her guesses full rein. As soon as she registers what is happening between herself and this voluptuous female, she runs to Macca for cover, refusing to admit that her wish to be alone with the Black Serpent is born of physical desire. She is confined within the puritan strictures of her community. Its values are hers, even when she rails against them. She and Blue are always sensitive to wagging tongues, although the gossip invariably posits the girls as harlots, not lesbian. That possibility cannot be spoken; it is taboo.

Steve, torn between the desires of her body and the values of her culture, is prey to self-loathing. She knows from the beginning of the novel that whatever sort of woman she is, she would rather be a man. She has internalised a hierarchy which begins with God and descends first to man, and then to animals. 'Man' is generic in this form. When the hierarchy becomes more specific, it separates man from woman. Man (soul) is closer to God, while woman (body) threatens a downward pull toward the animal.

Steve's prose is saturated with this way of thinking. Once, taking a lift with an Italian on her way home to Dandenong, she begins transforming the landscape into heroic terrain, waxing lyrical over 'these Italian roads'. The driver treats her as woman, stops 'the truck in alarm, and made me eat some bananas, with some vague Darwinian theory possibly rumbling through his mind'. Women are less evolved. They are closer than men to animals — and at their most alluring are serpents.

Steve, hating the category to which she has by her body been assigned, aspires upward: 'I knew that I was a woman, but I thought I should have been a man.' Then she would be soul, not dog. And . . . if she were a man, she could love women, the Black Serpent, her sister Blue.

In the novel's final section, Steve finds her femaleness repellant (not just undesirable, as it was in the beginning). Like Eve, she has fallen into a knowledge which alienates her from her body. Bitter, mocking, she parodies her longing to be a man:

> I became hard, masculine and truculent in manner, swore and blasphemed, became passionately fond of guns and bullets, killed every living thing I could see around me, and grew to love with a fierce mirthless joy, adventure and extravagant comedy. I was alert for men to offer me insults, so that I might take them as a cue and work them up into a

theatrical act, well rounded off, which I would perform before the Buccaneer and the Black Serpent.

But her performance of the masculine is always limited by her body. Her breasts give her away. As if they had a life of their own, they exaggerate and thus parody her femaleness while she is playing male. Why, asks Blue, 'do you wear the strap of your rifle under your breasts? It makes them look huge'. Steve's response to her femaleness comes straight from the Bible: 'I was ashamed.'

No, she says immediately to her sister, 'I shan't go home with you. I couldn't bear to be at your wedding . . . who knows, I might even wear the rifle strap under my breasts there, and confound the clergy.' The eyes of others remind her of her breasts. Only if she is by herself can she forget them. The novel finishes with the stark sentence, 'I was alone.'

There is pain in this, and power. Her stance is defiant, and uncomfortable. The love for which she hungers goes unsatisfied. Fame is only a hope for the future. But these are the desires expressed in passive mode, and Steve has successfully resisted their siren call. She remains the subject of her life and of her prose.

*　　　*　　　*

Eve Langley left Australia for New Zealand in 1932.[4] There, between March and the end of May 1940, she wrote *The Pea-Pickers*. She was thirty-five years old, the mother of two children under the age of four, and pregnant. Her husband, Hilary Clark, was a painter obliged to work as a labourer in a quarry to support his family. They were desperately poor, and the marriage was unhappy.

In writing the novel, Langley drew upon journals kept between 1925 and 1928 when she was an itinerant farm worker in Gippsland and the Ovens Valley. Most of that time she was with her younger sister June. When they first went to Metung, the shocked locals referred to them as 'the Trouser Women'.[5] More than a decade later, these seemed halcyon days, not just because they were days of youth and were past, but because in 1940 'this dreadful war was raging around us'.[6] Langley saw in Hitler and Mussolini the incarnations of gods like those Steve sought in Kelly and Macca; her enemies were the Japanese . . .

Langley's world, past and present, affects Steve's, but the connections need to be made with care. The novel is more than a writing up of the journal; it is an autobiographical novel, but that does not make it autobiography. Langley herself saw the difference in terms of a struggle between time and the author for narrative control. In a journal (or autobiography), time wins. In a novel 'the creative mind' holds sway. 'The surge and the mastery'[7] belongs to Langley. Narrative moves and is shaped as she decides. Time, fidelity to the past, no longer has her in thrall.

Ironically, the novel which marked freedom from time was written to an inflexible deadline set by the conditions of entry for an Australian award, the Prior Prize. Langley was bent on winning. To her delight she did, sharing the first prize of £300 with two other writers. By the time the book was published in 1942, she was in the Auckland Psychiatric Hospital, where she would be kept for seven years. Her husband committed her.

One further Eve Langley novel appeared: *White Topee* (1954). She submitted many more to Angus & Robertson, and among her voluminous papers held by the Mitchell Library are ten unpublished manuscripts.

In 1960 Eve Langley left New Zealand for a hut in the Blue Mountains of New South Wales, where she died in June 1974. Her body was not discovered until weeks after her death. She had been living, like Steve, alone.

LUCY FROST
Melbourne 1991

(1) For the most enduring example of this approach, see Douglas Stewart, 'A Letter to Shakespeare', in *The Flesh and the Spirit*, Angus & Robertson, 1948, pp. 30–38.

(2) Marion Arkin, 'Literary Transvestism in Eve Langley's *The Pea-Pickers*', *Modern Fiction Studies* 27:1 (Spring 1981), pp. 109–116; Harry Heseltine, 'Eve Langley, Oscar Wilde in the Blue Mountains', in *The Uncertain Self,* Oxford University Press, 1986, pp. 112–130; Joy Hooton, *Stories of Herself When Young: Autobiographies of Childhood by Australian Women* Oxford University Press, 1990, pp. 344–352; Joy Thwaite, 'Eve Langley: Personal and Artistic Schism' in *Gender, Politics and Fiction: Twentieth Century Australian Women's Novels,* ed. Carole Ferrier, University of Queensland Press, 1985, pp. 118–235.

(3) For a discussion of Steve as picaroon, and for many other insights into the novel, I am indebted to an unpublished lecture by Sue Thomas.

(4) All information about Eve Langley's life is drawn from Joy Thwaite's detailed and constantly illuminating biography, *The Importance of Being Eve Langley*, Angus & Robertson, 1989.

(5) Thwaite, p. 39.

(6) Quoted Thwaite, p. 378.

(7) Quoted Thwaite, p. 379.

CONTENTS

FOR THE BEST! FOR THE BEST!

I

*And reports from Bairnsdale, in the Gippsland district, indicate that Mr Nils Desperandum, of Sarsfield, will have the largest crop of apples, this year, for miles around.—*INTERSTATE WEEKLY.

ON a hot Australian morning I read the above advertisement out to June as we sat in the low-roofed kitchen of our old home in Dandenong.

"Well," said I, sitting back in the poet's corner, as my end of the table was called, "here's a chance to get into Gippsland, at last. I wonder if Mia has ever heard of Mr Nils Desperandum? Mia, little woman, do you know this name . . . Desperandum of Sarsfield?"

"Back in the airly days," said Mia, putting down the load of groceries that was needed to feed us when we were loafing around at home, between jobs, "I've heard my father speak of them. Why?"

"It says here, that he's got a great crop of apples this year, at Sarsfield. I suppose you know the place, Mia?"

"Many's the time I've ridden through it, down from Tambo Crossing, before you two were ever thought of."

"Well, it doesn't say here that he wants apple-pickers, but I thought I might write on the off-chance and get a job in Gippsland. You've made us love that country, Mia, little woman, and we must see it before we die."

"Ah," sighed Mia, sitting down among the parcels, "there's no place like it. Wouldn't it be wonderful if you two girls could get a job up there and see the old places I used to ride through when I was your age?"

Mia, our mother, was a Gippslander, first generation. She was a short, rugged little woman, as swarthy as a gipsy, with a crooked nose which she had broken into the grotesque soon after it was given to her, by crawling under a house and hitting it on a block there. Her eyebrows were enormous and her laugh was windy, coming from somewhere down a chimney.

Although she was a widow, we had found a lover for her in the person of an elderly man with grey, stormy whiskers and an appetite for strong tea and the rings and lockets out of Christmas puddings. His name was Bob Priestly and he carried on a thriving business in dried tea leaves from which he manufactured reconditioned tea. The work was done by night, and the tea leaves, to get the full flavour, had to be turned one by one on a moonlight night when a slow fine drizzle was sweeping across the swamps in which he lived, with his assistants, "The Twenty Trained", otherwise known as "The Twenty Trained Ferry-frogs". For the admirable man had mated the frogs and ferrets around him and produced a breed half-way between a ferret and a frog. Bob Priestly, and his ferry-frogs, or V-frogs, was an inexhaustible joke among us. He kept fowls, too; therefore, any ambiguous advertisement for a broody hen was considered to contain a proposal to "the woman", as we called Mia.

Our house, from the street, looked like a pile of rotten chips, and often as we lay in our beds, the remarks of casual passers-by whipped the blood up in our bodies with a short lash which struck home . . . literally.

"Time this place was in the hands of the wreckers," they said contemptuously.

Threats like this led us to practise harmless deceits against the town's health inspector, whereby, with many variegated roses, lilacs, ivies and grape-vines, we concealed from his unkindly eye the fact that our "kipsie", as Mia called it, was falling down.

But the house proper was thirteen giant plum-trees which held the soil in their hands and brought up snow out of its blackness every spring. It is lost to us now, but yet, how mysteriously satisfying it is to know that in the minds of my mother, my sister and myself the old house is embalmed, so that one may render to a forgetful other a fine correction of some intricate detail that has escaped her memory. It is a thought as sweet as heaven to know that in the minds of each of us the may by the fence still blooms in an eternal springtime; that the snowdrop has in our hearts a triple birth, and blooms in three separate minds, faultlessly. The river-weed by the tap may not, in the season of dehiscence, split the purse that holds its seeds and fling them far and wide, but the ghosts of its ripeness spring up seasonably in our minds and sow a ghostly seed. So that if all the flowers and grasses and hollows and hills of the old house were razed and mutilated—as they are now, I suppose—we keep them intact in three minds, each depending on the other to supply it with the delicate minutiae of remembrance.

It was on the kitchen walls, however, our peculiar fantastic minds showed in verse and drawing that the time had come for our strongest migration from home. My sister covered these walls with her imaginative drawings, which even now no one ever sees, for no one will bother to buy them. Well, who wants a fragment of ancient stone tinted with Hungarian rains, Chinese lichen and Russian sunshine?

Always her drawings troubled me.

"To where," I asked her, as I stood before the naked figure of an old man who stood alone in a desert, bearing a veiled woman in his arms, "does that sad withered hermit bear the veiled woman . . . she, who is veiled like those insects that set their tents in the tea-tree in springtime? I should like such a man to carry our youth, so veiled, into the ovens of the desert, and there burn it, that the escaping flame, our true selves, might vanish into heaven."

The poems I had written were delicately printed by my sister and set on the walls beside her drawings. Often we sat staring at these symbols of our coming years, while under our feet were the uneven wide red and white flagstones, and through the broken black fireplace a golden ivy crawled, etiolated and frail, putting its arms around tea tins and biscuit jars. In summer ripe plums dropped down the chimney into the pans from the branch above the house.

The corner of the table nearest the fire was mine, and here I sat, arms folded, breathing deeply, and made songs that to my mind were as rich as wine. All the timber in Australia couldn't give that wine enough bush now, as far as I am concerned.

My first illness was that one most common to the children of the poor . . . a bad education and, like the bite of the goanna, it was incurable and ran for years. My early arnicas of Matthew Arnold, small balsams of Wilde, Rabelaisian cauterizers, Shavian foments and Shakespearian liniments have only added to it and spread the offence.

At that time I theorized regarding my brain. It had four points of consciousness which I clad with scraps of art and literature.

I knew that I was a woman, but I thought I should have been a man.

I knew that I was comical but I thought I was serious and beautiful, as well. It was tragic to be only a comical woman when I longed above all things to be a serious and handsome man.

The third point of my consciousness was a desire for freedom, that is, never to work.

The fourth was a desire, amounting to obsession, to be loved. I suffered from it, as others suffer from a chronic delicacy of health. It haunted my sleep and impeded my waking hours.

I was short and sturdy, having twisted flexible legs like a ballet dancer, narrow hips, broad breast, very large arms and a tiny head with a freckled face containing a dram of green eyes, long-lashed, heavy with melancholy and dreams, a thin red mouth, crooked teeth, a long thin nose with dilated nostrils, fine black eyebrows and black-bronze hair.

June was taller and broader, having sinewy brown legs, big at the thighs like a grasshopper's, and the body and breast of an Indian wrestler. Her small sharp hands were yellow in hue, and held all things crookedly, while her head, large and out of proportion to the rest of her body, was covered with black hair that had streaks of copper in it. When she sat in the sunlight, these streaks appeared like subterranean streams of metal rising into a dark plain. The eyelids fell back cleanly from her alert brown eyes and she stared clearly and fearlessly at everything. Her full lips were cut well in the flesh with much red showing below a short straight nose; the chin was firm, strong and white, and her brow, snowy, wide and shining, was dominated by splendid black eyebrows. The white in her eyeballs was echoed by the animal beauty of her even teeth, and her carmine cheeks were an overflow on her golden face from the red fullness of her lips.

She had not long arrived home from a job in the Goulburn Valley, where she had worked on a farm and, disguised as a boy, had fed pigs and cut star thistles. But the lonely bush girls had become importunate in their misguided affections and she had fled to save her manhood.

Mia had encouraged us to wander; made restless by long hard years of gipsying through the Australian States, she found peace in urging us out to follow the echo of the aboriginal names of towns that had tempted her when she was young. And of all the provinces, Gippsland, she said, was the most tradition-haunted. She speculated on the conditions of those whom she had known in youth, and filled us, too, with a desire to know what had become of them. Mia knew and loved her Gippsland, and our childhood lullabies had been the names of towns there—Sale, Briagalong, Maffra, Redbank, Fernbank, Bairnsdale, Haunted Stream, Omeo, Tostaree, Tambo, Monaro and Double Bridges.

We had gone to sleep to the cry of, "Who killed Baulch's bullocks?" "Riverina Bob, are you coming out tonight?" and "Where's Jack the Packer?"

For years she had been saying, "You girls would love Gippsland . . . the Monaro . . . the Stream . . . the Tambo and the Lakes." For years she had laid the powder trail and the Gippsland apples were to be the crimson flames that would set us alight.

"Yes, back in the airly days, I've heard my father speak of the Nils Desperandums of Sarsfield. Ah," cried Mia, "I mind the days when there were forty hotels in Haunted Stream, and when the So-and-Sos of Such-and-Such, big social people now in Melbourne, used to gallop past in the double-seated buggy and people used to talk about their daughters because they painted their faces. You never saw paint used in those days. There were a lot of sons in this family, and they married the daughters of an Irish family that had rented a grog shanty from your grandfather, and they're rich and well known now. Or at least, their children would be. But the best people were the old bushmen."

Mia looked like an old bushman herself when she spoke of them. She went into a maternal trance for a few moments, saying as she stared into the sad distance, "M-m-m-mm!" and worked on the bushmen. Then she brought them forth into startling life with voice and gesture. They became men of genius and profound sorrow to us, men who had been let down in life and wandered into the easy-going bush, but had never forsaken their courtesy and their love of songs and sentimental feeling. And Mia, as she spoke, lamented her youth, the passing of time and the dreadful change worked by it among those she had known.

"All gone, now," said Mia. "All gone. Ah, it's sad. What days we had. I've told you about them for years. I think I can see old Blind George now with his fiddle in the green bag. I see the Wilson boys and the Svensons coming down from Monaro with remounts for India. Sometimes," cried Mia with the desperate energy of one faced with the death of her time, "I can't believe it. . . . I just can't believe that they're dead and gone. I wonder, if you girls go up there, will you meet any of the people I used to know. 'By-by', Alec used to say, 'By-by, I'm off to the Doubles.' He meant the Double Ridges, but it got to be a byword in time among us along the Tambo. What names," said Mia, "the Thorburns, the McDougals, the McAlisters, Wilsons and Svensons."

She was not merely a colonial historian then, but Gippsland incarnate. Her people held and were still holding large tracts of land there.

"If I'd stayed at home and not married your father and gone off into New South Wales," she mourned, "your grandfather might

have left me some of the land, too, and you girls would have had
property there. But after all my years of hard work . . . what have
I got? Nothing! And what future have you two girls got? No father,
no property. Of course you're young and you don't understand. It's
for the best."

"But Mia, you were happy with our father, wandering all over
New South Wales, weren't you?"

"Oh, yes, in a way," Mia replied, fingering her chin dreamily and
sadly, "but Gippsland's always been our home. I left a cow and calf
there when I went away," said she, waking up, "and when I went
back for a visit, brother Charlie said to me, 'See that herd over
there, Mia? They came from your cow and your calf.' Yes, I should
have stayed in Gippsland, and thought that one day I would have
children and that I should make some provision for them. You'll
go to Gippsland as workers, poor and unknown. Don't go near any
of my people, girls. Just look around and talk about the old days.
But don't let any of the family know that you're working on an
orchard."

"Ah, but we haven't got the work yet, Mia. And we don't care
about relatives. The poetry of Gippsland is lost to them. It's the
names of the towns that is taking us to Gippsland. And after that
we are going to follow the glorious aboriginal names of Australian
townships to their sources and feel all that there is to feel
there."

My sister and I, being of coarse and fertile earth, were more
sensitive to the etymon than to anything else in the world. At
night we sat down and wrote out columns of Australian place-names,
glorying in their ancient autochthonousness. English names, in
Australia, we despised. "Effete," we said. "Unimaginative. But . . .
ah, Pinaroo . . . Wahgunyah . . . Eudarina . . . Tallygaroopna
. . . Monaro . . . Tumbarumba . . . Bumberrah, and thousands of
others! How fine they are! We must be in the towns and speak
their names."

But the etymon, like art and literature, was obscured for me by
my passion to be loved.

In a torn newspaper under the portrait of a pale fat man I had
once read these words, "Lauré, Lauré! I am young and my plate
is empty! When will my two great desires, to be loved and to be
famous, be satisfied?" And I cried this out at every opportunity. I
wrote it everywhere and chanted it to every tune.

The very letter I wrote to Mr Nils Desperandum, whose crop
expectations were going to free us and take us to Gippsland, was

here and there shadowed by a pretentious and romantic softness. After I had posted that letter I grew alarmed thinking that he might shy off it, so I wrote another purporting to come from the town where I had been working. This one was in a wilder, freer tone, and I decided to act, when I met him, according to his choice of writer.

One week afterwards, he told us, on note-paper printed with apples and pears, that he had decided to take us on as packers for the season from February until May, and hoped that we should prove satisfactory.

"Ah, won't we just!" we cried. Nothing mattered to us except the fact that we were going to Gippsland. At last we should see it through adult eyes. We were eighteen and nineteen years of age at the time. Now that we're going to Gippsland, we said, we must put off our feminine names for ever. As we sat that night around the fire, myself in the poet's corner, little Mia opposite and my sister sitting on a low box between us, playing on her sonorous violin all the Gippsland tunes and old dance melodies that our father had played on the plains of New South Wales, we considered the question of names, and at last. . . .

It was decided that my name should be Steve, because the comic literature of the Australian bush has always had a Steve in it and, of course, we had always loved Steve Hart in that bushranging song that Mia sang to us now and again.

> Now, come all you young fellows, and listen to me.
> If you're wise you will keep out of bad company!
> Remember the fate of brothers and friends . . .
> Ned and Dan Kelly, Steve Hart and Joe Byrne.

In the corner of the kitchen hung a glistening picture of a hold-up in the early days. Ah, what grand colour in it! Against the silver and blue trunks of the eucalyptus-trees the bushranger's chestnut mare strained, as her rider levelled his revolver, his face hidden by his hat and a brilliant red handkerchief around his neck. The blue and sultry Australian sky seemed to ring with the words we had heard as children, while the elders talked at evening in the bush. Out from their quiet conversation, the brazen-sounding words had come suddenly and fiercely, " 'Bail-up!' said Kelly." Or at other times it was Ben Hall, or Thunderbolt or Morgan.

So I am Steve. We spoke of this new person as a long, crooked-moustached fellow who didn't care much for women and was sure to end up living alone, a hatter, in the scrub, through which he would ride wildly and with passionate sorrow on mournful wet nights.

> By at the gallop he goes and then,
> By at the gallop comes back again.
> Late in the night when the fires are out,
> Why does he gallop and gallop about?

They said to me, "That'll be you, Steve."

"But cripes," I answered, "I can't ride."

"Well, now we know why you gallop and gallop about. You can't ride; you don't know how to stop the horse, you see."

"But what about a name for you?" I said to my sister, staring at her short handsome figure clothed in old fawn riding breeches, with a khaki shirt over her breast and a red handkerchief around her neck.

She crossed her legs and said she didn't care what she was called.

"What about Jim?" I suggested. "You know how Lawson says that 'There are a lot of good old mates named Jim, working around in the bush.' But I've always had a feeling that we might pick up a mate named Jim, so I won't take the right of priority from him."

And we had just agreed on that when there was a hollow tumbril-like sound from up the street and a deep uncanny rumble rang through the black night.

"Whoa, there!" howled an agonized voice and heavy hooves scuffled on the rough country road.

Then someone burst in through our back gate, stumbled over the drain and, falling across the clothes line, was flung by it head-first into the wire-netting around the wood shed and, with his head in a mass of snails and nasturtiums, we heard him gasp despairingly, "Where the —— hell am I?"

A voice yelled encouragingly from the cart, "To your left, Blue. . . . Back-trapdoor!"

Stepping bravely forward now with his burden, he found his object. There was a heavy scraping sound. One was removed, and one inserted, then the laden Blue thumped heavily but contentedly over our onions, on his way out to the tumbril. As it rolled hollowly with a clanking accompaniment down the road in the late hours of the night, I said, "I think the name is Blue."

"Yes," replied Blue, putting the violin under her soft white chin. "That'll do me, Steve." And she broke into the reeling strains of the "Monaro", a bushman's waltz, upon which I solemnly rose and, tying a bit of black rabbit skin under my nose, putting a size eighteen collar around my neck with a crooked made tie in front of it, and holding a concertina in my hand, I advanced to Mia and, bowing, asked for "the pleasure of the next".

She rose and, in various clasps copied from old Gippslanders she had known, we revolved in the little six by four to the pealing strains of the "Monaro".

The first hold was the "pump-handle" in which the hand and arm of the partner were energetically raised up and down.

"Water very scarce now," I remarked as I worked for it, "Only two rims left."

I next adopted the "vase", which is characterized by the grace of the couple's arms stuck out from the gent's side like the handles of a vase.

Then followed the "dried fish", in which, without perceptible style, but with frozen eyes and set face and stiff carriage, the couple revolve in silence.

Last of all, came the "indifferent", where gent negligently holds the concertina behind his partner's neck and plays as he dances with her.

Steve and Blue were busy for the next few days, thumping the tailored trousers we were to wear in Gippsland, pressing silk shirts and ties and tearing the tickets off new khaki overalls for packing-shed wear.

Everything was spread out on the old dark green rug that our father used to take with him on droving trips; on top of that was a bluey, and the monstrous sandwich was neatly rolled up and bound with luggage straps.

Our new names delighted us, and we roared them out to each other as we worked.

"Wonder what we'll find up in Gippsland, Blue, eh? Old-timers . . . old music . . . strong horses and the memories of old days, I suppose."

"But, Steve, it might be all changed now. We think we're going up into a district that's a mixture of Mia and Henry Lawson. But a new generation's come since then."

"Yes, Blue . . . that's true, all right. We'll be two generations removed from Mia's old-timers. It's the sons and daughters of the young people of her generation that we'll be meeting, and I wonder what they'll be like? When Mia talks about the old days, you get a strong sense of a hiatus that was widening even then, between her generation and the bushmen that she loved. The young people of that day seemed to me to be hard, sorrowful and wild. I think as they grew older they'd scorn tradition, as Mia does sometimes now. They seemed to have a sense of being fooled by the long aeons of existence, at last. And their children, I wonder what they'll be like? What change will the deliberate years have worked on them? Time's a terrible thing, Blue."

"Yes, Steve . . . only got two days to go, now, before we set out," said Blue.

At night we sat around the fire listening to Blue playing the old Gippsland tunes, while I shouted to a phantom ballroom at Haunted Stream, "Change partners! First and second couple advance; swing in centre!"

"By-by, we're off to the Doubles," we cried and sang an old song of Alec Cain's (he was the saddest bushman of them all) . . .

"What more is a man than a leaf on a tree?"

And . . .

"Love, dear love, be true.
This heart is always thine.
When the war is o'er,
We'll part no more . . .
For Erin's on the Rhine. . . ."

Also, "Rorie O'Moore", and "My Father was a Frenchman".

Feverishly we made ready for Gippsland, that she might welcome us by turning back old times, and letting us see the days of which our mother had spoken.

II

THE day came, *"Der tag"*, we said, airing one of our four German phrases. "Well, Mia, we're off. By-by, we're off to the Doubles! Look after Priestly and the Twenty Trained V-Frawgs while we're away . . ." and in our wide-legged trousers, silk shirts and sweaters, we made off down the dusty Australian road to the dingy station and the palpitating train.

Our chief glory was our sweaters. Not that you need sweaters in Australia, which is a sweater itself, manufactured by the sun. . . . But the fine cardinal, gold and royal blue of those sweaters against our tawny faces (with our imaginary black whiskers of the eighties, which we stroked as we waited for the train to come) gave us the air which seemed to be necessary to enter Gippsland.

Our grandfather had come to it by bullock dray from Ballarat, wearing a scarlet and gold cummerbund, a bright Spanish hat, yellow moleskins, an embroidered vest with brilliant buttons, and rings of pure gold from his own mine hot on his fingers.

We looked at each other and felt that we hadn't let him down.

Under the dark interest of the travellers around us, we got aboard the train.

"Dandenong! . . . Gippsland line train . . . stopping at all stations!" the porter cried musically.

Outward it shuffled, deeply sighing and, picking up speed, fled grinding through the short green grass, and in its singing, lilting, grumbling, bumbling, knocking, rocking theatre we flew forth to Gippsland.

At some part of the journey, my hereditary Gippsland mind awoke. It was a totally different apparatus to my Dandenongian mind. A sweet shower had fallen in the country through which we were travelling in the fair morning, and I saw on my left a hillside divided into fields of such depth and colour . . . such blue earths, mauve earths, brown soils (to change my tune), red grounds, yellow clays, black malm and grey clods that I felt disappointed because the ploughman standing on the edge of his boots and ploughing therein, did not, with his horse, change into a chameleon.

I looked at Blue who sat on the end of the rocking seat playing her violin, from which not a sound came, because we were passing through hills that roared as wildly as the train. But I was comforted by the look of her, and if, as I believe, every fine memory petrifies into immortality that part of the brain into which it was entered, then there is a millionth part of an inch of mine that will never die . . . for Blue's big handsome head looked, that morning, just like the head of our father.

At every station men and women got into the train. The women carrying big bunches of pink, white and red heath, and the men carrying their coats over their shoulders, with the air of men come from the hills. This is the indisputable sign of the true Gippslander, especially those around the shire of Warragul, the country of the Wild Dog. This shire, through which we rushed, was like miles of patched quilts left out in the weather, and wherever the quilt had been torn a beautiful body showed through, silver and rapid in its movements. This was the rain. It was the rain married and settled down into rivers; willows round about attempted a few repairs with their green threads, where the fences were broken down.

The sight of the wild dogs (warrigals) flying across this country,

is given only to children and poets. What a swarming of tails and
males, of teeth and tongues, black and brindle, white and red,
yellow and sallow, as the wild dogs of all time follow the train to the
refreshment rooms at Warragul. They looked up, showing the
whites of their eyes, as they rushed along with the train. Sometimes,
they turned into tall men leaning on shovels, yelling, "Pape . . .
pape!"

"Whee!" they turned into white gates.

"Whoosh!" into the first houses outside the town; and then, with
a million snarls and clashes of teeth and frizzling, steaming and
puffing of their whiskers, they became the station and the rattle
of cups in the refreshment rooms—in which was secreted a most
potent drug which was dropped into the tea and coffee.

We went into the railway refreshment rooms and were intoxicated. But then, how little it takes to intoxicate those who travel
through Gippsland. How could we help ourselves, landing as we
did on the Warragul platform, exalted by the effluvia coming from
the celebrated blue clay, the streaked yellowish and red clay, the
red ferruginous earth and gravel, quartz pebbles of moderate size,
large quartz pebbles and boulders, blue and white clay, and pipe-
clay?

Exalted, I repeat, by these exhaltations, we added to it a pinch
of that opiate which dwelt in clashing white cups, the individual
coffee, the flying spoons and the starch in the caps of the waitresses,
and staggered out to catch the train again, drugged into joviality.

The guard with the bell in his hand, the whistle in his mouth
and the flag in his eye, sent us sighing and panting farther still
into the country of Gippsland.

At last, in the dry afternoon, we came to the town of Moe, which
is Gippsland's outermost door. Ah, now we near our Promised Land,
that country which we saw lying like a bubble on the hills one
morning as we went down into the red and purple paddocks of
Wandin Yallock.

Up from the dust rose the station and on the coppery gravel
platform stood an old Gippslander, tall, thin and long whiskered;
around his hat was a snake-skin, the small metallic scales gleaming
and the snake's eyes staring towards the low hills far in the
distance.

Near the gate stood a beautiful woman with bare arms and much
black hair which appeared to have been lying for miles on the
road, but had been abruptly chopped off just as we came along.
She looked at everything but the train. This meeting of trains and

looking beyond them is a custom of Gippsland females, religious in its punctuality and intensity. It is a form of worship among the young and unmarried, and consists of exposing the body to glances that exalt it, while the eyes are veiled from what is known to be there.

At Moe many passengers alighted and others joined us. These were wept over by women in black net veils which had thick furry insects lying on nose and cheek, and when the mourners had gone these new travellers sat in the hottest parts of the carriage, staring at their new dusty boots and disturbed and alarmed by the look of their wild hands against the new cloth in their trousers.

The fire buckets along the station wall turned into a man lying naked in a crimson coffin, as the great bell of the border of Gippsland walked along the train, ringing itself and crying. . . .

"O, go to the country of Gippsland then! For it is all ended, and your youth is over. O, be crushed utterly in the country of Gippsland, for love is not there. Labour is not sweet there, nor is time to be recaptured. Nor shall any die there. Yet, all is ended!"

The whistle ran about with the whiskers of the stationmaster hanging to it like a sporran and piped the song of the country of Gippsland, and the flag dripped blood and flew about on shoulders like a harpy, crying that we should never return as flesh from the country of Gippsland.

Mysteriously then, the train moved backward along the route we had come. It slid aside from that route and was raised and winged, and began to run with us swiftly into Gippsland. The angry sun of the late afternoon filtered in tiger shadows through the wooden slats of the window shades. Sliding apart the doors edged with green velvet, we walked along until we came to a part of the train that rushed back and forth like a concertina. Over it lay a mat of twisted fibre to hide the instrument from our sight, but yet we heard the song which made us hold to each other's hands and laugh and weep.

> The strong sob of the chafing stream
> That seaward fights its way
> Down crags of glitter, dells of gleam,
> Is in the hills today.

Listening to this song, we saw hanging in a frame on the trembling wall of the train a map of Gippsland drawn on the hide of a still-born native bear and, largely on it, "Bairnsdale".

"The dale of bairns," I said, and my heart opened up and gave out life and blood to the dreams that name aroused in me. . . .

There, I thought, the children would laugh as those who are beginning life laugh, and they should weep as those who are beginning life weep.

"Here's Fernbank that Mia told us about," I said to Blue, looking out on a plain of green reeds.

"But the fern . . . where is she?" wondered Blue.

On the dusty white road between the rough railway gates, an old teamster, his snowy beard lying on his chest, halted beside the long line of musing bullocks he drove, and halted in me forever.

Lindenow, the last station before the dale of bairns, sounded German, and should have had a green tree somewhere around. An old man limped out of the blue gums with a box strung around his neck by a dark oiled strap. He had a wooden leg and a black patch over his eye, and in the box lay many poisons wrapped about with red and yellow papers. These, he implored us not to buy, saying that the gods had sent him out into Gippsland to slay those who came looking for old days.

"But what about Bairnsdale?" we said. "What's it like?"

"She's a good big place," answered the old Gippslander. The wind blew among his rigging and his mast leant forward and carried him away, crying from a flute hidden in his beard, "Chocerlits! Pea-nuts!"

The train burnt its way through acres of grey maize, sawed through a fence and past a blue hotel outside which stood some Gippslanders holding bridles in their hands. Then came a bare desolate tangle of yards where cattle stood casting their wet mouths upward and rolling their eyes towards their ears, or backward, where death was waiting, just between the horns.

"Perhaps these are the bairns. . . ." I said.

The station came to us in that first unfamiliar line of light which is poetry, and I see it even now as a dark smudge in a darker place, outside which lay bright yellow sand. It was all veiled, then, in the excitement of being imperial, for ever young, for ever handsome and for ever unloved.

Catching Bairnsdale's one black cab, in which our mother had ridden years ago behind the same driver, now old, we drove along the main street, with black oilskin arms waving on either side and black buttons boring deeply into the seats on which we sat.

I felt afraid as we entered the gate of Mr Nils Desperandum, the orchardist, for on this journey into Gippsland I noticed that

Blue had grown taller, lovelier, wiser and more powerful than myself. I felt weak and lost . . . dependent on those about me to decide what I should be. Sadness overcame me. Had not the bell at Moe foretold it? Had not the flag and whistle cried it? My only reason for living at that moment was the remembrance of,

> Autumn bold
> With universal tinge of sober gold.

Who else among the Gippslanders knew this? I had brought a small book of Keats's birthday quotations with me, imagining that his entire works lay in it, and I turned to it whenever I was judged.

The dry garden behind the yellow fence was full of cosmos, those flowers I had stolen long ago in childhood and been whipped for stealing. I was afraid of them at once.

And when the door opened out came my punishment again.

Mr Nils Desperandum was a Gippslander of purpose. The map of his flesh was short and broad, and on it was drawn a keen harsh mind, kind to those it had studied and understood, and impatient of those who evaded it, not through any fault of his, but through some implacable twist in the character of the evader.

He saw at once that I was one of these.

When we had introduced ourselves, he marvelled, looking from one to the other, "that you two could be sisters".

The twilight in which we stood grew darker then, for me, and I laid myself aside until those who would come, in the future, should understand and love me.

Yet I respected the man, for he, like my father, began with a large head that terminated in a small rather crumpled body.

The sadness that came about me, when I knew that he rejected me, is, and shall be, about me forever. I regarded him as a collection of days and experiences in this loved country of mine, and with sorrow I saw that these things scorned me, and in the scorning almost denied themselves being.

For I had brought to the country of Gippsland a great marking power which held and judged all that I saw there, and any overturning or dismissing of that power by those I found saddened me, for it meant that they stayed outside my strength.

At the moment, however, I was only a woman in man's clothes asking for work on an orchard. After some discussion Mr Desperandum decided that we should sleep in the town of happy children for that night, and go out with him to look for board and lodging next day.

The cab raised its arms again as soon as the old horse flapped its feet along the street, and we moved off towards an ancient family hotel, which overhung the street with damp black towers and turrets, magnificently drawn by our unfamiliarity with the nights of Gippsland. In the dining-room which seemed to be sunken in a well, so strange and low were its lights, we sat at a cool polished cloth with the landlady and her daughter and, while we ate, they asked us whence we had come.

I said I did not know. In Gippsland the beginning of journeys do not trouble the travellers. Then the memory of my little book came to me, and the poet's fever made me say to the old lady: "While the wheels of the train shook our bodies to and fro, I thought I saw our souls leaping into the dust of Gippsland. If you could go back to that place and find that dust, you should know us and our ultimate ends."

No doubt it was of the drawing of the hermit and the veiled woman which Blue had done that I was thinking; and truly, my flesh was twining around those beautiful knees of his, and around that morose and hearkening face which I was to see in Gippsland. The passion of loneliness raged in me, and Blue was ashamed when I brought out from behind my chair a large blue and white packet of bran and began to eat it in front of the two ladies. I added honey to it, and chewed it like the ass in the fairytale.

On the next morning, at an hour when, in Australia, the clay of the roads is burning and sickly with the heat, we went to the house of the orchardist and he took us out in a mournful black car, a fit hearse in which to go searching for dead days. As we drove along the hot white road, the lukewarm shadows made by the flapping curtains of the car saddened me still more, for these inanimate things became, by reason of the heat, imbued with a greasy distasteful life in this country.

The road was a four-mile-long flake of white clay between hairy black trees whose sides were covered with dried red gum. About their roots lay a spirit drawn from the souls of those who had passed along this old road that ran from Tambo to Bairnsdale. Along this road my mother and my mother's mother had ridden and driven, and my gallant uncles, side-whiskered and button-holed, had galloped on fast horses . . . from youth to death.

Little dry houses lay on either side, and blue-grey fencing-wire held in its mesh endless dry grass, dusty trees, dry white gums and the gasping horizon.

"There is a little house along here, belonging to an old lady, where you two might get a room," said Mr Nils Desperandum.

We saw it, and felt that we were already sitting on a little bed in that little room sighing with the heat of the afternoon and waiting for night, or rain, to come, while Gippsland grew old outside us and within us.

First, we called at the orchard, and immediately we saw a little hut standing among the apple-trees. We asked for it, and got it. Striped apples, called Edna Mays, had fallen around it, with a little brown hole in the sides from which the sawdust of some carpentering grub welled; and down below the hut a long bed of tomatoes flamed ripely.

One night more we had in the town of Bairnsdale and walked the streets looking for the happy children . . . following their laughter down to a tall tannery with a high platform jutting from its side. Behind it moved the slow wide River Mitchell, named after an explorer of Gippsland's "airly days".

As we sat outside a house on the river-bank, a 'cello gravely sang to us through the dry flowers and the leaves. It was the house of the man who had built the romantic passenger boats that lay in the river below and took men and women down to the blue and flower-encircled lakes. How we longed to go into his house and become known to him and see the 'cello played before our eyes. For the Gippslanders are haters of walls when music sounds, and they wish to draw into it all those that love it as they do.

Of a certainty, had we been long in the town, we should not have hesitated to enter, nor would the inhabitants have forbidden us. Under the shelter of the hedge we lay. The old boat builder came walking in his garden and murmured to the night:

"O Gippsland, I have built boats for your rivers. The waters that swirl on their sides echo in my ears as I lie, old and weary, in my bed at night. But what avails it? I have never seen my country since the day I bowed my head to the making of these little craft. Beyond this town, in a village by the sea, lives a good man. He waits to give happiness to those who lie under my hedge listening to the vast violin that cries in my house. But I say to those who listen to it, 'There is no peace in Gippsland. All is disappointment and misunderstanding. I am the land. See, if you come to me, I shall speak in a different tongue, harsh, slow and diffident. Yet within, I am like the land, struggling with distances and depths. As old as the moon, and as hot as the sun. Endure, O young men that are not men, and prepare to lose all faith and hope in Gippsland.'"

The vast violin ended with a sob, and we arose and, bowing to his gate, returned to the town.

The morning came. We took our poor baggage with us and Mr Nils Desperandum ran us out to the orchard. Ran us out! Let us say, rather, that he jerked us out. I never saw a man handle a car so badly. The literature he wrote on the roads! The curving drawings of comic aspect that he laid on the hills! Looking back, I saw a line commencing with *"Lasciate ogni speranza"*, which ran from Lucknow to Sarsfield.

"Ah," whispered Blue, "where the —— hell am I?"

Mr Desperandum knocked his gates down to get us into the orchard, and called for help to raise them.

"Come up into the packing-shed and meet the men," he invited. By way of steep wooden steps on which blew a wind that came from some oven in a desert, we reached the shed. He introduced us to the workers, calm brown fellows in gilded leather aprons stained with apple juice.

"Now we'll go and have a look at the hut. I've had it swept out for you."

Beside it, a long fat ram lay on the sand, losing its wool by the inch. It had a striped black and white cloak flung over its horns, and as he drew near Mr Desperandum said, "I put that kapok mattress out to get the wind in it. You might be able to use it on the bed." We thanked him profusely.

The kapok mattress lived up to its ram-like appearance that night when we had gone to bed. Somehow or other, we found a way into its entrails, or perhaps it opened them up to bring us in. Towards dawn, the tongues of Gippsland descended upon us, and from that moment we were forever at variance, body, mind and soul.

"Gorstruth!" exclaimed Blue, through a mouthful of wool. She sat up in bed, with a white beard streaming down her breast, and a shower of white eyebrows, through which her eyes gleamed like a madman's.

"Lie down," I grumbled, "and let's get some sleep. We'll have to be up soon."

Shaving herself with her hands, she did so, and we followed each other into a dream, in which it seemed to me that I had hidden my working shoes in the belly of the ram. I bent double and went in after them. Blue pulled me out, and in the heat of the early morning we sat up and faced each other, covered with chaff and kapok.

There is a peculiar national merit in waking up like that in Gippsland; it amounts to a proclamation of manhood. The echoes of the proclamation soon died away and out we leapt to get ready for the first day as apple-pickers. A cracked bell rang from the packing-shed, and we went off to work, dressed in wide khaki trousers, covered to the knees with green and blue dresses, and flash scarves around our throats—mine being a passion vine climbing across a summer night with a touch of sea water rust and a few barnacles flung in; while Blue's was a smooth autumnal breast of silk, with brown leaves and purple berries, created by the lights she turned to.

The bell hung in the sky, still shaking, and I said to myself:

> The bell that in the sky you see
> Chimes clear and faint;
> A bird from the familiar tree
> Sings its low plaint.
> O, you who stand here full of tears
> That flow and flow . . .
> What have you done with those long years
> Of long and long ago?

"Good Verlaine," I cried, "come with me and make me forget with your stainless lyrics the condemning gaze of the Gippslanders!"

They were gathered together in the shed, the packers bending above their open cases. On a tall narrow desk to their left lay a pad of tissue paper which their fingers, ringed with rough rubber, grasped quickly and clasped about the apple that the right hand raised to it. The apple's core was thrust, bang, into the middle of the tissue. This coiled around it with a fine expansive movement that would have wrapped every apple in the world, and the fruit was pressed down into the case according to the formation of the pack.

We were taught while we watched, and got to work clumsily, our whole bodies shaking and wrapping and writhing with apple and paper. After some hours of this, two tall men, brothers apparently, brought in cases of fresh apples which were taken to the grader. The packers left their benches, and we stood at a machine called "The Lightning", invented, Mr Desperandum told us, by a local boy. I have been trying to understand him ever since,

and have now decided that the Gippsland lightning was dawdling
in the season he built the grader. The low monotonous rumble
stupefied me with a desire to sleep. I stood on one leg like a fowl
and dozed. "Treat them like eggs, ladies," cried the orchardist,
above the rattle. He stood at the chute end of the machine, feeding
it, and the two tall brothers worked opposite us, grave and slyly
mischievous.

They were called "the Harrisons" and what men they were!
True Gippslanders, from the turned up toes of their boots to their
whiskered faces. The eldest moved about without a word. His face
was full and white, as patient as a woman's. Sometimes his wild
black eyebrows twitched like a horse's tail, his wild black beard
and moustache moved when his mouth moved; but his glory was in
his weight, his silence and in that soul, the Gippsland soul, slow,
sad and puzzled, that lighted him from within. We felt that we
should like to know him.

His brother carried a bright red light on a brown cheek that was
almost a smile, and his fair moustache, not so kingly as his brother's,
spread from under an upturned shining nose. He looked too light. It
seemed to me that his mother had borne the darkest first, and
then the pigment had given out.

Blow-ther-Beard, another packer, was a shy young Salvationist,
with large brown eyes and dimples that worked together after we
got to know him.

The Trumpeter was a tall silent feline youth, addicted to practis-
ing the cornet by night. He bunked in the machinery shed, somewhere above our hut.

An emaciated boy with a hollow cough and that easy-going look
of the consumptive worked down under the shed, sawing and
putting together the cases. I sorrowed for him.

Around the grader hurried a timid little man, excessively
courteous, gentle and considerate. His arms were full of fruit-cases
and he threw quick apprehensive glances from under his drooping
green hat, which looked as though a terrible thunderstorm was
beating it down.

After work, when we got home to the hut, our timid little man
was sitting at the table having his tea. He introduced himself as
"Mr Homburg" of London, where he had been a civil servant. His
food was dry and grainy and kept in small black flecked tins, the
lids of which he closed with awful care, interrupting himself in the
middle of delicately decisive discourse to squeeze the last bit of air
out from the tea. I was sorry for Mr Homburg. I remember three

remarks he made. My reactions will serve to show what I was then.

"In this country, they confuse civility with servility."

I agreed with him profusely, because his civility frightened me more than a blow.

"I had never heard good English spoken in Australia until I met you."

I hummed and ha-ed and excused myself, trembling so much with pleasure that I nearly fell off the kerosene-box into the fire.

"Would you mind putting the lid back again on the tea tin, tightly, as you found it?"

This was when he had unwisely left his groceries in the safe over the week-end, while he went home to his family. We had been into them, and this was his only reproof, kindly delivered. But it gave us such a horror of theft that we learnt to cover our tracks expertly.

One night I felt so melancholy, so utterly downed by the lack of something, that I strolled down through the almond-trees and leant over the lichen-encrusted fence as a bad sailor leans over a rough sea. In the distance I could hear dogs barking faintly, and the "black" Harrison's concertina was going, making a wistful rainbow of sound as though he were throwing the instrument all around his head as he played. I found out later that that was just what he was doing. The sound of the concertina was old, sweet, sad and reminiscent of the days when the Thorburns and the Baulches roamed Gippsland, boasting of cattle and wool and long journeys, droving overland.

I felt that I must make a poem. In a few moments, the noise down at Harrison's was nothing to the clamour in my head. After a torturing half hour, out came something which consoled me for weeks.

> They dream, they dream, they weep in song
> Beneath the bow, these plaintive strings . . .
> Does not their agony, for long,
> Awake unwise rememberings?
> Does it not falter, does it not make,
> Slow tides of sorrow rise and fall
> Heartward and as lightly shake
> Those crimson blossoms from the wall?

I'll swear Harrison never played a concertina like that one, with its bows, strings and rememberings. And on seeing the house a few days afterwards, I found the crimson flowers to be there all right—in such profusion that the Harrisons were going for them, hammer and tongs, with weed-killer.

I congratulated him on his playing next morning, and discovered that he had a quizzical way of talking both with voice and eyes, and wasn't a sad man at all really, just a bushman who secretly found things amusing in a quiet way. He told us that we could come down and get our milk from them, if we wanted to; and our groceries could be left with them if we would go to the trouble of ordering them.

Finally, great excitement was caused by his simple invitation to "Come down tonight, if you'd care to".

It was Saturday. We knocked off on the half-day, and I remember with a memory as faint as the gleam on the galvanized iron roof of the packing-shed, the silent bell, the dry wooden walls, and that feeling within and without of joy and indolence as we went home to the hut, slowly and wearily. Saturday and Sunday were always to me, in Gippsland, blowfly days; trailing high and low with a weary cry, seeking something and then, on a fresh scent, disappearing from sight into the carcass of the week.

We dressed up that night with the greatest enthusiasm in the world . . . the enthusiasm of youth . . . to go down to Harrison's and meet the family. There was I ramming myself into trousers and sweater and trying to make my goblin face as handsome as Blue's; and there was she, carelessly tying a ribbon around her throat and getting effects that would have enchanted every apple in the orchard.

Mr Harrison was standing at the door of his house against a sunset, dusty and heroic in colour and immensity. The concertina was hanging from a strap on his thumb; his black hair fell into his eyebrows and eyes in a coarse fringe, and his dark beard bristled on his white face. "I only need a boomerang," said he, dashing his hands across his wild appearance.

Then out came his wife. A woman who looked like a lump of blue stone hidden in leather hide and showing out through the two slashes made for the eyes. And she had some autumnal red from a climate that doesn't usually give red, and it lay on odd places on her cheeks, chin, hands and breast. Those blue bitterly bright eyes of hers flashed over us, and she said in an Irish way, "How do ye do?"

They ushered us in and showed us the piano with its printed calico front. The small whitewashed passage between the front

room and the kitchen was choked with hair and giggles from the
moon-eyed children, who were upset by the look of our pants.

They politely put on the gramophone (which makes it sound
like an apéritif), and the bane of Australia at that time, Hawaiian
music, sobbed out mournfully. That most glorious sound! Ah, I
loved it. I lay back, weeping within, and making poems that shifted
around the guitars and the natives, disregarding their pipe-clayed
boots, white socks and bow ties.

There was something significant in the music that caught and
imprisoned the time of our youth. I forgot that I had come to
Gippsland to listen to the old traditional songs of bushmen.

Then with that peculiar dim whirling mixture of smells, hands,
smiles and defiance which dazes us when another sex enters the
room, we found that the "boys" had come in and were set bowing
by our names, and saying like their mother, "How are ye?" or "How
do ye do?"

There was Leo. We called him the Lion after we had known
him for a while. A tall thin lion was he, with meek blue eyes, a
crown of fair curling hair and a slow timid way of talking. His
white eyelashes were very conversational.

Bill, the son of the house, was mother, red rock, over again, but
with softer eyes and thick golden lashes that had some affinity
with his freckles. He had a lazy sneering laugh and a calm,
business-like manner. It was hard to believe that he was only a
pruner in an orchard down the road.

Percy, a fine looking boy with the auburn head of a poet, sat
among them too.

Moony, the youngest boy, was all black and white like a
mourning envelope.

Out of the dark through the door, came a short, bow-legged youth
with a great head of golden brown hair, two narrow blue eyes that
roved from side to side, a hooked white nose, and a flat red mouth
with two white teeth in it. The movements of the head, half eagle,
half vulture, predatory, uneasy and rapacious, ended in a pair of
dwarfed legs with boots and spurs crossed Crusader fashion as he
stood at the door.

"Hello, Kelly," said some other boys.
"Hello, Wilson!" said others.

Out of the conversation we gradually got his name, Kelly Wilson.
I wondered if this were one of the Wilsons that Mia had known
in her youth. I remembered her description of Myra Wilson, the

girl whom my uncle had loved. She, with her high head of brown-gold hair, her long flat red lips and her wild air.

So this was the second generation.

He sat across the room, staring at me with fixed hypnotic eyes. Afterwards he told me that he loved me from the first moment because I had looked so sad. There is a budding surgeon in some men, and the sick look of sad women makes them eager to heal.

There has always been in me a strong light which is only liberated when I am about to make a fool of myself. Out it darts, surrounding the object of my desire with such a fire and fancy that I am overpowered, and it takes years for me to re-adjust my vision. I have wasted aeons in recovering from being deceived, and it could happen tomorrow and in the tomorrow of immortality, too. Indeed, I can only imagine an eternal life, for me, as being involved in that eternal deception.

Down I fell, in love. And what happened? In feeling, incidents pure beyond pens, anguished beyond all telling. In fact, incidents silly to the point of idiocy.

III

IN the Gippsland bush, among company such as we were in, the demonstration of gallantry from the lover to his lady is to take her shooting . . . while she is in the ascendant, as it were. He borrows an old gun, oils it up, and buys some cartridges. He thinks of a gully where the rabbits are slowest, calls for his mistress, and they scramble away together for the afternoon. Conditions are best just before, or after, rain, but the mosquitoes grow thickest then. The conversation . . . mainly on rabbits killed in the past; their habits; their homes; eugenics and calisthenics.

I followed Kelly, the eagle, through reedy swamps and over slippery logs. The rabbits must have followed us, too, for we saw none before us.

"Have you anyone in your family named Myra?" I asked.

"Yes, my father's sister . . . Auntie Myra. We haven't seen her for years. She had an unhappy sort of marriage."

Then, I thought, you are, with me, one of the second generation of Gippslanders, and poor and outcast as I am. He was a bullock driver, although only sixteen years of age.

I didn't know what to make of it. Spiritually, there was much to make of it; but everything is done with words in the bush. When the words break down, time steps in and wraps you about, lettered and unlettered, telling you of your significance in her.

"My mother knew your father and your aunt, when she and they were young."

"What was her name?"

I spoke it.

"Oh, they're well known around here. I'll tell mother when I go home. She'll want you to come down and meet her." He was pleased to think that I was part of the early days. "Dad's pretty deaf now, but he's still got his big head of hair, like me. And he's working up in the bush near Tostaree."

"Still around Gippsland?"

"Yes. But his brother," proudly, "he's got a wine saloon down the line."

Next Sunday, he came down from Black Mountain, where he was driving the bullocks. And a bicycle ride was arranged for the amusement of all. I was the only one unamused, because I couldn't ride. The machines, frail, thin and, it seemed to me, almost transparent, were wheeled out on to the historic clay road between the hairy black gums. Blue mounted hers and swam off in swift shining circles down the road . . . her red sweater and scarf giving her the look of an escaped parrot, with slim legs in neat, tight breeches moving rapidly up and down. I was dressed in sad-coloured garments, and the hot day had made me expand from eight stone to ten. Putting one foot on the thorny pedal of that bicycle I thrust myself out, rising like an uncooked pudding as I went, and breaking in the middle as the bike curved inward—grasping its stomach and howling with laughter, as it were, before it flung me into the clay and dust.

They raised me up, accepted my explanations of a sprained ankle . . . watched me perform again, and pityingly offered to "double dink" me.

My shame had double damned me, and now, double dinked, I bent over the bar of Kelly's bike and off we went, his bow legs made as bandy as a tunnel under the load.

After a mile or two we got off and, making through the bush, halted at a great pile of rock, a district landmark. We climbed, and I was sure of my footing here and felt like a human being again.

Then, as in a dream, we found an old house, deserted and white-plastered within. We wrote our names on the smooth surface, with charcoal taken from the crumbling hearth. The sadness of the bush, silver-white and grey-green, sang about us as we moved from place to place, and the now unmeaning sun of that day made us breathe heavily with heat.

Kelly came down from Black Mountain every Sunday after that, and we went double dinking on his white mare, with its "Arab blood", as he called it. I sat behind him on her sweating rolling rump and Gippsland lay silent around us as we rode. There was a big bony house at the roadside, with yellow boughs twisted around it, the windows barred with wood and the sun, full of malevolence, forcing itself on the unfortunate walls. Kelly said vaguely as we passed it: "She used to wait for me to go by every Monday morning. One day I gave her a ring with a red stone in it, but she took it too serious, so I went to Black Mountain another way."

"That's the Cherry-tree Hotel," he said, as we passed another long flat yellow house, near a river. Below the bridge in the willows the bell-birds clink-achinked without a pause. They had been clinking and chinking ever since my mother rode along here, one Sunday in her girlhood. "They still tell around here, how your uncle stripped himself naked and climbed the flagpole to meet Cobb and Co.'s coach."

My uncle!

We passed a pair of old riding breeches lying on the bank, and Kelly reckoned they belonged to a drover he knew.

Silvery-grey houses, all deserted, were huddled in the timber that was still baked-looking from recent fires. The blackened trees stood in red, blue and golden ashes, and their young green leaves, hopeful and tender, swayed under their dead foliage. And all about was the silence of the Gippsland bush, the triumphant silence, the hypnosis eucalyptean, giving me indolence and dreams and sorrow for I knew not what.

On the way home Kelly dismounted and picked up a dainty little handkerchief that lay with the strange warmth of human rag on the road. I kept it for a long time, and have always connected it with a lady whose back we kept in view as she and her husband rocked away in front of us in a sulky.

Falling in love more deeply with the days, I dreamt at my work, sang monotonous threnodies that made Mr Nils Desperandum eye me anxiously, and ate cases of apples, which made him eye me more than anxiously.

He came in one morning with his starched white collar floating around his neck, and above it grief-stricken eyes that floated, too, in a mixture of tears, vexation and bloodshot sleeplessness, as though he had been lying looking at devils all night. A large consignment of his apples had been condemned and tossed into the sea, because of over-spraying with arsenate of lead.

We were at once ordered to wipe the apples free of the spray with wet rags and sat in the hot shed languidly playing housewife with the moist fruit. At lunch time Mr Desperandum brought out his big black bottle of tea, and drank long and deep. Then he spluttered and sat up rigid, with black ink running down his chin, and the words "Delicious apples. Hamburg, Germany" running around his white collar and shirt, as the stencil ink from the big black bottle that had stood beside *his* big black bottle did its work.

It required a doctor and a stomach pump to erase them.

The nights grew hotter, for the bush-fire season was fuming among the rocks and trees to the north. We tossed on our beds all night, and got up now and then for a cool drink.

We were both in love. Blue's was a long-standing affair in our native town. And, as we snored side by side in dreams, we toyed with each other's hands in joyful bliss. When we awoke, we recognized each other with a grunt of disgust and jumped over to the other side of the bed. Every morning we awoke pale, dispirited, ill-tempered and lazy and had frequent quarrels, after which I would go down to the almond-trees and devour nuts while I made verse.

Blue, eyeing me wonderingly, offering to share my hermit-like walks, was repulsed, and I went alone. One afternoon, in the throes of my unspoken passion, I walked far into the bush along a road to a farm called Waddel's. The road to it was set with those silent rusty flints one finds in Gippsland. There were post-and-rail fences on either side of the road, thick with lichen, and every mile or so there was an enamel placard on them, advertising soap. One of the saddest sights you could see. Another advertisement which must have driven more men to drink than the tongue can tell, was that long blue legend which affirmed that "Reckitt's Blue is best, Melbourne 300 miles". I met a swaggie leaning against a sign, talking to it earnestly.

"I've seen thousands of youse along this road," he said. "Youse have been the only living words I've known for days, and now I can hear youse chattering in me ears all the time. I can't think because of them signs. I get to wondering what the next one will have on it. If it's the same words I think I haven't moved a step; and if it's different words, I want to go back and compare them with

C

the words on the other rails, miles behind. Why can't the city leave the bush alone? We don't go milling around in the busy streets with swags and horses and dogs."

I shall never forget that walk to Waddel's: my mind was in that virgin condition where nature is merciless. Now she laid it onto the flesh with mystifying odours of leaves, glimpses of far-away ranges that made me tremble, sudden winds that blew gusts of loneliness into the mind, and the slow sweet divulging of a bush road, being covered by two human feet. I was in anguish and there was no escape from it. If I could have been dissolved into a flower or a pool of water it would have been all over. The late sun shivered with the lights of autumn, as I walked down to Waddel's. Hands, shares, wheels and hooves had ploughed the bush down and planted deep grass in a valley that had once been up to its neck in the sea. I wandered furtively around the heels of the deep-breathing bulls and made my way up into the chalk cliffs where the fossilized oyster shells crumbled in the open air. I picked them up and pretended to know something of conchology, in order to forget my passion and my pain; but, in reality, any sort of knowledge would have just chilled me, and made me stupid and sent me home dreaming. No, I was the victim of slow-moving time. As I went home, I climbed a little hill, thinking that if I should be able to marry Kelly I would have sons and daughters; so strong was this thought that I knew nature was thinking for me, and floundered to get out of her hands.

But she was even suggesting names for these unborn Gippslanders. "One could be called Gauntlet," I thought. The other might have been christened Hobnail, for all I knew, because, just as I topped that hill, I saw that which was my own, rightfully. Between us, these feelings of flesh and fancy, stood as obstructions.

I saw a miserable Gippsland township, grand with distance. It was a sultry purple day and dead and dry was the grass, but I looked from where I stood, on the side of the hill, and saw in a sudden stream of sun from a heavy cloud a few roofs, magnificent with the light, miles away. Some unknown town of which I shall never know the name. It had the pathetic beauty of an old crop of unharvested wheat left to melt and moulder under the storms of the world and, while I looked, rain fell there, or I think it fell, for I saw the arms of a rainbow outstretched, as though a great head lay on them and wept for the sake of the desolation in that place.

And one white roof that I watched earnestly smote me heartward, so that I turned on my heel, in an anguish of unrest and longing.

At length I went on, but would have as happily died, for my kingdom, Beauty, lay behind me forever.

Something gleamed on the dark road, and I bent and picked up sixpence with a quick hand and a surprised heart. Consoled, I strode off to the hut, my prize in hand.

Just as well it was in my hand, because when I got home, Blue, who sat peeling apples and glowering at the fire, said, "Did you take our milk money with you, Steve?"

Feeling pained, I felt in my pockets, saying, "Yairs . . . yairs, I think I remember taking it," while my fingers went through a hole in my trousers and found my leg.

"Oh, here it is," and I gave her the sixpence that had delivered me from sorrow and sat down for hours, wondering on the nature of life. I was still sitting there when she came back with the milk, and I sat there still while she prepared the tea: I ate it in the moody silence of the heroic who have faced life singly forever, and decided that my influence on Kelly must be an evil one, because of my distorted thoughts.

"I'll leave the country of Gippsland," I cried, "and let my lover be free. O Abnegation, how holy thou art! O Apostasia, what a nobility is in thy flying garments!"

"Where the hell did I put that butter?" Blue was grumbling, flea-ing the seats irritably in search of our fresh pound of butter. "Is it on your seat?"

"No."

"Get up . . . move aside and let me look."

I was just rising as it decided to fall from the seat of my pants, as flat as the Russian steppes, and as greasy as a steppe's coat. "Always dreaming," complained Blue. She turned me around, had a look at my greasy spot and laughed.

In two days' time it would be Easter Monday, and Mrs Wilson had invited us, through Kelly, to come with them to Eagle Point, a place somewhere down the Mitchell River, to picnic there. Ah, sultry thunderous Easter Monday, come out of your tomb again, you Lazarus, and unwrap your linen windings one by one.

The first, coming off in a morning mist, revealed us crawling under the apple-trees at dawn, picking up spotted fruit to take to Mrs Wilson. On the dewy grass the sand clung, and among the silver leather of the apple leaves the ugliest spider I have ever seen rode to the death.

The smell of apples when they get into a bag is like a jovial ripe lively conversation of which one cannot understand a single word, but enjoys each alien sound. We dressed; I to my buttered seat and Blue to immaculate faded trousers. There was some beautiful heat in that girl which used to tint the clothes she wore. She would wear an old blue dress into a fairytale tint. Poetry, music and beauty came from her clothing, and in their midst she bloomed away, independent of fear and sorrow.

We sat by the side of the white clay road, waiting for Kelly to call for us, our bag of apples between us. The light of youth made him look wild and rapid as he came tearing down the rutted track in a double-seated buggy drawn by a horse that had enough legs, manes, eyes and snorts for a dozen. The yellow eagle, our friend, stood up on the seat, howling, shouting, screaming and laughing, with a black buggy whip flying from side to side. The road seemed to be coming along with him and, just as I had a sense that chasms were opening out behind him as he galloped along, he drew up about fifty yards farther on, and had to back the buggy to let us get in. Then, with a swift turn, we scampered breathlessly back to his home.

His mother came out and greeted us quietly. She was a tall thin woman with narrow brown eyes that moved softly and nervously from side to side, as though she were trapped and looking for a weak place. Her toothless mouth moved and munched as she looked, and her cheeks twitched at every sound. He handed the reins into her restless but experienced hands and, mounting the white Arab, stood in the stirrups and trotted behind us rapidly to the township.

Whenever we looked back we saw the handsome embarrassed youth standing astride animated snow, harnessed with silver buckle and oiled leather; his planet of hair bursting with the rays of movement; his thin red cheeks rumpled with laughter under his long white nose; and a couple of wolf fangs standing clean and sharp in his naked gums. Had he and his mare taken to the sky by way of a drop of dew and ascended in mist, I should not have been surprised at all.

We passed old hop kilns where the lost pea-pickers, they told us, lay on wet winter days, and saw the kingfishers wedding the waters of the river with a golden flash of their beaks and claws. Past rows of hawthorn hedges in leaf, but lacking flowers, we trolled, until a tall yellow-brown cliff stood up in the River Mitchell.

"Eagle Point," they said.

Down we got and picnicked for hours. We swung on gum-trees

and looked down into the water from the top of the yellow cliffs. Misery began to oppress me again. I lay down alone, above the grassy thunder of the racers' hooves on the sports ground below, and the wintry sound of applause, and I looked up into the filmy heavens. A large white mask of a cloud, shaped into the face of an Egyptian woman, floated over: the mutilated lips trembling into dissolution, and the eyes seeking for something. This beauty wore a storm for a dress. It was sewn with lightning and she wore it until twilight, when she dropped it on our heads.

As it struck the ground, Kelly kissed me with the furtive whiskery kiss of youth, smelling of the sun and feeling like a blow from a hairbrush.

The kiss of youth is like the sip an old man takes from a glass of wine as he sits in the twilight; sipping, touched into life by the sip; trembling a little, and looking away until it is time to sip again. By the time the bottle is empty he is under the table.

And with youth, by the time the feelings of passion have gone, we are under the coverlets, wedded, bedded, with little interminable gongs called "offspring" that will not run down until they are jammed with bread and milk.

Kelly and I walked home together from his house that night, with the Arabian mare as chaperon. As we walked, and kissed, our blood mounted, and from the rear our staggering intoxicated gait must have been comical . . . the ballet legs and the bowed legs bending together.

Kelly exclaimed, "I feel like a bottle of yeast that must soon explode."

Afraid of desire, I tried to remember some saying of a great man. Tolstoi. "Women are like dogs. They have no soul," he said. "They have," I cried to heaven. I caught Kelly by the arm and made him run until he laughed and the Arab mare ran after us, the stirrups hitting her flanks and the bridle rattling on her jaw. The thunderous dress of my Egyptian still rose upon the horizon in the night, and from it a few hot drops fell. Kelly tied our Arabian chaperon to the orchard gate and we made our love, timidly and shyly, fearing even to touch each other.

There was the cold but happy ideal of the virgin in my mind, forever, a joy and a torment to me, and I laughed as we parted, saying, "We conquered . . . we conquered. Hands and heart go pure to bed."

"Oh, go on," exclaimed Kelly giving me a poke in the side, from which I retreated, pained and wondering. Always for me, the tea tin, the sixpence and the buttered trousers lay grinning in wait.

As I walked home through the grey orchard at dawn, that oldest sound in the world, the far-away screech of a cockerel, rang through me, and I wept at this natural voice of time. I have never forgotten that hour, for in it I was humiliated and my weak human spirit that laboured for the good in me was rendered weaker yet. Beneath my feet the grey sand lay, so calm, so still and, as if from the army that lay behind the trumpet-call of the rooster, a sigh arose, and moved by its sorrow the trees rustled restlessly. The hand of Gippsland had touched me and weakened me, and I doubted myself and the purity of youth and the worth of that purity.

Blue and I went down next evening to see Mr Harrison alone, feeling that we owed something of a homage to a man who had lived so long in our mother's country, and who knew and respected the colonial lineage of our peculiar family.

Mr Harrison sat on the tank-stand in the hot evening. He was still wearing the grey-blue flannel shirt we had seen him working in all day. It smelt of apples and sweat, and his underpants were turned over on it, like a sultan's girdle if you like, but mostly like white underpants.

He wiped his hand along his nose in greeting and shuffled the concertina which lay on his knee like a favourite child. We told him how we loved the old days when he was a youth, and revered the quality of time in Gippsland, and asked him to play us some old tunes, like "Rorie O'Moore", "Just as the Sun Went Down", "The Girl I Left Behind Me", and "My Father was a Frenchman".

Drawing it out to its full length and talking while he drew, he suddenly clapped the startled instrument together and rushed through, very sweetly, those old songs.

It was like rain falling through wet gums on a summer afternoon, and as the storm grew heavier, he raised the concertina in a rainbow above his head, and stopped the rain with it for a moment. The thunder of the bass prevailed, and down fell the rainbow and out rushed the rain of "Ring the Bell, Watchman".

His face was so sad when he played that the hands holding the concertina might well have come from behind the tank, while Mr Harrison listened as though he had toothache. Then he stopped and, shining his hair and whiskers with his hand, added in parenthesis, "Only wants a boomerang!"

At twilight we wandered from his place to the house of his brother-in-law, Rocky, the grey-faced, the bitterly blue-eyed, his rough hands cracked with rising early and harnessing horses. He filled these with snowdrifts of lard and complained bitterly as he sat by friendly fireplaces.

At Rocky's place we found a lot of fair people, two of them in motor-cycle mufflers and goggles.

Through them wandered an elderly man looking very severe and a little insane. On the couch lay a young married man who was at the stockinged-feet stage which is common among the married of Gippsland. After it, came the hanging-braces stage, but fashion will have banished that now. He was what the bush calls "a fine violin player", and could trill off anything on the instrument.

Blue was carrying her violin under her arm, and the stockinged-feet-stager offered to try "her" out with a tune or two, which "she" stood up to well. Then the elderly party with the severe yet insane look took the violin from Blue's hand and stood beside the door with it, looking as though he were meditating on a dry spell that had brought crows flying around the sheep and mortgages flying around the mail box, and on that violin he played, with an absent-minded hand, such tunes as Ulysses should have retorted to the harpies.

I only mention this house because the fair girl whom I scarcely noticed behind her motor goggles and scarf as she stood laughing with her lover, became known to me afterwards in the deeper part of Gippsland.

We called in to Harrison's on our way home. Kelly and the boys were waiting for us there. A small fair fellow dressed up as a comic parson was with them. His name was Florence and he had a hard open laugh that ended somewhere in the soft palate, or perhaps he had a hard palate and a soft laugh.

His girl sat beside him, the big bones of her chest rising and falling under the thin gold chain of the locket she wore.

Mr Harrison said, "I hear old Diddlie Herkits is looking for you fellows."

"What for?" asked the fellows, while Florence laughed harshly.

"He reckons you're treading his paddock flat by going every night to see Steve and Blue home to the fence."

"Aw, him!"

"And he's going to put a charge of saltpetre into your backsides if he catches you there again."

A riot of laughter like the squealing of pups with trodden tails rose from our heroes, and Kelly said, "By hell, I'll skin the old devil

when I get him. Let him dare come near me, and we'll do for him.
won't we, Moony?"

And Moony, who looked like a spoonful of ink spilt in a saucer,
laughed and said, "Let him try it on."

"You want to be careful, though," Florence cut in seriously. "He's
got a name for hardness around here: a tough old cove, they
reckon," and he gave another loud harsh laugh from his soft
looking mouth.

"By hell," exclaimed Kelly whirling his fists and spurs around,
"I'll eat him up, underpants and all, if he comes on me while I'm
crossing that paddock." The sight of his courage would have made
your heart leap. I drew near him and told him that I had written a
poem about him . . . beginning,

> O heart, let love die young,
> Then we'll remember
> His stripling soul, and shall we not recall
> His lovely body golden with December
> And the . . .

H-m-m, ah er—well, I hadn't quite finished it.

Florence sat in his corner beside the girl, twisting the parson's
collar around his neck and laughing about something.

The boys rose at last, to take us up to the fence as usual, and
with wild shouts of valour and defiance in the direction of Diddlie
Herkits's house. The night was full of exclamations like "By cripes",
"By hell", "By the gods", "By jove". Diddlie was torn to shreds, his
beard flung to the trees, his nightshirt to the sky, and his hobnails
to the earth, by those ravenous, danger-seeking bravoes of the
bullock and pruning knife, as they embraced the old fence and
told us their methods of attacking aged narks in their home
paddocks. Finally, with a loud defiant farewell they left us and
turned for home. But, remembering Florence's strange smile I
persuaded Blue to hop over the fence and trail them back across
the paddock. They straggled across the tufts of reeds, stumbling
here and there and still fulminating threats, as they advanced in
the night.

" 'Ere! Wodjer mean be . . ." cried a stern voice and a decrepit
form leapt up from behind a bank of reeds, with waving white
beard and a glistening gun barrel held up in the long scrawny arms.

Screaming like wounded brumbies, our heroes trampled each
other down right and left, tore from each other's sides and fled in
all directions, shrieking with fear and horror.

The rattle of their boots and the echoes of their yells had just died away, when Diddlie Herkits took off the sheepskin hanging to his ears, flung down the bit of lead piping he carried, and, disguised now as Florence, went laughing over the paddock to Harrison's, while we with equal laughter stole home.

IV

IT was after this that Blue met Jim, who was to take us to Metung with him in the following springtime, and be our mate for a while. She met him, one night, in Bairnsdale, when Kelly's mare, which she was riding, bucked at the music of the municipal band. Jim came up to choke the mare, introduced himself as one who knew the mare and her owner, and saw Blue home.

On the following Sunday there was a long lonely hoot down at the orchard fence, between us and Harrison's, a pitiful stifled howl such as the river boats gave. Blue said to me, "Come down and meet Jim, and tell me what you think of him."

"There are a lot of good old mates named Jim, etc.," I said.

Walking down, I was introduced to a young fellow of medium height, absolutely bursting out of his shabby brown long-coated suit with muscular development. On his fat pink finger was a broad gold signet ring and motor-cycle club badges were quivering their wings all over his breast. On his big fat red face was a smug sweet smile; he had good teeth, Nordic blue eyes and short crisp fair hair. I acknowledged him, and after talking aimlessly for a minute or two, I walked back unthinkingly to the hut, and away from the best mate that we were ever to find, and one who was taking us to the enchanted land.

Poor old Jim; he attached himself to us like a tick to well-wooled lamb before shearing time. He was dangerous to take out to Sunday tea, for I never saw a hand cross a tea table more unobtrusively, and depart taking such a ton of food.

Sunday afternoons, deepening into winter, were warmed by the rays that shot from his striped collar, and the imprint of his hoof (shod with the gilt horseshoe on his lapel) was over our paradise from that time onward. Two things haunted Jim, making him seek friendly fires and roll cigarettes that a wombat could have crawled into ("boree logs", we called them). The two things were Jim's Uncle Gus, and his days "When I was a kid". His voice crawled low, long and humble like a worm when he spoke of them, and he raised the boree log between his thumb and first finger, the big signet ring nearly weighing his hand down to his ankles.

He had a deep respect for Blue and when he stood at our hut door and said, "Are yer there, Blue?" his voice was like the hush before a flower opens.

Usually the flower thrust its head out of the window and said, "Curse you, James, what do you want?"

"I thortcher might like ter come fer a ride, Blue."

"Got the horses?" in a business-like tone.

"Too right. Down at 'Arrison's."

"Right. Be with you in a minute." And off they rode, farther into the country of Gippsland.

One morning, just before summer really shifted from the land with her umbrella and water-cart, Mr Desperandum took us down to a property of his on the Mitchell. We were to pack pears there, and I didn't want to go because I had diarrhoea; but when we arrived at the gate of that old orchard, and I saw the black trees imprinted with red flower-like fruit among which the hairy pigs rooted, my bowels adjusted themselves, held firm by admiration for a while. We climbed up a stairway to a dusty rattle-trap building and began to work.

Mr Desperandum took off his starched collar and joined us. But, alas, I was rupturing within and was approaching that state of mind when I wished to confide in someone who had once had an illness. Or more important, in anyone related to a doctor, or at the last pinch, a clergyman. The nearest to these transcendental states was Blow-ther-Beard, who was in the Salvation Army. Approaching him stealthily when he was packing pointed pears into their cases, I commented on the dreadful heat.

Blow-ther-Beard said, "Yairs, she is pretty warm."

Did he think that she was the cause of much intestinal trouble that was going around the district at the present? I didn't indicate the district most acutely affected at the time.

"Might be; never know."

Could he indicate a remedy to deal with such an undue irritability in an elderly person of refined habits, who was known to me and waiting in the extreme of patient agony until I arrived home that night with the remedy?

Blow-ther-Beard looked out on to the Mitchell, pear in hand, as though he had seen a fish there, and said slowly, "Starch is as good as any."

I looked around and about that bare shed while my bowels yearned for the sight of a striped packet with advertisement on it and dialogue between mistress and maid as to the virtues of Such-and-Such on shirts and collars . . . collars . . . ah!

Mr Desperandum's collar!

There it lay, clean and calm on his paper holder. I worked towards it, coiling and uncoiling with agony, and while he was out of the room I brushed it on to the floor behind a case of pears and let it lie there until lunch time. The extreme heat drove Blue and myself down to the wide river where we sat boiling our tea billy on a fire of willow sticks. The long white fish among the red water weeds flung themselves out like the arms of the water to embrace any fly that hung, buzzing an airy kiss above their cold snouts.

When the tea was made I drew the starched collar out from the middle of my clothes and put it on to boil in fresh water.

"By cripes," exclaimed Blue, starting up from the grass. "What have you got there?"

"The Nils Desperandum, a sure cure for diarrhoea."

A few minutes afterwards, the Mitchell took unto itself an Arrow, super-styled with reversible points, size eighteen and a half . . . and with it went my malady.

Kelly was still coming down, weekly, from Black Mountain, his memory quivering with the sight of wild brumbies that galloped down to drink at twilight by the big pools along the rivers. He pawed the ground with his feet while he talked of them, his hair crackled and his eyes sparkled with male wildness, and his voice grew deeper than his age warranted.

I was beginning to sense, through other things, that my tragedy of love was an inverted comedy, and the wisdom of Gippsland came to me and I began to laugh outwardly at everything, and mock and make fantasy. I rode with Kelly through a little bush town, called Bulumwaal. The thunderous aboriginal name haunted me, for it meant "The Land of Good Spear-wood".

"In the old days," said Kelly, "the blacks came here to get wood for their spears."

We rode towards the home of a man named Rusty Organ, in the hope that we might get a few plump ripe grapes. The sight of the grey bush with its millions of little fine dry twigs was like a hopeless thirst in me, and with a vindictive appetite I longed to throw the gum-trees down and give the kookaburras that sat raising and lowering their tails on the bows, the rich elms of some other land. I longed to build palaces and set galleons sailing on every drop of water I saw lying dull and rusty in the waterholes.

Every look in every direction enfeebled me with despair, while torment muted me.

Rusty Organ's lean-to was an architectural mingling of a sty and a fowl-house. He lay in a broken bath in the shed, reading a paper two years old, and took off his shattered black derby hat, to me.

"We got very few grapes this year," said Rusty in a creaky voice.

Apologizing for disturbing him, we crawled away. He lay back, and as a sign that this sleeping beauty of the bush would dream his aeon away, the blowflies chanted to each other and bound their wreaths funereal around his head.

"You're a beauty," I said to Kelly, as we lay under a gum-tree, biting the acrid twigs.

"Well . . . last year, he had heaps of them."

"I've got a good mind," said I, sitting up, while my old friends, Verlaine and Keats, lay their length on the grass and held each other's convulsive hands, "to go to New South Wales for the maize-picking next month, when the apples give out."

"They reckon yer make good money there," said the love of my soul.

"If youse care to wait around here till spring," Jim told us, that night, as we sat around the fire at Wilson's, "I'll get a job for both of youse and me down at Metung on the Gippsland Lakes, pickin' peas."

The brave wood in the open fireplace waved its hands over our faces, and I thought that I had never seen Kelly look so terrifyingly beautiful as at that hour, so at the mercy of time, which was blooming in him, not with the sensuous lights of maturity, but with the pure gleam of early youth, when the lips and eyes are innocent and merry. At that hour, I imagined his colouring to be the immortal part of our lives—every flush and tint was the beginning of eternity for me—but now I perceive that it was the words of poor old Jim that were the portals of new life, such as it was.

"What's this town of Metung like?" we asked, made languid by the fire.

"It's near Nowa-Nowa . . . round from Colquhoun . . . by Swanreach in a way . . . above the Nicholson and not far from Johnsonville. . . ."

That was the sort of idea we got of it, and then the names of old families there were spoken, but they meant nothing to me. For I was tired of Gippsland.

"No," said I, sad at heart, but mocking them all, "we're off to New South Wales." A wildness came into my heart and I spent myself with a free hand on imaginary adventures there.

It was in this way that I decided to leave Gippsland.

As we stood on the veranda of Kelly's home, the summer lightning flashed through the iron lace below the guttering, and Kelly's mouth came out of that flash and bent, wild and sorrowful, to my mouth.

It was a look, and then a kiss, that said, "I am the earth of Gippsland, and while I endure I shall bring to me and send from me, lovers, wives, sons and daughters unending. But you, I do not need." Then he stepped back lightly and silently on his insect feet that trod the ground as though tapping it for honey wells.

A great broken crying sounded among the leaves of the orchard, waking us early, a few mornings afterwards, and we leapt out of bed and sought the throats from whence the crying came. Big brown and white birds were hopping furtively from bough to bough, moaning like heart-broken women. "For the best, for the best, for the best! Oh . . . ho . . . oh . . . ho. Aye . . . for the best! Oh ho, oh ho!"

They were the harbingers of autumn, the brown and white jays come around the coast from New South Wales, driving workers like themselves from the orchards into empty bush huts to wait for work, or down to the city to seek it there, unhappily.

It was after that, that we began to pack older fruit: King David apples with purple stains on their rounded gold; and little pears, perfumed and harsh skinned. Then did the bell stop ringing; the inactive grader was full of shadows, for the shed was closed, and Blow-ther-Beard was seen only among the Salvation corps that croaked testimony in the main street of Bairnsdale on Friday nights. Mr Homburg, enthroned in a sulky, wrapped in a green coat, with a new high hat curling about his kind eyes, rattled away with his tins and his little daughter beside him. The Trumpeter's note rose no more defiant from his straw mattress, and the consumptive packing-case youth died all untimely in his dismissal.

The early winter rain came side-on into Gippsland, the apples on the ground were sandy and those on the trees streaked with tears. The Harrison brothers picked no more of them, but staidly ploughed the soil between the trees.

The packing was over, and it was now time for us to be off. Willingly, we would have stayed in the little hut for the winter, but we were not wanted.

One last walk I took alone down to Waddel's to see that land of the stormy light again; but it was like grain that had been ripening, and while I had been absent a reaper had come and cut it down and bagged it up in a great black cloud which lay over the spot where I had looked at lost beauty.

But I was consoled by finding the largest mushrooms I had ever seen. The cows were chewing them down on the flat. I picked some and took them home and cooked them.

One last ride with Kelly; one last halt on the mysteriously greening hill above Harrison's where the lights of autumn, tearing at the flesh of the grass, bared its veins and mystically the blades shook in the late sunlight, their gestures making an acre of great declaration as sombre as decay.

The long clay road, in its dampness, was like the frozen floor on which little Kay walked in the palace of the Snow-queen, and on the black and hairy legs of the gum-trees, the small beads of red sap showed.

It was then that I tasted that despair which comes to us, the humans, who long to be joined to time; and I hated the day because the meaning of life was full in it, and richer than we could ever be. It retreated, taking with it that which it was intended we should know.

In me, there is not water in vain: for me, the flight of the clouds at evening in apostasy; I, too, am cloud, and should have been invited to go. Even the coming of the stars implies a scorn, for they came and I did not come with them, and at night, all night, I am made drunken and laid away so that I may not share in the rites of the hours. Day was begrudged me and night was denied . . . Love was permitted to join me and half explain, until it, too, became part of my own ignorance and could teach no more.

These were the thoughts I had, while I sat in the saddle on the hill above Harrison's, looking down on their smoking chimney.

It was the last night at Wilson's too, and I sat beside Kelly in the front room overlooking the ancient road from Tambo, and stared at his father who had that day come from Tostaree for a holiday. Out of the bush he came, with hair as grey as the wattles there, and nose as hooked as an eagle's below eyes of brilliant bush-

sky blue. The quiet deaf man sat in an easy chair looking at us. My
mother had known him years ago; they had been boy and girl
together, and now I sat by his son, in love with him and the old
traditions of Gippsland.

My mind, held ecstatically in a body rich with unspent life,
towered like the music of a symphony and fell to terrible depths
of loneliness again, making me smile and shudder.

The old grandmother and the grey father sat oblivious of us all,
of the music and the kerosene-lamp which had overflowed on the
glass and was soaking up the grey moths in the patterns around the
stand. My mind writhed and sped far into the future, and I
dreamed with surety of a day when I should return and see Kelly
again. Then, then, I should not be silent and unhappy in their
midst. I thought that I should come to him, and sitting in this same
chair, soft and green and old, I should sing in an alien tongue,
unceasingly, like a siren. Above me rose a jungle of rich thoughts
and ecstatic sensation, and through it I writhed like the serpent
Lamia, with speckled crown, dappled throat and a blaze of sweet
fire beaming from my folds.

Beyond the room, the square window and the dry veranda, lay
the white road with its darkness of rain in rut and hollow. It
curved and it crawled, mile upon mile, into the bush to which
Kelly was returning—to Black Mountain.

Ah, mythical name! Ah, name of dark and lowering splendour,
shall I not some day come to you?

The levels below the window were white, and flashing with the
slow lanterns of buggies, the swift cars with their rattling hoods
and curtains. On one side stood the ranks of red gums, rough-
barked, bleeding with thick sap in the night . . . their roots littered
with the hieroglyphics of twig and nut.

That old remembrance of my childhood returned and I clung
to it, wrestling the full sweetness from its colours and command of
time, its coherence, its god-like sanity in oblivion's lunacy.

The rain gleamed on the white clay road, the wheels of the
coach ground together as the horses reared under the insensate
flogging.

My mother screamed, and I, hovering, it seemed, above it all,
must have screamed too, for she cried out, "I'll get out, Mr Frazer,
and walk. . . . Stop the coach, I'll get out and walk!"

"No, no. Stop where you are. I can manage them!"

The whip rang out. Oblivion seized me and held me at its
will. . . .

Now, grown adult, and in partial command of my body, but still held slave to time and blinded by it, I sat looking out on the white road and the black trees that bled in the night, while oblivion clung and held the minds of those passing along it.

But surely . . . away from all this . . . in the grey paddocks, lay poetry and love?

The mass of desire in my mind moved together and ground huge shapes laboriously one against the other, moved forward by an avalanche of poetic power. The first line escaped into poetry; fled clear for a moment, but returned to the edge of the conflict and was sucked down; fought, was clear again, but could not entirely free itself until all its fellows were with it, and the mass of conflict that had fed observation was discarded for . . .

> I see across the plains, the cup,
> The lover-haunted space.
> The little hollow that gives up
> Their murmurs from its face.
> I see, as now, upon occasions
> Faces and breasts that shine
> Faintly in that fiery basin,
> Faintly in its pallid wine,
> Flashing like slender fish about
> Their small ecstatic sea,
> A delicate, swift and careless rout
> Of uneager lechery.
> The stemless cup with its fevered wine,
> Its lovers and limbs that slide
> From lip to lip, and without sign,
> Into the gloom subside.

A meagre offering this to come from the singing multitudes in my mind, I thought, and swore to return one day and sing Kelly an alien song in which all my love should be shown.

Kelly's mother, her toothless cheeks softly hollow, nervously twitching, sat as restlessly as a fox in her chair, her brown eyes constantly looking towards the door. There was no ease in her. I could not understand that she had given it all to pad the souls of her sons and daughters. Now she appeared to be hunting in some never-ending forest of her mind.

I went over and said to her, "I should like to have known your husband's sister Myra. My mother told me that she was very beautiful in her youth. I believe that my uncle loved her."

"Yes, my husband told me that she used to work for your mother's people. I've got a photo of her somewhere. She said she was coming up here, soon, for a holiday. Her husband's left her and she's had a hard struggle."

"I'd like to see the photograph, if you could find it."

"M —— mmm," said the tall wiry bushwoman, glancing restlessly from her nervous eyes. "If you come into my room, we'll have a look for it." The father sat quietly on the couch, never noticing. The son sat opposite him, breathing quickly.

Gran slept in her daughter's room. The old lady had got into the white cotton bed with its dry bush smell of the Australian sun, and it spread widely around her, fold on fold. Her little white head was a mere speck on the pillows, but the power of old womanhood came from it and she silently despised us and our hunt for the photograph.

"Yes," I remarked, to fill in the awkwardness of the search through old trunks and drawers. "Yes, my uncle loved her once. It's strange, you know, to think that we've come back to this country where they lived and loved long ago." No one answered. Things were tumbling out of boxes and tins, bringing with them sad perfumes of forgotten days. "I have a clear picture of your sister-in-law in my mind. My mother said, 'Myra was a pretty girl. She had a high head of golden brown curling hair, piercing blue eyes and long flat red lips. She was always singing.' I am sure my uncle would have married her. We had a photo of him at that time. He had just come back from India. A nervous, tense-looking fellow with a wisp of moustache and fair hair parted at the side. You remember those old coats they used to wear, with the little lapels right up to their collars? He wore a grey coat and a little spray of lilies in the buttonhole. A wild, nervous, useless-looking fellow, but she might have made him into something. I often think I can see their last parting. His family, our people, didn't want them to marry, so she decided to leave them, because she couldn't bear to be with him, and know that. The coach drew up . . . my mother said . . . and Myra came out on to the veranda, dressed to go away in it. He came forward to shake her hand, but she flung her arms around him and cried bitterly until he had to put her gently in the coach, and it rolled away. I think, I always think that it was sad. Ever since I have met Kelly her brilliant blue eyes and her golden brown hair have been in my mind. I think they must be alike."

"Here's the photo," said Kelly's mother, handing it to me. "Of course," she added apologetically, "she's changed a lot. She was young then, when your mother knew her."

It was a cheap postcard. A tall woman stood in front of a papier mâché landscape. She was dressed in a clumsy costume of serge, and she had a large flat face, long distorted lips, lost hopeless eyes and a head of high waving hair. A little girl held her hand.

"Ah," I said. "Yes. A fine face . . . thoughtful, sad. Yes, very fine."

Next day, Mr Nils Desperandum took us into the railway station, and we asked him might we come back next year.

He half promised and he half refused; we heard afterwards that his wife had pinched the two into full denial and that we were to return no more to the old orchard.

Kelly came to see us off, and thrust his head of golden palsied curls into the carriage for a moment; but a bunch of flowers hanging around us from someone's hands extinguished him, all save a bony throat, a gilt stud and a shyly bitten lip.

Jim came, too, talking huskily to Blue about the spring crops of peas in the town called Metung.

The station bell wrested itself from the master's hand and rushed down the platform to me, glaring at me brazenly and clapping out in unisons, "You shall not forget the country of Gippsland and the old orchard where you loved."

Outward fled the train.

V

Once more, we stood on the red and white flagged floor among our drawings and verse, while the plum-tree bough swished along the top of the roof.

"Well, Mia, did you get all our letters? How's Priestly and The Twenty Trained?"

Mia hurried around her house making tea and cooking food for us. What a tiny creature she looked . . . how frail and mortal, and this house, how futile it seemed after wide Gippsland!

"Well, little woman," we repeated for the hundredth time, stroking our imaginary moustaches, "we had a great time."

The walk to Waddel's farm rose up, the traitor, and tried to elbow me out of the way to tell the truth, that I was growing up and getting to a marriageable age; but I said steadfastly again, "A great time, little woman. And now, Mia, we're going to Noo South Wales to pick maize."

"No!" exclaimed the little woman emphatically.

"We are. Have you got the *Weekly* here?" (We got most of our jobs from the agricultural pages of an interstate weekly.) "We

must look for a job. Give us a cup of tea, little woman." We leant
above her stroking our long ginger moustaches and kicking each
other in the shins.

"But did you see any of the old-timers?"

"Yes . . . old-timers? Dozens of them. Heard the old names, you
know . . . the Thorburns and Baulches and Svensons and Callinans.
But, it's not the same, Mia. The new generation's on the go now,
and they don't care for the concer. Rather have the gramophone.
We told you about the Harrisons, didn't we? And the Wilsons.
Kelly, the son, is just like Myra, too."

We gave a great performance that night . . . a mime of everyone
we had met up in Gippsland.

Mia was enchanted and begged us to stay home for a while, but
we attributed her softness to hardening of the arteries and, lifting
her up on to the kitchen table like the Dormouse, we operated on
her clothes with a bread knife and cupped her into the tea pot.

That night the atlas came out, the weekly paper came out and
our cash had an airing, too, in between strokings of imaginary
whiskers, the playing of old songs Blue had learnt from Mr
Harrison and our imitation of a bush ballroom.

We settled down for a few days; myself, in the poet's corner
where the ivy came down by steps and stairs through the old
fireplace and bound a bitter wreath around my head as I sat hour
by hour, thinking out lyrics. These were printed in a large book
and a drawing done opposite them by Blue.

I wrote many letters to Kelly, but he wrote only one, saying in
it, "I can't forget the old orchard." The words turned into grey leaf
and heavy fruit and the sorrow of love before my eyes, and I
mocked as never before, imitating the Gippslanders and stroking
my beard as I stood at the door with my hat drawn over my eyes
like a bushman at a dance. The unrest was on me, and I hurried our
plans to leave for New South Wales as soon as possible.

VI

Grape pruning has begun at Rutherglen on the Murray.
Good crops of maize are expected this year in Gundagai and Tumut,
although floods are apt to cause some damage, if the heavy rains continue.—
Interstate Weekly.

"Well, Mia, we'll go to Rutherglen first and see if we can get
any grape-pruning to do. . . . If not . . . on to Gundagai and Tumut
to pick maize," I said, finding something at last in the paper.

I waited for days for a letter to come from Kelly; but we had to strike out, at last, and early one morning we caught the Sydney Mail from Spencer Street Station and began our journey to Rutherglen.

In the warm corridor, the most unstable things were the big-globed lamps hissing in the roofs of the carriages. They looked faintly ectoplasmic. The footwarmers felt like discarded hot-water bottles, a trifle indecent, from someone else's bed. We sat on first-class seats with second-class tickets in our pockets, looking out of the window and mumbling and trembling in awful mutual conversation whenever a guard passed the door. A richly dressed young man, heavy with suitcases, came in and made himself comfortable in the corner opposite, and we felt from this intrusion that the scene was ready for our unveiling and our humiliation.

In came the guard, hand and clipper. "Tickets please!"

Mournfully, ruefully, stupidly, we brought out our second-classers and said "Yes", to "This is first class, you know".

And "Yes", to his, "You'll have to go down second"; and we crawled out under the unseen but imagined contempt of the rich young gent.

"Tickets please," said the guard.

And a few minutes later, with much scrambling of effects and defects, the richly dressed young gent followed us down to limbo. But the turning out was in the nature of a good turn.

The man from Mount Bulla sat in his corner, second class, clasping a hot-water bottle to a couple of broken ribs, and talking to the man with the glass eye and the thick moustache. Above the roar of the train, this individual's only contribution to the conversation rose frequently.

"Bunkum," he said.

"Bunkum," again.

"Bunkum," forever.

A little dark woman with tender eyes and a toothless mouth sat beside him, in the expectant silence of the stranger who wishes to get into the conversation at some time or other.

In the corner by the landscape window sat a frail young man, with his white chin in his bony hand, drawn along, dreaming, through the dawn which had lit a fire for itself on the edge of the country and was sitting around it, warming a pair of cloudy hands.

The man from Mount Bulla took the water bottle from against

his ribs, and poured something steaming hot and yellow from it. This he drank from a glass, refilled, and passed to Bunkum.

We were passing over the plains and could hear through the silence of the carriages the sonorous sighing of the engine which seemed to have forgotten us. The dawn's fire spread, and the white tents of the roadmakers had a weary, sleepless look about them as we passed, and over fine fires in front of them sausages leapt and sang in the morning bath of dripping.

"Wah!" roared the carriages as we shaved the galvanized shed near the line, that seemed to leap to meet us, turn with us, try to run with us; but we left it behind, staring across the plains.

Far ahead, the engine chanted and bore us towards Rutherglen and the poetic Rhineland wine and songs of our old fairytales.

That communicative feeling which travellers over steppes and plains entertain and do not dream of repulsing, animated us all: the silent flat journey hypnotized us into a dreamy pleasantness and questions were simply asked and as simply answered.

The man with the glass eye put his arm around the woman with the cross eyes and forgot to say "Bunkum". Through grey and showery country over fern gullies where bushmen walked clay roads, we flew. Blue took down her violin and we walked out into the corridor, where she played, while we stared down into leaves of the wet bush. The rich melancholy of youth, the reverie of the heart, was coming over me again, and bowing me into my hands, while my large bosom and broad knees intruded themselves, it seemed to me, on everyone.

The old man from Mount Bulla said he'd like to ask us up to stay with him for a while; and with the eagerness of the workless looking for work—that they hope they won't find—we tried to pin him down to the essentials of when and how. But he, with a sense, I think, of "the wife", put it off, and it would be too late now.

The train stopped at the dreary station of Springhurst. A hotel, long, dark-browed, silent under a drooping brown hat of a roof, returned the look of travellers with as great a variety of malevolence as could be achieved by odd doors and windows. It seemed that the early colonizers had felt some need to declare the place a township and had made their statements in sentences composed of wooden rails and vine-like houses to which bits of leaf clung. A gentleman named Dust, who could easily be imagined as sailing up the main street all summer, had taken to bed and lay moist under a sheet of water on the roads, through which local sulky wheels splashed and into which rain fell sadly.

The next stop was Rutherglen, the vineyard district to which we had come prepared to pick, cut or burn grapes. We were ready, as the picker is always, to leap out of our tailored clothes and mutilate anything in exchange for a hut and a few shillings a week. The flat country looked to me like a sick old man, and over it the skeleton-bare vineyards bowed, doing Holbein's "Dance of Death", peering, grimacing and saying "Come with me".

Rutherglen was not like Bairnsdale. Autumn had given it the look of a rusty tin. Amply feminine in our masculine clothes, we got out of the taxi at the hotel and sat down in the hotel bedroom. It was one of those blurred pieces of atomic life that are responsible for feelings of class inferiority. Passing through the plains I had felt manly, melancholy and potentially great; but the washstand, the crockery jug and the basin changed me into a masquerading pea-picker in a few moments. What despair!

How could one talk about it, hedged in as we were by our own clumsy flesh and the worse flesh of our needs, as expressed by this stuff. And then, we were so utterly outside settled humanity. Because, by way of travelling, we were just rolling stock and immoral, until proved.

Now, for the vignerons. We had been advised to meet them as they came out of the local bank where they were holding a conference. I imagined them to be all Verlaines; fine young Frenchmen, young poets, seeing us as we saw ourselves, working in the shadows of the cellars, racking the vine. Or on a hot Australian day, plunging our hands into the solar system of the vine. Messieurs, we are the salt of the earth; we are the poets to be; the artists whom men shall love forever. Give us work with you; let us make poetry under your patronage.

Down the stone steps of the bank they plunged, a motley lot of brown-clad men, jovial, with wine-clear skins, stout with youth and well tailored.

We stepped forward to meet them.

Ah, heaven, that first step forward to meet the employer; what a killing thing it is!

"Good afternoon," we said, stopping the general of the troop. "We have come from Gippsland to search for work among the grapes."

They swirled around us; some unwilling to stop; others pulling them back with a "Hey . . . one moment! Do you know if. . . ." Intimate mumbling followed into the ear of him who had turned.

The rest looked at us with an expression that said, "Curse these what-are-theys. What do they want?"

The poetry of toil, messieurs.

A big brown face with a swollen nose bent over us; a watch-chain winked and rattled on his warm chest. The large vigneron heard us out and then turned to the others. "These young ladies want work in vineyards. Has anyone a vacancy?"

More milling and murmuring, while our blood grew hot and ashamed, and we struck an attitude midway between calm unhappiness and an eager defiant simper.

"Well, you see," they replied, one against the other, in rising and falling tones, "the picking is over, and the racking is done by men."

"But the pruning?"

"We—ll. Have you had any experience doing that? You need good strong wrists." Ours withered under their merry critical looks.

"I know a woman who does pruning," one of them exclaimed, and a vast feeling of awe at his charity in knowing such a person spread through all of us.

However, like a troop of jolly porpoises that have been stopped in their gallop to the sea, they shook us off, slid us off, gaily, happily and kindly.

Somehow or other, we found ourselves on the other side of the street, talking to a tall thin man with a delicate hand and short moustache. There was a small man, there, too, with a piercing glare and an inquiring mind. Behind him stood an old building . . . its cracked grey window bearing the fatal legend of the local newspaper, with which we, fools that we were, never associated him.

Said he, "Why don't you try domestic work? There's plenty of that around here."

"That job can go into the waste paper basket," we replied. "We are out to see Australia."

Those common words were to look awful within a few hours' time in the metropolitan Press. They were to make us feel that our delicate judgment of this world was childish. But the tall man with the short moustache had a daughter who was just like us.

In our private vanity, we wouldn't allow such a thing. No one was ever like us.

So he took us to a terrible café . . . and a café in an Australian town can be a terrible thing indeed; and there we drank tea with him and ate the pink icing cakes that have followed the white race all over the earth.

That man was kind. He pushed you on towards the adventure of suffering. The others only tried to push you down into the domestic mire. Time enough for that, messieurs. We shall not need pushing when the hour comes.

That night I could not sleep. This contact with men, and the effort to meet them and interest them in us, had made me into a wasting dynamo that tossed all night and fought the world, wanting it knew not what.

Love? Yes, love; but more than love. Something into which this enormous stream of power might be turned. I wanted to make things; to orate powerfully from a mind of genius. And then, my terrible loneliness tormented me.

The evening in Rutherglen had been as wild and sweeping as the wind. We had walked through the little back streets, and men and women had cried out to each other, wondering what we were. One rather likeable woman had even rushed after us, holding her hands under her red sweater, while she drew in our youth and our oddness, and told us, "I'd have known this one (Blue) was a girl by her hips: but I couldn't tell from you."

We caught the first and only train early next morning. A man in a khaki coat sat with his wife opposite us and stared hard at us from Rutherglen to Springhurst, where we had to catch the Sydney train again. For Rutherglen is a branch line.

The sun shone into a shower as we got out of the train and stood among a group of jockeys and their trainer, bound for Albury races. Other jockeys or lads were gently pulling the heavy timid horses out of their vans, and their medieval rugs turned the day into a carnival for me.

Blue, impelled, stepped forward, took the reins from the hands of the lad, and led the animal out.

We joined the jockeys. The trainer was a dwarf, with a tiny wizened face, fascinating in its miniature ugliness; on his feet he wore wee buttoned boots with white spots in the middle of the black buttons. The jockeys, honest country fellows, young, fresh and smelling of straw, with thick gold rings on their fingers, walked with us across the railway line into the township of Springhurst.

We parted there; put our luggage in the parlour of the hotel and prepared to settle down to the two-hour wait for our train.

A red road down to the local butter factory was a little slice taken out of time, and soon we were in the damp concrete rooms, looking into tubs of butter and tasting whey that the manager gave us to drink. He was a dark serious man who had lived in Rutherglen.

But we didn't want to talk of that Aceldama.

We were drinking, and trying to put all our intelligence into understanding the making of butter, and hoping that he would offer us work of a good kind when in walked the tiny trainer, the jewel, the little lump of worked leather, and his jockeys.

Drawing us aside, he said in just the wrong sort of voice, calculated to arouse a storm of emotions, "Two detectives and a police sergeant have arrived from Rutherglen to find out who you are. Can we help you to make a getaway across the railway line?"

"What on earth for?" I asked, and knew for a moment that this was the part of life that held for me something that work could never give. Here was argument, conflict and victory. Here, in fact, was acting, which I loved.

The trainer and his jockeys walked a little to the rear, advising Blue to cover the gold bracelet on her wrist, and muttering a lot of other advice that would have been too sane to take.

Ahead of us, in the red road, stood a tall green-grey overcoat, inhabited by a severe ginger man.

"Are you two girls masquerading as boys?" he asked as we drew up to him.

With a puff of power that seemed to make the words epic, I advised him that we couldn't discuss the matter on a wet road; but . . . to our suite, our boudoir, come, fair sir, wrapping the grainy gaberdine about your fox-like form.

Springhurst, which had, when we arrived, opened an empty mouth to us, was now filled with the usual set of rustic dragon's teeth. In retrospect, I thank them. I multiplied them into thousands that day, with the power of an amateur producer managing a mob of ten into two hundred.

Two large impersonal sort of men, standing under the veranda, joined us in the private parlour of the hotel. Outside, the multitude brawled and seethed, I hope.

I was beaming, chuckling, shivering within, over my words, my act; and as I sat down in a chair, with the sergeant riding side-saddle on one beside me, I felt genius pouring through me, and if I could have rendered these men down into ink and used their bones as nibs, I should have done it.

"Now," said the sergeant, "what does this mean? Are you two masquerading as boys?"

"Where," said I, "is your authority? First show me your authority."

"I'll soon show that." And out it came. A little book saying that Sergeant Picklebottle of So-and-So could ride in a tram as far as he liked without paying.

"But we are not trams," I objected. "This won't do at all." A stamp fell out of the book, too, in a homely fashion, and the sergeant bent to pick it up with the blood rushing to his head.

"That has nothing to do with it. Here is the authority you asked for." And he put the free tram ride back into his pocket again.

"Well," I began; but suddenly, staring at the grey wall and one picture with a splash of blood across its ugliness, I cried dramatically: "How can refutation be made in such a room as this? A colonial bar parlour, with walls the colour of badly cooked steam-puddings . . . with a picture like that . . . who's the painter?" I went over to it and had a good look. "Bah! No name. I thought not. Sirs, refutation to any charge cannot be made here. I demand the rich laboured spread of century-old tapestry, the scenes and perfumes of other lands, the mocking glances of slaves that bring wine to us. You ask, in this hermit's cell . . . are we masquerading as boys. No, we are masquerading as life. We are in search of a country . . . the Promised Land, seen one morning, rising bubble by bubble from the clouds above the hills of blackberry vines."

"Well, why not wear women's skirts and thick woollen stockings?" said the sergeant.

"The blackberry vines demand more."

"Two good-looking young women like you have no right to be getting around like this."

"We are not young women. We are life, sorrow, loneliness, searching. . . . God knows for what."

"Are you looking for work?" asked the now smiling detective.

"Work? Yes. If maize be the poetry of life, the maize that leans rotten and bemired, waiting for the sad-faced picker, cold and unhappy, and without gifts of brain, to raise him from his wandering life, then we are looking for work. We are going to Tumut, to pick maize."

"Is your father alive?"

"No."

"Mother?"

"Yes."

"Have you any relatives whom we could notify or verify your statements by?"

"I have an uncle, a magistrate in Melbourne," I cried proudly, although the good man was an out and out bad 'un. Never mind; his name rang through the room like the last trumpet call that finishes hostilities.

At his name, the flesh before us bowed and—saying, "Well, I suppose you can look after yourselves. You seem able to." Gone was our sergeant, our smiling detectives and the hour.

We sailed out of Springhurst, with the blood of victory in our faces, and played the violin and sang and talked, in our youth remembering not any Creator, trusting in our own purity and love of beauty, forever.

That night we stayed at the hotel in Junee, and on, next morning, to Cootamundra. We reached it at night, and came into the hotel lounge with our long overcoats belted around us, and wide trousers showing below. . . . Our dark heads were shining and our healthy young faces were vivid with life.

The elderly proprietress entered us, and up the stairs we walked. Empty as it reads now . . . it was life then, working towards destruction, perhaps, it may seem to others. But had that way of life been always followed by us, it had not gone so ill in after years.

As we sat in our room, on the white cotton bedspread, staring out at the ironwork in the backyard below, the proprietress rushed in with clean towels. We had taken off our coats, and I dared not look down to see if my broad bosom was apparent. Blue looked suspiciously feminine to me, as with a gay "Here are your towels, boys", the lady plunged in, with a piercing stare. "By jove," we exclaimed, as she went out, and we stared at each other sternly.

"Did I look like a girl, then? Did my bosom appear large to you, old man?"

We fretted over that for a while, until at last we slept, while the long iron chimes of the clock struck.

Early in the morning, the sad, static housemaid came in with a cup of tea, in the saucer of which reposed a biscuit that looked like a finger-nail she had slipped. I love all servants when I am travelling. I sorrow for them and the eternal cleaning up that has to be done. I want to take them with us, too, masquerading, basquerading, and let work be hanged.

As we sat in the taxi, waiting for it to move off, the landlady came up the street, her well-kept head firm under the umbrella on which the rain pattered sadly.

"Good-bye, girls," she said.

We moved not; spake not; thought not.

Articulate was the wave of time that encircled us as we sat in the
Gundagai-Tumut train. Blue had never looked so beautiful. The
gold bracelet shone on her wrist, under the red sweater, to the
bewilderment of the passengers; her bow swept over the violin and
her face hung over it in full flower. The morning of life was in
the carriage, and our heavy flesh encumbered us with the agony
which is called self-consciousness.

The Tumut train is a very small one, and the driver is travelling
on a curved line that brings him face to face with you, all the time.
Leaning out, we smiled at him, as the bleak plains and the low
foothills accompanied us to Gundagai. Under the hot sun the flood-
waters lay over the maize we had come to pick. It was grey and
broken and had been picked some time ago.

We were too late; it was useless to look for work in Gundagai
or Tumut. My melancholy overpowered me again and I sat
bewildered and in pain throughout the long miles, thinking of
Gippsland and the old orchard, and Kelly.

Through the rust-red waters we came to Gundagai, looking out
sentimentally for the dog that sat on the tucker-box, "Nine miles
from Gundagai".

I saw a low-roofed hotel there, and from the vase in the refreshment room stole a yellow rose, and sent a telegram to Kelly, for
the sake of romance, saying that I was in Gundagai.

As we left the bush town and crossed the rumbling red surge of
the Murrumbidgee, a woman waved to us from a house above.

It was still morning when we got to Tumut, and the mid-winter
heat was stifling. The sun burnt on to our skulls as we walked
heavily from the station to the town; and right through the little
main street, past the glittering glass around the hotel and the cry
of the fat proprietor, "I say! Aren't those two . . . girls?"

The town ended at the Woolpack Hotel, where there was a
bullock team drawn up outside, with a pack-horse sleeping at the
back of the wagon and dusty dogs stretched out, chin on spotted
paw. We stood outside a Chinese hide-store and reverenced our
country at the altar of a bullock wagon, and mighty were the
deaths we wished to die for it, but not for the fat hotel proprietor,
whom we had to pass in diffidence, as we went back for something
to eat.

A little Chinese girl served us in a green room full of old pictures.

The hot red and white little carriages bore us away from Tumut
and onward back to Gundagai, which we reached by sunset. The

man from Gundagai stepped aboard at the last minute, flung in on us, crying: "By hell, I nearly missed her that time. I come in eighty miles on a scooter to catch her, and I had to go and get a bottler wine at the pub, and by cripes, I nearly missed her."

The lights were lit and hissed above us, slowly, while the man from Gundagai, wild, dirty, greasy-collared and vacant-eyed, drank. We got into his carriage and listened to him. " 'Ave er drink . . . 'ave er drink," he said, passing around his flask. "No one? All right, 'ere's the Woolloomooloo spit." He spat and drank.

"I been to the war, you know," he said, gasping after his draught. " 'Ere's me pay book. Three hundred and sixty-five days . . . that's three years, isn't it? Yairs. I got no luggage, but I'll soon have some."

He retired into the toilet and returned with the towel, a bar of soap and the coir matting from the corridor, carefully rolled up. This, he put on the seat beside him, together with the foot-warmer, and said, "Now I'm as good as any commercial. 'Ave er drink?"

In the next carriage sat a fine looking young Chinese, and beside him travelled, with slow majesty, the moon. There was a grave beauty in it, that slow Eastern face with the moon gliding beside it, and from the wild land outside came sad exhalations of time and growth.

> "I have the moon to supper, the most grave
> Genii of Dreams attend my breakfasting,"

we said to each other, quoting from a poem by Furnley Maurice.

Sitting down opposite the young Chinese, we began to talk to him. Our lonely minds that had desired for so long to flow in young, kindly and handsome company, now became eager. We told him of all that had happened; a big, tall, blue-faced man sitting by listened hungrily.

The fine honest face of the Chinese was alight with pleasure, but behind it all . . . what melancholy, what unrest and frustration!

O God, to stay the flow of time. How could I be happy? Even in that far youth, secure in it, I was crying, "You are passing, passing. I shall soon be old and this will be no more."

I was afraid, but thinking that there was some philtre which could preserve me against the wrinkling of the flesh, I sought. Outside ourselves, in youth, what is there but man? And man, I thought, can stay all these things. To be man's is to be eternally young, happy and rich in imaginings.

The train bore us along to Cootamundra again, where we had to change into the train that would take us towards home again, workless and almost broke. While we stood drinking black coffee with the young Chinese, the man with the blue face came in whispering, "The detectives are here, looking for you two. Come with me."

I think that I shall never know such sorrow again as I did on that night when, through the lights and the noise, we followed him, knowing that each of these new steps meant the ending. How could I enjoy youth knowing that it ended in age? White were the lights and grasping was time flying with us in its arms, as we followed him in a walk that seemed like a Dantesque journey to me, so much of the spirit was it.

We went out on the railroad, past the black steaming face of the Sydney Mail's engine, and over some colder lines where a little box-like carriage stood at the end of a cattle train.

Up we climbed with the young Chinese. Blue-face disappeared, and we heard next the spitting of sausages in a frying-pan in the guard's van.

The train took to the line, following the moonlight through rough stony country, beautiful and aching, like myself, to be at the end of all things and to understand all.

Blue took out the violin, and in the dark played Dvořák. The Chinese sang to it, the sort of voice that has strained until it is good enough for some choirs. It was stilted and disappointing, and I couldn't understand why he didn't open up his throat and be Chinese to the bottom of his larynx.

On went the train. The big dry boulders stood in the moonlight and the sorrow of life ached in me and cried for immortality; that this night might be forever.

The melancholy of one who has to die young stung me, although I was heavy with healthy flesh then. Suddenly the train stopped and we stood motionless, as though we had come to an end; had died and the whole universe had died with us, for the dry boulders stood with us and the moon moved on.

By the time the train had reached Junee we had told the young Chinese all; and as a poet, as part of that Eastern sky from whence the sun rises, we felt he would understand that we were not sex, but spirits.

Alas, and *eheu,* before we could avoid him, he kissed us both swiftly, as we parted for the night. "My sisters," he said fondly, and his strange mouth tasted like a bubble of meat.

Good night, sir; thank God, one writhes.

In the morning he was there to see us off; we evaded the kiss with an expert hand, and were heading for the border, back home, broke, but vastly entertained by corrupting the Chinese name into a noise that sounded like "Borrelerworreloil".

As we passed through Ettamogah and Gerogery, Blue played an old march our father used to play, while pools of rain dyed blue by the heavens shone in the green grass. A dark girl named Rose sat opposite.

"Good-bye, Rose," her father had said as he saw her off, and we clung to that part of her entity whenever we looked at her.

At Albury, a hideous hatred of Blue came over me. Yes, she looked so beautiful that I hated myself and I hated her, for I felt that I was a heavy ugliness doomed to eternal loneliness and sorrow. Yes, it was her slight flushed beauty that I hated as we walked, and in the golden poplars of Albury we quarrelled, and I walked away from her in self-loathing.

By my hatred, I had stretched a hand out into the future and helped to destroy her, and I knew it. Fear overcame everything, and when I saw her walking along the street, small and lonely, I came to her, overcoming my dislike that sprang again instantly at the sight of her beautiful face.

Poor Bluey. She took me in to dinner at the Border City Hotel and we ate between us a steamed pudding that took the edge off me, and I couldn't have hated anyone after that.

We caught the next train and settled down to listen to a beautiful rich voice in the next carriage. It came from a short ugly man who wore a tweet hat, and was apparently a foreman of the works on the Burrinjuck dam. He swore like a trooper, but his voice was vibrant with strings that wouldn't have disgraced a 'cello.

At Strathbogie, in the Kelly country, we peered out to see if we could glimpse the burning hotel and Kelly staggering out to meet the troopers with his arms and legs broken by bullets. But no sign. Two men got in, and their ugly faces, grotesque with the light and shadow under big hats, were uneasy as they settled their luggage. They had swags with them, and their clothes had a damp smell about them, as though they had been locked up in a gum-leaf wardrobe or lying over the flypole of a tent.

A drunk got in, too, announcing to all and sundry that he had no ticket. "I'm jumping the rattler, and I don't care who knows it," he bellowed.

"Tickets, please," said a calm precise voice down the corridor. The drunk searched hurriedly through his hanging pockets, and was looking under the seat when the guard came in; he was peering under beer bottle labels and combing out his whiskers as the guard neared him.

"Now, then, where's your ticket?"

"Lorst."

They searched. The drunk raised and brushed the very specks of dust on the floor, to gain time.

"No use," said the guard calmly. "You'll have to get off at the next station."

And lo, when the train lights stayed for a few minutes on a patch of green grass and barbed wire, down the line, the ticketless one, with howls and cries, was rushed off into his native bed.

Haunted by his lonely cold night ahead, and wishing that I could have paid for him, I turned to resume the conversation which the incident had permitted us to strike up with the two other travellers . . . possum-hunters from Strathbogie.

The eldest and ugliest was very anxious about a mysterious hidden quantity called his "little dorg".

"Mister," he appealed every time the guard came through, "how's my little dorg getting on?"

"All right, all right," returned the guard irritably.

"I wouldn't lose her for fifty quid," the possum-hunter explained to us. "And I hated putting her in the dorg box. Mister, how is she?"

"All right! All right!"

"We just come down from the Strathbogies today, miss," he continued. (Whereupon, the guard, who had said to us casually when we got into the train, "You two boys going home on school holidays?" to which we had murmured, "Yairs." . . . now looked grim and morose.) "And we're off to the city," chanted the possum-hunter, oblivious of the mortification going on under his eyes. "Yairs, we took the tent down this morning, and we've got the skins in that bag there, and we'll sell them in town and in a few days you won't know us, as you see us walking down Bourke Street, with our flat 'ats and our little walking sticks. You'll say, 'There's a couple er nobs all right.'"

"What did you live on, up there in the ranges?" I asked, wondering if we could take up possum-trapping for a living. "Did you make a go of it? What sort of equipment do you take with you?"

"Miss, you got to 'ave a good little dorg. Wish that guard'd come along. Aye, there he is. Aye, mister, how's my little dorg getting on?"

"Oh, he's all right; I told you before."

"Well, yer got ter have a good little dorg, for a start; and a few traps, a good tent, and a little pony and trap to take your stuff up for you. We been living on McAlpine's flour ever since we started out. Arh, you can't beat McAlpine's, miss. You mixes it up with a bit er water and baking powder. Yer throws it in ther pan, and there you are, the best little damper you could knock up anywhere.

"An' if you're going to town and yer want a nice clean collar . . . give her a bit of a rub and leave the rest to McAlpine's. Just dip her into it and give her a squeeze . . . hang her out . . . take her in when she's nearly dry, lay a hot brick on her and there you are, natty as any bloke in the city. This scarf I got on," he pulled a dirty matted looking mess of torn wool out of the front of his coat, "she was pretty dirty, yer see, miss. So I just boiled her in a mixture of soap and McAlpine's, and look at her . . . white as snow. And when yer find the blankets are wearing a bit thin, just you run them through a drop of water and McAlpine's, miss. That puts some body into them and they keep you warm . . . just like the best Onkaparinga."

(His silent, saturnine mate, standing on the swaying floor of the train, kept up a stealthy grin under his wide hat.)

When we told him about our search for work, he applauded it. "Just keep on having a good time and enjoying yourself, miss," said he.

At Seymour he got out and begged us to have a "little cuppa tea and a sangwidge, miss". But remembering all the hard work he had had to put into trapping possums, we said "No, thanks", and sat alone, thinking.

The helmeted head of a young good-looking policeman plunged through the window. "Are you the two girls that the Rutherglen police are after?" he asked.

Affronted to the soul, I said, "Yes."

"And where are you going now?"

"Home."

"By jove," he said generously, "I wish I could get something on you two and have you locked up." He looked so handsome and

kindly and human as he said it that I was speechless, preferring
to believe that an ugly animal down in his stomach was enunciating
those good words.

I had a treatise on romance and the spirit of Australia ready
for him, but the words wouldn't come. Goodness and trustfulness
sank in me, then, and I have felt ashamed of our journey ever since.

VII

WE had been a shamefully short time away. On leaving we had
promised that the letter-box should be full of mail and much gold,
so that Mia was bewildered by our sudden arrival and the way
we thrust our imaginary whiskers through the window and
announced, "We're home, little woman . . . whattaboutacuppatea?"

Hiding our humiliations from her, we put on beards and
moustaches of black rabbit-skin and performed before her until
morning, acting the parts of all those we had met.

"Well, Mia; there was nothing doing at Rutherglen," we
repeated, "and the maize was picked early this year at Tumut,
because of the floods; so we'll have to hang around home until
work turns up."

Blue said, "I'll write to Jim. He promised to get us pea-picking
up at Metung."

"Yes, drop him a line, and say we want work at once."

"We can't get it, Steve. What's this? May? Well, he said the
pea-picking doesn't start until the end of August, so we'll have
to just resign ourselves to the winter at home. That's if Mia doesn't
mind."

"I'll dig the garden for you, Mia, to earn my keep," I said,
anxious to lose some of the overwhelming energy I felt mounting
in my body.

Long days of rain and inactivity followed, but whenever the
weather cleared, I got out into the garden, lifting heavy shovels
full of black earth from here, and putting it there; while forever
I dreamt of my lost Kelly, the blue-eyed and bandy-legged, who
was bullock driving up at Tostaree. I bought many sheets of
unlined paper and military dispatch envelopes. Long and artificial
were the letters I wrote to Kelly and long and natural were the
silences that followed them from his side of the fence.

I grew sadder and sadder, while the wind laughed in the
chimney with Mia's windy laugh, and the old plum bough on
top of the roof dribbled raindrops down the side of the stove. The

purple, red and yellow bricks in the yard shone all through the wet days, the leafless rose boughs knocked against my bedroom wall and I, unloved, saw no reason to be alive.

I dreamt one night that I went over to the bookshelf and took down the copies of the old *London News* of 1816 that Blue had bought at a sale in the Goulburn Valley. Where they had been, a door stood open. I walked through it into an old deserted house from which bees flew, mumbling the song of nectar while tall dark trees kept their shades cool under the heat of the sun. I awoke next morning in a furious temper . . . quarrelled right and left, flung "Twilight" (a Luxembourg painting that I had bought for Blue in the days when I was a printer's devil in the city) down on the floor and smashed the glass. Then I polished my shoes and went out walking alone for miles.

Yes, past the first farm I strode, where the crumpled wet manure flowed in the bails; along the lonely road of gorse and tall dry gum saplings I walked, with body and soul aching for my mate. Turning the corner and climbing the steep hill before me, and panting like "Youth with his face towards the upland hill", I found myself, once over its brow, in a land of lights. Long, mauve straight lights fell across the acres of green cabbages, while blue and golden lights were steeped in apple orchards, and biting bitter-sweet was the odour of the land, crying to the fresh earth in me, breaking it down into a loneliness that would kill in its effort to be accompanied. Many hues were there, in that land of painter's lights where lonely white paddocks spread out, smeared with yellow roads, mauve-green crops of turnip and cabbage, and golden searchings of the sun.

I climbed the rocky hill in front of me and came to a large stone house lying well back among the trees, the trees of my dream. I walked in. Beyond the cold darkness engendered by the leaves, the sun shone strong, and the mossy joints of the stone veranda steamed. Then I heard the bees, and their voices were like the sun singing aloud down through many flutes; long, low and banked by the fires of work were their murmurs, as they streamed out of an empty room in which they had their hives. This old house was a mingling of wet mossy stone and dry wood; little cell-like rooms lay along its passages; blue glass doors locked the halls, and over all lay the silence of distillation. Everything that could have been taken from those who lived there once had been taken and now was breathed out again. The human life in that house was still active. Yes, from old books that I saw scattered around, from old rags and bits of crockery, an oblique sort of family was formed by the house in its loneliness.

In the yard I found a large wooden dome above a deep cold well; the pump handle was broken and the grey galvanized iron drain was dry for want of water. Because of the house above the pump, I thought that I would call the property "The Pump-house".

Hurried by the triumph of coincidence with a dream, I gave a few looks around and then rushed homeward by another road. Soon I was sorry that I had left the old house, for the road took me by the scruff of the soul and shook me until I was weak and heavy with melancholy. Rounding a corner where the gums hung in soft fine leaves, I saw an old dray coming along, driven by a small white-bearded man through whose fingers the reins slipped and slid back and forth as the horse snaked forward sinuously.

On the cart was, "W. Beerneer".

I at once changed it into Beesknees.

"Mr Beesknees," I said meekly, "I have come a long way and I'm hungry. If you are going home . . . I thought you might pick me up and let me buy some lunch from you."

The old bush eyes looked me over, and the beard of ice and age moved first before the Beesknees said slowly, but suspiciously that "You might get a bit to eat, if you like to hop up and come home with me".

I hopped and upped, and in ten minutes (I like to think; for the silence between us was absolutely sinful) we came to a place made of thin sticks gummed together by insect fluid; opened out bags made into squares of shade by hanging them over four sticks sheltered a few perspiring fowls from the sun. A bench nailed to the wall welcomed us with a basin of someone's ablutions, on which the foam was subsiding. In we went to the kitchen where Mrs Beesknees was cutting off crumbling slices of hot steamed pudding.

Dad showed me; I showed my money and sat down, knowing that they wouldn't take it.

Dave, their bush neighbour, had opened his heart to the steamed pudding. He sat opposite me and planted it with ardour all over himself.

"Arrrh!" he breathed, pushing the empty plate away with a bump and a rattle.

"Another helping, Dave?" asked Mrs Beesknees.

Dave didn't mind if he did.

He didn't mind three times; but when Mrs Beesknees, with anguish in her voice, asked if he'd mind for the fourth time, Dave turned to the door with a roaring laugh and, undoing his belt so that it leapt off his waist and hit the cat in the eye, he bellowed, "Aw no, Mrs Beerneer, ther novelty 'as wore orf!"

Then he wore off into the bush . . . somewhere.

When I got home I told the tale of The Pump-house to Mia and Blue and apologized for my fury of the morning.

After many letters, Kelly was still silent, and out of my pain I wrote verse upon him. It was keen agony to me once, this poem, and now it is such a minor thing, written in an un-Australian language. It is not even a thing . . . it is just . . .

> June chimes with drowsy calls and distant bells, dear lad,
> That cry your name. Your name is very fair
> With echoes of lost years remembered well . . . with sad
> Old dance tunes played and heard . . . I know not where.
> June has not many songs, as has her daughter
> The wine-red lipped July across whose knees
> The early spring complains with cries like water
> Bubbling across the plain beneath the trees.
> June has for me, one melody . . . one only.
> A ballad of a never-ending pain,
> Of passion that awoke in two hearts lonely,
> And, satiated, fell asleep again.

My heart was never less like sleep and satiation in its life; but I pretended in verse. Long, therefore, were the nights I spent sleepless, wandering tormented around the countryside.

It was useless to stop at home, because the tick of the clock grew unendurable at about 3 a.m., when I'd get up and take the pendulum off the hook, or punch the hands until they stopped, bruised, in their cruel theft. I climbed over hills, halted before sheets of wind-blown water teeming with moon and stars; and I suffered the agony of youth and desire as firmly as possible.

I remember coming home from a night-long walk on the Dandenong road, past the brick kilns, and meeting a sturdy contemptuous working man who stared with disdain at my woman's body in men's clothes.

"Blast your good soul," thought I; "there is but one thing to do, and that is, to kill . . . and remain, myself, a god."

"But . . . I went on!" as Rupert Brooke cried to himself, to me, to thousands of us, the young of the tribe.

Aching with my agony, I took Blue out to The Pump-house.

The bees were still filing along the murmurous corridors of their sunlike singing, but the old rooms were not really deserted now. Far away across the hills we could hear steel ringing in a quarry which was hidden from us by a breast of blue stone and green grass, and often the heart-leap of an explosive told us of the passion of detonators.

Yes, the old room with the fireplace was lived in now, and it smelt well of a working man and his mate. They had lit fire upon fire in the creamy white ashes with their brown markings like the plumage of an owl, and they had played at cards around the fires.

They were beautiful cards, old, slippery from the handling by greasy fingers, and dark around the edges. I took those cards and loved them for years. They held the smell of The Pump-house and the quarrymen for long.

We made a cup of tea in the still-glowing fire, coloured it with dried Australian milk which smelt of The Pump-house, cooked a pot or rice, and ate, read and talked, secure in our youth and its loneliness.

The orange blossoms blowing clear and sharp near the stone steps hurt my heart with the wildness of their perfume. From the dark earth it came, and I had no lover.

However, although grand with loneliness I was not above a trick of the meaner sort. Blue saw a piece of scarlet Paisley lying in the passage and picked it up to take it away. Blind with longing for it, I begged her, in the sacred name of ghostly hospitality, not to do so.

"For," said I, "who knows—not even He who lit the torch in the first rose—how long this has lain here, or to what end it is destined. This rag, perhaps, on which the blood of old Scotch art has bled, gives out to the night the spirit of love; for since it was torn from the breast of some young girl as she in haste fled down the years. . . ."

"Don't," expostulated Blue. "That's almost pure Francis Thompson."

"Anyhow," I continued, "don't take it. It might have all sorts of germs on it, you never know."

The obedient one followed me and left the red rag alone. But I didn't. We took out the pack of cards when we got home, and the piece of Paisley slipped from my sweater at the same time, *eheu!*

I meant well. But Blue's reproachful glance rose and sought out God, and He hated me for a moment.

I had an old black book full of superstitious lists of various conditions in life that accorded with the numbers of the playing cards. Spreading them out, we told our fortunes. "Letter from old friend. Much happiness through fair man," I told Blue. "Have you written to Jim lately, Bluey?"

"Last week."

"We might get a letter, then."

It came next day. Jim wrote it on the soft raggy pages of an exercise book.

Lower Nicholson,
12 August.

Dear little Blue just a line to tell you that I received your last with pleasure it is raining pretty heavy up here at present you were asking where I was working I am still working at Nicholson wood-cutting still that is about my main job that horse I have got is one I got from the man I am working for at Nicholson he bought it in the yards the other day it was very wild and he couldnt get any one to break it in every one was afraid of it so he told me if I rode it and made it quiet he would give it to me so I am riding it to work night and morning everybody told me I would get my neck broken off it but it has never offord to buck or kick with me and I have been riding it for a fortnight it is a very nice looking pony something after the style of Kelly's pony it is a bay it is pretty quiet now I was going to buy it in the first place Metung is twenty miles from Bairnsdale by road and about twelve by boat from where we will be picking it is about a mile and a half to Metung the man's name that is a question I dont know myself I only know him as Jerry he is an Indian he has known me since I was a little toddler he knew my mother and father before they were married when I was a little chap I used to curl up in his possum rug he is a very nice old fellow he has been in Australia for fifty years last Sunday he told me that if ever I was out of work to go to him and he would give me a job so if you come up as soon as you get this letter I will meet you at Bairnsdale and we will go down all together in the boat to Metung the peas will be ready soon I dont know where we will camp I will bring my tent and you and Steve might get board somewhere I have relations in Metung an uncle I think I am well known around there be a lot of people your loving

JIM.

After which unpunctuated screech to us, I suppose Jim fell down on the floor of his hut, purple in the face.

Delirious with joy, we lit huge fires in the stove and the crumbling flat irons were pressed to every rag we possessed. The hiss of iron and wet cloth meeting above our best pants turned the kitchen into a foundry, while the thump of the yellow clothes-brush as I banged it down on the creases deafened passers-by.

THE GLITTER OF CELTIC
BRONZE AGAINST THE SEA

I

AGAIN, then, on one hot late August day, we took the train to
Bairnsdale. The same journey, but now my heart ached, yet
hoped to meet Kelly. I did not speak his name, out of pride, but,
tethered to him by time and circumstance, I suffered until we should
meet.

At Moe the great bell cried out when it saw me, "Lo . . .
returning again to Gippsland to forget sorrow and find it again,
deeper than before. O, flee from Gippsland, for it is pursuing you
even unto death. The spear from The Land of Good Spear-wood
will never rot; it shall pierce you and be proud of its name for
strength among the warriors aboriginal. Their ghosts cry, 'Bulumwaal . . . Bulumwaal!' in praise of the spear."

At the Bairnsdale station stood Jim; but Kelly was not with him.
I did not ask. My vile heart, sick with sorrow, took no pleasure in
anything and the cruel Fates that pursued me lived in glee,
mastering me and numbing me to life.

The signet ring on Jim's finger glittered with joy, and he loved
us as he took us down in the cab to the steam boat that waited
in the Mitchell River. After one curdling whistle to let all know
that she was departing, she steamed away down the wide river,
with piles of light, thin wattle-bark on either side.

Only in heaven shall I recapture that ethereal feeling of being
an angel in a vast blue-purple paradise, or of being the twilight
wind, the first star beating out light in vivid flames, or of being
the earth going to the earth. O, vast and sweet and terrible were
you, Gippsland, that evening, as we stood high up near the wheel,
entering into your river and your lake and going to Metung, the
town that shall hold me forever.

The dry grey reeds in the river entered me, like barbs; the kingfishers drooping from them were my blood drops, and the hop
kilns were the houses of fairies, miscalled pea-pickers out of
work.

Under Eagle Point we slid and I remembered the Egyptian mask in the sky and the thunderstorm that held the kiss of Kelly. Then the boat turned her bow and trembled into the lakes with the same Ulyssean sense of splendour that the old hero felt long ago.

> To sail beyond the sunset, and the baths
> Of all the western stars, until I die.
> It may be that the gulfs will wash us down:
> It may be we shall touch the Happy Isles,
> And see the great Achilles, whom we knew.

Not old, not idle kings were we, but young adventurers, as humble as they, unbarred by pain and the years, fresh with the great godliness of youth which age crucifies slowly.

Purple mists came swimming across the silver sedge to us, and in that mist was God, was all eternity. Purple were the waters and brown and blue the twilight, chill the wind and solemn my heart above the mother-hushing waters. White pelicans stood on peninsulas of sand and opened their mouths as we passed, giving a silver salute of fish; above flew white cranes. And I loved that land with the intensity of death.

Far ahead of us glittered the dry white Hillside of Metung and our young eyes saw it as a citadel of splendour, peopled by kings and their sons, by men with generous hearts and women with romantic loves, by children who would love us for that fairy belief.

Drawing near to the foreshore of the town, we saw a little grey shed lying among the dark bush, with nets spread out before it. Then we rounded the point, drew to the jetty and the boat crashed softly against the piles. And . . . it was not the fairy town that we had seen afar. Yet that vision had been true. Within itself, Metung was more glorious through the lives of its people, and they were indeed kings; but I had to be crucified before I could understand them.

Here was Metung. A jetty, a weatherboard hotel and a post-office, with houses scattered around . . . all splendid with the lives of those who were to be joined to mine for some years to come.

Just as the boat steamed away, Blue remembered her violin . . . lying on its deck. "Never mind, you can ring their office at Lakes Entrance," said Jim, "and they'll bring the fiddle back tomorrow morning."

A beautiful dark girl stood in the doorway of the hotel as we entered, and she showed us into a sagging room, while Jim went to camp, heaven knows where. We had a wash. In those days the ceremony of the wash was a splendid thing. One performed it with the scrupulousness of the bushman and was pleased by the young innocent face that came glowing out of the towel.

After tea, we were entertained in the private parlour by a fair young woman, who, delighted by our love of music, found "Ben Bolt" for us and ran it off on the shaking piano.

A voice rumbled through the passages that were still odorous of dinner, and a face that was a cross between a mushroom and an old hairbrush looked around the door.

"Ah, here's Steve," said someone.

"Where are the peas? I want to start in now. I'm a good picker. I put up ten bags a day last year I was 'ere," bellowed Steve. Tilting himself well back from his boots, he began to sing, "When ther feels are white with daisies, I'll return. . . ."

"She wept with delight when you gave her a smile," we chanted feelingly.

"When ther feels are white with daisies I'll return," bellowed Steve.

"If they could see you now, Steve," said a voice, "at home, they'd plough the daisies in as soon as they came to the surface."

"I can pick peas with the best of men," averred Steve. "When ther feels are white with daisies, I'll return."

The barren "feels" chased us out of the room eventually, and into the dark we wandered. As we stood on the jetty, watching the dark and glistening waters that murmured around the old wood, a youth came along with a peculiar ambling walk. Standing beside us, he lit a cigarette that gave us a glimpse of a large dreaming white face, full-lipped, heavy-eyed and stubborn-jawed.

"I meant to go to a dance tonight," he said slowly.

"What are the dances like around here?" we asked for something to say.

"No —— (shocking bit of profanity) good!"

For the moment, we stood dazed, but then remembered that, being dressed as men, we had to take what they would have received.

"Ah," we said and moved slowly away to find Jim.

He was rather late coming in. "I been looking around for that uncle of mine, Blue. But I can't find him yet. I met a bloke from Bairnsdale that I know. Macca . . . his father runs the mail-car here; he's down for the pea-picking, too."

"We met a vile youth on the jetty . . . language. . . . Gods! Ah, Metung, I fear for thee," I sighed.

"What was he like? Short, fair bloke with a slow voice?"

"Yes."

"That's Macca. He's not a bad sort. He couldn't have known that you were girls."

"I like him not. Come, James, away to your couch."

"Yes, we got to be out early tomorrow to see ole Karta Singh about picking."

"Where can we board, James? The hotel would be too far away from the work."

"Too dear, too, Blue. I'll see Karta about a place for youse two. I got me tent."

Unforgettable first morning in Metung! Alas, our youth . . . where is it? O dawn, that came red from the burning furnace of time. I feel that I shall go mad if I cannot recapture it; and I never shall.

Yet the earth that morning was filled with an indifference that was comforting. The dawn spread wide and red; the sea-gulls flew quietly through the skies. Down to the water's edge we ran with Jim, to where a tall crane stood meekly thinking over his diet of worms.

"A crane, Jim, a crane," we cried, and hurried with silken garments flying to where stood the apparently trustful emblem of this apparently trustful land.

It stood while we hastened, and it stood while we stopped and rapped it on the head. Then we turned and went back to the hotel, for the crane like everything else we ran to admire and trust in, was a takedown. It was stuffed.

"We better go out and see Karta Singh," said Jim, "and there's a place near his hut, I heard about, where you can board for about twenty-five shillings a week."

"We'd never earn it. Besides, Jim," we argued, "we want to live like bushmen and pea-pickers, in old huts. Freedom . . . freedom, James, my boy!"

We set out; well-tailored and innocent-faced, trusting in everything; we walked along the foreshore where the blue lake rose and fell singing among yellow stones. We were young and it was morning.

The sun shines differently now. Our carelessness and innocence was in it then, as it fell all dewy among the native bush in the gullies. The black sun lay on the rotting leaves, a golden sun bent on the ferns, a green sun moved the living trees back and forth and on the snowy supple-jack the white sun blazed for us along the damp and wheel-marked road.

"There came a soldier marching along the high road. One two! One two!"

Yes, here he was, that lovely mythical man, with a fair comrade beside him, gold-haired, blue-eyed and smiling.

"Goot morning," said the fairy soldier, a brown-skinned slant-eyed fellow with a broad Japanese face. They passed and we were afraid, then.

"They are Germans," we said, and went on still trembling with the shock of meeting man in this flowery bush.

Coming at length to an old hut made of wood, tin and bags, that stood in the corner of a large dry white paddock, we saw the peas; long green rows falling over to one side. A dozen little men in brown velvet pants stooped, with their posteriors in the air; long bags slipped in under their belts gave them the look of kangaroos. They peered around their legs at us, with great brown startled eyes. "These are Chinamen," we said moving quickly away.

"Karta might be down the paddock," said Jim, so we cautiously moved down the rusty wire fence with its hanging dewdrops until we saw a tall old Indian, grey-bearded and turbaned, ploughing near the road under a dead tree which raised its grey and white limbs above him.

As we followed Jim across the ploughed field, we felt very common indeed . . . to be walking, dressed up like tailors' dummies, on the soil of Gippsland, and not to be owning an inch of it.

Karta Singh pulled the horse back and stopped dead, looking down on us cunningly and amusedly.

He was a tall old Indian with a brown hooked nose, brown eyes across which a smoke floated as from the funeral pyres of the Ganges, and his grey beard was coarse and uncombed. The dirty white turban on his head had a rib of blue in it, and he wore a navy fisherman's jersey too short for his long arms. Most marvellous of all was the silver bangle on his wrist. On his thin legs were cotton trousers of a grey and black stripe ending in the serpent coil of puttees.

Jim stepped up. "Don't you remember me, Karta?"

We found later that Jim's preliminary was always the same, marking a man who made little or no effect on the memory of those he had met.

"No. I not know you. What your name, you fella?"

"Jim. Don't you remember me calling here about a fortnight ago and you said you could give me work?"

"No, you fella."

"Don't you remember . . . you knew my father and mother before they were married and when I was a little fellow I used to sleep in your possum rug?"

"Oh! You Jim? Who this fella?" indicating us. Even our morning suits and our silk hats could not bother Karta. We remained, through all our vicissitudes of fortunes while we knew him, "this fella, Steve and Blue".

"What you fella Jim want?"

"You got any pea-picking, Karta?"

"Might be got little bit, two or three weeks' time. You like for wait, might be you get some work . . . God willing. God not willing, you not get."

"We wus looking for some place to camp in, Karta."

Karta pointed to a strange hollow-looking house far up on the hill.

"One Afghan fella live there in that house, belonging Mr Whitebeard, another grower. Might be you ask Mr Whitebeard, he let you stay there. I not know, you fella."

Respectfully, we drew back from Karta, and he, shaking off the dew of the morning, dragged on the horsehair reins and, with a strange high nasal cry, staggered off behind his floundering plough.

We got over the fence and walked up to have a look at the house. It faced the rising sun, had a small shed to the right of it, in front; a poor garden behind a wire-netting fence, a broken tank on one side and an unexpected wire door attached to the back door. There was no one at home and we could see no furniture in the rooms. A post-and-rail fence divided it from the paddocks of Karta Singh, so that we would be near our work. There appeared to be four rooms and a bathroom to the left side, which overlooked a lonely gully scattered with sad grey wattles and dry white fallen timber.

At the back of the house a large paddock went up the hill to a post-and-rail fence dividing it from another property. Going through this, we found ourselves, after crossing some crops, at the house of Mr Whitebeard. By tacit consent, Blue and I left the interviewing of this gentleman to Jim; I think we had an idea that he mightn't let the house if he knew that mixed sexes were going to inhabit it.

Jim came out triumphant. "I got it," said he, "at two and six a week. The Afghan, Akbarah Khan, has got to share it with us. Now," said Jim, "I think we'll go around the foreshore and I'll see if I can find out where my uncle lives."

What a wonderful place that foreshore was in the morning of early spring! The very rubbish littering the coloured pebbles on

which the waters fell was romantic. Clouds blew lightly and
airily above us, bush birds sang out broken phrases, and the blue
lake chanted in its blue and white depths. I felt that there was
something about the place that would hold me forever . . . that no
other place in the world would possess me as would the foreshore
of Metung.

Jim couldn't find his uncle, although he stared up at houses on
the dry yellow cliffs, wondering which one was his; so we returned
to the hotel in the growing heat of the day. The heavens had
contracted and grown hotly dark and blue; the tender green gum-
leaves turned violet and hung heavily from their scarlet twigs.

· We had not breakfasted, being short of money; but lordly was I
in those days, and when the three pea-pickers arrived back at the
hotel, they ordered black coffee, and it was good black coffee, too.

As we sat drinking it in the sun, a short fair fellow in dirty torn
khaki pants and an officer's coat with the bronze "A" on the sleeve
sat staring at us. His contribution to our conversation was "Pon mai
word, ha, ha".

He was a boarder at the hotel, and in those days my reverence
for a boarder could not be expressed in a word.

Yes, and he also wore a military uniform. While the sun blazed in
our coffee cups, we stared at this marvellous being and tried to
make friends with him. But no; to all our timid inquiries he had
but one answer . . . "Pon mai word, ha, ha."

At length, hearing us discuss the best way to spend the first
night in the bedless house which we had rented, he volunteered:
"Pon mai word, ha, ha. . . . Ai have heard that one can make an
excellent bed, pon mai word, ha, ha, and sleep quaite soundly, if
one cuts a few gum boughs with the leaves left on and sleeps on
them . . . pon mai word, ha, ha! It seems, you know, that the boughs
are springy and just like a wire mattress . . . pon mai word, ha, ha."

Overwhelmed by this courtesy, this opening up of indifferent
springs, we besought him for more; but no, upon his word, ha, ha,
that was all he had to say.

"There's Macca that I met last night," remarked Jim, putting
down his coffee cup. "Is that the same one you were talking to,
Blue?"

"Wait till he speaks," we said.

In the wild sea-sunlight, he came towards the jetty that blazed
in the palpitating air. In the daylight, he was a short broad youth,

sandy-haired, with many freckles, heavy blue eyes, full lips and pigeon toes.

At that age, you would have thought none save his mother could have loved him. That is untrue. Lo, an Australian Sappho had seen him, and in him the blue sea, the terrible dying day, broad blazing and sounding of many waters, and she wrapped them about him, saying, "Here is Gippsland."

On that instant began one of the great love stories of Gippsland, of devotion, of fidelity, of poetry unequalled.

I forgot the obscenity of the previous night. "This man is a poet," I said. "He is myself . . . his oaths are part of his sorrow in the face of life. Like me, he has been unhappy in love, and has grown hard and bitter. Youth, I understand. I shall work on him, and make him more complete in body, mind and soul than the gods."

"Good day, Jim," he said, nodding to us, and taking off, slowly, a wide black hat. "Going over to the other side to get some apples. Care to come?"

Eagerly we crowded into a frail little boat, full of dry white crabs, and were ponderously rowed over the rising and falling waters. The boat was drawn up outside a little black shed on a burning white patch of sand. There the nets of the sea, old Neptune's veils, were kept, but no apples saw we. It was a Greek day, with the earth rising in pure columns against the cloudless blue sky.

"What are you going to do this afternoon?" asked Phaon as he rowed us back again in the heat.

"We got to go out and shift our things to the house we rented from Mr Whitebeard. It'll take us two trips. I wouldn't take my portmanteau out till last thing," answered Jim. "I don't trust them Indians, and I got things in that portmanteau that I wouldn't like to lose. I 'ope it's all right at the pub now. Keep going, will you, Macca, so as I can have a look before the boat comes in. Might be some more pea-pickers on it, and if they got their hands on my portmanteau that'd be the last of it. I got things in that port that might interest them."

I nudged Blue, and we determined through our nudges to have a look at that portmanteau on the very first day Jim was out of sight.

"My pop's got a lizzie. He'll take you out there tonight for a couple of bob," said Phaon dreamily. "And your portmanteau will be safe with him, Jim."

"Will you be coming, too?" I asked.

"I might," he replied, looking at me heavily. My trance began

at once. It was to last for over five years. How can I explain? It
was the heavy, languorous cynicism that he practised which irritated
me, and at the same time, enervated me.

I knew, too, that no matter how coarse he looked I could, when
I had battered myself into the right state of mind, make him to look
beautiful through my hypnotized eyes. I had to love and be loved,
or suffer alone in torment.

Once more we started out for the hut of Karta Singh, this time
carrying Jim's tent done up around his mean belongings. The long
day—ah, the days were long then—was still terribly hot; walking
through white dust, we tired and, carrying the swag between us,
we left the road and, climbing a green hill, clung to the fences
of the houses on its crown. There was a tarred-looking house that
we passed, where a tall man wearing a black felt hat sat mending
shoes on the veranda. He looked out at us keenly as we passed.

Now we were in the bush, nearing Karta's hut, and walking in
the dazzling heat on brown gravel road. Under a tree stood a group
of dark, volubly chattering Italians, who grew very quiet as we
drew near . . . sepulchral as we passed, and deathly as our backs
dwindled in the distance.

We were sensitive, Blue and I, thinking that everyone would
recognize us as women and laugh at us.

By roundabout ways we found ourselves at the rented house, and
Jim, bringing out his bushman's axe, started to cut down a lot of
gum boughs to make us that comfortable bed, pon mai word, ha, ha.
There was no one at home in the hollow house.

At dusk, a huge bearded Afghan, wearing a rusty brown turban,
came rolling up out of the bush with an axe over his shoulder; he
invited us into the kitchen and we stayed till dark talking to him
among billies, syrup tins and old lamps.

"You see Missa Whitebeard about this place, too true?" he asked
finally.

"Yes."

His black beard parted, showing rolls of red lips, tongue and
white teeth. "All right, you come tonight, you like."

That had been our very intention.

In the twilight, made Biblical by the tall bearded Akbarah Khan,
we walked down to the gate, and mother Australia laid hold of
me; she, with her twigs around the gate, thin and aromatic they
smelt; she, with her big white chips sliced from trees that had
been ringbarked years ago, with her sad twilight, brown, outward

curving, full of dry smells and the first star. Desperately in the agony of brief human flesh I laid hold of her and mourned, while I was young, that I must grow old; and wept, while I was free, that I must marry and bear children; and was maddened to think that, while I lived, I must die.

Akbarah, big and proud of his strength and agility grinned through the twilight of his beard, and leapt the gate.

"We'll be back soon," we assured him, and Akbarah, thinking that we were all men, hoped obscenely that we would, and blasphemously wished us *au revoir*.

Turning back, he went striding up the hill.

Late in the night, we bundled into the lizzie belonging to Macca's father and, with the precious burden of Jim's portmanteau weighing us all down, we rumbled along the road, making the rabbits scurry back and forth and churning the post-and-rail fences into serpents with our distorting lights around the curves. I sat, sad and high-thoughted, beside Macca, attempting to draw out of him a confession of immortal poetry. The jangling of our newly bought billies spoilt it and Blue loudly begged Macca to look out for her violin on the boat next morning.

Until far past midnight, we stood with Akbarah Khan drinking tea and making merry while the candles thrashed the shadows around the kitchen. The place had gone completely masculine, for the want of a woman's hand. There was nothing like that for miles around, and we were satisfied. At last we were men. We stood with Jim and Akbarah and were accepted.

However, one must sleep, pon mai word, ha, ha, and we went into the front rooms which we had rented. Jim retired to the bathroom to fix up a divan for himself in the tin bath. Dragging our gum boughs inside, we laid them, shining and sweating in the night, across one corner of the room. Little black ants could be seen running madly along the white limbs from leaf to leaf. Hoping for the best, we took off our stiff white collars and red ties, our tight tailored coats, braces, shirts and pants, and put on pyjamas (the candle out first, in case the moth, Akbarah, be attracted to the delirium of the light) and settled down on the rug, under which the springy boughs lay. Even at first, I cannot say that we were comfortable; but the body, tortured by the day, will rest anywhere for the first ten minutes. We were so tired that we slept. Then the ants marched. I have ever commended a serene and patient endurance of all things. To raise an ant from the leg is but the work of a moment, and as you do it a line from one of the poets might well flash into the mind and elevate it. My favourite was,

> Love never dies, but lives, immortal lord
> Of all the black and misbelieving horde
> Of fears and sorrows that infest the soul.

Soon, I was running out of quotations and still raising ants from my legs; later, without a thought of quotations, I was frankly and brutally squashing them on the limbs.

We were indeed infested. Meanwhile, the gum boughs began to protrude, and stick into us as though in search of their ants. The leaves felt cold and slippery through the cold rug.

Our irritation mounted until, on some trifling pretext, while searching for an ant, Blue thrust her elbow in my eye. It was the best thing she could have done. We sat up in our singlets and began to fight with swinging fists, while the leaves soughed around us, the ants refereed and from the bathroom next door came the thump of Jim's boots against the tin, as he bounded about in his dreams, perhaps defending the portmanteau.

All night we fought, we tossed and shifted the gum boughs, from my back to hers, from her back to mine, or we exchanged ants. One large meat ant for fifty black ones, or three small high-smelling sugar ants for a crawler of unknown species. And Akbarah snored and Jim hit the tin bath until dawn, when we got up and never said a word about it, pon mai word, ha, ha, but just set about looking for a better mattress.

We took the doors off the fowl-house and, stripping the bag off an old shed—it was peerless bag, weather-worn and silver with the rain and wind—I filled it with straw. I dragged in two large charcoal logs and rolled them on the floor, one at either end. On this frame, I set my fowl-house door and my straw mattress.

It was a windy day, following a dewy dawn, which we had discovered by looking out on a paddock of short green grass. Sitting on a polished rail in the old shed, we played the mouth-organ until Akbarah came along, looking at us curiously; at our long trousers, ribbon floating from our coloured sweaters and blue smocks over our maiden figures.

"You funny looking boy, you fella," remarked Akbarah wonderingly.

"What you mean?"

"You got on half boy clothes, half girl clothes. Why you do that?"

"Oh!" At last we comprehended his bewilderment. "Our mother

and our sister . . . they like us dress like this. We never go to school with boy; we never work among men before. Our mother, our sister, they bring us up, dress sometime like boy, sometime like girl. This thought very good in some place in this country."

"I see, you fella. I not see before. Ten years I live in this country; nine years I have camel train in West Australia, but I never see any Australian men like you before. You tell me now; I see, you fella."

And Akbarah went up to see someone else about it—Karta Singh perhaps.

I was in my room when he came back, entering with an apology to take out some belonging of his. "Karta Singh, he say you two fella girl," he began, with a curiously vile leer, which looked like a small pig in his eyes.

In a deep angry voice, I replied, "Let him say. We are men, as you know, Akbarah Khan."

"Oh, yes, I know," answered Akbarah Khan; but he bent forward and quickly seized the front of my sweater, gripped it and let it go.

Nothing was said. He grinned and walked out of the room.

The day went by, flinging the forgotten splendour of passing life through us, and I worked around, making myself comfortable, and hating Akbarah Khan.

The first Sunday was devoted to a walk along a back track that led to the Tambo River. We passed a deserted house and arrived at last on the main road. Just before we left the back track, Jim leapt over the fence of an apparently empty property to steal some limes that hung temptingly from the trees. Just as he touched them, the scene changed. His touch had brought forth forty mongrels of all breeds, and they made our heads rock with their concerted clamours. Pulling Jim back into safety again, we rushed off, pursued by shouts and barks.

We had early determined to have a look into Jim's mysterious portmanteau at which we used to sit staring and conjecturing on wet days. One day, when he had gone to Metung, we opened it up, after appointing Blue as a watchman in case we should be surprised in the act.

Cautiously, I undid the straps, for I was afraid of that portmanteau and lowered my voice when I spoke of it, as though it were a proud, quick-tempered sort of thing, swift to avenge a slur. I jerked the mouth open and began to laugh loudly. Blue came running in from her post.

"What is it?"

I laughed more and, picking up the portmanteau, tipped it upside down. A pair of dirty socks, a tram-ticket and a Testament fell out. Blue and I rolled on the floor, writhing with laughter, crying like children.

"He said he didn't trust anyone with that portmanteau!" Blue said in a strangled voice.

"Wh-hacks of collars and suits in it," I held the tram-ticket out in a shaking hand. "You can wear this one. I'll wear the socks, they suit me better."

"Put everything back," warned Blue. "Everything! You know Jim. He's got everything numbered. Ah, what suits . . . what linen!" We laughed for weeks.

That night we lit a fire in the wide hearth and sat about it talking. There was a rather fine overmantle of polished oak; I stood and leant against it as I talked, and it fell to pieces all over me, flinging me into the arms of Blue and Jim.

"The white ants," they said. We went to bed before the termites could get into our tired timbers. At midnight, a loud voice cried liltingly out in the bush, "Ulallah . . . ulallah . . . ulallah!" A light shone, and the tall figure of Karta Singh came slowly up the paddocks leaning on a long staff, with a lantern hanging to it; his beard glowed in its light and a battered turban nodded on his head.

"You fella picker, open this door," he shouted. "My son in Punjab, Lahore. I want you, my son in Punjab, Lahore, India."

Jim went softly and opened it, saying, ingratiatingly, "What is it, Karta? What do you want?"

"You fella, open door. I want come in, you fella." He came in, and stood among us, smelling of methylated spirits. "You fella come and sit down on couch." He dragged us down with him on to the fowl-house door. "Now you fella, I love you like my chillen. What name, you fella? You fella, what you name?"

"Jim," croaked the owner in a rich bovine voice.

"Blue."

"Steve," I said angrily, "and what do you want at this hour of the night?"

"You fella Jim . . . I call you Lovie. You fella Blue, I call you Duckie, and you fella Steve, I call you Darling. And I love you all three like my children."

"But what do you want?"

"You fella, I want breathe in your ear. This make you millionaire. You my three children. Let me breathe in your ear and make you rich man."

He was so huge and looked so delicately poised on the edge of violence with his dreamy dead eyes, quivering mouth and animal expression that we had to let him blow in our ears. But he had no idea of the extent of an ear apparently, for he almost blew me off my feet and gassed me with the smell of spirits.

"Look, we want to go to bed. We can't be bothered with this rot. What do you want of us?" I said bad-temperedly.

"I want to tell your fortune, you fella. You fella Jim, give me your hand." He nodded his dangerous drunken head above it, saying thickly . . . "You fella Jim, you make lot of money and marry woman with plenty children. Now you fella Duckie," he took Blue's saffron hand with its grotesque fingers, the hands of a fantastic artist, "you fella Duckie got good hand for needle. You marry one day and have six children. You fella Darling," he took my hand, dribbling from his beard, "You fella Darling, get married and have plenty children, too."

We sat silent, like lumps of grease around a flame, waiting to be caught at. Karta took a piece of writing-paper and a dirty envelope from his pocket.

"Now you fella Jim, you write letter to my son in Lahore. My son a policeman in Punjab. Now you write. . . ." He closed his eyes and began to drone. " 'Dear Son, I write you letter for tell you this good year for crop, and hope you are well.' You fella Jim got that?" he asked, waking up with a start. Jim was holding the paper and staring at it. "Why you fella not write?"

"We got no ink, Karta," Jim explained in a gentle humble voice.

"You fella got pencil! All right! 'Dear Son, you not see me again for some years. Long time I not write. . . .' You got that, you fella Lovie?"

"Got no pencil, either, Karta," breathed Jim.

"You fella too poor. I not give you job." Karta swept out of the room, through the middle door into the quarters of Akbarah Khan. In a high pealing voice he shrieked, "Sal—a—am, Akbarah Khan!"

And in a gruff rumbling voice, "Sal—a—ahm, Kar—tah Singh," enunciated the Afghan.

Then, until dawn, followed an argument between a roll of thunder and a cat having its tail trodden on.

On the following night, a small fair man came to the door and, taking off a large dirty felt hat, showed a mop of splendid bronze hair, dirty blue eyes, no eyebrows, dirty false teeth, and a skin full of womanish wrinkles and blackheads. In a weak light voice, he told us his name was Creeker, and that he was a pea-grower. Being pickers, growers were objects of reverence to us. He was invited in and sat by our fire. Here, in the hollow house, in the bush, he told us tales of the war . . . yarns of the "What no shave?" "What . . . no razor?" type, and promised us work when his crop was ready. Macca came in, too, and I, sitting back in the gloom, eyed him deeply; and deeply, I remember, he eyed me in return. Ah, my cry is, if only I could live again, I should always be what I really am . . . a clown, and clowns should not love. Punchinello told me that as he crouched on a roof in the moonlight, weeping for Columbine.

What have I not missed through staring at the fire of love? And yet, how could I have lived and not known it? Oh, my despair as I lay on that fowl-house door thinking of love, pure idealistic love which I was carefully nurturing in my heart for Macca.

There was a hurried knock at the door. Jim opened it. A short black-cloaked woman stood there, stormy looking, hurried to and fro by the strong wind blowing along the veranda. "Is Billy Creeker there?" The little fair man hastened forward.

"Look here, did you say that I said these two girls were no good?"

"No, no, Mrs Rotterdam, I never said anything of the sort!"

"Well," agitatedly, "everyone's saying that I told Billy Creeker that these girls were no good and they say you're over here, trying them out."

"Absurd, absurd, my good woman," I said smoothly. "Time alone can try us out. What is within us will destroy us. Nietzsche, if you will remember, declares that in order that a temple may be built, a temple must be destroyed. We, in effect, are that temple; and when we tire of our present form, we shall destroy ourselves and rise again in splendour."

"But they say. . . ."

"What say they? Let them say! Do go home and remember us as gods. Anything that you may say about us cannot disturb our lives." So I spoke, assured by youth that I was not, and would never be, what they said I was. I felt high-minded and triumphant that night, for I had got two graceful letters from the young Chinese, Borrelerworreloil, and to ease my heart I poured out my ashamed soul to him in reply, next day.

The slow-moving days brought Akbarah Khan to love me, and I hated him, for I felt that to be loved by an ex-camel-train driver from the East was an abasing thing. In all Keats there is not a remedy for the evil. Akbarah took my pyjamas down from the line where they sprinted in the fresh breeze, and pressed them with a brick. I came in and found him mending them at a delicate point with black thread. "Here . . . what the devil!" said I snatching them and staring at him furiously.

"Ah," murmured Akbarah softly, "white girl . . . black man . . . many camels!"

The master of symbolism, indeed.

As I was eating my lunch in the kitchen, Akbarah, fully enamoured of me, reached out to embrace, and I, with a billy lid of hot stew on my knees, flattened it out on his face. But of these dainty repulses he thought little, and as I walked through the dark kitchen at night, he seized me. Upon which I drew a long narrow stiletto I carried and drew a little of his blood. We became almost enemies.

Every morning, on awakening I heard a faint roaring sound, continuous and poetical in its resonance, coming from over the hill. Only in poetry had I heard of that "melancholy, long, withdrawing roar". Bemused by its beauty, I listened all day long, asking no one, fearing to be told.

And all day long we were hungry, for our money was running low and the peas were not ready. This, too, bemused me. I listened to my rumbling emptiness all day long, asking no one, fearing to be told.

At last Akbarah got a job cutting scrub for Billy Creeker, and our starvation ended. As soon as his tall shambling knock-kneed figure went off into the bush, rusty turban rolling on his head and axe over shoulder, Blue ran around to his kitchen and I strolled after her, meditating on the passing of tragic time and the probable coming of love. She prised open the wire window and got in. I sat in the sun dreaming sadly.

"You keep yow, Steve."

"Right-o, Blue." I dream.

Blue emerged with a cup of oatmeal and some sugar, a few potatoes and carrots. As in a dream I helped her to cook the meal, but I was well awake when I ate it.

That day we decided that our new home needed a romantic name. The pangs my forsaken heart had suffered there led me to call it "Avernus". And I was engaged in carving that on the door when Blue and Jim called me to go for a walk with them through the various pea paddocks, and to the foreshore. I had reached the syllable "Aver . . ." and left it.

When we came back, Macca had been there, and had picked up the knife and carved it into "Averdrink". So, Averdrink it remained.

At night, he used to come out to see us and drink cocoa with us. To see us. Those words mean nothing now. Then . . . they meant a dramatic twilight when youth was in the heavens and the flesh, and we were gods with soft rounded limbs and flushed faces. The straw mat lying on the floor and billowing up and down in the draught was cloth of gold to me, and the sound of the gate clicking, meaning that Macca was coming, rang through my mind's heaven like a twanged harp string.

Akbarah, by our grace, was permitted to sit at the fire and sing to us, one wide flushed twilight when the trees sang etched against the sky. Between his knees was an old oil-drum, and this he struck monotonously while he howled in a strong resonant voice love songs from the Afghan hills.

From his bearded mouth rolled words that made his rusty turban shake.

> "Ulladhin . . . ulladhin
> Ulla, ulla, ulla, ulla,
> Ulla, ulladhin!"

"Bang! Bang!" on the oil-drum.

After one particularly massive song, he said complacently, "This song of one boy that want one girl. He sit outside her window and sing, like me."

"Impossible!" I exclaimed.

Thumping the drum again, he howled in agony for some time. Then he said, "This song of man what want marry sister of his wife. She no let him."

"Dear, dear."

Blowing a huge stream of smoke from his mouth, Akbarah boasted, "I knock down any white man, if I like, by blowing in his face."

Macca said, "You can't knock me down, I bet, Akbarah," and knelt down before him, laughing, and appearing, by comparison, slim, golden and white.

While he lit his cigarette, Akbarah, pipe in mouth, inhaled until his buttons burst. Macca puffed a large cloud into the Afghan's face, and he replied with a relatively enormous quantity which brought the Australian to his knees, coughing and choking.

Then the champion went to bed, and soon afterwards came a sound as though water was being poured from a great height into an empty kerosene-tin. We lowered our heads and said nothing.

The coals in the fire broke and fell, but we stayed silent long after Akbarah began to snore.

It was morning, and all around us the green lonely paddocks lay with the wind from the dark sky turning the grass confusedly. A little white-haired aboriginal leant against the post-and-rail fence near the shed, and languidly, in a well-bred voice, offered to throw exhibition boomerangs for us. He appeared quite unsurprised to be black with pinkish palms, and sent the decorated boomerang wheeling and winging out across the paddock on a slanting angle. We bought two at one and threepence each.

"What do you make them from?"

"Oh, I find a wattle-tree that has a root shaped somewhat like a boomerang, and I work on it with a piece of glass or sharp tools until I fine it down," said the aboriginal and, collecting his money, he strolled off into the bush.

Akbarah smiled at me. "You have magnificent teeth, Akbarah. What do you clean them with?"

Akbarah mumbled, "Might be get little bit bark from wattle-tree and rub on tooth." Watching Blue and Jim throw their boomerangs, he said: "I love you!"

"Pah! A black man!" I said cruelly, watching the wind blow over the stormy grass.

"Yes," he replied angrily. "Black man, all right, but I own train of twelve camel in West Australia and one boy to help me."

"But," I retorted, in explanation, "a black man." And in my soul I was seething and twisting with hatred.

That night he tried to touch me again, and I stroked his chest deeply with the knife. After that we were indeed enemies, and when in the clear amber morning he came to the door, asking in an insulting voice, "My broom, you fella!" I flung it at him, saying, "Here you are, my man," with quite a trace of old England in my voice.

The broom hit him in the face. Perhaps there was old England in that, too.

"Thank you, you fella!" he said bitterly, and went away muttering to himself.

In the evening, Mr Whitebeard, the owner of the house, came

to the door, and told us that we must go. The Afghan had complained of our immoral behaviour and our company of villains whose clamours kept him awake all night.

Only by talking sheer Keats and Biblical prose could I keep the roof over our heads. The good man really believed in me, saw something of the struggle for existence in my words, and permitted us to stay; but Akbarah Khan was given notice and departed, savage with hatred.

We rejoiced deeply and I took over his small room whose window looked out over the pea paddocks of Karta Singh. There was a stretcher in it and a table made out of boxes beside the bed; from the one side of the window hung a torn bag. On the table I put my volume of Keats, a small translation of the *Aeneid* (with the Latin words alternating), my dictionary which was called among us "Farrago", and a bottle of blossoms picked from the beautiful foreshore where wild flowers and bush shrubs grew rich in purple, gold and crimson sprays of an unbelievable perfume. Blue took the room to the left of the house and Jim had the front room with the fireplace for himself and Campo Santa, an unfortunate baby possum which we had rescued when the poor mother was shot against the moon one night by some thoughtless murderer.

Campo Santa was well named, poor creature. He was about a fortnight old, long and racy looking, like a greyhound. We fed him carefully and Jim took him to bed at night in the breast of his shirt; but he was soon gone from us and we mourned for him.

Before Akbarah left us, he had had a concourse of dark visitors, with whom, we thought unhappily, he was conspiring to murder us. The young German whom we had met coming down the road with his fair comrade on our first morning in Metung stood for hours at Akbarah's door, talking.

Within, we listened, trembling with apprehension, but determined to defend ourselves stoutly. Jim said, "I'll look after youse, Blue."

"Youse look after youse-self, James," said Blue.

The young German said gutturally and pityingly to Akbarah as our bewildered, anxious faces peered out of the window at twilight, "Very yong, I think. Very yong!"

Yong! What contempt in his voice. We shrank back and hated him.

An hour later, a short dark young man swept through the garden where the warm red roses were; in the cold wind of the night, his black cloak swung outward over his shoulder; the curls on his head swung over a brow of ivory, while black eyes and white teeth gleamed at us, and we shook and trembled.

Another murderer.

So it was that we first saw Peppino, who looked so villainous and was so manly and compassionate.

In the paddocks of Karta Singh, the Italians (whom we had thought were Chinese) worked. There was just enough in the small crop to keep them going. When this paddock was cut out we should be starting to work, too. Over we wandered, one afternoon, to make their acquaintance. I knew a little Italian, and on the strength of it embarked on long philosophic discussions with handsome young Antonino Crea. Up and down their rows we flitted, helping them out before sundown and crying to them, *"Bel giovanotto!"*

"Bella ragazza!" they cried in reply.

"Mio caro marito é in campo santo!"

"Si! La stessa é la mia cara moglie!"

On the next morning, we awoke and heard the most shocking profanity from the paddock nearest the house.

"Baggy-knees! You know —— well, you're on my —— row!"

Out we rushed to kill the profaners of the holy morn; but we stopped in our tracks. Karta Singh's motley crowd of pickers who had been lying around under bags and mia-mia's for the past month were coming down through the peas, snatching them up in thousands.

"The peas are ready; out we go!"

II

AT last, after many days, we were working; we were honest; no one could point at us now.

The hut of Karta Singh stood on a hill in dusty earth, among small saplings. Around it the long rows of peas grew down to the post-and-rail fence that divided his property from the one in which ours stood. On the crop frontage, the golden cape-weed grew on juicy green and white stalks, and its yellow flowers, black-eyed, became part of my heart and soul.

We strolled over to work, Jim wearing black split pants and shirt and a brown hat with a hole in it through which his curling hair sprung. On his little finger gleamed the heavy signet ring, and between finger and thumb smoked the boree log.

Blue wore khaki trousers, neat socks and shoes that were polished to the depth of an old fiddle. A blue smock, covered with tan flowers in silk of her own working, protected her clothes, and she wore little white gloves to keep her hands clean.

Jim tied them on her wrists as we walked along.

I wore something the same, adding to it an old felt hat I had found along the beach. It was too big for me, but by bandaging my head with scarves and towels and fastening the hat around my head with a luggage strap, I managed to look dashing and seductive.

The Australian pickers were lined up in a villainous looking row at the top of the paddock. There was Baggy-knees, a hideous old fellow with a frizzed moustache, stiff with beer; he leered at us out of a crooked eye and pulled his burst tweed cap to one side.

His mate, the Yank, was a thin silent fellow with a bitter brown moustache. Blue Snake, a short squat man, tattooed over the arms, and capable of both a basilisk stare and an agreeable glance, stood with them. Poor Moss, who was afterwards found drowned in the Tambo River, stood talking to a tall thin man with an educated accent.

They all frightened us, and we went down to the bottom of the paddock, where an elderly, grizzled, but courteous, New Zealander lived in a little mixture of kerosene-tin and tent.

"Ah, yes, I worked for years among the Maoris and I know their language well," he said in the course of conversation. "The women are called wahines. They are a very fine people."

The two Italians with whom we had talked on the previous afternoon came in, greeting us with *"Buon giorno!"*

Their pants were of brown spotted velvet; their socks of a bright green shade, their shirts embroidered, and on their heads they wore fine brown hats of a primitive sort of felt. Their pretty shirts of a soft material embroidered with little red flowers and green leaves enchanted us, and we liked the handsome Latin faces, innocent brown eyes and courteous manners.

Labouring under the heavy weight of my past love for Kelly and my coming passion for Macca, I took hold of a rusty kerosene-tin and, under the direction of Karta Singh, I began to pick peas. One row apiece is allotted to the picker. At the top of it, he leaves his bag or his hat, so that it shall be marked, and not picked over again by a late comer. Heavily hung the peas among the blue-green leaves in this poor soil which was a mass of cape-weed and sorrel between the rows.

To be so near the earth, face to face with it, and groaning beneath a load of unrequited love past, and a hopeless passion to come, was torture to me.

At first I was slow and unwieldy and my tin was only half full when the others rushed by on their journey to the bag to tip out their picking. But within me is a latent fire that burns brightest only in competition, and so I left the threnody of love that I was working on, and began to pick fiercely and wildly everything in sight. I would have picked Karta's beard off his face, if it had been around, and thrust it, with his turban, into the bag. Awed by my flash of speed, the others saw me race past them, with that dancing step of the pea-picker which can best be imitated by getting down on your haunches and walking half on your feet and half on your knees, while you drag a rusty tin after you, with a few peas rattling in the bottom.

I tell you, my loves were forgotten for a while, as I raced and sped, stripping leaves and clods and thrusting them into the tin. I panted in triumph every time I ran to empty it into the bag.

"My word, look at Steve . . . can't she go?" said Jim and Blue.

The hours passed, my bags filled and, with the stubborn pride of a shock-worker, I Morris-danced over the rows, leaving the others behind.

In the fiery fury of work, now, picking everything as I went, I could leave my body alone while I attended to the needs of poetry.

"Sweetheart!" I muttered, looking down into the dry white earth, red speckled by the sorrel. "Be thou a mare, O Sorrel, and bear me to the arms of my love."

A howl of agony arose from where Karta Singh squatted sewing the bags.

"You fella Steve! You fella Steve, come here!"

Knocking my tin over with fright, I went along to where he sat throwing rubbish out of my bag and frothing at the mouth with fury.

"You fella Steve, you dirtiest picker in this paddock. You fella got everything in this bag essept the barb-wire fence! Why you not marry Baggy-knees?" pointing to the execrable creature with the loathsome ginger moustache who knelt grinning, with bags tied around his knees, a few yards off. "You two go away and get married, you dirtiest pickers in my paddock."

Moodily returning to my row, I began to pick again; but slowly now, while I forced a love song from the torture of my brain. It was a song about Bulumwaal, the town through which Kelly used

to ride; the name that in blackfellow language, means The Land
of Good Spear-wood. And it was from the timber of the bush there
that the aborigines cut their best spears. Ah, into whose heart was
the spear thrust?

I called the song "The Land of Good Spear-wood". Here she
goes.

> The wind clouds leapt to the north,
> And northward I leapt, too,
> And all my despair came bursting forth . . .
> Shouting, "He's done with you."
> That spear will pierce me at Tostaree, at Delvin and Meerlieu.
> Man, if at last you've done with me,
> I haven't done with you.
> How can I be done? Though we've come far
> From kindliness, though all that's fine,
> Has strangely vanished . . . still you are
> Indubitably mine,
> To swiftly canter with, through all
> The forests of the brain
> Until the spears of Bulumwaal rot and I'm well again.

As I grew quieter and fell into step with the other pickers I had
time to touch on their characters as they divulged them in the bits
of conversation we had in passing. The tall educated man whom I
had admired a little, as he stood waiting to start work, came along.
I thought perhaps that in him, too, lay poetry and an immortal fancy
that might turn to love.

Close at hand he was a little disappointing, being very lanky;
his hair was black and thin and his nose burning red. I envied the
sang-froid with which he leant back against the peas and ate them
as Karta passed, with turban wagging.

"Within the hearts and minds of men lie unguessed at things,"
I remarked in passing.

"That's nothing to what lies in that bag of yours, I bet," he
replied.

I felt affronted.

"I had imagined that I would find in you a man of education
and profound thought," I returned, praising him a little, for with
a good suit on, a hair massage and baking soda after every meal to
cure the red nose, he might have been a very impressive man.
"I thought I saw, in you, one who had charted the kingdoms of the
mind."

"Pardon me, for remarking it," said he, "but that one black tooth
of yours, just in front there, quite spoils your appearance."

I have never smiled with the same easiness since that day. Back into myself I retreated with my dreams of love.

Slowly, however, with kindly sun and wind, with long hours of beauty, the bush was making me glad to be working. At twilight we knocked off and made for home across the paddocks to eat a rabbit stew, and I was in paradise, supple, passionate and imaginative through every nerve of my body.

Macca came out later to see us, bringing some large lemons for Blue who ate them raw and used the rind to clean her hands. As we sprawled on the dark veranda, he remarked slowly, "The police have been down to Metung, making inquiries about two girls dressed in men's clothes." Disarmed by sadness, I said weakly, "What is it now? Why are the police and men always pursuing us? We do nothing."

"It may not be you, Steve. There have been other girls dressed in men's clothes around here. Different to you two."

On my first free day I took a walk out along the back track to the Tambo, remembering the sorrow which I had felt when Blue and Jim and I had taken the walk that first Sunday afternoon at Averdrink. Once more I walked through the grey trees that had been split by lightning so that their stems frizzled outward, splintered and old, from the heart of their being. A crooked cart track wobbled through the bush. There were really two tracks. One which was used in summer and one was a ditch when the winter rains came; the other was a detour made to avoid the summer track in winter.

Enormous charcoal logs lay on every side with little pools of clear rainwater caught in the hollows made by broken branches, and drifts of charcoal lay about them. Underfoot, the soil was clay, covered with a small red pebble of a mournful dimness, and the sky above was gloomy. Through the lonely grey delicate feathers of the wattle, mobs of crimson-crested cockatoos flung their black bodies, like flying aborigines, and as they went they cried harshly and savagely like wire being strained over posts and leather being thrashed against trees.

I was dressed in khaki trousers and shirt, wearing the hat I had dragged out of the sea, and I was unshod, my leathery feet walking easily on the sharp pebbles. But O God, the anguish, the melancholy of going poor, unknown and unloved through this bush! I felt that I was condemned by those who did not know me; that I was to be further condemned, while far ahead lay terrible years and an anguished life.

A khaki-clad horseman galloped past me on a panting shining horse whose stout body seemed to encompass my own and fill me with triumph for one moment, but when it had passed it left only shuddering fear. I looked back after him—horse and rider fled up the hill, scattering the dust—and bowed to pass under a drooping gum-tree which was the veritable king of the hill, standing on a throne of dry grass against post and rail and native sky.

I thought of love until I should have gone mad, and when I had come to the deserted house among the fruit-trees I looked through it, and then returned to Averdrink.

The front room was full of Italians; and among them was the short handsome villain who had one night visited Akbarah Khan. Blue stood among them, drawing her bow over the strings of the violin. She began to play "O Sole Mio", and the villain, with his cloak swinging from his shoulder, dropped to his knees at her feet and in a rich robust baritone sang,

> "Che bella cosa, l'urnata sole.
> L'aria serena dopo la tempesta.
> A! L'aria fresca comme un' giorno festa . . .
> Che bella cosa l'urnata sole!"

I felt half excited, half irritated to see these Italians in our room. We seemed to have descended another step in the ladder of our race. They really meant nothing to me, however, for I counted them as primitives, children, animals or deaf-mutes. Their faces pleased me, but the blankness of racial difference held me apart from them.

The beauty of Antonino Crea was not dangerous and sad like the beauty of Kelly or Macca. These men, it seemed to me, passed by those who decided not to fraternize with them. Accepting their inferiority, they extended to their superiors many little courtesies that pleased.

Crea stood beside Blue, smiling gently, red-lipped, white-toothed, green-eyed and black-browed. Beside him stood Sebastian Paolo, a little dark mouse of a fellow, clear-complexioned, brown-eyed with pink in his olive cheeks and, in his voice, a broken lilting complaining note.

Their quaintness pleased and excited my curiosity, and the comical English made me laugh and secretly ridicule them.

When the song was finished on a last high note that dragged somewhat, showing that our villain had been overworking it for years, Antonino said softly and maliciously, "Dis Peppino . . . mai friend . . . now, your friend." He dragged the dramatic Peppino to his feet.

"I nebber hear dis tune of my country played so sweet," he said to Blue by way of acknowledging the introduction.

He was a little fellow, Peppino, his blue-black hair cascaded over a brow of ivory, and his face was like the face of that old hermit who carried into the desert the veiled woman of Blue's drawing; handsome, sensitive, anguished and primitive, laughing like a boy at one moment and then lapsing into a seriousness aeons old and simian-sad.

Macca came in and we sat Peppino down on the fowl-house divan and began to examine the peculiarities of his clothes.

"Why do you wear green socks, Peppino?"

"Dese my mudder make!" he explained with a wide grin that showed red gum and white tooth.

Around the socks a piece of tape was tied; we traced it to a modest inch farther and found attached to it a pair of striped underpants, decorated with flowers and butterflies. "Dese my mudder make."

"But why have you got them tied to your socks?"

"They no fly away with me, then."

He wore no vest, and a huge chain attached to his watch appeared to be holding him together.

After a while he took a mouth-organ from his pocket and commenced to play as I have never heard anyone play since; with a rich shuffling vamp, with turns and twists and wanderings quaint and wonderful, he played to us, old, old Italian folk songs. There were litanies and marches and Fascisti hymns, love songs, and old men's dance tunes.

He held his head high in the air, gazed unblinkingly above our heads, and chanted sonorously, huskily, with genius, on the mouth-organ. Under all the music ran the primitive stamping beat of the accompaniment.

He stopped suddenly.

"Oh keep going, Peppino . . . please, please!" we cried.

"Too sore my troat," he explained, rubbing it.

A bottle of eucalyptus was brought out and we tried to dose him with it, but he wouldn't touch anything out of a strange bottle among a strange race.

"Well, look, just a drop like this," we said, "on a cigarette. See? Now you light that and smoke it at once. All gone, sore throat, Peppino!" putting it between his lips, he applied the match, but whether the eucalyptus had been poured too freely on the cigarette, or whether kerosene had got into the bottle by mistake, I don't know. Up she went in flames that singed his hair and eyebrows, and a great sizzling took place, during which Peppino hopped up and down while his friends hit out the flames, and he cried, "You killa me! You try for killa me all right. I go my plice . . . good night!"

And we didn't see him for days after that; not until the night we were asked up to Sunday tea at 'Ardy's.

Jim conveyed the invitation in his rich humble Norwegian voice: "Blue, them people, 'Ardys up on the hill, said we could get milk offa them every night if we liked, and they asked us to go up and 'ave tea with them tonight. They reckon Mrs 'Ardy's a good cook."

Pea-pickers invited out to Sunday night's tea are more scrupulous than the masonic brethren in their toilet and general behaviour, at first. Cans of water were heated, towels were washed, shirts laundered and the household brick was passed over pants, ties and collars. Jim, who was never satisfied with his suit, took a reef in the back of it for the occasion, and let down the legs of his pants. I clasped a cutting collar around my neck and, finding a small tin of Brasso, I polished my gold tooth and, breathing out gleams and Brasso, I hurried back and forth in tight trousers and a white shirt without a tail, over which my braces strained.

Blue, who was always lovely, didn't bother, but sat playing her violin while we made ourselves look uncomfortable. Among the empty kerosene-cases and the fowl-house door beds we moved, making ready, and at half past five moved with dignity up the hill to 'Ardy's.

Mr 'Ardy was a small brown man with startlingly false teeth, a short moustache, round brown eyes and a high jerky voice. He was a Seventh Day Adventist and usually avoided by all youthful pea-pickers, because he asked them to work on Sunday (Saturday was his Sabbath) and even the native bush seems to condemn you when you work on that day. Mrs 'Ardy was a tall brown woman, gentle, kind and self-sacrificing. She had a fascinating high moaning voice that was distinct for the first five words and then ran into a rapid shrieking jumble that it was enchanting to attempt to elucidate.

Most important of all, a large white table was spread out with cakes, scones and butter. We had not had butter for a fortnight and hadn't known that cakes were cooked in Gippsland. Now at the genial table of our host spread we our legs and, with bright remarks and kindly to the children, waited in patience for a start to be made. Our mouths watered so that we could hardly speak, and when we asked the little girls what grade they were in school, a flood of expectant saliva lay along our lips and brightened them like cherries. The stitches in the back of Jim's coat cracked ominously as he stretched out his hand to grasp the first slice of bread he had touched for weeks. We lived on Weeties, syrup, carrots and rabbits.

"We don't drink tea," Mr 'Ardy said brightly. "It's against our religion. Instant Postum's what we drink."

This was immediately and secretly corrupted into Stinking Possum among his graceless guests, and hands were pressed and ribs shoved as the cup of the dark unknown was passed along.

Jim's hand went in and out, mechanically propelled by his stomach, until every dish was empty on the table, and Mrs 'Ardy hurriedly rose to lock the safe door.

After tea, a family concert was indicated. We sat around the large whitewashed room on hard chairs and looked cheerful while Mrs 'Ardy, with the gentle courage of a mother, induced the little girls to give their items.

"Lindy an' Dot," she wailed in her peculiar voice, "come-an-do-yer-dialogue! It's a lovely piece," she assured us with a tender yearning look.

We said that we knew it would be, and gently added our encouragement. At last, the poor little beggars did their dialogue to a thunder of well-fed applause.

Then Peppino came in, smiling brilliantly and talking breathlessly, and after him, a tall Dantesque man, brown-skinned, dressed in brown velvet. He lived in the little bark hut just below the house; we had passed it on our way up. They had taken the Dantesque Domenic to their hearts. "Ar-r-r! poor Domenic!" chanted good Mrs 'Ardy. "'E's got a wife and family in Italy."

"In de Nord," said Domenic bowing.

"An' he misses them, too, doncher Domenic?"

He did.

"Calvin loves 'im. Ar-r-rh, Calvin loves Domenic." The baby, in the arms of the smallest girl, was urged forward. "Say 'Good-bye Domenic!' Ar-r-h, 'e loves Domenic! Domenic brings 'im lollies. Say 'Good-bye Domenic;'" And then with a wild terrifying change of voice, to the little girl: *"Lindy! Look out! You'll pull 'is little arms out!"* and the infant was grabbed and flung out of sight.

"Ah, here's another Domenic! This is Domenic Gatto."

"Tomcatto," I translated to Blue and Jim; they writhed about in their chairs, enjoying his name.

"Good naight, missus, mister, little girls!" said Tomcatto, a short, stout, dark fellow, clad in green corded velvet breeches and coat, with black leggings around his calves and a dark green hunting hat cocked on his head. It came off with a fell swoop and his thinly haired head, hooked nose and vain face smiled around impudently.

"What about singing us a song? Ar, Domenic can sing, carn't you, Domenic?"

"Yes, come on, Domenic," his boss urged heartily. "Give us a song!"

Without warning, Tomcatto grabbed from the mantelshelf a bunch of dry weeds and flowers sacred to some funeral urn and, taking Mrs 'Ardy's shrill cry of sacrilege as a cue, romped into grand opera.

Mincing from chair to chair around the room, with his mouth wide open, his eyes glaring and his posterior bouncing as though wagging a tail, Tomcatto mewed through a dozen of Donizetti, a couple of Bellini and a Mascagni.

"*O Lola, che ti datti la camicia,*" he wailed thrusting the flowers under Mrs 'Ardy's nose; and coming up to me with wide staring eyeballs he shouted while he lunged the flowers at my heart: "*Eri tu che miacchiavi quella bella vita mia!*"

Then turning to Jim, he shouted with a look of mute adoration, as though he knew why the rash Fitz-James was there, and why the stitches had burst in his coat, and why his face was rapt with satiation. . . .

"*Vesti la giubba!*"

"He says, 'Put on the coat'," I translated.

"*E la faccia infarina!*"

" 'And put flour on your face'," I continued.

"I'd rather put it in me inside," said Jim richly and humbly. Onward passed the Cat with heart-rending howls, dainty mincing steps, waving the bunch of weeds which he held, now before and now behind, until with one long hoarse caterwaul he fell into a chair, mewing faintly at our applause. "In Italy I do-a dis, all-a night," he explained graciously. "No one sleep . . . not-a one."

Now fell silence in the big kitchen, and above the scrubbed boards and the white kerosene lamplight time kept its kingliness alone.

Then Blue stood alone in the room and played "*O Sole Mio*" with such power and sweetness that before she got beyond the opening phrase, she was applauded with sheer happiness. Tomcatto had made the way easy having gone before. But the girl had always a gipsy easiness in her playing and her beautiful romantic face, like that of an innocent boy, resting on the brown violin made all who watched her remember and love her.

Peppino stood beside her and sang loudly and strongly, again, that . . .

"Che bella cosa l'urnata sole!"

When she had played it out, he took from his pocket his magical organetta and chanted swiftly with an ancient shuffling vamp that sounded like the feet of aged Italians thudding on the floor around the circle where the young danced. His black curls shook with the violence and speed of the half-forgotten folk songs.

As we sat quietly after that, Blue noticed a harmonium standing in the corner.

"What? You've got an organ here! Who plays it?"

"Ar-rr-h, Riy-plays-it-Blue," Mrs 'Ardy chanted. "Come-on-Riy-play-us-a-tune-on-ther-organ!"

"Aw, I can't play," protested Riy, a tall pleasant-faced youth with a lot of tender yellow whisker on his chin.

"Arr-r-r, you-can-so-Riy! Come-on-play-Shall-We-Gather-At-Ther-River-Riy!"

"Come on, Riy," we bellowed jovially, "give us a tune. Let's hear yer play!"

"No, no, I won't. I can't. Not for anything," protested Riy.

"Yes, yes," we chorused. "You must!" Mingled entreaties arose: "Play-Shall-We-Gather-At-Ther-River-Riy!" "Come on Riy. Give us a tune. You must play. We'll torment you till you do."

In a panic Riy arose and rushed out into the night, his long thin bare legs in the hobnail boots beating the earth rapidly.

We visitors rose as one and pursued him madly . . . over roots and rabbit-burrows, bog holes, rusty tins, tangled fencing-wire, old cultivators, heaps of bones and broken bottles. At last we ran him to earth under the flowering lucerne where the fowls had scratched deep holes in the dust, and we tickled him until he nearly strangled. On our knees and his hobnails we begged, implored, beseeched that he play . . . one note, one mere thump of the fist to show that the organ was a real thing and no vile imitation.

At last he consented.

Blinking, into the light we came, clamouring for the master-touch, for some abstruse movement from Beethoven or, at least, a song bubbled by bushmen in their cups.

"Play-Shall-We-Gather-At-Ther-River-Riy!" cried Mrs 'Ardy.
Riy thumped it out.

Ah, how we wished that we had let him run madly away in the moonlight! Nay, better than that; why had we not followed him with stones and sent him flying over the sliprails to Karta Singh's . . . treed him up in Billy Creeker's bottom paddock, left the magpies to guard him and returned in time for supper.

Late in the night we went home, past white fences and dead trees and Domenic's bark hut. Our faces were blanched by the silent Australian moon, the vast and delicately bouncing moon that mile by mile filled the sky, while Mars to the left of us bit redly and vindictively into our eyes.

Strange and wild were the cries we flung to each other.

"You fella . . . you have cup of Stinking Possum, you fella?"

"James, what did you go and eat up everything like that for? We'll never be asked again."

We weren't.

"I never ate much, Blue," huskily and humbly.

"Go on! Your coat's split. I can see the white threads fraying out from the reef you took in it."

And then an awful cry of *"Lindy! Look out, Lindy! You'll pull 'is little arms out!"*

And an answering roar of, *"Come on . . . Riy! Play th' organ, Riy!"*

And a piteous shy wail "Aw, I carn't play."

"Come on, Riy; come on, play for us. We know you can play," wheedlingly.

"Ar-r-r-r go on, Riy! Play-Shall-We-Gather-At-Ther-River-Riy! He's only been learning three weeks!"

While Peppino cried in a minor tone below it all, "I want go fill my bell' tea and cake Mrs 'Ardy."

The big soft feathered Australian owl flew overhead with whirring wings and its liquid cry deep in its throat. Blue and Jim could imitate it perfectly. The sheep in the dry paddock around the hut rushed bleating from the dusty reeds that had a sort of dry white cork running down the centre, when the thin bark was peeled off. Dead trees, with never a leaf on their boughs for fifty years, stood in terrible silence against the stars. We climbed over the post-and-rail fence between us and 'Ardy's and stood talking and dancing little pastoral dances with the Italians in the moonlight, while Peppino played on his mouth-organ the tune we called ever afterwards Peppino's folk dance.

On the next morning we again stood, ready for work, in a row with the Italians from whom the night had washed a romantic whiteness, and who had dwindled in their sleep. With us stood Blue Snake, the low-faced but eager-looking, the Yank, and drunken Baggy-knees who had put fresh sacking around his shanks and pulled his beery moustache while he waited. Country Gardens, the red-nosed and educated one, was lounging along towards us. Harry Grant, the Maorilander, far away on the hill, performed a wild silhouette dance with his tin for partner and the split legs of his trousers waving a fine fringe in the early flush of the morning skyline.

The talk all morning was of 'Ardy's, tea and cake, Riy and pulling little arms out. Karta Singh came majestically along to get the grocery orders from the pea-pickers before he took the peas down to the river boat at Metung.

"You fella Steve, Blue and Jim, what you want? Weetie and syrup?"

"Yes, that's all, Karta." We had very little to go on with until he paid us.

"What?" mockingly. "You fella eat nothing but Weetie and syrup?"

Everyone in the district knew by now that that was all we had to eat, because our groceries were left standing on the post far away from Averdrink, right on the open road where facetious youths could put a pea-rifle bullet through them.

"Yes," we had to say, "a packet of Weeties and a tin of syrup."

Little Ram Singh, Karta's partner, came down to oversee while the big one went away. A gentle comical dwarf of a man was Rammi, very like an old woman if you caught him early in the morning hanging his head of long curling white hair over the fence, without the turban tilted on top of it. He spoke timidly and giggled he-ehe-he after every opinion he put forth.

He liked Blue at once. "Bluey, you like snuff? Quick, you take bit. Karta Singh not like me taking snuff." Out of his pocket he brought a brown paper bag to which he put his nose and sneezed heavily. At that time, Blue and I had a habit of asking everyone we met (like the fellows in Hilaire Belloc's *The Four Men*) what was the best thing in the world. By doing so we hoped to collect a philosophy, a faith and a truth. Therefore, we tackled Rammi.

"Ram Singh, what is the best thing in the world?"

Rammi stood up and giggled. "Best thing in the world? Why, Bluey, enjoy yourself . . . that the best thing in the world."

I listened and determined thereafter to do that . . . to enjoy myself; but I didn't seem to have the necessary equipment like Rammi, who had an innocent and childlike mind.

Later in the day, when Karta Singh sat in the afternoon sun lazily sewing bags, while the clear wind of evening was flowing slowly towards us and shading the delicate white clouds in the sky to a lilac hue, there came, striding over the golden cape-weed, a tall, red-bearded man who waved a rusty revolver in Karta's face and shouted out, "I am Captain Kettle. Give me the wages you owe me, or I'll shoot."

Karta Singh arose and flung the captain over the barbed-wire fence, and into the bush he crawled, being seen no more.

III

THE paddock was almost cut out and my love for Kelly was gradually fading before the splendour of my love for Macca. I walked alone whenever we had an idle day and found places full of lonely twisted trees that appeared of great significance to me. Down to the foreshore I went, by a difficult route and, seeing black pigs rooting on a naked hill with but one broken tree on its top, I followed them and went down to the grey and desolate shore. Here, I meditated on many things and, returning, took out my sharp knife and carved the names of poets on the tender young saplings. On one afternoon in particular, I remember following the sandy gravel road that went straight past Averdrink, to where it forked into an old forgotten track that was half grown over by gum-trees and wattles. I have always sorrowed for forgotten things, so I stepped on to the track and walked a pace.

The harsh voice of a bird high in the trees shouted, "Go back! go back!" It was a bird known in Gippsland as the "wattle-bird". "Go back," it barked. "Go back! Go back!" There was a canine harshness in its voice. I turned and went back, overcome by the sad mystery of the bush. I said to myself, "I shall know much sorrow on that road. The bird is good; it means to warn me. I should never return again to Gippsland; for I see that it holds sorrow for me, and the beginning of the end. Nevertheless I shall come back to it, again and again until I am hated by it, and I, too, hate."

All night the moon covered the roads and fields, giving hills the look of ancient temples, making roads look like fair rounded statues. Yes, from the Greek lands had come the moon, full of the memory of Grecian art, and through the broken columns of the night I wandered in search of my love, while from the withered moonlit bush on each side of the road came a distressful watching, a sadness and a melancholy unspeakable. I waited by the road under the shadow of a superb hill, which was on the property of Billy Creeker.

At this hill I gazed, crying, "O rounded Australian hill, covered with grass like the hide of the kangaroo, above you burns the familiar stars in a clear, sad and naked heaven. Often shall I look on you in days to come; yes, with a forlorn eye I shall look at you, for from you comes sorrow only. You are earth, waiting to become man."

Now I climbed the road, deep and dusty in the moonlight, and came to the hut of Karta Singh. In the day saplings that moved murmuring around it, stood three caravans, their dry canvas hoods billowing in the night wind, and from the hut of Karta Singh came such a clamour of mingled tongues that I was astounded. It seemed to me that within that small hut some two hundred cats lay shrieking, cheek by jowl and, passing and repassing over their tails, strode Karta Singh, screaming joyously. I stood by the sliprails, wondering greatly under the stars that shone on the white caravans, and listened to the lunatic din inside the tiny hut.

The small door opened and an old Indian came out, dressed in dark clothes. On his head he wore a snowy turban and it nodded from side to side as he came to me. Together we leant over the sliprail and his spotless beard shone as he spoke.

"You want see Karta Singh?"

"No. I come to look at the stars. But who is with Karta Singh, O venerable one? Who is it mourns within his house?"

"Six my countrymen and me, we come stay for one week with Karta Singh."

Nine men counting Karta Singh and Rammi in that hut; certainly I had never been in it, but it appeared small on the outside.

"Yes, we come. We talk of many things to Karta Singh." Looking at my figure clad in the best suit, garnished with stiff collar and tie, he asked, "What you name, boy?"

"My name is Steve."

"Where you live?"

"With my sister in a house on the hill over there."

"You good looking boy, you fella."

"So also was Adonis, but yet he came to dust. But I must go, good ancient, away to my guests who await me and robed in splendour do chant that I come. Farewell, *addio!*"

"Good night, you fella!"

Macca was at Averdrink when I got there, and into the moonlight we walked; the moonlight of youth, that fell crucified through the boughs of the dead silver trees; that made the shadows of the leaves as small as it could so that it might gleam abroad and lie on all the earth. To him, I had nothing to say. Only, I looked night long into his white face, saying, "This is a Greek urn that will pass away with time. Therefore, O eyes, look your fill and tremble with the coming sorrow, for life is flying."

I walked with him down to the gate, through the dead trees, and picking up their white chips in the moonlight I said to him:

"Words come after thought as slowly as music follows the unwilling bow trailed over the violin strings by listless hand. The moon is ardent tonight; she tires of human restraint. At midnight drops of blood will fall from her. If you are about, gather them on a brazen shield. Only the naked young have brazen shields. These only shall catch the blood of the moon; the red and silver drops will moan within the goblet. Heed them not! Do but anoint your breast with them. We, naked, splashed striplings, shall dance to them. . . ."

Macca said, leaning over the Cyclone gate, watching two hooded bush women quietly passing, "Steve, say 'Bucket of firewood' very quickly!"

I did, in perplexity, and he laughed loudly.

"Ah, you are not worthy," I said, turning and leaving him. "But some day I shall make you worthy."

On the following day we finished up the crop down near Averdrink. I was sorry, because I had been able, now and then, to slip over to the house and put on a cup of cocoa for us. That is past. Carrying bags, twine, needle and scales and tins, we went up to start in the peas on the dry chalky land right in front of Karta's hut.

All through that hot day we laboured with the tins and the poor peas. The sun was a warrior whom I gladly contested and whom I overthrew. Dazzling and magnificent was the sun's arm on my back and joyous were the blades of sweat that came from my pores and vanquished him. Sometimes, from the intoxication of work, I arose and, half delirious in a fantastic world, got a drink of cold water from Karta's little tank in the shade.

Once Sebastian Paolo gave us an effervescent drink in his enamel mug, and we were branded with the beauty of that gesture, forever.

At lunch hour we were asked to enter the hut of Karta Singh and eat curry and johnny cake with him. Decorously, gracefully, we entered, feeling for him, sometimes, a respect. The man had an ancient lordliness about him, a querulous and brutal majesty which subdued us.

He was over six feet tall, and he sat before a roaring fire on a stool about four inches in width and three in height. The hut, a lean-to about five feet long by three wide, was like a hive, with cells made of stringybark poles and bag beds slung on them, all the way up the wall. In these lay the Indian friends, their eyes quivering like mercury as they smoked and screamed conversationally.

Karta had three johnny cakes ready and, splitting their smoking roundness open he filled them with curry and rice and handed us the dish. He was very drunk, but drowsy and harmless.

After eating, we wiped our mouths and thanked him. Taking a pea-rifle down from the wall he put medicine bottles out on the fence in the sun and asked us to test the weapon. The purple glare from the sides of the bottle hurt the eyes, and we missed often, but Karta Singh, of the English cavalry in the Indian army, missed never. Old Rammi busied himself, rushing around in a circle of a few inches that was to spare, giggling and exclaiming, "Well, well, Bluey!"

Tin in hand, we walked out and began to work again. As I laboured in the palpitating heat that came in swift rhythms from the sun, with easeful and cool withdrawings at regular intervals on my body, I was gently poked in the ribs and, looking up, saw my patriarch of last night.

A foul breath drifted into my face as he said gently with an apologetic laugh, "I think you boy you come last night."

"Don't mention it. The mistake was pardonable, for by moonlight I am all things."

"My name Leep Singh."

"Indeed? Any relation to Spring-heeled Jack, O venerable acrobat?"

Poking me again in the ribs, he asked, "What you take for fun?"

"Fun? You mean wit? The Attic?"

"You come my wagon tonight, we have fun."

"Humour? Burlesque? The jest?"

"I pay for good fun."

"Tonight, then, shall see us duly assembled before your wagon, doing the Falstaffian at your pleasure. And now, worthy Leep, vault aside and let me on with my honest labour."

That night, by the light of the moon, we four, Blue, Jim, Macca and myself, assembled before the wagon of Leep Singh, crying, "Lo, Prince of India, we come for fun! With jest and persiflage we come to make merry your heart. Welcome us, therefore, into your caravan! And ere we go, pay us in the rupee, the cheroot or the pukka sahib while we wallah in your punkah."

But the Prince of India, on seeing us, was dismayed and angered, and sent us forth to wonder while he cried in the distance that he had not meant that species of fun at all.

In the earliness of the next morning, he was at our door. I was fumigating my room with liberal shovels of sulphur found in an old bag, when our door was gently knocked, and lo, before it, stood with a dirty bag over his back, the Prince of India.

"What you got to sell?" he asked with a crafty smile.

"You," I responded, "and in this wise. Come, enter, thou gorgeous and voluptuous gourmet of the East. O, that Solomon had seen thee in thy purple before he went to the tents of Sheba! Thou, with the baldrics of Calcutta scarlet, with thy shoulder-knots of string and tar, made by the craftsmen to dazzle all time; thou of the painted cheek (the rouge of the methylated spirits jar), thou of the breath given by the glorious goddess Pyorrhoea. . . . Come then, into my chamber, fall, and be in Elysium."

And with a hasty look to see if the room was dim with sulphur I pushed him in and locked the door.

He got out after an uproar and fled vomiting across the fields, and I had to nail a piece of wood over the window to take the place of the glass he had broken in his agony to escape.

I stood in the sunshine beside the old tank at Averdrink. It was Sunday afternoon. The sun was shining on my strong round arms. I flexed them derisively in Macca's face. "Well, are we going for a walk? You said you'd take me to a gully where I could hear the leather-heads singing."

"Well, all right; come along." He picked up his rifle and I followed him. It was a wooing just like Kelly's. I wondered how many bush girls, on a Sunday like this one, would be following Australian males armed with guns loaded against bird and beast. This was how the bush courted. Man and woman, bird and beast, this was how they wooed. The male strode ahead through the gum-trees, and struck for some vague satisfaction of his own, and the woman admired, because through admiration she struck at the man.

I had hardly time to look at the leather-head before it was lying at my feet, flung from the branch by death, clothed in a shivering mist of deep blue feathers from which its black eyes looked coldly and dryly past us. The gasping golden beak with its sharp tongue looked intimately of my own flesh.

"So that's a leather-head? Why leather-head, I wonder?"

"Oh, it's only a local name. I don't know its real name. It's supposed to have a tough piece of skin under the feathers on the head."

"It needs a leather skin in a country like this," I exclaimed, brushing a swarm of mosquitoes off my arms. As I sat on the dry twig-strewn ground I made a little mia-mia from the thin sticks.

"I should like, some day, to marry and live in a house that would look over the sea; and all night I would lie with my head on the arm of my love and listen to the water's broken voice on the shore."

"Steve, that's strange! I always thought that if I married I should like my wife's head to rest on my arm all night. Yes, marriage could be beautiful!"

"Instead of being a procession of perambulators," I replied.

He laughed. "A procession of perambulators! I shall remember that," he said.

"Let us go down to the sea, now."

We rose, leaving the gully behind, with a strange crop of forgotten peas, belonging, it seemed, to no one, on the steep hillside. We climbed the hill up which I had climbd in the wake of the feeding pigs some time before, and when I saw the broken tree on its summit I sighed, remembering my lonely meditations that day.

"Stevie . . . Stevie . . . Stevie Talaaren . . . Talaaren! What is that, Macca?"

"Those birds are called peewits or grallinae, Stevie."

A flock of delicate black and white birds, shaped like little Greek oil lamps, flew overhead crying in rich rollicking voices, but faintly lonely: "Stevie . . . Stevie . . . Talaaren . . . Talaaren!"

"My name, Macca!"

"Yes, Stevie! That's what they're saying. How perfectly they say it!"

"But what would Talaaren mean? It sounds like very old English."

"Among peewits and young pea-pickers, Steve, it might mean, 'I love you!' "

My heart leapt, dragging me forward into a new existence.

"Stevie Talaaren!" said Macca, taking my hand.

Silently we walked to the sea.

The shore was dull and sandy today, strewn with dry light wood into which sea-worms had eaten. From bush to bush a lonely little bird flew, crying rapidly, "Three bishops . . . three bishops . . . three bishops!" It was very concerned for their graces and threw the sand and leaves about in agitation as it searched for them.

Far away in the bushes, the burgher-bird that used to sing about my home in Dandenong fled searching for his lost love, "Pretty Jorea . . . pretty Jorea!"

Macca took a small pair of bathing trunks from his pocket and hastily put them on behind a bush. Then, casting his false teeth into his hat, he wiped his mouth with his hand and, turning his face away from me, waded out until the water was deep enough to dive into. I watched him bobbing up and down in the grey water with the toy-like movements, the sense of celluloid, given by the swimmer far out.

When he came out of the water, we lay until nightfall talking in the warm sand. He made a fire from the dry punkwood, as he called it, and it burnt blue and green, flinging its wild spears across the shore and into the returning tide.

"Where did you work before you came here, Macca?"

"I picked maize all last winter at Orbost; but on the other side of the Snowy River, at Newmerella, I had a good mate. Streak's his name. A strange fellow. We lived together in a hut up there in the Snowy, and went into the township and got drunk on Saturday nights."

I was grieved to hear my colonial Keats talking like this. "And did you love anyone there?"

"No. But I knew a peculiar girl in that town. Her name was Monday. She was so moody and passionate that everyone in the maize paddocks called her Muggy Monday."

"What an utterly vile name. Oh, that was horrible," I cried, all my poetic instincts outraged.

"Yes, but that was her name and it had its own beauty, if you thought of it. Think of a muggy day in Gippsland among the tall green maize. Or if you're cutting sunflowers that they grow over in Bruthen. You ought to see them, Steve. About thirteen feet high, bending above you with jet black faces swelling with seed; and the hair, Steve, I mean the petals, standing out golden in the sun. You're down below slogging away on the damp black muggy soil, and there might be a sultry storm coming up in the north-east. Muggy Monday sounds a good name then. We had a song about her . . . it went. . . ."

"Don't sing it, in the name of the gods! I've heard enough." Lying back on the sand I mourned for want of great company.

> "The stars, a jolly company,
>   I envied, straying late and lonely;"

"I like that, Steve. Any more of it?"
"Yes, but I forget it. However, there's

> "Your hands, my dear, adorable,
>   Your lips of tenderness
> Oh, I've loved you faithfully and well,
>   Three years, or a bit less.
>   It wasn't a success.

No, that's not good, really. But 'Libidio' is fine and then that wonderful

> "Love, in you, went passing by,
>   Penetrative, remote, and rare,
>   Like a bird in the wide air,
>   And, as the bird, it left no trace
>   In the heaven of your face.

I am vain. Macca, I have always wished that face to have been mine. I don't want anything to leave a trace on me. I want no change at all, in myself.

> "O, infinite deep I never knew,
>   I would come back, come back to you,
>   Find you, as a pool unstirred,
>   Kneel down by you, and never a word,
>   Lay my head, and nothing said,
>   In your hands, ungarlanded.
>   And a long watch you would keep;
>   And I should sleep, and I should sleep!

Ah, Macca, if only I could come back to you like that. When the pea-picking is over, I must go, perhaps forever. Oh, if I thought that I could come back to you like that. Remember, promise me that you will remember that poem; and when I return, let me

> "Lay my head, and nothing said,
>   In your hands, ungarlanded.

I want no more than that, forever."

"I shall remember, Steve," said Macca solemnly.

"Well, here's another fine thing of Rupert Brooke's:

> "Down the blue night the unending columns press
> In noiseless tumult, break and wave and flow,

Dash it, I've forgotten the rest. But O God, how a night lives in that! How the large skies of the South Seas with their vague majestic clouds live in that! He saw that with a lonely heart, knowing that he would die young.

> "O little heart, your brittle heart;

That's the worst of it, I can only remember fragments.

> "Like the star Lunisequa, steadfastly
> Following the round clear orb of her delight,

and

> "Day that I loved, day that I loved, the Night is here!

or

> "I have been so great a lover; filled my days. . . ."

"Is he dead, Steve?"

"Yes. Died of fever in the war. Let us go home. Here's the moon, too,

> "The moon leans on silver horn,
> Above the silhouettes of morn.

A poet named Francis Ledwidge wrote that. Dead, too. You don't know how I have mourned for them. I came out into the world expecting to find all men like the poets I loved; that's the reason for my madness and confusion, you see. The world is here, but the poets have fled it."

As we walked through the moonlit bush, the plovers high in the sky cried in thin Russian (as I fancied) their song of the silver shower and the little bell. Down fell their voices like the ghost of rain, and in a hollow among the fern the curlew wept alone, saying piercingly "Eo . . . Eo . . . Eo!" so poignantly I stood still and was heart-broken by the sad wild cry. Oh, to be loved!

"Lauré, Lauré, I am young and my plate is empty. When will my two great desires, to be loved and to be famous, be granted?"

At the broken tank in the garden of Averdrink, we stood and looked down into the molten water glittering there. "Wait, Macca, I have a poet here who looked down on this before Christ was born!"

I ran into my room and returned with the *Aeneid* which I had stolen from the farm where the women had starved me a year before.

"I have words to fit this water flung from side to side by the moon. See how it ripples on the eaves of the house and on the ground throws a faint aura. Virgil noted this long ago," I said, peering at the small italics by the light of the outpouring moon, and cried,

> *Sicut aquae tremulum labris ubi lumen ahenis*
> *Sole repercussum, aut radiantis imagine Lunae,*
> *Omnia pervolitat late loca, iamque sub auras*
> *Erigitur, summique ferit laquearia tecti.*

Those are words for you!"

"They're like the water splashing about in the tank, Steve. What's the meaning? Let me look."

"Here, then—'As when the trembling light in brazen vats of water, reflected by the sun or by the image of the radiant moon, flits over all places far around, and now is tossed up towards the air and strikes the fretwork of the top of the house.'"

"The fretwork on the house, Steve! Fretwork, think of that! And this was written before Christ was born. I didn't even think they had houses then; but here Virgil says they had brazen vats and fretwork on the eaves. I can't get over that."

"Well!" (The usual Australian "Well!") "Macca, I must go to bed. We'll be out late tomorrow night. Jim has found his long lost uncle at last. He is a fisherman, I believe, and we have been invited out to tea with them. His name's Edgar Buccaneer and, like Jim, he is of Nordic blood. From what we've heard of him from Jim, he's rather a grand figure."

"I must get to know them, too, Steve."

"Good night then, Macca!"

"Good night, Stevie . . . Stevie . . . Talaaren." His voice broke into the rollicking cry of the peewits.

In those days, we were almost inseparable. I had not long said good night to him before he was at our door again, sitting around watching us prepare to meet the family of Edgar Buccaneer. I swung from room to room, large and muscular in my trousers and shirt, looking for a lost stud. Jim's concession to the evening was to wash his sweater, a tight white woollen one with a red striped V around the neck. It had dried in the act of climbing half way up his chest and not all our assembled weight pulling on it could bring it down. He let his coat out at the back, since this meal was to be a family affair, and took out the reef he had put in his trousers.

Again the tin of Brasso came out and he cleaned his gold ring and I, my gold tooth.

In the warm grey night we made our way under the drooping trees, from which small clicking insects fell, to the house of Edgar Buccaneer. Climbing a steep yellow cliff that stood above the lake, with the main road running under it, we entered the gate of that tarred house we had passed on the morning we lugged Jim's baggages out. And out to the door came with a shy, strong step the tall man who had looked out at us keenly above the shoes he cobbled.

The Buccaneer, in those days, was a figure to gladden the heart. The great drooping bulk of the man was alive with tenderness and laughter. The sea-blue eyes, bright with brine, tense with the sun, shone in his handsome brown face. His hair was black with a twist of white in it, and his golden moustache, bleached by the sea, was full, over his dark red compassionate mouth.

As he spoke he gave sweeping gestures outward with his arms, all embracing, as though we were a shoal that he was intent on netting. And his eyes had a curious power of changing instantly from the wildest look of merriment to a steady serious gaze, honest and un-wavering. The soul of the man was in his eyes.

"Ha," said he. "Good evening. Pleased to meet you. Come in." As we walked before him, he was talking away muffledly behind us, laughing and exclaiming. "I saw you and Jim go past the first morning you landed here, you know, and I said to the wife, 'That's one of Violet's boys, just gone past; I'll swear it.' Are you there, Jess? Here they are." He introduced us.

The coquettish face of his wife lit up as she came out. Her red lips, with little straight lines above them, curved over her darkish teeth on which patches of white glittered. It was a face lined with power and wit, kindliness, anxiety and courage. Under the brown skin a flush showed dimly. She took my hand in her own sensuous clinging one and pressed it warmly, while she smiled, catching her lower lip delicately with her teeth, and her breasts swayed as she moved towards the bedroom taking us in to talk for a moment, after saying easily and with the power of a woman whose marriage has been fertile and happy, "How do you do?" She gave one to understand that she, at least, did well, and was going to arrange matters so that we should be equally favoured. This drew me towards her.

Hitherto, I had lacked someone to whom I could turn the full face of my loneliness and my desire to be loved. Nothing of what

I had really wanted from life had, thus far, escaped me among my mates. With Blue, I was moody, or humorous and restless. To Macca I showed a scornful attitude of scepticism towards love; or a petulant, intensely sentimental outlook. At other times, in despair, I tried to be a man, and put on the boxing gloves with him when he came to see me. A ridiculous figure I must have looked, with the big brown gloves on my fists, attempting in the bewildering smother of boxing to strike him fiercely and master him in that way, if none other.

I had now met a woman who would mould me firmly back into the sexual mould from which I had fled, but which I secretly desired with all its concomitants, love, marriage and children. My life was to be ruled by this visit. On Blue, it had no effect. She went her own way, needing no guidance, strong in herself.

The Buccaneer's house was of unpainted weatherboard. There was a grey wind-swept garden in front, high up, looking directly out on the lake waters. Wattles, blackwood, salty grey shrubs and blue flowers leant sadly around grey wire-netting, beyond a wide board veranda. The house was well made and as strong as the Buccaneer's boats; he had built it himself.

They were not wealthy, and yet I think that about their house the air was denser and more luxurious than in any home I had ever been in. It was chaotic, tangled, rich, sensual, obstinate and passionate with love, marriage, births, and illnesses of a petty kind, and with an increasing contentment.

They, like Kelly, perceived my overwhelming loneliness and by many compassionate signs drew me to them, showed me favour, and gave me a confidence in myself which I had been lacking.

The Buccaneer's wife talked to me about books. She was fond of those that dealt with girls who had been disappointed in love and had become masculine out of masochistic desire to hurt themselves; and then, ah, then, love had stepped in and they had become perfect mothers and wives. I agreed with her that that was ideal, but difficult to find. She lent me the book in question; but I really preferred Wilde, Virgil or the dictionary, because I thought that the desire to be loved should not be troublesome, nor should literature be made from it. It amounted to a pathological complaint in my case, for which I knew no remedy. I only hoped, sadly, that these contented people knew of one. If the desire could only be stopped, so that I might get on with the task of my life, I should be grateful.

But I was happy that night. What a tea Jim ate! Without fear he piled into tea and coffee rolls, which our hostess made, and his good greasy red face shone with joy and shy pride in his new-found uncle. Very late that night, we left, promising to come again and bring Macca with us.

I carried the book my friend had lent me. "I had another splendid one that I would have liked you to read. It was called *On the Trail of the Black Serpent.*"

I laughed all the way home, and determined to call her, ever after, the "Black Serpent", for I felt that I should always be trailing and creeping around her, for sympathy, company, love—anything she had to offer.

From the dusty road we could hear the squeals of Karta Singh, Leep, Gungah and Naran, as they gyrated around each other's turbans. In a bag mia-mia at the back of the Indian's hut lay Tom Country Gardens, the educated gent. His candle was still burning.

"Hello! May we come in?"

"Do."

There he lay in his pole and bag bed, a piteous, comical man, but with a curious dignity about him.

"I am employed, as you see, in the triple occupations of eating a red herring with tomato sauce, combing the dandruff out of my hair and looking for fleas."

The Indians shrieked deafeningly, almost in our ears, it seemed. Their boots beat the shingle walls and they flung themselves back and forth in their bunks, clamouring and miaowing furiously to high heaven.

"What a row! How can you sleep?"

"Quite easily, really. I take a caraway seed before retiring and that seems to soothe me," said Tom Country Gardens. The candle-light blustered over his coarse bag bed, his thin black hair, red nose and red herring. We left him to it.

Next morning, with a letter from faithful Borrelerworreloil in my pocket, I took a walk over the immortal hills, rolling with white clouds and gulls in the morning wind, free-limbed and full of poetry, and I was struck to the heart by romantic glimpses of far-away trees, enchanted by distance into human shapes. I thought of Macca, so that he filled my heart entirely.

But O afternoon, long dry lustrous and windy! Afternoon of shining boards, empty sheds, as lonely as parched bones, you saw me lying on a bed of tinsel gum-leaves in an old house with a galvanized iron roof. There the sea wind roared; I lit a fire in an oil-drum to keep myself warm while I listened to it, bearing the voices of men, women and children about the earth, and prophesying in my ears the enormous future. Full of visions was that air and murmurous with words spoken in other lands. Far away in the bracken, the curlew cried, "Eo, eo, eo!" so brokenly and sadly that I wept.

At night I went outside and stood tormented under a tall crimson-limbed gum-tree, its black leaves making a huge wig for my head, a wig of boomerang-shaped leaves; and there I wept again, because I was young and unloved and life was unknown.

When Macca came out I sat with him beside the lowering fire and heard the curlew cry in the encircling darkness, "Eo, eo, eo!"

"Macca," I said, "what does that cry mean?"

"It is my heart," he replied sombrely.

Then without a word I loved him. I chained myself to him for all my youth. I set my heart down at his feet, and it became his. To me, in reward, after a long season, came the outline of my soul.

To comfort myself I made cocoa and ate biscuits with him, but Blue heard us and, being an irritable soul, wanted to know: "Why the hell don't you eat in the daytime and be done with it?"

We had finished the peas in the paddock of Karta Singh and after a lot of argument, telling of fortunes and blowing in the ear, we got our little cheque. On the very next day we started in on Billy Creeker's crop.

The day was wet; the peas were poor. And we were so miserable by midday that we went up to a little hut at the top of the paddock and knocked on the door. Out came the young German whom we had met on the first morning and who had called us "yong". The hut was warmed by a little red fire which the fair-haired comrade stoked. We sat yarning the afternoon away, and found that we had been mistaken in the young German. He, too, like Peppino, was an Italian from Piedimonte, and his name was Domenic Olivieri.

The fair comrade who wore a wide leather belt covered with tiny buckles was named Frank and he was even more melancholy than myself. But with reason. When his girl came out from Italy to marry him, he had met her at the boat and, in the ardour of the meeting, put his suitcase down beside him for one rash moment. A wild Australian had lifted it, and his clothes and hard earned cash as well.

Addio, la nozze, mio povero Figaro!

Now, they'd have to wait.

"Arnd Frarnk . . . he bur-r-r-n!" Domenic remarked succinctly. They both looked as though they had been burnt. Italians shave their heads every autumn and get a good crop for the coming spring. These two had scarcely a covering on their heads and, in deference to our stares, they put on little white calico nightcaps.

Domenic impressed me. He was a short, stoutly built but tigerishly lithe man, with a calm yellow mature face; the writhing lips of a Dante, the narrow eyes of the Mongol race, and the suffering look of a man bent on making money and getting on in the world.

Billy Creeker's peas were no good. We had to give them up after a week or so of work; anyhow, he was on the last picking. Billy Creeker attracted us greatly. He was a dirty lazy handsome little fellow with a squeaking groaning voice and a habit of pushing his wide hat up over one ear, whenever his own cleverness as raconteur struck him too forcibly. He, as you might say, patted his own intellect. And the splendid hair fell down over his brow.

Machinery lay rusting all over his farm, and his house, into which we had not been asked, was locally described as being a wreck. However, he didn't do so badly for a widower with five children to look after, and I always thought of him as a great man and an artist, although he had little to say of things like that. Anyhow, he came out into the paddock and yarned to us while we worked, or stopped us and got us to talk with him, as though the work wasn't important. He wasn't anxious about money, and he didn't want to get on.

Domenic watched him with a quick glitter of amusement in his brown bulbous eyes, but pulled his mouth down deprecatingly when he spoke to him.

Macca, who was working for Greenfeast over to the left of 'Ardy's, took us along for a share in the crop. Two of the local girls were there, decorous in skirts and stockings. They stared at us searchingly and their presence spoilt our day. We didn't care much for women; they had no sense of adventure, we said, and didn't know how to live in romantic leisure.

An old man named Snowy (half the pea-pickers in Gippsland seem to have been baptized in the Snowy River) was working in the next row to mine, and he told me how to save the knees of my trousers by sewing patches of leather on them. He looked so old, cold and forlorn that I grieved for him. It was a sad condition for a gentleman to be in, among wet peas, and sleeping in an open shed all night. I secretly swore to get out of this harsh furrow into which I had fallen some day. But for the present, there were on the sloping hillside the khaki-clad figures of Macca, Blue and myself, Snowy and Jim in old suits picking the cold crop above the spring. Greenfeast, the owner, a carven-faced brown man who wore a plaited leather hatband, sewed our bags contentedly. It was a magnificent crop, and we picked many bags.

As we went home together, in the wake of the milk cows that trotted with creamy swaggering udders before us, stirring up with their swinging feet the golden mist of dust from the earth, we saw Mrs Greenfeast, a wistful-looking, tall, gaunt young woman, pegging out children's clothes on the line.

Some days afterwards our cheque was politely brought down to us.

'Ardy's crop got us next, and we had to work on Sunday with the whole family. One unforgettable morning I walked with Macca across the paddocks to the peas. The ecstasy of youth was churning the earth around me into splendour. There was a clamorous glory that is beheld but once. Swiftly I observed the shape of flower and tree, of dim Gippsland distances, grey and feathery, and these things communicated their genius to me. "It is a fairytale," I cried, holding his hand tightly, and walking lightly in my old faded trousers and sweater, ridiculous felt hat that I had picked up on the beach, and ribbon tie. "I am living in fairyland."

"Ar, don't get married, Blue," cried Mrs 'Ardy dolorously to Blue who was always thinking about it, since she had an importuning lover at home. Through the dry purple wings of the crop the morning flashed in glory. "Ar, don't get married, Blue!"

"Go on," said her husband cheerfully, "I'd get married again tomorrow if I were single." Ah, how he smiled.

Macca and I worked until moonrise that night, long after the others had gone home. Even the moon was young, that night, for it was through young eyes that it shone. When we had finished, we wandered away together in our innocence and listened to bull-frogs croaking in the bog-holes and dams; and with a dream-like splendour shone the moon.

IV

IN the afternoon the dust rises in the air of Gippsland and takes bat-like flights, all gilded by the declining sun, from bough to bough of the lustrous red and silver trees that are shot through with silken purple and gold. Even in the pastoral patches where there is grass, the dust comes and for hours, until night takes its place, it is a part of the air, just as the birds are.

Blue and I walked through it, along a lonely track with rainwater hollows on its surface, and we saw the Italians picking for Mr

Whitebeard in his crop on the opposite hill. Going through a rusty Cyclone gate that literally ran out of our hands in its eagerness to be opened, we climbed a small steep hill with stringybarks and bracken growing on it, deep in the dim dust. The Italians chattered brokenly in loud voices as they worked.

One of them in a clean white shirt went up and made water against a thistle. No one saw us. Delaying a respectable while, we went through the broken grey gate into Mr Whitebeard's property. Peppino came over to the fence, a scarlet wild pea hanging over each ear, and grinned sweetly, with much brilliant flashing of teeth and tossing of black ringlets.

"Hello, Pep. You'll soon be finished here."

"Yes, tomorrow we finish for sure. Then I go to Maffra for de sugar beet."

"Many people working there?"

"Oh, yes, lot my countrymen go dere. Why you no come, eh?" It was a soft hurried question, urgent, deep and ardent. He grinned after it. "I think go too soon now. Why you no come?"

"Fill my bell' tea and cake Mrs 'Ardy, Peppino," we said, falling back on our stock phrases. "Oh, we've got a good hut; we like Metung and Karta Singh wants us to pick for him."

"No good beans Karta Singh."

"Oh, well . . . might be we have fun," we answered, falling back on another stock phrase earned from experience with Leep Singh.

Unfortunately, despite our real liking for Peppino, our conversations with him, at times, were like those ranges far back where saplings are spaced widely and have no connection with each other, yet contribute to the whole.

"I come your plice one night for sing and tea and cake, before I go," he promised.

He did, too, and sang *"Gigolette"* until the house shook and Tom Country Gardens came down from his hut up in Billy Creeker's where he was now camped, and congratulated Peppino on his lungs.

"I could hear you bellowing grand opera half a mile away." Peppino thanked him shyly.

He sang it again, and as I sat on the fowl-house door bed with Macca I could feel the vibrations quivering through the wood and almost making the wire-netting lay eggs.

Peppino with his face lifted to the ceiling and his mouth rounded, sang in farewell.

Two mornings later we accompanied him to the wharf where,

decorated from one side of his chest to the other with medals, tin birds, clockwork mice, lead frogs and metal butterflies, he waved farewell to us and set forth for Maffra to cut sugar beet. Following the boat around the foreshore, we waved and cried, "Good-bye, Domenic" to Peppino, punctuated with howls of "You'll pull 'is little arms out!" as our friend leant over the rail, gesturing dramatically and glittering in the hot sunlight that struck fire from his haberdashery.

During the week a letter arrived from him, written on the stationery of a leading haberdasher in Maffra, to whom, we surmised, he had gone for a fresh stock of glory to trail across his breast before he attacked the beet. The letter had been written by the haberdasher as Pep dictated. This communication revealed an unsuspected passion for Blue which endured for years.

Dear Blue, I send you this name because I forget what you were at the boat. You ask that I might give you this place. Sorry I did not give it you yesterday. Remember me to Jim, Mac, also your sister. To you I give my right hand. Last night I was sick for you.

(Poor) PEPPINO.

The haberdasher added the "poor" sympathetically!

Then general exodus of the Italians commenced now. Experience had taught them that the bean crops around Metung were sparse, for the land did not take kindly to pulse. Huts were to spare, fortunately, because Mr Whitebeard had sold Averdrink to a family that wished to enter into possession at once. We had to shift.

The Nordic Domenic whom Calvin had loved departed for Maffra also, so the good 'Ardys invited us to shift into the bark hut lately occupied by him.

Packing together our rags, bags, boxes, cocoa tins and Weetie packets, we jumped over the post-and-rail fence and climbed the hill to the bark hut. This place marked a definite period in our lives; it was, and will be forever, our youth. What a power it had of projecting itself on us! We, at its mercy from the first, saw only a two-roomed lean-to of inch-thick bark that smelt like seed potatoes. This was the sole remaining part of a gaunt milking shed that had once stood on the naked hill among the dry reeds. The grey shining rafters and uprights were visible for miles around, and the cow bails were overgrown with nettles. Other than a few clumps of dried bracken and three huge trees from which, by their anguished look, the bark hut had been cut, there was no sign of vegetable life. There was, truly, a pumpkin vine placed behind wire-netting by the Italians, to protect it from the ravenous rabbits, and kept going on

a diet of precious dishwater; but this miracle was more in the nature
of an orchid than common vegetation. The grass around it had dried
to dust.

Within the hut was an empty fireplace of tin; to the right, a log
seat was bound to the bark wall by thick fencing-wire. In the bedroom stood a bark table and two bark beds; there was a small
window, too, with a fantastic pane of wire-netting stretched across
it; through it, the tall dead trees shone black against the blue and
gold lake in the red sunset. Eagerly searching with the poverty-
stricken eyes of the bush people for some sign of life, we found a
few lovely things that Domenic and his friend had left; things that
simple creatures like Blue and myself would hang on to for years.

A strip of flowery rag from an Italian shirt; a religious text and
some small cards depicting the burning of various Italian saints;
and, last but not least, a magnificent and imposing photograph of
Domenic's brother-in-law perhaps, who leant, stroking a gigantic
black moustache, against a white icing harp covered with pious
mottoes. Yet another figure had apparently leapt on to the top of
Saint Peter's and stood there with his thin legs debonairly disposed
and every rag fluttering in the breeze of that altitude.

How we loved such things! How we loved the bark hut!

Jim was ordered to work with a tea-tree broom to cleanse the
rooms while we carted our rubbish up from Averdrink and disposed
things in a cultured manner around the luxurious halls. Macca
brought a bowl of golden roses for the bark table in the corner; Blue
spread our father's old travelling rug over her bed and hung the
watch up on the nail. Jim had hardly time to get his tent up before
night came rushing through the stars, and we wouldn't have cared
if he had failed.

No, secure and inviolable in our own home, at last, where there
was no rent to pay, we rejoiced. Ah, and so did the fleas. No matter;
they were our own, and we sympathized with them; they, too, paid
no rent.

Jim was ordered out of his bed, in a lordly fashion, early next
morning, to make tea for us and bring it in. We drank it out of
little bowls. While we sipped, Jim swept out the hut, the signet
ring glinting on his little finger, and the good nature on his honest
face a very mask of reassurance. "Hurry up, James," Blue said, "and
sweep up under that table there."

"Orright, Blue." Jim shifted the moist dirt a little nearer the door.

He and Blue, towards evening, held a caterwauling dialogue
about going up to 'Ardy's for the skimmed milk.

"Go-r-r-rn!" Blue growled in a low rich voice, advancing towards him with a growl, like a tom-cat meeting another on the roof.

"Wo-o-o-on't!" snarled Jim obstinately.

"Gor-r-r-r-n!" A questioning treble crept into the voice.

"Wo-o-o-o-n't!"

"Go-o-oo-orn!" a high fiendish scream, the last warning given before the tom-cat jumped, and made the fur fly.

"Awr-r-r-ight!" with a low abandoned purr, meek and soft, and putting out the hand with the ring shining fiercely on it, Jim took the syrup tin and, buttoning the windy evening out from his sparse brown coat, he pushed his brown hat farther down on his curls, gave a hurried look from under it and went up for the milk.

And 'Ardy's tame magpie snapped at his ankles all the way up the track.

Long, thin and black against the crimson sunset, Riy brought the cows in with his lonely musical cry, "Ooo-oo-wuh!"

It was October and the beans would not be ready until late November. Mr Whitebeard gave Jim a job in his shearing shed and all through the long fiery days while we were going through his suitcase for the hundreth time, turning over the silk shirt, the cotton socks, the tram-ticket and the Testament and wondering greatly thereat, Jim was shearing heavy sheep.

On the first night following his hard day's work, he retired into his tent early. And we, as usual, went early to our bark beds. But a strange light shone in the night, and, rising up, Blue saw Jim's shadow outlined sharp and black and huge on the roof of his tent. It bulged and circled there, struggling with something; it bent backward and performed contortions unknown to pea-pickers. Then a giant hand emerged from a shadowy shirt and placed a small object carefully right in the middle of the light.

"What's wrong, Jim?" cried Blue, standing in her pyjamas at the door of the bark hut.

"Nothin', Blue," answered Jim in a low unctuous voice, humble and fervent. And, blowing out the candle, he got into bed.

When we went out into the hot yellow morning to go through his portmanteau again, we saw around the top of the candle, which stood humbly in the dust, a long circle of ticks, standing dead but dutiful around the wick.

Jim immediately became known between us, as Hegbert the Tick, or Heggie for short.

Far from entertainment of any sort, our sole social interest at night, after that, was to wait until Heggie felt the afflatus and arose to light his candle and perform. What a writhing of legs, arms and hands! The roof of the tent was turned into a jungle full of snakes, and when he arose and examined himself seriously, carefully and with consideration, his silhouette was a thing to run miles from. There was something fearful in its grotesquerie.

Half mad with laughter and fear, we stood watching his arms go up in shadow on the canvas; or a leg being raised, seemingly, to an acute angle above his head; or his head, apparently, lying under his knees with his arms locked through all and waving about, until, after a few moment's intense feeling on all sides, a sharp finger and thumb would unerringly steer a tick to the radius of the light and deposit it therein . . . returning with a sense of freedom and renewed interest to another search. And often, in his haste and anguish, just at a sublime moment when his body was coiled about his head and his hand covered the active spot with a view to encircling the parasite . . . ah, at that very moment, with one wild awkward sweep, Heggie would inadvertently put the candle out, and where a boundless and amazing activity of a lunatic sort had existed before, all now was an unanswering black.

At that, we would rush back to bed and get under the blankets to bellow with joy. While Heggie swore, then sighed, and got creakily into bed.

A natural morbidity appeared in his nature from then onward, and he began to trap rabbits as an outlet. He felt that he had to catch something, and catch it well. But even there he was frustrated, because Blue, unable to bear their tortured screams, arose from her sleep and went out, lantern in hand, to liberate them.

Then again, Blue ostracized him harshly at all times, retaliating cruelly because he had dared to say that she loved him. It was, "Jim, do this; Jim, do that. Jim, sweep this dirty room out; lift me over the fence; clean my shoes; make my tea; take that dirty shirt off and wash it"—until it was not surprising to find Jim being led home drunk, by Macca, one hot evening.

They came along by the frail and beautiful fence against the skyline, and Macca comforted Jim and murmured masculine sooth-sayings to him.

"He went and got drunk, Blue, because you're cruel to him, he says," Macca explained delicately.

"And I bet it didn't cost him a penny," said Blue.

"Karta Singh shouted for me," sobbed James and made motions

as though looking in his portmanteau, declaring that therein among other luxurious appurtenances, a razor was packed, with which he wished to cut his throat.

"Try the tram-ticket, or the old socks. They'd be quicker and more merciful," Blue advised unkindly.

But she did relent a little after that and I heard her, that very night, pointing out to him the real way of life and his duties towards God and man, while assuring him that, so far as he was concerned, she felt quite incapable of any matrimonial feeling.

Jim accepted this fact from that night onward and became an exemplary mate in every respect.

A grey showery morning blew Mr Greenfeast to the door of the bark hut, inviting us to come over and pick his early beans. This was tantamount to telling us that we were considered good enough to pick for the rest of the season. Gladly did we go. On the second day he said to us in the loud voice of the deaf, "Care to come up to tea on Sunday night?"

His full crooked stammering lips formed the words nervously as he sat "sewing up". It was easy to see that they were nervous, reserved people who did not invite friendship.

Timidly, thinking of Jim' capacity, we said, "Yes."

Inwardly, my discontent was increased, for we were now being asked out to tea; that was a sign that people were being interested in us, as problems which they would attempt to solve. They designed to try us for what we were, and secretly, we knew, they would attempt to break down our way of living and thinking. They were disquieted by two girls living in a bark hut, dressing as men and conducting a masculine friendship with a mate picked up casually in their travels.

Forgetting all in the promise of a fine meal, we turned up to Greenfeast's, threatening Jim on the way and begging him to control his hands and his appetite.

Once again, we sat before a good meal; but this time the table-cloth was a linen of careful purchase and the shining designs on the dull starched background were as brilliant and dry as the everlastings that used to grow around our selection at Slap-up in New South Wales.

I thought of that tall secret Mongolian drover who had come to the house at twilight and talked with my father. Looking up from the lid of a biscuit tin which I had been twisting in the blackness of a child's oblivion, I had been revived and brought into life by the sight of that lean sharp face with the frail moustaches and the sun-closed eyes; that downward stare of the bush creature, the immortal riddle of the dust, the long road, the drought and the drover.

We ate. The cucumbers were deckled, slice by slice. Mrs Greenfeast, young, tall, thin and blonde, had a faintly skeleton face, often seen in some Irish types. She laughed with the shaky laugh of a woman who has just stopped crying, and behind her glasses her innocent, childish eyes shone wet and wide. Their two little boys, pale, intelligent and freckled, cocked their grizzled heads on one side and regarded us gravely and politely.

We ate slowly and told them of our adventures, such as they were, and they laughed gratefully, all of them; for the bush is a lonely place.

On the mantelshelf stood high boots and chains, carved from wood.

"I picked up those bits of wood from the beach after a storm," said Mr Greenfeast. "Yes, ah, yes, I made those."

He laughed as we admired them, the loud, clear, refreshing laugh of a man who is seldom amused. Everything that was to be appreciated in the little house came before our eyes and rejoiced us. It was marvellous to see how he had carved the chain, link by link, with no sign of beginning or end.

"It was quite easy, really easy." His clear brown face was in shadow as he sat at the top of the table with the sewing machine behind him. Blue and I had our heads together at the mantelshelf, grasping the carvings and talking softly about them.

The house was fit to be one room, really, but it had been divided into four. The last and lowliest was the wash-house, a dusty place with bags around it and tubs on a bench. All the water had to be carried from the tank around the corner.

The entire property was parched, grey and sad. Every inch of the soil held an ingredient of sorrow, infinitesimally small, mingled with the constituents and insects. It breathed out grief and loneliness and a tragedy that must dominate these two mates, however hard they worked, no matter how often they smiled and sang.

In their loneliness we felt our visit to be a burning, to which our absence would contribute only a longer-lasting material. They would heap us on to that little fire for days afterwards; and when the glow showed the least sign of subsiding we could be invited again and made to burn with a different flame, so that despair might be kept at a distance. They had no daughter, for Mrs Greenfeast was not long back from a still-birth confinement and she was pitiably easy to awaken to tears.

Talking our way out, we left them, and as we went back to the bark hut we tried to explain to each other what it was that had saddened us there.

The day the bark hut was almost burnt down brought forth from Peppino a Laocoön-like fragment of literature which has remained with us for years, still arousing curiosity.

Jim had lit the fire on a windy morning and gone up to get the milk from 'Ardy's. While he was away, I lay dreaming in my bark bed of that blue and white sea which I could hear roaring loudly over the sand dunes, miles away. Suddenly, it seemed very near; it was in the kitchen, by jove. Good heavens, it was in the very bedroom.

The bark hut was on fire.

"Blue! Wake up; the hut's on fire. Jim! Heggie! She's on fire!"

In rushed our butler, flinging himself out again with the flames on his tail, singeing his handsome apparel. Then, with a kerosene-tin full of water, he galloped up on to the roof and flung the water wildly over the flames, and Blue and me, who were just rushing out.

"That's fixed it, Blue," he bellowed, as the water smashed into our faces and half choked us.

"Come down, Jim, you fool!" Blue was yelling, when through the rotten roof James descended as swiftly as in a city elevator, and was among us.

"You do what you're told sometimes, anyhow!" grumbled Blue, as we sorted ourselves out.

Watery, smoky, dingy and blackened, we waited around while James built up the fire he had put out, and made us a cup of tea in the ruins of the bark kitchen.

Blue wrote and told Peppino about it all since he had professed his tenderness for her. And he answered her. The opening has all the marks of a solitary struggle with the unknown.

Dear Blue, I send to you this letter because I sende to you letter I give one may friend I tell you go Boisdale im tell me yes post this letter im purne in fire im geve my sorry.

As one in a delirium he struggled with the language, and in despair hailed, as we imagined, a careless Gippsland passer-by who stepped in and took charge, so that things looked up culturally for a few minutes.

Dear Blue, sorry your hut got caught on fire you were lucky you didn't get burnt. I can't tell you for sure that I will be up there to pick beans because I haven't finished down here yet, after I finish I will come.

The visitor, presumably wearied, left and dropped our poor friend back into the soup again.

Dear Blue want come soon for to see you because I like you very much no write too much because too much work today and going to bede my eye too much sleep I can writ no more dear little flower I must conclude Peppino remember me to Jim and Macca and your sister Steve. *Buona sera:* good naight. You have look in letter, you find something.

Blue looked and found a small tin bird on a piece of green ribbon, flown from the aviary he had carried on his robust, singer's chest the morning he left Metung.

Often we talked of Peppino, and in memory of him sang his songs "O Sole Mio" and the dramatic "Gigolette".

Sebastian Paolo, who had gone away to pick early beans at a little seaport called by the Italians Portalinkon, sent Blue a sepia post-card of a weatherboard pub standing alone in a small empty street of unphraseable dreariness. Not daring to soil the masterpiece, he wrote on a separate piece of paper in his stately Italian hand, with many a twirl and linked curve.

My dear Blue,
  I thank you Very much for The Tour Card. I send you one P. card of Grant Hotel in Portalinkon Main Street.

I remain Tours old friend
SEBASTIAN.

Here, indeed, was one who had seen Naples, and truly died. Art could stir him no more; its miraculous draughts were drained, and feebly he added to the list of great technical achievements the Grand Hotel in Portalinkon Main Street.

Sitting outside the bark hut in the sweltering night which was blue with bush-fire smoke, we waited while the small light coming up the hill glowed large into the figure of Karta Singh, his lantern, his staff and his turban.

"You fella Jim, you fella Steve and Blue, you ready for come pick bean tomorrow morning?" he shrieked in his high wild voice, breathing out hot glazed fumes of methylated spirits.

"Orright, Karta! Where you picking?"

"Might be pick crop down near road, you remember where you come in paddock first day I see you fella? Might be there. You come, you fella." Turning to us: "How you fella Steve an' Blue? You got nice boy yet, you fella?"

A harsh fashion in which to speak to an idealistic poet and a fantastic artist; but there it was. We said as delicately as possible, that we wanted work, not boys.

"Why you fella not get married? Then you not want for work!"

The very land and its tillers rejected us, we thought. The earth that we loved would have none of us.

"Well, good night, you fella; you come pick for sure tomorrow." Karta tottered away down the hill, his lantern glowing red through the blue bush-fire smoke.

Starting out early, with bags shoved under our belts and rusty kerosene-tins in our hands, we began to pick the poverty-stricken beans of Karta Singh. The earth was grey and marked with the tracks of the tiny creatures of the night and by faint rain-smelling dew.

When the sun rose the sandy soil grew red and then gold, but as the hours passed it became just hot grey earth. In the afternoon it burnt white-hot and fierce under our bare feet and blazed angrily in our eyes as we crawled miserably and tiredly from plant to plant, snatching off the few long green beans from under the wide leaves and languidly throwing them, with their rasping skin to which strands of thistledown clung, into the tin.

It became a delirium at last. The country spun within me and became a particle which clung to an incident like a brother atom, and through that atom lived on.

As we worked under a gaunt dry red tree, Tomcatto, 'Ardy's operatic star, came stealthily up through the heat, and a man of means looked he, in his green velvet hunting suit, cocked hat, black leggings and dainty boots.

Sweating in torture, we looked up at him and his friend, a small handsome fellow with a petulant conceited look, who brushed away the myriad flies with a languid gesture, as though tipping them to keep off. We stood up to rest our broken backs for a moment, and kept our faces calm and well bred although agony was twisting our burning spinal columns.

Tomcatto and his mate were not, of course, staying for the bean-picking, but departing to pick grapes at Rutherglen or Swanhill, so they idled away the hours until their departure.

I

Tomcatto leant absorbedly over the flushed beauty of Blue's face, while the petulant one, Puglisi, looked wearily at a small red book of French fables that I took out of my pocket in an effort to interest him.

"Ah! *Fables de la Fontaine.* I read dis. Where you get?"

La Marquise, a wandering woman picker farther down the paddock, had given it to me.

Puglisi stood aside and watched Tomcatto stepping daintily back and forth from the plants to Blue's tin, and mewing faintly as he picked for her.

"Give me wan kees. Just wan kees, pliss!"

"You keep on picking beans," said Blue laughing wearily and despairingly.

The soil under our feet looked rough and dry, and we sweated while Tomcatto in his spotless hunting suit leapt lightly on the beans and, plucking them one at a time, tossed them into Blue's tin. "Wan kees; just wan." Airily he sang an old Italian song.

> "Son tornate a fiorere le rose
> Nella dolce carezze del sol';
> La farfalle s'inseguon festose
> Nell' azzuro col trepido vol!"

Mewing and scratching, now at her hand, her cheek, the beans, and his hat, he worked a little while longer.

"Blue, Mees Blue, you come our plice tomorrow naight for say goodbai? We go too soon. You come; we have too much tea and cake and sing little bit. You come, and bring your sister and Jim. I sing for you, too much!"

Blue and Jim shuddered, but accepted the invitation, since it would save them the trouble of cooking tea when they were tired out after the long day's work.

But I didn't want to go, because I had already heard the cater-wauling of Tomcatto in the house of another, and trembled to think how long and never-ending it might be if one were left alone in a hut in the bush with him. Opera is many and long, and Tomcatto was more than willing; he was desperately eager.

Back and forth he prowled, lashing his coat-tails behind him, until he had helped to fill the tin, and then, with a last cry of "Wan kees, pliss, Mees Blue!" he mewed a forlorn farewell, waved a claw, raised his tail and leapt the fence.

The small birds fled into the trees, as up through the bush he strolled, sniffing and stalking everything that crossed his path.

Jim and Blue had met the Marquises one afternoon when they were walking over the paddocks to see if their rabbit-traps had got a catch. They halted and talked in the lonely paddocks where the twilight winds blew forlornly over the grasses as though saying, "All is futile; generations come and go; still, I blow over the grasses!"

The Marquis was a little sandy man and La Marquise was a tall fat woman with a coarse face and dark greasy hair. They said that they had come from "somewhere down the line" in a van drawn by a tired horse.

The Marquis complained of not being able to get a haircut, so Blue, who could do practically anything, offered to cut it, and went with them over to their caravan behind the fence of Karta Singh.

The Marquis sat on a box and Blue cut his hair. She trimmed it carefully but with a feeling of repulsion, for his face was the purple-red face of a sandy man, and his ears filled her with an inexpressible sickness. She avoided them as well as she could, but in her over-anxiety cut a slice off one, and the Marquis leapt into the air, biting out an oath.

La Marquise had a dress that was too long for her. She had no idea how to turn it up and hem it, so Blue offered to do that, too, and, bringing it over to the bark hut, made a neat job of it.

When she took it back next day, La Marquise confided in her that the Marquis was not her husband. Once she had been the wife of a steady man, with a home of her own. They had one little girl whom they loved; but their child died, and the husband turned to other women.

So, in her unhappiness, she went away with the Marquis, and they travelled through Gippsland together in the old van, sleeping at night on a rough bag mattress that was inside. And whenever they got their money at the end of the week they went down to the hotel and stayed there drinking until it closed, and then they came home and fought like cat and dog all night.

Every Monday morning La Marquise came to work with an inflamed black eye, and the Marquis was sullen all day.

The evil years and the unhappy experiences had made La Marquise hard and reckless and foul-mouthed. Her heart was bitter towards all men. I trod warily when I worked with her, sensing terrible wrath that would spring and devour, if aroused. The sorrow of her life gave her an immortal quality. Poor crushed being, the pained home of a little dead bush child.

Sometimes I could almost see the delicate little girl moving around her in the glaring sun in that dry paddock, helping her as she worked and comforting her with childhood's funny innocent language, and admiring her, and seeing in her huge bulk, which others despised, only a great softness to which it could run and rest.

At such times, as I worked in the merciless sunlight, my heart was dull with sorrow for La Marquise.

She gave me the little red book of French fables which she had picked up, and was conversational enough, but apt to let fly some hideous bit of obscenity that made me shrink away from her.

I recall her as a shadow, black and irregular, that for a moment took the sun off me as we passed, squatting on our haunches. She was a point of life, united, with me, to the sun; and the majesty of her huge bulk, the funereal cut of her black clothes soiled with white dust, drew me towards her.

At noon I went to the bark hut, far across the paddocks, to have lunch. When I made ready to go back to work, I had to put on a blue veil over my hat, for the heat was blinding. The veil swam before me in watery blurred folds, and my face, when I left the hut, looked lion-like in its flushed imperial beauty of heat and toil and virginity. The golden purity of the tender flesh in such heat, the clean blood running unwaveringly through the veins in such a furnace of a land, made me sorrow, for I thought as I stared into my mirror, "Why cannot the one I love see me now? Why cannot that one whom I shall some day discover to be as truly of my body, heart and soul as I am myself see me now? It is all wasted, wasted."

Had I remembered God, I would not have thought in such a fashion.

I walked barefoot over the yellow grass hill to Karta Singh's and the little black pills of rabbit-dung rolled beneath my feet in hundreds, for the land was eaten up by rabbits. The dung was hard and shining, and the mind, through the touch of the foot, was repelled by them.

The sun streamed over me in waves; the dry grass blazed with heat through every dead fibre.

As I worked beside La Marquise, she looked at me with a hard deep look that told me unwillingly, "You are beautiful today. In time, you will grow hideous, but the day has seized you and made you beautiful at this moment."

"How old are you, Steve?"

"I am twenty."

"What? Why . . . I am only twenty-five!"

I smiled, but felt shocked. "Only twenty-five are you? Yes, you are only young," I said.

"But what has aged you?" I thought. "You appear forty or fifty to me. Will life do this to me, also, at twenty-five?"

"Yes, you are not much older than I am. It is good to be young."

The Marquis walked swiftly past us with a full tin. "Hurry up!" he growled; his shadow struck the white ground with a thick blackness, and his breath came with a quick frightening intimacy as though he was dying. "Hurry up! Don't be magging there all day!"

And I, I hurried, too, guiltily, as though I were his second concubine. That was horrible!

For comfort, I said to myself, "Surely, since I am beautiful today, Macca will come and sit with me tonight, and we shall stare in a trance of innocence at each other's faces, by toil and thought made lovely. Yes, he will come. I shall come back after tea and work until starlight, alone, for Blue and Jim are going to say *addio* to Tomcatto. From this hillside I shall be able to see Macca as he goes back to the farm." He was now working down on the Tambo River.

Therefore, all the afternoon, I fled before the sun, picking the beans from the dry plants that sent out roots desperately in every direction for water. But there was none.

I kept my loveliness in face and heart until evening, and went home to eat my wheaten tea with Blue and Jim. When they had gone to feast with Tomcatto and Puglisi, I washed my face and set out across the hill again to Karta Singh's.

The grassy hill was changed now: the wind of evening was making it shiver, but yet, what loveliness was abroad that night!

I trod the hill of yellow grass; the land was veiled in the blue smoke of the still-burning bush-fire that was wallowing in red seas from some desolate shore to the end of its journey. Above the dry grass the blue smoke wandered, and in the mystical twilight I cried, "O Patria Mia! Patria Mia!" and my naked brown feet kissed the dear earth of my Australia and my soul was pure with love of her. "Patria Mia! Patria Mia!" the grave face of Italia on the old school book we found in the bark hut chanted in my soul. Divine was my love then, and with an uplifted heart I strode into the empty paddock, and alone there, crouched in the twilight on the earth I loved, began to work.

"O, it is painful," I thought, "to be a woman; to long for love and fame, for the immortality of all things; for love and the unborn and the dust of all countries, to be caught and held. Forever. Not a being lost, not a grain of dust lost or a gesture of love wasted. At last, perhaps, when all men have been born, it may be found that there is no more earth that is inarticulate. It will have been transmuted into men, and it shall, with a living and immortal soul, move and love, even as man."

I knelt, tired in the twilight, working alone in the vast paddock; the sky, heated, vermilion with the day's wrath, became at last a warm blue and wept stars. I worked on; staring up the road for the sight of that one small human figure that would give me joy; but no one came.

So I arose and went home, in sorrow and loneliness. "It was wasted," I said. "That which La Marquise admitted to me was wasted; tonight I have been young and lovely in flesh and mind, and no one came. O ye gods that set me there, I cry to you in anguish tonight. Was it not good to you, the humility of my toil and expectation; the poetry of my abased body dragging tiredly from plant to plant, while I waited for my love to come? He did not see me; no matter. I thought that a multitude watched me while I knelt. The years hold me back from them; I shall never know them. But these, at last, shall find me and mourn with me, for I shall spread this twilight into their hearts, and make it beat there, shade by shade and star by star and hour by hour. You, O brown road," I cried, turning to it, as I stood on the hill, "wild and lonely, downrushing and empty, shall be with them then. And you, vast paddock of dry soil and thirsting plants, shall be as a dream to that one who will come to you, mourning, saying: 'Even here, even here, she who is gone from the dream of life stayed late and lonely, thinking on immortality; and love did not come to her!'"

Blue and Jim got back early to the bark hut. "Well, what sort of feast did you have?" I asked them. "What happened?" Standing beside my bed, in the hot sickly night, they told me of how they said farewell to Tomcatto and Puglisi, and of how they ate of the delicious meats put before them by the weeping, departing pea-pickers.

Tomcatto's hut stood in decay on top of a high cliff, and below it was a criss-cross of fences, paths, bushes and fallen logs. Like most Gippsland huts it seemed inaccessible at first glance, and the two guests looked around for a topographical tin-opener with which to get into it. The darkness increased and the night wind blew drearily through wire fences and thin bushes as they climbed the cliff and skirted chasms that poured down to the lake. At last the hut was seen to be close at hand; the front door appeared, but since it was almost ten feet from the ground, a knock would take a long arm. They clambered over broken posts and trailing vines until they reached the back door, and with thoughts of a hospitable brightness within, of long swaying tables spread with the feast in mind, they knocked at the dark door . . . for a long time.

At last, Tomcatto appeared, *en déshabille* and bewildered, inquiring dazedly why they had come.

"To say good-bye to you. Don't you remember, you asked us this afternoon to come to feast with you?"

"Dis afternoon? Oh yis; but I no think that you come."

He ushered them into a large deserted room; some sheets of newspaper lay on the floor around a candle stuck between two nails. From the chamber beyond where a bag bunk hung between poles, the handsome Puglisi advanced, bowing.

Tomcatto hurried past him, mewing anxiously, and after rattling around in the dark, brought out a bag of small broken biscuits with hundreds and thousands scattered over them, and two bottles of ginger ale to carry the multitude down.

The guests sat on the newspaper around the candle and ate mightily. Tomcatto passed around the viands and afterwards amused the company with selections from grand opera, executed with verve and fervour in the bare room where the newspapers rattled in the draught. After which he took out a sheet of transparent paper and, in honour of the company, described on it with a compass many circles, a few acute angles and, in the midst, the Australian coat of arms, carried by an emu like a mosquito and a kangaroo like a decrepit rat.

"Viva l'Owstralia!" cried he.

A tune was then chanted on the mouth-organ, and into the dance the handsome Puglisi swung the beautiful Blue. Over the stifled gasp of the newspapers they trod in the lounging one-step of the time, and while they danced Puglisi said morosely of his own beauty: "Rudolph Valentino . . . he not dead while I alive."

We said that for a long time afterwards, to each other, on days when we looked particularly ugly after a long dirty day in the crop.

The old hut shook to the rough music and the proud step of the handsome Italian, while Jim's hand went stealthily into the bag for the rest of the biscuits and gently outward to the bottle for the last drip of ginger ale.

When the dance ended, Tomcatto stepped forward with a caterwaul of triumph and mewed wildly. "I no true pea-picker. You see, I great artisto, too! Any time what I like I paint the picture," and he waved the Australian coat-of-arms around until the mosquito-emu and the rat-kangaroo should have bitten him. "I sink like-a-da Carus' too; if I like, I start now and sink all night, through da grand opera. All dis Owstralian bush . . . I spit on it; dis no like Michel-angelo: dis no like Raphael. Dese people in dis bush no hear of the Michelangelo and de Raphael. O, O, Italia!" And with a few high, shrill miaows he subsided.

Blue and Jim wished them both a pleasant journey, and then went off home.

V

IN the primitive slowness of the hour before dawn, everything inanimate is articulate in the bush, and whispers as distinctly as mankind. The walls move, garments hanging on them writhe and murmur and grin in folds and rumples. Man was shaped to come forth at this hour; he gave to all things the texture of his being in an effort to try them and taste them.

I arose and, mad with unhappiness because I had worked and waited so long for that human soul whom I had marked for mine to comfort me, I went out into the wide dry yellow world; and as I did, the flames of morning, bearing their own individual mark in the place of the solar system, rose in the sky, fled into it, thrust before him by the sun. The time that was roared overwhelmingly about me, fixed me in its socket, and I to it clung and was carried forward.

"I am unloved," I cried, and ran screaming out of sight of the bark hut, down the soft dry grass; leaping naked, crying, sobbing, cursing and dancing in the terror of the lonely red morning.

The male sun moved above me and outward with a giddy spinning, a palpitating that was endless, that beat like my own heart, but forever. The heavens grew redder, with the primitive gleam of fire in a shell under whose colours the pigmy cell life thrives and loves. Ah, shell of heaven made by the thought of the Enormous Cell, how long must you outlast me? I, tethered like the bivalve by the throbbing knot of life to this one circle of vision; corded to you, O heaven, and to you, O base of the heavens, flesh of my flesh, the earth!

I leapt, I ran, I cried insanely, but love did not come.

"O God," I said, "if only at this hour, I could release myself in poetry! Flow forth, words, and chant me into the trance of oblivion."

But nothing came, and tired, wan and dispirited, I returned to the bark hut. There, Blue lay sleeping; I crept into bed and slept too.

The day was so hideous with heat that La Marquise's social call on us was perfectly timed, and her costume, another black one, had the uniquely awkward appearance of a pall on a coffin.

Her visiting card was her first remark, "Ole Karta Singh asked me for some addresses of women in Melbourne, but I wouldn't give him any. I know a few but I wouldn't insult them by sending him along. All these old Indians are the same, you know."

We said, gravely, that we didn't doubt her at all.

"Youse gotter pretty hot little place here, haven't youse?" She sat on the edge of the bark bed and stared at the bark wall which was splitting, bending, bowing and twisting awry, every sheet of it making manifest its own radical infirmity under the harshness of the weather.

We had no refreshments to offer her, except a pie-dish full of a bluish block of junket made from 'Ardy's skimmed milk; and while we hesitated a blowfly skated across it, did a figure eight and was lost, sitting down with extreme firmness on its concertina pants.

"He told me he wasn't satisfied with me picking, the other day. Him and his old beans. I told him where to put them." She rose to go, confident and dark, wiping her sweating face with her handkerchief, and, bending low, waddled outside. We followed her out, awkwardly, to the door and stood dragging it to and fro.

Shading our faces with our hands, we peered into the mixture of glare and smoke that was our view, and, reckoning that there was a big bush-fire somewhere, we gradually forced her to weaken her social hold on us and draw away.

'Ardy's now requisitioned us. We began to work in their also poor beans. Forlornly, we set out early, walking tall and dark, with the cathedral drape of the figure in smocks and trousers. The weather was so hot that my nose bled continuously and I was forced to work with a handkerchief tied under my nose and over the top of my hat, like a Mussulman's moustache. Just when all was perfectly in place and my face looked a fool of a thing, my figure bulky and awkward in tight khaki pants and shirt, Macca rode past the paddock going down to make hay for his uncle on the Tambo, which ran a gleaming blue thread in summer and a dragged brown one in winter through the maize country to the lake. At the sight of the white handkerchief moustache under my nose and knotted on top of the hat (and a smart Homburg hat at that, with a fine shot blue silk lining) he turned athwart politeness and laughed and rode by.

When we had finished work for the day, Jim said as we shut the weatherboard gate behind us, "What about going for a swim Blue?"

"You run home and get towels," replied Blue.

We paced slowly onward meditating, while our butler ran back a mile to bring the towels. Twilight had brought the ghosts of roses into the waters of the lake and they flowered on everything; the very beach was flame-coloured, the water was red wine around which the trees blackened and softened more as the minutes passed into night.

"Now, James, you go in farther down the beach, and we'll go in here."

On to the dry stones our clothes dropped and lay there like old men, brown and withered, but we, rounded by toil and health, stood splendid in the twilight waters, and I, gazing at Blue, felt the anguish of life's brief poetry and the short gasp that is language, no matter how sublime, when beauty is seen.

We lay in the water which curled about us its liquid roses, and behind us, over fields of blue and rose, the sky retreated with a blue step, pure, without the strain of the worldly and faintly mocking stars.

"You look beautiful, Blue . . . and I?"

"You look nice, too," and she laughed and hit the water. Her teeth with the faint light on their strong white edges were just that shade under real brilliancy which is so sad, so bewildering and so lovely. A heart of rightness, in the mind, is struck by it, pleased by it and longs for the impact again and again. About her cream throat the rosy waters frothed and the spray she struck from it rose into the air in a smother of small pearls.

Such loveliness, it appeared to me, should be earning for itself the truest courtesies, the most happy wisdom; but was wasting, day by day, in the bean fields among rustic lovers, with chance companions, little food, poor clothes and miserable wages.

Far down the shore, Jim beat the water with his huge feet and bellowed and spluttered; we laughed and got out before the light faded and went home, smelling of the salt water.

Macca was haymaking for his uncle, Adam, down at the mouth of the Tambo, and had bought a mare called Kitty to take him back and forward to his job. In the evening, with tantalizing rareness, he called back to see us at the bark hut and lounged talking with his lazy Gippsland smile in front of the wire-netting window. The setting sun shone full on his face from among the black trees. Looking at his face, in its glow, I grieved, knowing that the years were passing and bringing bitterness.

"I've been looking for a bunch of roses, red roses, for your room, Stevie," he said to me. "You would like red roses, and they will come from an old house. I have got a job up at Kingscote, working for two elderly ladies . . . doing up their garden—the garden that I brought the golden roses from. Kingscote is so old. I shall love working there."

One night, sleepless through the heat, I heard the little hard hooves of his mare come scuttling across the dry hill, and he dismounted and stood by the bark wall, near the head of my bed. I tried to force the bark apart so that I might see his face. I had a feeling that it looked like a bunch of cool white roses, and in that close night I longed for the fresh flowers. But the bark was tough and wouldn't part. At the beginning I felt sure that I could have forced it apart, so strong was my desire to see his face. No, it wouldn't part, and I felt ridiculous, for he laughed triumphantly at my deathly struggle to break open the wall. And when he laughed I knew that I was unloved.

Often, in the bush, the longing to be with him would fill me to the exclusion of all other things, and I went out of the paddock, before the wondering eyes of Blue and Jim, to the bark hut, and got dressed and set off to find him—perhaps to call in at the Black Serpent's and sit there talking to her, and waiting for him to drop in, for he was a frequent visitor at her place now.

I talked in a tortured way, letting her know obliquely that I cared for him. Even to find him was useless. With a moody humour he stood in the road and fended me off, in a kindly fashion.

"You don't know what you want, Steve. What is it all for, anyhow? Well, Steven, what are you after today? How is Jim? And Blue?" With an amused stare at me, he stood, knowing his own power and my stupid bewilderment.

"Macca, last night I tore a bough from a tree of flowers and heard the tree screaming."

"That's a lovely thought, Talaaren. Well, you can come shooting with me, if you like, around the foreshore."

"Thank you, Macca. Will you go and buy a packet of those biscuits we like? Here's eightpence. I'll walk around to the shore and wait."

I leant against a sandy bank while he was away. My impatient blood and my poor bewildered mind fought for the meaning of these years. There was no directness in them. No one spoke the truth to me about anything; no one save the Buccaneers, and their truth was that sex and marriage were the only real things. No, I wanted poetry, and love of the earth, I wanted morning, noon and night spent purely with the one I loved. But don't talk to me of sex, I said. I fear it. I only know that there is beauty. I do not know that there is God. I have not offended Him yet, so I do not know. The dark green trees bowed heavily to the dusty road below; centuries old were they, and centuries ahead lay their ruin. I encompassed it all in one sickening second. All this was apparent. It was gigantic. Did no one notice it?

"Macca, when I am with you, I am happy. Yes, I am happy. Do you believe that?" I put my arm around his waist as we walked awkwardly on the rough road. I was wearing trousers, too, like him, but with my usual touch of the ludicrous had added to the outfit a woman's blouse and a straw school hat of ridiculous droop.

A small dark girl, plump and faintly moustached, passed us with an amazed stare.

In the depths of the cool ferns along the track we found a place to rest, and there I sat with him and wrote in delicate printing on a dry white stone, "Don't ever leave me, Macca!" I put it away in a little dry place that I should remember, under a log.

"I shall come back in the years ahead and take this out and weep over it, for you will not be here."

"We'll come and find it together, Talaaren."

"No, you are intending to leave me. I shall be utterly alone . . . all my life. Yes, that's going to be my tragedy. What have I done to earn it? Why am I not loved? Or, if that is wrong, why am I made so that I desire to be loved? I wish to circle above things, unhurt and not hurting anyone. Tell me, now," I leant towards him, watching his jaws as they chewed bits of grass and flower stems, "what are the women like, whom men love?"

"They're different, Steve. They know more; they can hide themselves. In fact, they have a hold on themselves and you haven't."

"It's torturing for me to have hold of any one part of myself. I suppose they find themselves comfortable and soothing to know. But I'm afraid of myself. It is so lonely and melancholy."

"Well, you only want to impose that loneliness on me!"

I groaned. "Can it be only that? The earth tortures me. The colours of that hillside, all rusty with ferns, are agony to me. Don't you feel that an awful sadness is hanging over it all? Don't you imagine that it is living and suffering and breathing out despair, quivering with it? Everything is, and I know it. It's pressing me down and crushing me. I feel that you're not affected, so I am only asking to be very near you, within your safety. Don't you see?"

"Well, let us make some cocoa and eat these biscuits, Steve."

It was twilight now. The rough buffalo grass about the lake was breathing moistly and sweetly. The shapes of the trees were like those of fine soft people, courteous and kindly faced, murmuring each to each.

The sad afternoon had worn into the peace of evening.

And oh, the lake, how broad, broken and shining it was! Even in the coming night it was as blue as in the daytime, because far away beyond it, in the sky, was a red and yellow light, expansive and all-embracing, a watery picturesque light, a childish glow that delighted ineffably with fine plumes of feathery cloud leaping white in it, and stars as big as comets, blazing with fringes of light. Macca set a fire in front of a log and its red flames leapt up smoothly, advancing and retreating against the colours in the sky, while from the black log little insects ran in an agony of terror. Over it, he placed a long stick and hung the billy on that.

"An old man up in Orbost taught me that trick, Steve."

"Yes, and I am happy now, Macca. How is it? Well, anyway, the night is just black and hides all the colours of the earth from me; because they are sad dying hues. All I care for is light, but when it is divided into hues I am borne down by their heaviness. A star dances and that brightens me, you know. Or the moon reaches out and pulls as she travels and her strength makes me calm. The sun is all right, in a way. Here, in Australia, we've got to bear its thrashing and we feel that God will reward us for our patience. But the earth, with its colours of dust, is too melancholy; it is yearning towards me. Perhaps within it lie the constituents of generations to come, and, knowing it will be such a long time before they are liberated, they are mad with unhappiness. But to be with you, and drink with you and eat . . . like this . . . I am happy!"

We sat watching the flames performing around the log until the fire died down. Through the starry night we went home to the bark hut. At the door of the hut he turned to leave me.

"Wait, Macca! I'll come with you down to the last dead tree."

He leant on a long staff that he had picked up along the foreshore, and he looked back at me with his tender humorous smile, clear-drawn in the glowing Gippsland night. Away to our left, Mars burnt small and red and the dim Seven Sisters flickered overhead.

"Well, just a little way, Steve. I'm tired. I want to go to bed."

"And it's such a long way to the village. Gods, I'm so sorry to be selfish and send you out into the bush, away from me. Wait, we'll say good night here. Look, under this tree." I drew him over to a tall dead tree, charred and leafless. I struck its warm body loudly with my hand. Under my flesh, the dry silky wood slid from knot to knot.

"What hideous desolation! Ah, you understand, you must, what I meant today, Macca. This tree has no bark, and in the night it is unnaturally hot, like our bodies. But it is only the heat of the sun that warms it. This tree is like the moon."

"And the moon is like our love, Stevie Talaaren. See it? There it floats high and pure, above all human sorrow." He turned his face to it, and the moon, with her light, seized him, placing on his features an ethereal line or two which made a god of him. I ached at the sight of such transient beauty.

"Macca! Macca! We are young . . . we love. Soon—do you hear me?—we shall be old, and we shall have forgotten each other. O dreadful night, hideous tree and vile moon, you are mocking us. This country of ours, which we love, is withholding all things fruitful and rich from us. That's what I think. Look, the tree hasn't a leaf. Those stars whirling above it are its only flowers. And, every time she returns to these skies, that moon is making of you and me the same dreadful hardness and coldness that she has made of the tree." I grasped him by his shoulders, feeling the smooth straight skin slipping away from the silk of his shirt. "You must love me. I demand it. You are Gippsland; you are Patria Mia: and you must love me. If you don't, I feel that I shall be lost. Tell me to stay with you forever. Speak the words that I wrote on the white stone today. Say to me, 'Don't ever leave me, Steve!' "

Leaning against the tree and enjoying, in his power, the depth of my sorrow, he said, laughing, with a moment's pause: "Steve, I can't say that. You've got to learn to stand alone, and trust in life. You won't give yourself up to it."

I tore the long staff from his hand and thrashed him furiously with it; he leant still against the tree and smiled at me, painfully enduring, knowing that in the days to come I should suffer more than he. I felt the skin under the thin shirt leaping, bouncing to my blows. I thrust the staff back into his hand.

"Here, take it. O gods, what do you make me do? I shall be punished for this, and you know it. Your whole heart is savouring it, now. What do I want? If only my whole life, my future could come to me at this moment and unfold, year after year, eternity upon eternity. I am immortal and I suffer, suffer, suffer. What I am saying is nothing, you see? What you are saying is only flesh and air. Realize with me that we are being used, you and I. See with me that we are being directed by the unborn. It is cruel. They are searching for their own commonplace matrix. I don't care about the matrix. I am the soul. I'll come again to this tree, in the years ahead, and mourn beside it when you have gone from me and found your love. I'll cry madly to the stars, the false flowers of the tree. Futile, futile," I said in a deep moaning voice, and moved away from him up towards the bark hut.

"Forgive me, forgive me . . . or don't forgive me. It is all a trick of time. I am saying, now, words that will be meaningless in years to come. I am avowing a love that will be foolish in my old age. Who says it? Is it I who cry love? Is it you who deny me? It is not. What is it? Ah, I seem to be on the very verge of knowing, but something steps in between me and the light. Leave us alone, thing, time!" I cried, whirling my arms about in the air. "Now, I laugh at you. I named you and you are shrinking. Wait, Macca." I ran back to him. "Don't leave me tonight. Come back to the bark hut and lie on my bed, and sleep, sleep or talk. Come along. Blue is asleep. She won't care. As for me, well, all Metung calls me a harlot, perhaps, but I am only wild with the sorrow of life . . . with vague Wertherian sorrows."

"What are they, Steve?" asked Macca interestedly, turning and walking with me towards the hut.

"Wertherian? Well, Werther was young like myself. He loved time, saw time as something that could eventually be identified with the individual and bring joy instead of sadness. He looked about and found that he was a spirit who had been thrown aside by the vortex of time and was able to survey it with a free, clear eye. It is when one is in the maelstrom of time that he cannot see. But to be thrown aside by that gulf which draws the rest down, and to watch them being drawn . . . that's a chance. I watch you, and I cannot tell what will exactly happen to you; but I feel that I know your relationship to time."

"What is it? Tell me."

"Now you are going to be amused and think that I am a fool and a liar. For I can't tell you. But I feel that you are one of those in the maelstrom and I, who stand clear from it, in pity follow you to the edge. You beat me away; and I, fool that I am, instead of being happy, I am so enchanted by the speed of the current that I try to get into it, long after you have disappeared into its depths. I shall get in yet, and be happy and accursed, like the rest. My time is to come. Like Aeneas,

> "... *multum ille et terris iactatus et alto*
> *vi superum, saevae memorem Iunonis ob iram.*"

"Steve, bring out the *Aeneid* and let us read it again in the moonlight!"

"No, let us only speak the words we read together at Averdrink. Do you remember the moonlit water trembling in that broken old tank, Macca?

> "*Sicut aquae tremulum labris ubi lumen ahenis*
> *Sole repercussum, aut radiantis imagine Lunae,*
> *Omnia pervolitat late loca, iamque sub auras*
> *Erigitur, summique ferit laquearia tecti.*

What old nights are in those words! I made them into a song the other day. Yes, it goes like this . . . to the tune I put to 'Ante Aram'. I finish off Brooke's,

> "Or the soft moan of any grey-eyed lute player.

with

> "As when in brazen vats trembles moonlit water;
> The long lights strike the carven roof,
> Swift strong strokes, and the shorter
> Dimpling glow spreads out below,
> Returning to the water.

Sorry about the 'shorter', but I couldn't get anything else."

We tiptoed into the hut and lay decorously on the bed. Excited by the events of the night, I tossed beside him and could not sleep. I wished to talk of verse and cry out passages of the *Aeneid* all night. He began to breathe with a monotonous regularity, slowly and evenly, opposing my short passionate breath. His calm animal sound maddened me, at last. I could not bear it. I appeared to be breathing my life away, two to his one. Then he snored faintly. Enough! I struck him sharply.

"Go home! I cannot sleep. If you won't talk to me of the *Aeneid*, go home!"

Sitting up on the straw mattress, his figure black against the wire-netting window and the bilious clayey light of the moon, he said cruelly, "Steve, you're a little cow!"

"Then, O, to be in India where they worship them," said I. "There I could eat milk tins in the very streets, and wear a hat on my horns and who would dare to cry me nay?"

"I'm going home. It must be nearly daybreak." He went out angrily and I, left to my own quick wild breathing, fell asleep.

I awoke in the blazing, copper-coloured dawn and looked out on dry grass, grey earth and dead trees against a livid sky.

Last night, I thrashed Macca! I must go to him. O gods, what recompense can I make? Blue and Jim walked with me up to 'Ardy's to get the morning milk. All around us a mist of smoke held steadily. The grass rustled dry and sharp with seeds below our feet and burrs clung to our trousers. We walked through the smoky country with the red flame of the day burning along the hills.

"Goin' to be 'ot today," said Jim, giving the usual summer morning salutation of the Gippslander.

"Yairs, going to be hot all right, Heggie," we replied languidly. "If this drought keeps up, there won't be a second picking off the beans."

Gone was the roman moon and the brazen vats of moonlit water. The only water we saw that day was half a kerosene-tin begged from 'Ardy's on the hill. We kept it in the coolest corner of the bark hut on the earthen floor.

I lit a fire and put a brick in it.

"Steve!" exclaimed Blue angrily. "What do you want to light a fire for on a day like this?"

"To press my pants."

"Take them over to the bush-fire, then, and let us keep the hut cool. You're mad!"

I pressed the brick carefully over my trousers and shirt, put them on, and set out to find Macca. He was, as I expected, leaning over the scrubbed table helping the Black Serpent to hull strawberries.

"Stess!" cried the Serpent. She loathed my adopted name of "Steve", and had decided to call me a mixture of it and "Tess", from an unreadable novel she had lent me, called *Tess of the Storm*

Country. Disdaining to read it, I had not discovered what parallel lay between my character and that of the detestable Tess.

"Well, Steve!" said Macca lazily, eyeing my apparent passion and yearning amusedly.

I sat down heavily. "Pretty hot!" I said. I had no classics this morning; the heat made my tongue loll drunkenly.

We hulled strawberries in silence.

The Black Serpent smiled at Macca; she raised her eyebrows and poked her tongue out slightly as she smiled with a writhing of ripe mature lips over her teeth, which she didn't clean often. I rather liked the look of the clean mossiness on the strong crooked teeth.

I sat sullen and clumsy between them. Macca worked away with his short thick hands, the golden hair gleaming on the backs of them as he turned the berries over into the dish. He breathed that calm animal breath that had angered me in the night. His downward strained head made deep dark lines from his nostrils to his upper lip, which was dewy with heat. A few golden hairs gleamed in his nostrils and the top of his sandy head blazed in the dark kitchen.

His lips were full and moist and pursed in an outline that gave the impression of pretence at wisdom and worldliness. He looked false at those moments and I itched to dash his lips apart into a startled cry. Their protrusion and the dewy langour of the eyes came from within the brain where everything was complacent and self-satisfied; showing to me the conscious projection of a small self being achieved for view on the crown of the lips.

I was thin-lipped. I had no surface on which to deposit vanities. Mine were confined to my skull and they pressed about in a frenzied confusion that maddened me.

"I got a letter from Borrelerworreloil," I remarked, touching it in my pocket.

"Ah! Devoted as usual?" The Black Serpent raised her greying eyebrows.

"Oh . . . I don't know. Borrelerworreloil's a good chap, you know. I feel that I shall be punished some day for taking him so lightly. I ought to write and tell him that I am not what he thinks I am."

"But he may not think you are," said Macca lightly.

"He writes fine letters. He's an educated man. I should be honoured by them."

"You are so easily honoured, Steve, by any man," replied Macca with a cold bitterness. My heart leapt. Was his anger and contempt a sign of love?

After we had drunk coffee with the Black Serpent, I said, "Well, I think I'll go home now and answer the letter. Care to come down around the foreshore with me, Macca? I saw some rabbits there on my way in. Care to come?"

"Life is all care when I am with you, Steven," replied Macca; but while I trembled because he mightn't come, he picked up his rifle to follow me. I had a strange feeling of wrestling him from the hands of the Black Serpent, who, as I went, caught me to her and kissed me broadly on the mouth.

The iron latch of the gate clicked behind us; we got under the thick wires of the fence, passed under the dark trees and walked over the children's hopscotch squares, with their crude markings.

"Macca forgive me! Forgive me for that . . . last night! Today, I am not sane, either, but I am penitent. I can at least see as others see. Forgive me, forgive me, *marito, mio marito solo!*"

He whitened at the words of intimate Italian, and the sight of the blood draining from his face gave me a soaring sense of drunken happiness.

"Look, let us go to Reynolds' hut and sit there until evening, listening to the lake beating on the desolate shore."

"Yes, Steve," he said subduedly, "we will go. You and your *marito* will go and hear the waters beating against the earth."

Drunken with joy and love, I walked beside him, my strong limbs scarcely able to move, so stumblingly thick were they with the mystical glory of life and love, and that untouched and unhoped for portal of sex. My heart and mind swam ignorantly around in their circumscribed ecstasies, knowing that there was a gate through which all could pour, but not daring nor desiring to flow through it and lose the beauty of the earth.

I felt that the earth loved me for my virginity and would be with me while I kept it.

Around the curving white shore we walked together, silent, and came at last to the rubbish-strewn shore, where, against the coloured stones, the broken and bright jewels of the beach, oily cloud-reflecting water ran up and struck the land softly, lappingly, bearing long tear-shaped shadows on their unbroken waves.

Macca looked at it, and said, " 'A grim, grey coast and a seaboard ghastly.' That's from a poem called 'The Swimmer', by Adam

Lindsay Gordon, Steve. I must get it some day and we shall read it together."

Sitting among the nets and sails in Reynolds' hut, we stared out together on the water that was slowly rising as the tide came in. There was a dry rustle along the rafters above our heads. We looked up and saw a long black snake writhing above us. It was gone before we could strike it down.

"Steve, we shouldn't be in this hut. The mate of that snake may be lying here among the nets."

"And that would be very beautiful, indeed, Macca. Forget the snake. I am not afraid of them. Why, this morning, did we not hull strawberries for a Black Serpent, and drink coffee with it, afterwards? Tonight the moon will rise, *marito*.

> "This eve at Foo Tzoo shines the mellow moon;
> My love's wet eyes are watching it above.

Ah, the Chinese poets make rhymes as simply as their writing. Just a few gates, birds, fir-trees and bridges and they have written a letter."

"Tonight, Steve, when the moon rises, and with her the tide, the water will fall against the piles of the jetty with that sobbing note of the violin when Blue plays 'Alice Benbolt'; that surging, crying note when she double-stops the strings. Steve Hart, you know that I love you!"

His reluctant words were precious to me. How I valued that admission which I had forced from him! They pained me; they gave me no happiness, but I loved them. Through the long twilight we sat in the dry old shed, surrounded by the shells of the sunset, flashing in the sky.

"*Marito*," I said, "why should we not marry before we settle down together for the night? Why can't we marry here, with the heavens robed in priestly vestments of gold and red and blue, to perform the rites. Let them set the last molten ring of setting sunlight on my finger. The vast body of the sun burns green and red and palpitates against the horizon like the egg whence all life comes. Does it not appear fluid to you, that sun? Yes, it is molten fire. That shall be the ring for my finger; and the sky shall speak in the close small Anglo-Saxon of the stars, little cold words that hold much. Let the wind and the tide blowing through the pipes of the jetty be our organ song and the fences and nets shall be our lyres."

"Yes, we will marry, Stevie Talaaren. We will be married by the priests of the sun. You put your hand in mine." His thick clumsy fingers closed about mine, and he said, looking sad-eyed out into the wide lighted heavens:

"I take you, Steve Hart, to be *mia cara sposa*."

"And I take you, Macca, to be *mio caro marito*."

"My one love ever."

"My one love ever."

My heart ached sadly as we sat there, wordless, in the calm twilight. I longed for his touch, his kiss, but to myself, I said, "His love is too pure for that. I am coarse and vile."

It seemed then that the fishing hut put out sails from its roof, pointed its doorway into a sharp prow and floated out into the sea with us, flinging its nets far and wide, bringing up, from the deep, love and more happy, happy love, while the black serpent and its mate sang in the rigging and writhed joyfully. Evening burnt into night and we floated on in the fishing shed, talking and exclaiming with joy as the deep organ sound of the tide thudded against the jetty. When the moon came with many stars, we spread the sails out, found two soft pillows of nets for our heads and lay down together, innocent and undesirous, side by side to sleep, awakening often through the night to listen to the tide, double-stopped, against the timbers of the jetty.

Then . . . the red sun leapt into our eyes over the water's edge, biting keen through the folds of the sail we put up to shade ourselves with.

"Steve Hart, you look beautiful in the morning," said Macca, as we walked over the large coloured stones and washed our faces in the retreating tide. "I had a cousin once who looked lovely one night and I fell quite in love with her. It was at a dance, and I took her home. I said to her, 'In the early morning, I'll come and take you away over the paddocks for the day.'

"So I got up early, and I went and threw a flower at her window. She opened it and put her head out. But she looked so altered from the beautiful girl of the night before that I was frightened and went home. But you look just the same as you did yesterday."

"I am glad," I said rising with a wet face from the sea. "Give me your red handkerchief to dry my face on. I am hungry, too. What can we get to eat?"

"Let us go to Kingscote. There are some lemons up there and red roses, too, to look at while you eat, Steve Hart.

"But you should call me *mia cara sposa*," I exclaimed, hurt by his forgetfulness.

"Sometimes, but I like Steve Hart or Stevie Talaaren best."

We left the hut and retraced our steps back through the dewy bush, silent, calm and individual, borrowing from us, at every pace we took, some pre-arranged magic that made it immortal. Coming to a long dark lagoon with bright green weeds around it, Macca climbed up the bank and I followed him, dreamy with joy at the thought that his strong and pure young life was now part of mine.

I followed him over a fence, up a pine-needle covered hill with rotting cones lying broken everywhere, and over another sagging wire fence into an old orchard. The jays or robber birds flew away from the trees, silently, for it was not yet autumn and their passionate sorrowful cry was not ready. A peewit flew overhead, snowy white and burning black, crying, "Stevie . . . Stevie . . . Stevie . . ." and deeply in a gurgling voice, "Talaaren! Talaaren!"

My heart seemed to spread all over my breast and down into my loins with sad roots striking and imploring for soil in which they could rest and be nourished.

Macca stretched up and broke the fruit from the tree. Would the tree cry out as in my dreams? Should I tell him of my pain? If the tree cries!

"Here you are, Stevie." He handed me a large lemon. I ate it rapidly, looking at the dark red roses that nodded above the wet golden grass. When it was eaten, I belched, and Macca laughed.

"Just like a little baby, Steve!"

I hadn't thought of babies as belching; in fact, I never thought of babies, at all. I thought of nothing save love and beauty and sorrow. He filled a coarse sugar-bag full of fruit and, leaving the orchard, we walked back to the bark hut.

Blue and Jim had gone to work, leaving a note to say that 'Ardy wanted us to pick, and I could follow if I came home. Not able to bear the separation for the day, Macca walked over with me to their paddocks and, taking rusty tins from the fences, we picked together. I, too engrossed in the fascination of love and the splendour of the night to think of anyone, or consider what was being said about us. Far ahead of me, Macca crawled along a miserable row, and behind him I crawled, unhappy clown, palpitating with sorrow and passion. I felt angry and struggled to forget myself. But the desire to be with him was lunar in its strength. Finally, I skipped a whole row of beans, and got level with him, saying sullenly, "I had to come!"

And he said quietly, "I wanted you to!"

Released by his friendly sympathy, my evil nature fled, and a great joyousness came to me, although I still felt heavy with that merciless and sinful unknown power.

We worked until the twilight which was full of smoke and wild lights of sun, and red wind clouds. Walking home through the dead white trees we plucked at the fresh green and red gum sprouts springing from saplings cut down. We chewed these gum-leaves and the acrid taste brought the saliva rushing into our thirsty mouths.

"Lake's old horse is dying," said Macca. "I hear they are going to shoot it tonight."

"Ah, I had a feeling that the gods were going to make a sacrifice tonight. See what a splendid night they have set as a funereal feast for its eyes to rest on."

"It won't see much of it, Steve, because it's blind. That's why they are shooting it."

"The hide is not blind; the lips are not blind. This twilight, full of fire and fury, of dead tree, white and smooth and blue smoke behind it and crimson violent sky above it, will come fast into the hide of the horse and make it part of the clot in the blood of the universe that is man."

"There are the Lakes standing around the horse now," he said.

The grey-white gum-trees, dry and dead, towered over them with fantastic black charcoal writhing around their swelling trunks, and at the foot of one the old blind horse stood with drooping head. Two men stood beside it; one had a black gun hanging from his crooked elbow. Behind them blazed the high red sunset from which we emerged. They turned and stared at us, blinded by it, seeing us as dusty figures, half transparent, and we peered at them through the blue smoke that was behind them and around them.

We, coming from the sun and sea, stared at them; and they, coming from the smoke and hills, glowered at us, their hard little bodies carved out in the clay of Gippsland and bitter-brown with heat and toil.

"Come into the hut for a moment, Macca," I remarked, for the sake of saying something and interrupting the flow of feeling between us, the four human beings in that big dry paddock.

He followed me into the dry potato-smelling hut and we sat down on the log by the empty fireplace.

A crackling metallic roar burst out from an implacable source and circled around the paddock, making for the ranges and singing shatteringly there.

"That's the end of the old blind horse," I said.

Through the bark door we saw the little hard men slowly gathering the big white branches that lay dead and deep in the dry grass, their curved tusks, snowy and sun-bleached, sticking up to betray them. They put them together over the dark heap of the dead horse and, at the approach of night, it burnt high and crackling, smacking its lips exultantly; and the smell of burning flesh, hide and bone, saturated us and made the nervous sheep fly pattering and bleating over the hill.

Unable to bear the heat of the hut, we stood under a sad and dusty she-oak down the hill, our feet stirring awkwardly among flat cakes of cow-dung which smelt rich and negroid to the nostrils. The reflection of the fire rose and fell on Macca's face, drawing it with great delicacy and making it irresistibly beautiful with a native massiveness of feature at one moment, then blotting that out and showing a sad sensitive profile whose helplessness filled me with pity.

"Macca," I said, "what is it that I have been feeling in my flesh all day? I am innocent of it, but it persists. Yes, I am innocent. What do you think?"

"You are the victim of your own hypnotic thoughts, Steve. The fascination of the moment, and my presence, overcomes you. I try to save you from yourself and keep you to the way of poetry, but I have a secret feeling that you are not grateful."

"But you . . . you," I cried angrily with upraised fist, "are so cold and self-sufficient. That is what makes me feel hideously myself! I am self upon self, all passionate and eager, but returned to myself, without ease. Why can't you do these things kindly? Why can't you teach me freely, telling me what I am to do? I know nothing . . . only that my flesh tortures me and your nearness is unbearable. Do you feel this?"

"No, Steve. My love for you is pure. I do not need to touch you. I am with you; that is enough. From other women coarse satisfaction may be obtained, but you give the uncloying cleanliness of your mental passion to me, and I am satisfied."

"You talk, and I feel deftly trapped."

"Hello, the tree's caught fire!" exclaimed Macca, with that irritating quickness of bush boys to be interested in natural phenomena. "The fools," he added slowly, "to burn a carcass under a dry tree."

"There is more than a carcass burning under this tree, yet you turn away from it to look at a dead horse setting fire to wood."

"It is going to be beautiful," he cried.

From the pyre, the flames had run and caught hold of the lowest branch of the dead tree. One little flame, shaped like a hoof, laid itself on the bough and took hold of the trunk. It beat there in a rapidly galloping movement for a few minutes, while the men shouted below. Then one long foreleg rose right out of the fire, and a great head, maned with fire, shaking bridles of flame, rushed at the tree. The fire followed, laying hold and galloping up the dry white wood. It rushed to the top, light and airy, breaking into restless reeling shadows down on the ground. The entire fire in the shape of a blazing horse leapt up the tree, crackled from the craggy top in neighing defiance, and, shaking its mane, set to work to graze a little nearer the stars.

"The horse beat them after all," said Macca.

"Ah, if only you loved me," I mourned. "Yes, when I am gone, it will be the end between us. Last night, the gold-robed heavens married us, but what has it meant? You teach me now to keep a firm hand on my love. You will not even kiss me."

"Because you don't understand life, Steve. To you, it is a dream of poetry. To me, a kiss might mean, as you said once, 'a procession of perambulators'."

"Then you do love me?" I asked, wrestling with the ancient hold of women to extract the final cry from him.

"Yes, yes, oh, yes." He sighed. "My poor *cara sposa* . . . my Steve Hart, I am poor; but my love is as rich as the sea. If you had a net you might gather it; if I had a net I would gather it for you. But nets are dear, and we are only pea-pickers, Stevie Talaaren."

The tree fell, roaring and hissing, sending up gouts of flame and smoke that made our eyes wince. The men beat out the fire in the grass, as soon as it was safe to come near the breaking tree. Against the red glare they seemed to be extensions of the earth's substance reaching out a hand that was shaped into a creature called man. And this hand subdued and pushed back into place earth's own bowels of fire.

"I must go, Steve."

"I must see you, tomorrow night. Will you come?"

"Yes, just for an hour or so. Will you wear a dress, Steve, because I'd like to see you in one. Wear that dark green dress, of Scotch plaid, with black stripes in it. I'd like a shirt of that stuff."

"When I go home, Macca, I'll buy material and have one made for you. That would make me happy. I could bear to go if I knew that you were wandering through Gippsland, wearing a shirt made of stuff like my dress. Tomorrow night, then?"

"Yes. Good night, Talaaren! Sleep well."

"The horse will gallop all night through my sleep."

VI

IT was so hot that it was impossible to sleep. The agitated sheep came over to the bark hut for company and stamped bleating and munching outside the walls, just at the head of our bunks. At a late hour, Blue got up and, flinging a long white blanket over her head, rushed out, screaming and howling, "Fun! Fun! I come for fun! Rudolph Valentino, he not dead while I alive!"

In a frenzy of terror, the sheep raced down the dry hill into the hollows, with a pitter-patter . . . thump . . . thump . . . thump . . . baa-a-a-a . . . baa-a-a-a . . . bar-r-r-r! they were gone.

Blue came back swearing and, scraping herself from head to foot to get the fleas off, she flung herself into bed.

She said to me in the morning, "Steve, do I look thin? Do I appear pale to you?"

"No," I replied, not bothering to look at her. "You're all right."

"But I'm not all right," said Blue. "I'm starving to death."

"So am I . . . and Jim always shows the symptoms when we're dining out."

"But this is different, with me. I'm deliberately starving myself to death. I don't want to live. Kay hasn't written to me for a fortnight. It's all over between us. I'm going to kill myself by starvation. I haven't eaten for five days, but you haven't noticed anything . . . too wrapped up in your own feelings about poetry and love."

"Do you mean to say, Blue, that a tragedy like that has been going on before me and I haven't noticed it? Ah, if only all my life could be passed like this, absorbed, like Dante, in a noble passion. So, you're not going to eat?"

"Well, Steve . . . this is how it is." Blue was sitting on her bed, smoothing her rich waving hair, and the gold bangle slipped up and down on her saffron wrist. "Mia is sending me a birthday cake weighing nine pounds, and I don't know what to do about it. I've taken an oath to starve myself to death."

"Then give me the cake."

"You're heartless."

"I am also foodless. When is the cake arriving?"

"Tonight. I shall go down and get it myself."

"Then it will never reach the bark hut."

But it did. I could smell it when she was down the track. What an odour! Brandy, raisins, cherries, nuts, rich butter and eggs mingled with the flour and sent a drunken wave of perfume through the bush.

"I'll put it under the bed in the tin trunk, so Jim won't smell it," said Blue. If she had buried it fifty fathoms deep Jim would still have smelt it. She cut off two small slices for me and Jim; then she locked the trunk. "I'll leave it. I don't want any. I've no desire to live," said Blue languidly.

"Then have a slice of that cake. Gods, what a mixture. I shan't survive it."

I put on my plaid dress and waited for Macca to come.

"Well, Steve!" his voice made the earth, the sky and myself, one.

"Ah Macca, I live again."

"I can't stay long, Steve. I have to be at work in the morning; and I'm tired."

"Well, just an hour, then. Come and talk to me. Can you see the plaid dress in this light?"

"Yes, it's misty around your throat and your arms are broad and white in the sleeves. That's red tulle you have at the throat, isn't it? You see, I know quite a bit about women's clothes. You look better in that than you do in men's clothes."

"I'm sorry to hear it. Every day, I long more feverishly to be a man. Why? Because then I shouldn't desire man. I should have woman to work my will on; and she is tractable. What did you do today, Macca?"

"I worked up at Kingscote. Today, for the first time, I saw a little cousin of mine. She's a grown girl now, Steve. That's strange to me. Her plaits are quite long, and she's got elfin eyes, like yours. I wonder what will happen to her?"

"Sorrow, I suppose. That's the only thing that the elfin eye looks for. The poet Verlaine had green elfin eyes, you know. He fell on the cold floor of his garret and died, and his mistress let him lie there all night. God help all poets. I'd rather be a pea-picker all my life. I would rather be a wife . . . a woman . . . 'with child, content . . .'

"Poetry is to be feared. It has a fearful force which it wields back and forth, from the poet to the world, and from the world to the poet. And God has a habit of cropping the poets young, as though they were too beautiful to live. Yes, the ripest apple goes first and the most beautiful flower falls before the rest."

I sang, as I walked with him down to the straining post at the corner, Verlaine's *"Chanson d'Automne"*:

> "Long songs begin
> On the violin
> Of autumn trees,
> And my heart throngs
> With that sad song's
> Monotonies.
> Aghast and pale
> I hear the wail
> Of an hour that dies
> And dreaming, gaze,
> On withered days
> And slow tears rise.
> A curst wind blows
> Me where, who knows?
> With respite brief,
> It hurries me
> As wantonly,
> As a dead leaf."

I leant against the straining post and looked at him in the white starlight, remembering the songs the lads of Rokeby and Jindivick used to sing when I was a child. As they went home carrying demi-johns of beer across the Tarago River, they sang clearly and sweetly, "Good night, starlight, good night to you!"

Shudderingly rich from its downdrawn throat, the mopoke cried: "Quork. . . . Quoke!" That cry broke the bush open and started an alert spirit moving in it. It was dead timber no more. It had its voice. "Quork. . . . Quoke!"

It was a figure draped in stringybark, rising above the gum-trees; it was one of the clocks set here, to fill us with fear.

"Macca, one day you must die! You, you whom I love . . . you whom I love so well! Some day it will come to me that you are dead." I pressed my face into my hands and wept.

Macca was calm. His face, large in the moonlight, shone pale as he stared at me.

"We must all die, Steve."

"Ah, no; that is not the answer. I feel that it is not. You are being blinded and muted, so that that answer will escape from you . . . telling me nothing. All my life, I shall go on . . . hearing that message, receiving it from those about to die; but from each it will be succeedingly stranger. Never plain and honest, but mystical and grudgingly communicative, so that, at last when it has beaten upon me for years, I shall know and wonder no more: and I shall be too much a part of it all even to weep. Ah, the maelstrom! But you must die. *You*, pure, young-hearted you!"

I wept again and, walking away from him, entered the bark hut and flung myself down on the bed to weep into sleep.

I walked, haunted, along the foreshore all next day without food, and thought upon love and death. But at evening I remembered the glorious smell of the cake in the tin trunk under Blue's bed and I steered my way to it, with speed and aim unerring.

On the bed lay Blue, groaning.

"What Blue? Haven't you eaten yet? Are you still starving?"

"Ah, Steve, I wish I were. Ah . . . oh . . . that cake!"

"Yes, may I have a slice?"

"Ah . . . Steve. It's gone . . . I ate it all."

"What? In one day? Nine pounds of cake? No."

"Yes, I ate it all for lunch. Fancy . . . nine pounds of cake after starving for six days!"

"Sweet fancy roams at the thought of it; I haven't the imagination. . . ."

"Well, I ate it, and I felt so ill that I went for a walk along the cliffs."

"To think that I sat hungry below, while you, above, waddled fat with nine pounds of cake!"

"Yairs. Ah . . . I felt so ill that I lay down in the sand and went to sleep, and I had a nightmare. I dreamt that a big man with red whiskers was bending over me and kissing me. Then he crawled back on his hands and knees and stared at me, and came forward to kiss me again. I woke up screaming."

"It was the ghost of Bob Priestly whose fowls laid the eggs for the cake. And what about your love? Is it any better?"

"Oh, I don't know. I don't know anything, except that I feel sick."

"Then the cake has killed your passion, and you will be well again tomorrow. What a recipe for that knight who loved La Belle Dame sans Merci. Well, I am as in much need of such a panacea as you were, but it has slipped through my fingers. You are cured. I must suffer on."

Blue didn't answer. She fell asleep and slept for two days.

While Jim and I were wondering whether we should wake her or not, a strong wind blew in from the lake, promising rain, and blew the hut down on top of us, as we stood by Blue's bed. She woke up then all right, and we rushed outside into Jim's tent. When the wind calmed a little, we made the hut firm again, and got ready for a breaking-up of the drought. It rained for two or three days and we knew that this meant a resumption of the bean-picking from which we had had a rest because of the dry weather, which hadn't brought the beans along.

On the first fine day, Macca came out to see us again.

"Steve," he said, "I was working at Kingscote the other day, digging up an old garden, and I found a beautiful thing . . . the marble head of a child, lying deep in the soil under a rose bush. I brought it out into the sunlight, and I was so happy. The old ladies there said I could keep it. If only you had been there to share my joy! But then, I found something for you, too. Yes, not far away, among a lot of faded flowers, I picked up an old book of fairytales by a man named Hans Christian Andersen. Ah, they are so lovely . . . you can't imagine."

"Yes, I've read them, Macca."

"Oh, what a pity! I thought it was going to be a surprise."

"But I want to read them again; and to read them from a book that you brought me would be as miraculous as the tales themselves. It is, in its way, the sort of fairytale I have wanted to happen to me all my life. What story did you like best, Macca?"

"Ah, well, Steve, I think the 'Field of Buckwheat' appealed to me most. You know the field that is arrogant and prides itself on its power, and then it is suddenly blasted and blackened by the storm. Yes, I think I like that one best."

"No, I don't. Arrogance and punishment mean nothing to me. My choice since childhood has been 'Gerda and Kay' or 'The Old House'. No, 'Gerda and Kay' is the one I really like. You must read it. All my life it has haunted me. Read it tonight, and see how faithful Gerda lost little Kay and sought until she found him. Oh, I feel that I am Gerda, and that you are lost Kay. The splinters of worldly glass got into his eyes, just as they will get into yours, and I shall lose you and come seeking you. Promise that you will read 'Gerda and Kay' tonight and remember me while you read."

"All right, then, Steve, and tomorrow night I'll bring the book to you. What are you doing tomorrow? Can I bring it early?"

"No, not very early. We are going with Greenfeast to a sale at a place called Bell's Point. Do you know it?"

"Oh yes, the Bells have lived there since the early days. Their dead are buried in the paddock, on a high hill in the sand. Look for the tombstones as you pass."

"You'll come tomorrow night, then, Macca?" He had grown pale and stifled with some inner coldness and pride. Moving away from me, he walked down the track, his broad awkward body squirming a little as he went, throwing me off.

"I may, Steve. I don't know." His suave cold voice hurt me.

"Now, what have I said?"

"Nothing. I may come. I'll see."

He was like that, I thought, turning back to the hut. For a few moments he would be warm and free in his manner; his lips would part, and he would smile and blush and his shy dewy eyes would flicker as he looked at me. Sometimes he opened them wide and stared at me, laughing. Then, without reason, he relapsed into his habitual cold, calm indolence, becoming wary and suave and eluding me.

Through the mist of the morning we travelled in Greenfeast's buggy along the road past Averdrink; turned into the Tambo back track and then cut off to the right along a narrow and lonely road. Trees stood silver-purple in the middle of it, swinging their violet leaves idly from red stems. Broken and rusty fences hung on charred posts, and in square pits of rusty gravel lay a few inches of muddy rain-water. The bush smelt of dogwood moistened by the rain. We rattled down a steep hill. . . .

"Toe-rag Hill," yelled Mr Greenfeast, over his shoulder.

The road went far into desolate bush through which we twined and turned until the mist broke away from us and right in front loomed the bluffs of Kalimna, deep in the lake and covered with curling timber.

Down an old lane we jogged, through the sliprails, and drew up among other buggies and sulkies and saddle horses. There was a large shed in the farmyard; we climbed the slope from there up to the back gate under a cedar-tree. A large water-rat's skin hung dry and thin on the bough. From the littered veranda we walked into the kitchen and waited for the sale to begin. In it there was a long board table, with a form behind it, under the window which looked out on the lake. Through the small cobwebbed panes the grey waters heaved sullenly in the misty day.

Blue sat down, soft and glowing in her warm-hued clothes, at the fire burning dimly in the blackened fireplace.

When the auctioneer began to clamour outside the door, we strolled out to see if there was any odd thing that we could buy for Mia. The people gathered around were of a surprising sort to have come out of the bush. They were such tall, well-bred looking people; their intent, fine-lined faces looked appraisingly and calmly over the goods. One tall old man of astonishingly aristocratic demeanour and feature, stalked about, accompanied by a handsome youth. Refined habits had engraved him into the likeness of an ancient coin; about his clothes and around his hands and face, certain lines were pencilled by conduct, and distinguished him from the rest. A tall auburn-haired youth, with rich locks curling about a marble white face stood beside him. Through their elbows peered two brown, grinning middle-aged men of an antique appearance, with something of the turret effect of Flemish architecture, thirteenth century, in their pointed heads and grotesque nobbly and crooked features. Their eyes sparkled with a serene and interested pleasure.

Nudging each other, we watched them.

Presently a fine blue jug, admirably cracked and with black earth in the break, was put up for sale. I bid for it, and obtained it for one and sixpence. Not having the sum on me, I begged it from Billy Creeker who stood beside us under the veranda and made little humorous remarks in a weak whisper. Now and then he raised his hat a little, perhaps to cool his burning hair.

The misty rain fell softly over everything, and high up on a hill in the paddocks we saw the tombstones of the children buried there in the early days.

How sad and green the track below the bark hut seemed as we went home in the evening, blown to and fro by the wind. Blue went to bed, tired out, but I sat waiting and watching the earthen floor until it grew too dark to see. I walked out and stood away from the hut, where I could see the wire fence hanging in low etched lines against the evening sky. Into its soft blueness came plunging the rounded body of the black mare, and Macca, reining her in strongly, was bent against the heavens and the first stars in the pose of a dark and shapely centaur.

Holding out a large tattered book to me, he cried, "The volume of fairytales, Steven!" and, wheeling his mare, cantered away into the darkness.

All next day, I lay in the green grass around the foreshore, suffering the uncomprehending pain of young love. My maddened body and my excitable mind tried to find, somewhere in this barren bush, an outlet for my formidable energy.

On the stormy grey and white lake behind me, the green pea boat rolled up and down, shining oily and pearly in the yellow morning light, plumed with smoke. I peered into the grass with half-closed eyes and saw ancient pictures there, made from crossed grass blades.

An antique king and queen greeted each other with stately bowing and bending; stars of dew glittered on the grass green breeches of the king and his yellow weed cloak. "I shall draw these things," I said to myself. "The king and queen of the grass and the pearly hues of the boat shall be formed afresh by me . . . anything . . . anything, ye gods, so that I may not be troubled by love."

I arose full of new energy and hope to begin my drawings, but after a few paces the bush seized me and hypnotized me with its animal eyes into a mood for love and sleep.

Between two trees I saw a fern whirling about with a desperate movement of light madness. There was no breeze there at all. I sat down and stared at it, feeling an affinity with it. For about me there was no sign of love, nor any man, nor the rich luxury of imagined voluptuousness; but yet, I, like the fern, was whirled giddily around and around by a power like that unfelt wind which moved the fern on its exhausting dance.

At sunset I made for the bark hut. When I came to the broken white road below the house of the stout Mrs Rotterdam, I stood beside a gum-tree and, with my eyes on the closing apricot of the evening skies, I thought of my lost love, of the years to be, of loneliness and despair, and putting my head in my hands, I wept long and brokenly. It was good to weep there, for an audience of gods and heroes in the sky gathered to behold me, and their armour shone carved golden as they moved towards me and away from the sunset.

For a while I enjoyed the thought of the Greek heroes; then I thought that God Himself must be watching me, and would so pity me that He would let me be happily married to the one I loved. But at last, running out of images, and being, at that time, a fierce pantheist, I wept because a giant pity was enveloping me and enjoying my pure tears. I stared, wet-faced, into the sunset and wept.

The dust rose about me in a haze, swept by the wind as it passed, and the long golden sunset strayed into images of waters and figures over Mr Whitebeard's poor crop of beans.

L

VII

THE growers were giving the beans time to catch a bit of fullness from the rain. Picking would be in full swing in a week's time. Jim had been doing a bit of trapping for a long while now, and making a bit on the side. He went along and borrowed some more traps from his friends the Grabbems, and came home earnestly talking about "Mrs Grabbem", who was, "a nice little woman, Blue. Yer oughter go down an 'ave a yarn with her."

Blue, who had an aversion to women, snorted.

Jim cut up newspapers, and went off clanking in the evening to set his traps.

Macca was engaged in painting the house of a wealthy retired squatter who had brought a team of builders up from the city to renovate his home. Macca discovered that they were going down to the city on the coming Friday night and returning the following Monday morning. He thought to himself that we might like to go down to our home with them for the few days, so he asked on our behalf and was told to bring us along in order that we might talk it over.

Wherefore Blue and I went down one night to see the builders about it and, finding them decent fellows, we arranged to be on the road early in the morning and travel with them to our home.

This amicably settled, we withdrew in good order and were strolling out through the garden, watching the clouds foaming over in gold among the purple gum-trees, when the very tall squatter came out, like a newborn from some meditating eternity of his, and very softly said to us, in a voice that inferred his tolerance of us as lights o' love, but not, no certainly not, in his house . . . "Look . . . I don't want you girls hanging around here."

"Sir," I replied, bowing in a courtly manner, "yours is indeed a low gibbet. There were better in Montfaucon, if I may say so." And left him to be gathered to his fathers, full of years and honour.

The night came, and with it a dance, at which Blue and Jim wished to be present to perform the light Terpiscorpion, as the Black Serpent used to put it.

Ah, what revelry, what anxiety as they performed their toilets. I assisted them; doing the Figaro to their *"Qua e là . . . su e giù!"*

Jim brought his mysterious portmanteau out into the open and thrust his head into its depths, where the tram-ticket, the dirty socks and the Testament still slumbered. "I dunno whether to wear a silk shirt or a linen one, Blue."

"Give us a look at your wardrobe, Jim," said Blue, "and I'll advise you on the matter."

But Jim shut the port with a bang and swept it away into the tent. After reckoning, audibly, that his things were too good to wear to a bush dance, Jim emerged, wearing his usual white woollen sweater with the red V neck. It was a little changed this time and was streaked with red in unexpected places.

"What have you done to it this time, Jim?"

"I boiled her, Blue!"

"You spoiled her, too, Jim. You should have worn that tramway shirt of yours."

"Which tramway shirt, Blue?"

"That one with the hole punched in it . . . right down at the bottom of the portmanteau."

"I don't know what you mean, Blue." Jim grinned all across his fat red face and puffed away at the boree log, from which the signet-ringed finger stood out refinedly.

"I done me coat up again, Blue."

"What is it this time, Jim?" asked Blue, getting into my double-breasted coat which was always requisitioned on dance nights.

"I done away with ther pockets," gurgled Jim, turning and showing us the monstrosity with the pocket flaps sewn down flat along the sides. "An' I took in the knees of me pants."

This was a truly great sartorial achievement for a man in the bush, armed with only a darning needle and cotton as thick as twine. He aimed at the Oxford-bag design, then popular, and had achieved it by making the trousers fit bone-tight to the knee and so accentuating the narrow leg into what he fondly fancied was an Oxford-bag breadth.

"How does she look, Blue?"

"Awful. But the stitches might break before we get to the dance."

"Well, I don't care," said Jim with his queer sulkiness. "I'm tired of wearing it one way all the time."

"Turn it inside out, then. Come on, James, lift me over the fence."

He groaned as he raised her nine stone up and lowered it gently over the post and rails, and his stitches twanged faintly with the strain. Blue looked immaculate in her wide tailored trousers, silk shirt, college tie and double-breasted coat. She looked back at me, her white teeth shining in a curved line behind her red lips, her face warm and full with youth, and her white brow half-hidden by waves of black hair with threads of Celtic gold glittering here and there.

I watched until they were out of sight among the bushes and fallen logs, then slowly and sadly I went back to the bark hut. Why couldn't I go with them, and be happy at the dance hall as they would be? Why couldn't I be satisfied with lights and sounds, instead of longing for the unattainable, for dangerous desires? I put more wood on the fire and threw the brick in to heat up for my trousers. At two in the morning, I must be at the roadside down near Averdrink to meet the truck on which Blue would be sitting with the builders.

As I was pressing the brick over my shirt and trousers, Macca came softly to the door. The stars shone behind his back and the furry edge of the bark door was soft in the blue night.

"Macca! Oh, thank you for coming out here to this lonely hut! It seems feverish to me tonight. I shall be glad to get home for a few days! Are you sorry to have missed the dance? I feel that it is selfish of me to have asked you to wait with me, here, until morning. You are not like me. You would rather be among the people of your own age, dancing and making love; while I, who am one year older, feel as if a million aeons have passed since I first swam into being."

"But that shouldn't affect your legs, Steve. Why don't you learn to dance?"

"I feel heavy with sorrow. I can't do anything for the pain of life. I can scarcely work for it. I only really lose it when I work like a madman; and that is how I work nowadays."

"Well, in the dance, if you go fast enough and laugh enough, you get like that. There is no time for sorrow."

"But a dance is so mournful. One thinks, as the dancers whirl by in each other's arms: they have to grow old and be parted, even as you and I. And what is now will no longer be in time to come. This very hut, which is now poorly but humanly lighted by candle and fire, must soon be dark and deserted, overgrown by nettles and companioned by bats and snakes. Perhaps I am all humanity in composite; old, very old. The cells of my ancestors falter and fail in me, at last. Or is it because I am unloved. I have never been loved."

"I love you, Steve."

"Your love? Bah! I tell you, the day is coming when you will hate me, when you will hear of me with indifference. If you love me, why are you going to let me leave you and go away to another district?"

"But you are coming back within a week's time."

"Yes. But I shall have to leave Gippsland after that."

"Well, you will be back next spring, for the peas."

"Ah, yes, and because of that, Macca, you will not be here."

"I shall be here, Stevie Talaaren."

"No. The sorrow in my heart is not a liar. It is an eye that sees far into the future and groans in my breast at the sorrow it beholds. It will not tell me, but it groans, and by its heaviness I know what lies ahead. Sorrow and despair . . . disappointment, hardness, deception, crime, and death. You are going to sin against me. Mind you, it is not your fault. You are driven, like me. I have tried to entangle you. Yes, that's true. I have tried to make a poet of you and fit you for life with me. I am masterful. It was I who decided that you should be my mate. You had nothing to do with it. All my life I shall select like this, and always, I feel, unwisely. Men respect the severe gods that have ordered me, on pain of death, to remain virgin. Therefore, they leave me alone; alone in utter despair. For I know no joy in remaining vestal and serving the gods. Yet to sin will mean death. Once, virginity pleased me. I often stood alone, thinking with pride and joy, 'All my life I shall be virgin. All my days in the flesh shall be pure. I do not desire any other state, and shall go hence as I came, unsoiled.' But now that ancient vestal joy is gone. I feel no happiness in serving the gods. If I did not fear them I would break their tyranny tonight. I say it now, and mean it. But yet, I shall never marry; nor shall I ever forsake the gods. What are you thinking of there, with your head bent low in the darkness?" I asked, glaring at him through the heat and shadows of the little bark kitchen.

"Steven, I was crawling towards you on my hands and knees, then. Towards your vow of virginity and your purity."

Why was I unhappy, then? I didn't want him to crawl to me, but to come to me and take me as mistress and bride.

At midnight we lay together on the bark bed, and the tin clock that Macca had found in the sea ticked sturdily, but quiveringly, on the bark table. Scornful and angry we lay in the dark, without kisses or embraces.

"Macca, I shall have a plaid shirt made for you, and bring it back with me. And you will write to me, one letter, on that coarse paper you used when you write that letter to me, telling me to trust in love. Send me down between its pages a red rose from Kingscote and when I come home have a large bunch of them on the table. Take my books of verse home with you tonight, and look after them.

Soon I shall sit at home under a shelf of books and read your letter in the company of magnificent minds. Their portraits are the half-remembered portions of their poetry and prose that spring to mind when the form of their work is dwelt on. To me, there is a sort of feature in this broken fragment:

"And I said to my friend, that I should like to taste all the fruits on the tree of life.

and

> "The lonely tunny-fisher with his bobbing net.

and

"Far off, like a pearl, lies the city of Heaven; a child could get there in one day.

That's Oscar Wilde. Then there's Shaw:

"CAESAR (calling over the sea):
   'Ho, Apollodorus! (points skyward and quotes the barcarolle)
   The white upon the blue above'
"APOLLODORUS (swimming in the distance):
   'Is purple on the green below!'

And Ruskin, calmly, beautifully, opinionated:

"So also, a common workman even in this barbarous stage of art might have carved Eve's arms and body a good deal better; but this man does not care about arms and body, if he can only get at Eve's mind and show that she is pleased at being flattered and yet in a state of uncomfortable hesitation. And some look of listening, of complacency and of embarrassment he has verily got . . . note the eyes slightly askance.

"Ah, it will be good," I ended, "to be home again."
"I should like to go with you, Steve."
"Some day . . . when we are married," I said boldly.
Ah, how wrong the words sounded when they were spoken! How helpless and unsupported, unwanted and unrejoiced in!
"Forgive me, I should never have said that. Ah, let me remember something immortal to wipe out the folly . . .

> "Women with child, content; and old men sleeping;
> And wet strong ploughlands, scarred for certain grain;
> And babes that weep, and so forget their weeping;
> And the young heavens, forgetful after rain."

The moon flowered white in the bark room, and her sudden bloom made me restless.

"Let us get up and go down to the road and build a fire there. We shall talk until the truck comes."

He carried my suitcase down over the paddocks. I strode forlorn and shivering beside him. Over the white ground we stretched our hands and caught up twigs and light boughs. Soon a clear hungry flame was leaping up towards the green leaves drooping above. The night wind was cold; the whole world about us was blanched, secret and sad with the reflected light from the dead moon.

"Tonight, Macca, I think of my father, that twisted moody failure, who despised me, and set in me the seeds of destruction."

A terrible picture came into my mind. I set it aside hastily out of consideration for the dead, and began to talk of his love for the bush and the heavens. A rooster crowed far away and I recalled the old orchard and Kelly. Behind me lay the back track to the Tambo, down which I imagined, when I first came to Metung, he might ride, searching for me.

The truck roared down the road, blazing-eyed, and stopped. Jim got off, and I took his place, saying hastily to him and to Macca, "Good-bye, we'll soon be back with you!"

"Good-bye, Steve!"

It moved off. I was among a soft sense of rugs, cases and tired men braced for a long night's journey. This feeling gradually infiltrated, until I grew tired, too, at last, of watching the gloomy clouds, the flying fences, rushing leaves and trees, growling bridges, sluggish rivers and the animal-patient houses, square-eyed in the moonlight.

When dawn came we were moving across a long, grassy, dry plain; a huge dead gum-tree stood at the side of the road, and heavy yellow and white flowers moved on its boughs. The tree whirled by, the flowers flew off, raising their sulphur crests and screaming raucously . . . a mob of white cockatoos.

I looked sleepily at the dry country.

At eleven o'clock I was so drunken with fatigue that when we got down and drank black coffee in a bush shop I became utterly intoxicated.

I remarked to the driver on the beauty of these Italian roads, being firmly convinced that we were in Italy. He stopped the truck in alarm, and made me eat some bananas, with some vague Darwinian theory possibly rumbling through his mind.

At three o'clock in the afternoon, we were home. I flung myself down on my bed in the small dark bedroom with the bit of tin

nailed to the doorstep and slept up and down the universe, whirling
in deep fatigue from night to day and day to night.

I was not happy at home, either, although Mia was so glad to see
us. Waiting around for a letter from Macca exhausted me. At last
one came, together with a box of lemons and a fine Gippsland
rainbow trout. The world burst into bloom.

All the red roses are gone, Stevie, my one love ever, but I am sending you
a bloom from our garden. I shall have a bowl of golden roses waiting for
you when you come back. I am writing this to you while the moths are
leaping around the oil lamp, and on the roof the rain is falling cleanly, as
pure as our love. I went down and sat on the jetty last night, thinking of
all the gold in the sea, and the richness of my love for you.

I read and re-read the small rounded writing, that verged on the
fantastic with its trembling curves and mannerisms. It was as
though I gazed into his pure face, and saw the heavy eyes stare
into mine, while the shy tremulous lips smiled. I sat all day, holding
the letter in my hand, tasting ecstasy that was tinged with fear and
distrust of happiness.

Then, I went down and bought the material for his shirt, a dark
green plaid like my dress. A little woman living in a house surrounded by pomegranates promised to have it made up by the
week-end.

Blue was the unhappy recipient of a letter from Jim that made
her leap into the air and react more strongly than I did, to *her*
feelings of fear and distrust. It arrived with a big black snake
drawn under the address. Blue ripped it open, snarling, "Wonder
what's wrong with Heggie? What?" she shouted, reading it to
herself. "What? Hat? Bah! Hat! I'll get him a hat all right! He
won't need a hat when I see him again."

She threw the letter down and sat brooding awfully for an hour
or so.

Dear ole Blue (ran the cause of the trouble), Just a line to tell you that the
bus will be coming down on Friday night. It will be leaving here pretty
early. It will be leaving Melb. about 10 o'clock on Sunday night.

Well, Blue, I am going to suggest something I am wanting you to pick
me a hat I am coming down as far as Dandenong in the bus and if you
or Steve don't mind would you meet me where you got out of the bus and
then go straight away and get the hat then I will catch the first train back
to Warragul because I have to be there at half past two to do some business
I think it will be about 9 o'clock when we arrived in Dandenong. Mr Hawser
said he will be leaving here about 9 or 10 o'clock. well Blueie there was
some person or other broke into the hut on Monday and took a 10/- note

out of my back pocket and a ½ of bread 1 pound of butter out of the tuckerbox, but who this person is I do not know Mrs Bugwun missed some things out of her house about four days ago no body has any person about any where that would do it there is things been pinched at different places about I will explain them all on Saturday morning when I see you well dear little creature I started work this morning at seven and didn't knock off till quarter past seven tonight and I am pretty tired so I am making this letter pretty short it has been raining since yesterday dinner time and until ten today by gee I wouldn't like to spend another fortnight in this tumble down old shack it is like being all dressed up and know where to go and nothing to see or do. Macca has only been out once since you left I haven't been anywhere either too tired to write any more I will close living in hopes of seeing you both on Saturday morning

> yours with love from Heggie and the ticks. I put urgent on the letter in case it dordles on the track.

"He'll dawdle on the track when I get to work," threatened Blue, and on the back of his letter she shaped various messages directed to his employer, the builder, for whom Jim was now working.

"I'm not going to have him down here, looking for hats. Fancy picking hats for that head! 'Tell Heggie will be away Saturday.' How does that sound?"

"You are really going to send a wire and prevent him from coming down?"

"I am. Here's another effort: 'Tell Heggie not to come; no shops; no hats. Blue.' "

"Let him come. I'd enjoy picking a hat for Heggie. Think of the jokes we could crack about the tent and the ticks . . . and the portmanteau!"

"But he'll propose to me on the strength of the hat-picking. I know he will. No, I'd rather go pea-picking all my life, than hat-picking for one hour with Heggie. How about this, then: 'Put Heggie off at Warragul. No good dis plice.' "

"I think the Italian would confuse his boss a little. 'Dis plice', so far as Mr Hawser is concerned, might be one of the Seven Heavens of science. No, let it be simple: 'No hope; no Heggie; no hats.' "

"But seriously . . . what about this?—'Heggie is to get off at Warragul.' "

"That would do; but you could have let the poor bloke get off down here, and we should have a great time hat-picking for him."

But the wire was sent and Heggie went hatless.

The bus called for us very late on Sunday night. We jumped up

sick, out of our sound sleep, and scrambled into our tight clothes
(we were getting more muscular every day) and, saying a sad
farewell to Mia, clambered aboard.

I sat in front with the driver and the lighted road tediously
unrolled before our eyes all night, smelling of damp ferns.

Towards dawn I grew sleepy and, taking Macca's hand in mine,
I dreamt that we were going across the horizon into the Promised
Land, where the rainbows of light made turrets in the sky and the
swords of the compass clashed lightly at our coming. "Look! We're
nearly there," I cried aloud.

And so we were. The driver had fallen alseep beside me and the
truck had reeled off the road into a steep gully. My ecstatic cry
had awakened him. Whirling the wheel madly, he dragged us back
to life again and took me away from my Promised Land. At last
we were all a little unbalanced from lack of sleep. The driver asked
me pleadingly to hit him on the nose with my heavy walking stick
whenever he closed his eyes; and I was so irritated by our narrow
escape and the sleepless night that I tapped him with such a will
as to make his nose bleed, and almost closed his eyes permanently.

I woke up on the bush track near the gum-tree where I had wept
in the face of the setting sun, and solemnly and stupidly directed
the driver to take us up to the house of Mrs Rotterdam. But Blue,
sane among us all, energetically told him to take us down to the
Cyclone gate. From there, we toiled sleepily, suitcases in hand, up
the track to the bark hut. There was the narrow drain near the
fence, and the dear white skeleton of the dairy above the hut. I
loved it. My heart stirred warmly in my breast. Heggie, who had
come out casually to have a look around, saw us first, and rushed
down the hill crying out with joy and hugging us frantically,
repeating over and over again, good fellow, "Dear little creatures!
Dear little creatures! Gee! It's good to see you again!"

And lo, Macca, there too, leapt on to his black mare and galloped
down the paddock towards us, waving his wide black hat and
shouting out welcome. That was one happy dream, at least, that
had come true. Ah, if only all dreams could be so realized, I thought.
It had never happened to me before. I rejoiced and was grateful,
but feared . . . it might never happen again.

The joy and the agony of seeing Macca again; the feeling of
having vanquished time and change, so that we met as of old . . .
that was best of all. I gave him the plaid shirt. We walked outside
and stood by the paling fence at the back of the old bark hut. How

wide and dry the Gippsland paddocks looked after the tiny culti-vated garden at home. What different emotions were generated through the eyes that beheld this dry sad land. I was drunken and trembling from loss of sleep, but rich and teeming with my love for Macca. Despairingly I looked at him, as he stood calm, kind and happy before me. My love and pain made me brutal with despair, and then he said softly: "If you hadn't come back, Steve, I would have gone down."

"What?" I said stupidly and cruelly. "Gone down? How? Are you so weak?"

"No . . . no, I meant I'd have gone down to see you and bring you back again."

Oh, I said to myself, why do I always place a mad fantastic meaning on all things? Why am I insane, I asked myself? There was no answer. I stood in the unbelievable day, communicating my drunken weariness and passion to the land around me, to the day that threw me and my energy aside into limbo; the day that wasted me and set me aside for destruction, as calmly and kindly as Macca set me aside, without embrace or touch or hand or lip. So was I set aside.

So did I return to Metung and to my love.

Within the hut, Jim was explaining all the thefts to Blue as though he had committed them under the guidance of her master-mind, and was assuring her of his success. The words "back pocket . . . half of bread . . . one pound of butter" poured out with a grovelling smoothness and Macca winked long and slowly at me.

"And how's the trapping going, Jim?" Blue asked.

"Pretty good, Bluey," said Jim anxiously. "I lost a good few, though. But it was better after you left, Blue. I 'ope you don't take them outer the traps now you're back, Blue.

"I lost a big bagful one day, Blue. I took them down, about twenty of them, in a big bag to Grabbem's, to wait for the bus to come and take them into Bairnsdale, and I was going to kill them at the last moment and put them on board, fresh. And when I heard the bus coming I made a dive for the bag to stretch their necks, and when I picked up the bag, Blue, there wasn't one in it. They 'ad chewed their way out."

"Glad to hear it. That'll teach you, James."

"Got to live, little creature," said Jim ingratiatingly.

That day . . . in full force, we rushed in on the Buccaneer and the Black Serpent, talking racily and absently while we ate of a splendid meal. After it, we walked about a lot on the wide veranda, with our hands in our pockets. Edgar came up the path under the green trees and beside him walked Macca, laughing, with the plaid shirt on his broad shoulders. He walked a little pigeon-toed, which endeared him to me, and in his hand he held my fiddleback walking stick. A broad black felt hat shadowed his face. I looked at the shirt and his shoulders and a sweet uncertain possessiveness tormented me.

After dinner we separated. Heggie and Blue went back to the bark hut along the main road; Macca and I took to the foreshore and sombrely ploughed our way along through the thick dry sand. I was really overjoyed at the magic which had permitted me to return and find the village and Macca unaltered. Blue begrudged this parting. She hated to see me leave her side. She was right in this, knowing well that through my incurable sentimentality I was weaker and younger than she. With her lay sanity and peace won through a struggle with loneliness; but I fought restlessly to be with Macca, as I had fought to be with Kelly. The earth changed when we were together. It became an exquisite torment that always hovered on the brink of a dissolving peace.

Leaving the dusty track we walked through Reynolds' dry property, past sheds cracked by the heat and carts lying fractured in its blaze; our feet crashed over dry thistles that liberated their snowy seeds.

"Macca, should you like to be married and live as Edgar and his Black Serpent live?"

"Speaking paradoxically," said Macca slowly, for paradoxical was a new word of his and he used it often, "Edgar and his Black Serpent are not married, in this sense, that they seem to be inviting everyone to taste their enjoyment of a forbidden pleasure. They assume, as they kiss, that the rest of the world is jealous and lonely, don't they?"

"And isn't it?"

"Of course not. It's entirely matter of fact."

"But they do those things with such splendour, Macca. I envy them."

"No, without thought. That's why you do envy them. You think too much."

"But," I persisted, "would you like to be married as they are married?"

"No. Of course not. They're too sensual."

I responded unhappily that I thought they were, too.

"Besides they have too many children. I fear the sensual, Steve; it clogs and destroys."

Starvedly, a few days afterwards, I walked along the barbed-wire fence to find the Black Serpent. I did not fear the sensual. I sought it without ceasing. From one person at least, I obtained sympathy in my search . . . the Black Serpent, Edgar's wife.

What meaning smiles she gave me when we met! Plump-armed, she stood on the board veranda that winced under the heat of the sun, her rich red lips twisted over her stained teeth with love and delicious enjoyment at my coming. Negligently, she leant out and caught me up against her heavy warm breasts and I let my head rest there, while her fingers, roughly, intimately and demandingly, caressed my hands, and she looked far out, triumphantly, mischievously and mockingly, over her dry country.

"You are like the rich purple sarsaparilla plant that breaks out of the clay in the heat of summer. Do you know it?" I said.

She smiled, catching her lower lip in her teeth, and kissed my hand.

"That purple plant with the tough root and the few leaves, Stessa?"

"Yes. The flowers are like little crushed grapes; as though a hoof had pressed them down. Ah, I love that flower."

"Have you ever tried to uproot it, Stessa?"

"Ah, you can't! It won't come. You've got to break it to pieces to get it out of the ground, and then you hate yourself. Oh, how it spreads out on the dry ground like the stain of delicate wine, the strong sinewy arm of the root holding it back from you. It may not really be sarsaparilla, of course; but an old bushman told me that that was what it is commonly called."

Pressed close together, we walked into the dark kitchen. I saw the grease on her frock, the spots and ladders in her stockings and the absurd but childish way she had of pointing her toes outward as she walked, so that her stout legs were put forth at an angle; but her immense fecundity and knowledge, her happiness and her faithfulness encircled and enchanted me. If I had been a man I should have married just such a woman and toiled for her thankfully, and she would have enriched my body as she enriched my heart now.

I tried to discover from her Macca's true feelings towards me; but she only smiled and raised her eyebrow. I went home feeling friendless and frustrated.

The next day was a stinger; and we had to pick in Greenfeast's dry, starved bean crop. It dawned sultry red. The kookaburras, black against the exploding sky, lifted their tails up and down with an air of deliberation, as they sat high on the naked trees. Just as the sun sparkled over the horizon, they stretched their necks out on an angle; with swelling throats and open beaks, they gave the savage premonitory "Quahrr-r-r-r! Quah-r-r!" and off they went, "Hoo-hoo-hoo-hoo-acka . . . ooh-hoo-hoo-hoo-acka!"

Then they sat raising their tails up and down, and cocking their heads at some bush crawler that lay on the ground, until the sun rose; after that they disappeared in the shade.

There was a pearly stormy hue in the sky and the dawn wind blew coldly as we hurried across the fields to Greenfeast's. I wondered if Macca would be there. He had given his word, when we picked the first crop, to come and pick the second; that seemed so long ago.

But there he was, after all, and my depressed spirits rose again at the sight of his freckled face under the wide black hat. He had nothing to say to me until later in the morning, when a dramatic light spread over us and the sky flamed with merciless sunlight, hour after hour, until we were dazed with it.

"Steve, we'll sit under the she-oak over there, and have lunch together if you will?"

"Thank you, Macca; I needed the thought of something like that to sustain me."

I moved off, crawling first on one knee, then on the other, to ease the pain of the cramps that the picker gets. The sunlight was shouting at me and deafening me. Not a bird sang; the leaves hung limp and sickly. I thought of Keats, home, love, our next job and the years ahead, until Mr Greenfeast got a cooee from the house. At that, we all knocked off, and Macca walked with me to the sparse shade of the dusty she-oak. The sky was so brightly blue and near that I fancied I could have cut it with a knife. It bored into my eyes. I lay down and hid my face in Macca's knees. Bending down, he took from the blue kerchief around my throat a cheap silver arrow I had picked up and stuck in it, for lack of a pin.

"It doesn't suit you, Steve Hart, that arrow. Too cheap and tinny. You seem to ask for noble adornments, for you are fine and noble."

"No, Macca, only tired, hopeless and passionate . . . and for what?"

"Why shouldn't you be? What are we? What have we to look forward to? You come of a family long established here, Steve. They seized the land, as pioneers in the early days; and some of them hold it still. But, we, the offspring of weaker laterals, have been trained along other ways, and cut off from the family property. My mother was one of the Svensons of Monaro. . . ."

"Oh, my mother often talked of the Svensons to us. They used to bring down cavalry remounts and ship them to India. At evening when they made camp, they cut logs and made chock-and-log yards to keep the horses in."

"Well, the Svensons are still keeping part of Monaro under their hands; but what am I? The pea-picker; the bush odd-job man. So we are proud and dream, and read too much, finally ending up in nothing . . . or worse still, the city. The others, by fate or fortune, have cut us out and got the land. If we had it, we'd master it with the appreciation of poets. Ah, what's the use? Steve Hart, there are hundreds of us, roaming up and down Gippsland, dispossessed by unwise marriages . . . or love, as our parents called it. I distrust love. I suppose your mother lost her share like that?"

"In a way; but her gipsy love of change and wandering got her cut out, too. She had worked for her people for ten years or so, and got nothing except calico underclothes and a few shillings a week as pocket money; but she had to ask for that. And she didn't just lie around. She was up at five in the morning, taking the hotel washing across the Tambo on horseback, to wash it where there were conveniences on the other side of the river. The old Chinese cook used to make her a special pancake and a cup of tea in the dark morning, before she set out. 'Ah, Mia,' he used to say compassionately, 'you poor girl, you work too hard.'

"But one morning, instead of putting the washing on the horse, she packed her valise and put that on, and rode on, and out into the world. Grandfather just forgot her when the property was being handed over. After all, she was only a woman, you know. But look at the ramifications of it! Your mother was only a woman, too, but she bore you, a son, and you have much to give to Gippsland. Macca, I'd like to buy a bit of land here, put up a bark hut on it, and work the soil of Gippsland till I die. I love my country . . . Patria Mia."

I raised a handful of the dust to my nostrils and smelt it. "Ah, that aboriginal smell! We tread on the soft black dust of lost Gippsland tribes, Macca! Yes, I should like a bit of land and some stock to drive slowly to the Bairnsdale yards every week or so, and I would become soaked in the old traditions of Gippsland. The heroes of my *Odyssey* should be Thorburn, Baulch, McAlister, McDougal, Frazer, Bill Grey, Alec Cain, Jack the Packer and old Blind George. Gippsland, Gippsland, I love you. I want to make you immortal, and die in you and be loved by you."

Mr Greenfeast came back into the paddock. We got up. "Back to it, again!"

Painfully, with aching backs, we knelt to serve her; Gippsland, the lordliest Her that we had ever known.

"Stevie Talaaren, tonight I'll bring you that book of Wordsworth's poems I mentioned to you some time ago. It's got 'Why art thou silent!' in it."

"You've said that to me often lately, Macca. I wondered where it came from."

"It's a sonnet.

> "Why art thou silent! Is thy love a plant
> Of such weak fibre that the treacherous air
> Of absence withers what was once so fair?"

Kneeling in the dust beside his rusty tin, he murmured, "I like it. That poem embodies all my love for you. It is a plaint like the sorrow in your glance. 'Why art thou silent!' "

He drew ahead of me and was silent for the rest of the day; but the sun was now a maze of glory to me, a rapid stabbing blade that I would have had in my heart forever. I cried to the day, "Be forever."

After work, that night, he brought a little faded green leather-covered book, with an owl stamped vigilant on the hide. We read it together while the light lasted.

"Yes, after 'Why art thou silent!' I like the sonnet of 'The One Ship', Macca. What striding colour of sail and swaying deck, of heaving sea and evening sky! If you don't want me; if Gippsland doesn't need me, I'll take ship some day, I think, and stride, full-sailed and bright-coloured, to another land. Who knows?"

We were moving over towards his mare; she was tied up to the old cowbails at the back of Jim's tent.

"Well, in the meantime, Steve Hart, remember that you are a woman and look out for yourself when you walk around among these old posts at night. I dreamt that you struck your breast on one of them, and I felt very unhappy about it. Be careful!"

"Yes, I will." Advancing with one hand over my breasts, I followed him.

A bad season of bean-picking was over, and we had very small cheques to show. There was no more work in Gippsland for us now until autumn ripened the Bruthen maize. That was too far ahead. We had to live. It was now December. In the *Interstate Weekly*, we saw reference to hop-picking on the property of a grower called Mr Padrone, whose fields were situated at the foot of the Australian Alps.

Blue said to me, "Write at once, Steve, for two places."

"But what about James, Bluey?"

"Jim's not coming. We don't want him with us. It would give us a bad name if we landed there in the company of a man."

"Oh, Blue, Jim's all right! He's the best mate you could ever find! Let him come along, too. Why should he have to stay behind in Gippsland now that everything's worked out? Poor old Jim!"

"No. No Heggie! We don't want him."

"All right!" I sat down on the log by the fireplace and carefully and with my usual romantic artistry, applied for accommodation for two hop-pickers.

"How's that, Blue?" I handed it over.

"That'll get the jobs."

"But are you serious about Jim? He's a good sort, Blue. Look at the way he makes tea for us in the morning, and how he lifts us over the fences when we go out walking through the bush. Let him come. The other day, you know, when we were walking over to the lake, you and I, one on each side of him, how he laughed and hugged us when we said that we three would wander forever! The boree log was sticking out between his lips, burning like a bush-fire; and he had such a fat, happy, far-away look on his face, as he stared down at the green patch of grass we were walking on . . . and the clear wind blew us along."

"That's the worst of being a poet, Steve. You see too many sides of the question. No, I've made my mind up about that. No Jim. We've got a bad name in this village through being with him; you know that."

And I had to concede that we had.

VIII

Two days before Christmas, Jim was ordered to go into Bairnsdale and buy presents which we were going to give to Macca and the children of the Buccaneer. He took the reef out of his coat, sewed up the red V in the neck of the sweater, and stood in front of us, licking a boree log that he had just made, and listened to our instructions.

"Orright, Blue! Orright, Steve! I'll do me best, little creatures. "Hurrooo!" Off he went, through the dead gums, to catch the boat to Bairnsdale.

Idly we wandered around when he was gone; wondering if we would get a satisfactory reply from the hop-grower. After we had tidied up the bark hut, I said, "Come on, Blue, let's fix up a Christmas tree for Jim, and hang presents on it!"

M

"Where'll you get a Christmas tree around here? And the only present around is the one we're living in."

"Bring the hammer. Where's the nails? Come on, here they are. Follow me."

I ran into Jim's tent and brought out all his old clothes. I put them down at the feet of the dead trees outside the bark hut. We nailed his hat to the first and stuck a magpie's feather through the hole in the crown. The tree had two big knots shaped like eyes about two feet above the hat, and a long arm-like branch that appeared to be gesturing; so that it looked as though it were holding its hat against its chest and staring over the top of it at us.

Blue printed its remark on a bit of cardboard and placed it at the end of the branch:

Good morning. I am a deaf mute, with thirteen children, so I don't notice it. Could I interest either of you gents in a line in lady's refined undergarments?

At the foot of the tree we placed Jim's portmanteau with a few thistles sticking out of it. To the second tree, we nailed his pants, green at the knees with sap from the crushed plants he had knelt on, and attached a recipe to them:

Pea-soup pants. Soak for two days in alcohol, boil until the buttons rise and flavour with a hard kick from the rear.

On the third, we nailed his working shirt, with a legend that ran:

Shall we join the ladies, Colonel?

For this tree had one branch entangled in the tree beside it.

The fourth tree got Jim's socks, and it sank back in its hollow as we nailed them to it. The very nails bounced and bent their backs, but we drove them home. Not able to waste much time on those socks, we just wrote out a brief ticket:

Humming birds; small; rare: *Avismella Petersenia*; Gippsland, Victoria.

We ran off out of range, and collected all the old boots around the hut, finding about twenty. They are the flowers of the Australian forest. In some places, you won't find a blade of grass, but you'll always pick up an old boot, as hard as stone, its little round tin-metal-edged eyes gleaming malignantly at their bad treatment.

We mingled these with Jim's dancing pumps and working boots, and hung them on a bit of wire around the straining post. No remarks were attached here; we knew that Jim would do his bit in that direction when he came to untangle them.

He came home late that night, when we were in bed, so he didn't get the full pleasure from our thoughtful work until next morning, when he rose to go and do a bit of work for Mr Whitebeard, who had asked him, on the boat, to come over and do a fencing job.

After cursing and hunting for his clothes everywhere, he went to work in his good ones, and passed his old rig-out hanging to the trees on the hill. The tussle with the nails holding the socks and the wire-entangled boots at the corner warmed him up for the day's work ahead, and the blood ran like wine in his veins.

He had brought home all the presents for us. Athletic singlets for Macca and crackers for the Buccaneer's children. Then, with a timid pride, he presented us with the gift he had bought us. A large red case of mock leather, which when opened revealed needles, cotton, scissors, thimbles, hooks and bodkins lying on a field of green plush.

Macca, who had been given the money for Jim's gift from us, returned with a solid leather belt, which we handed over to our old mate. "There are a lot of good old mates named Jim. . . ."

On Christmas Day, we turned up late at the Buccaneer's. It was a scalding hot day; we sat sweating over roast pork and plum pudding, pulled fiery crackers with the children, and swooned homeward after tea, to unbutton and throw ourselves down on to the bark beds.

Within a fortnight's time, we got an answer from the hop-grower in the alps. We were addressed as Messrs Steve and Blue, and advised that bins and accommodation had been reserved for us for the season. Picking would commence on 28th February.

"We'll leave here at the end of January and have a few weeks at home," Blue decided. My heart grew heavy; soon, I should be leaving Gippsland and Macca . . . and poor old Jim.

"Not a word to Heggie," warned Blue. "We'll just tell him that we're going home for a while, and we'll write and let him know if we've got anything, and he can follow us."

That's how we let him down, and made ready to leave him forever.

I filled in the last fortnight with long poetic wanderings. Macca was working at Redenbach's on the Tambo and I rarely saw him.

One splendid day, Mrs Greenfeast lent me a novel called *Jane Eyre*, and I took it over hill and hollow, until I reached the road along the foreshore where Macca and I had walked, it seemed, so long and long ago. Sitting in a small damp leafy glade, with my back against a gnarled branch of ivory-green wood, I read all day, enchanted by the melodious romance, the staid yet tragic story of those two lovers who spoke so beautifully. I marvelled at Jane, who kept so firmly to one line of conduct all her life. I also, with excitement, determined to do so; but felt that I had not the miserable dignity of a governess's profession to uphold me in my wanderings. It was sunset when I closed the book and sat with it, and a headache, and a slow-beating heart in the elfin wilderness. The sea flashed into gold before me, and two fishing-boats fled across it, aboriginal with shadow.

Many afternoons of promising storm hung over the land. The sky leant dark-breasted, heavy with rain; the sand on the shore was a flashing white, articulate with signs; every leaf in the bottlebrush-trees above me was distinct and sad in the bright sunlight, but athwart the sun and over the storm-dark water in the black sky flashed the red portal of lightning. From columns of straight cloud, the hasty figures writhed and fled.

That night I looked with a keener sorrow into the faces of Jim and Macca, as they sat about the fire with us, knowing that never again should I see them. I listened to their plans for the years ahead with pain and despair.

I said, "Let us go down to Averdrink tonight, Macca. I hear that it is not occupied yet. Let us go down and spend hours there, think-ing of the past, for I know that when I go from you I shall never see you again as you are now, as I have made you . . . the poet-youth, ideal and innocent-thoughted."

"Yes, Steve, we will, just for the sake of the old days."

In the darkness, we lit a fire in the hearth, and fed it with the mantelshelf which the white ants had now entirely destroyed. Lying on the piece of old matting, which billowed up eerily, as of old, we spoke of the past.

The light of the fire flowed over Macca's face and his features looked splendid bathed thus in the glow.

"Macca, we are beautiful creatures, of a frail loveliness, caught in a web of destruction. Have you always understood the torment of my heart when I have been with you? If you have, then there is a debt that you must pay in the years to come, because you compre-hended my agony and did not stay to help me. You don't know to what you are contributing; you cannot imagine the ends of our being. Many pictures haunt me here, in this room to which we have come for memory's sake.

"The song of alien Peppino is not, to me, more rich than the roses you brought me. I shall keep their dried petals for long, and even when they have gone from me they shall be powerful. Behind us, in the darkness, the years are waiting. It is remarkable to me that you are not saddened by their coming. Don't you understand that they are parting us, and are you not sad about it?"

"Well, even if we are parting, we will see each other again, Stevie Talaaren." The boy's face was contented as he looked into the fire. "I shall see you here next year, I think. Of course, I don't know what will really happen. But if I am in Gippsland I shall return to Metung in spring and meet you and work with you, *mia cara sposa,* my one love ever. But now that the crops have finished here, I must get out and find work, too. Where are you and Blue going?"

"Home, first, and then up to pick hops at the foot of the alps. Blue doesn't want Jim to know. Anyhow, we may not go there. We have almost decided to go on up to the Murray River first, to look for orange-picking. The grapes will be ready at Rutherglen soon, too; but, no, I'd never work in Rutherglen after that experience we had."

"Well, remember when you are working in the alps, Steve . . . Metung in spring; I shall be waiting for you."

"No. I shall not see you here when I return. We are parting now forever. And you don't grieve at all. You don't mourn for all that I stand for, although it is passing. Don't you see that I am not woman, but youth, your youth, and it is passing. With me will go some of the safety and happiness and innocence of your life. Why are you not grieving? 'Why art thou silent!' Well, I shall never marry. You will all marry; yes, that's true. I feel it. Blue will marry; Jim will marry, and you too. But I, no, I shall never marry. All my years shall be dedicated to mourning for our youth."

"What is our youth, Stevie Talaaren? I often think that I am a very old man. We don't know anyone young. They're all old with worry and fear, inside. I shall never marry, either. But you say I will, and perhaps you know best. Our love has been pure; I've clung to that word ever since we spoke it together. And now I haven't any more love to give you. What I gave was rich, as rich as the sea, and as pure as the long-awaited Gippsland rain. But now I'm emptied of it, and your love to me seems too sickly sweet and sentimental. I want a cold feeling from woman, for a change."

"What does that matter to me? Do you remember that night I stood with you at the corner of the fence and cried because some day you would die and I should mourn when I heard?"

"Oh, yes, I remember that night."

"Well, then, a more terrible sorrow has come to me since then. I have been thinking that when, at last, you die, I shall hear and not care. It will have been too far away and long ago. That's really terrible . . . terrible to think that all our self-importance is just self-preservation gone mad. Every day that I have spent here I have used up my entire mind in an effort to chain this part of my life to me so that I shall never lose it. I cling to every moment with a pitiful passion. A certain grain of earth, a peculiar wind blowing, a look on your face, the very sole of my shoes, with their polished edges, haunts me. I am astounded by the intricacy of their being. Don't you feel all this, too?"

"Steve, I have never heard anyone talk like that before."

"What is going to take the place of the lost years? I must wait and see. I cannot think that the pain and the ecstasy with which I regard everything can die, at last. I fancy myself to be mounting up in feeling from the observance of these lowly things to the worship of something greater. What could be greater? What is there greater than time?"

Towards dawn, when the fire was greying, we left Averdrink and walked through the sweet-smelling grass to the post-and-rail fence between us and the bark hut.

"It is true what I said, Macca. I shall never marry. You and Jim and Blue will marry, but I . . . never."

"No, you may not, Steve."

It hurt me to think that he took my vow of faithfulness so calmly.

I spent most of the days left to me at the house of the Buccaneer. He was out late at night, netting, and came home just before I left, joyous with the sympathy of the Black Serpent.

"Wa-aah!" he said, striding in. "Waa-ah!"

Taking the dripping oilskin off his back, he twisted the rain out of his sea-golden moustache; his eyes stole slowly sideways in the wrinkled flesh of the eyelids, and he quivered with a kind, passionate mirth as he looked at me. He had a high lordly ridicule for all unmated ones of the world.

The Black Serpent flung herself on his chest and they kissed with the full measure of twenty years of married life and seven children pressed down and running between them.

And when they kissed, they looked at me and laughed. "Ah," said their mutual look, "you poor lonely beggar, you envy us! Go out, find yourself a mate, and rejoice with us!"

I was so impressed that I determined to do so. Only my ideal love for Macca held me back.

Macca came to see us again. He had been to Bairnsdale, and was changed by a few days' holiday and the local dances. A new dance obsessed him. He called it "The Charleston".

"I practise it every night in the cowshed," he explained, doing a few rudimentary steps before our awed eyes. "And it's so hard to do that it fascinates me." Turning his toes in and squirming he whistled a quick tune to which he moved. "That's called 'The Belle of Barcelona'. It's just out. I do the Charleston to that. It's an American dance."

"Oh! American! Pooh!" Blue and I said. Anything American was anathema to us. We thought it strangled the originality of our native land's expression.

But now was Wordsworth forgotten and the fairytales despised, while the champing Charleston was performed before us and talked about, until I was sick of it.

Then, for a whole week, he didn't come to the bark hut at all, although he was working only a mile away from it. And in three days' time we were leaving Gippsland. So one night, broken down with loneliness and the sense of being unwanted, I walked down the track where the wattle-bird had cried to me, "Go back . . . go back!" It led to the farm of Redenbach for whom Macca was working.

I walked there with a sense of fear and guilt. Big logs lay about on the rough grass, and small trees had fallen over the track. I sat waiting until I heard the rapid regular stamp of his mare's hooves, then I arose and walked out to meet him.

> "Why art thou silent! Is thy love a plant
> Of such weak fibre that the treacherous air
> Of absence withers what was once so fair?"

I cried, halting him.

"Well, Steve," coldly.

"Come, dismount, and walk with me through the forest of the warning-bird." It was my habit to speak dramatically when I felt that I was despised and unwanted. I felt that the language, if nothing else, would hold his attention.

He got down and walked silently beside me.

"Macca, why have you never been near me this week? What is it? Are you tired of it all?"

"I'm working hard now, Steve. Also, I go to a good few dances."

"That's how it is, you see. You are forgetting me, and gladly. I am only a bundle of books opened here and there to let a verse show through. I am not, I know, like other women. You could scarcely take me out into the company you have been in lately. But then, you could scarcely bring that company to me, either."

"I just want to enjoy myself and be happy, Steve. Life is so serious with you. And what does it all mean?"

"This!" Stopping in front of him, I kissed his cold mouth that trembled under mine. He stood pale, silent and unhappy for a moment afterwards, as though I had awakened within him a voice to which he listened troubledly.

It was then that a full poem came to me, singing and swirling through my mind in loud ecstatic tones. It was imperfect at that moment; it needed to be fashioned. Oh, if only I could say it to him now, and win him by the power of poetry! I felt sure that he must succumb to the truth and penetration of the verse.

> Ah, what a lip of silence was that wood,
> Withered and never opening into song
> Or laughter; dark and quiescent, it stood
> Upon its knotted limbs, a whole life long.
> Ah, the dark wood, and your great pale head drooping
> Heavily in its gloom, than clay roads whiter,
> Wrinkled and scarred by thought weals and the trooping
> Of rough emotions . . . You, the contemptuous fighter,
> Weakened and shaken and sickened by my kiss,
> With wide frail eyelids wavering at their doors
> And brave lips sad and wordless. Oh, was this
> My friend, that would not be a friend any more?
> Blue and gold sang the sky, above, about and under
> A skeleton strife of wings, and so set screaming
> Bands of black robber-birds that passed in thunder
> Leaving you still at heart, trembling and dreaming.
> I was afraid and lost, with hurt eyes prying
> Into the very Grail-heart of your pain.
> What was this I'd awakened, that was crying
> In bitterness, to be asleep again?

"Let us keep going, Steve," he said at last, rousing himself; and silently we moved on through the bush. As we came out on to the main road with its rolling grit underfoot and the ochraceous cliffs showing faintly in the twilight, a tired little blackfellow leading a tired little horse stepped up to us and said mildly:

"Excuse me, do you happen to have seen any cows wandering around through the bush here?"

"No."

"No, none at all, and I've just come from along the Tambo," added Macca.

"Oh, I've lost them, then, I suppose. They might be over at Swanreach. I suppose I had just better keep going. Thank you." And he moved off, his white breeches and black face making a fine fresco against the cliff.

I had to halt at my turn-off, for Macca put his foot in the stirrup and mounted the mare.

"So you are going away down to Metung, Macca?"

"Yes, Steve, I'm going to have a look in on my mother and father."

"Will you come out and see me on Sunday at the bark hut? It will be my last Sunday here."

"I may, for a few moments, Steve."

"Macca! What have I done to you?"

"Nothing, Steve. I said I would come and see you."

"But with what coldness . . . with what indifference!"

"When I first met you, Steve, your motto was 'To the indifferent comes all good.' "

"Ah, but I can never practise it."

"So you are only jealous of a conscious mind effort I have made, and in which I can stand firmer and longer than you."

"Macca, I love you!"

"That's a sort of intellectual full-stop with you, Steve."

"Well, what can I say? Come out to the bark hut, if only for a moment, on Sunday, please. Soon, you know, I shall be going away; on Wednesday morning, Blue says. But, it appears to me that you have started on your journey away from me before I have even thought of packing up."

"I'll see. If I can possibly come, I shall do so; but I'm cow-cockying now, Steve, and I don't get any days off."

On Sunday a brilliant bay horse brought him over to see me as he had promised. In the cold windy afternoon he dismounted and stood on the dusty patch outside the bark hut. He smiled with shy pride when I praised the bay.

He sat on the bark bed and talked to us. Blue looked beautiful that day. Her hair waved back from her brow in black and gold undulations. Macca stared at her with delight. Then he looked at me, and laughed. I looked like a harassed country compositor, as I stood with a white cotton smock over my khaki overalls and a broken green eyeshade tilted over one ear.

He was off again within a half hour, galloping the bay across the golden grass, while I, alone and forsaken, sat in the blackened heart of an old dead tree on the hill. How cold the wind blew and how

I shivered with sorrow as I sat there in the sunlight! I felt physically weak and exhausted by unrequited love.

"When shall I be loved?" I thought. "Ah, Lauré, Lauré, I am young and my plate is empty. . . ."

I tried to fill it on the Monday night. "Jim," I said, "I'm going down to see Macca. While I get ready, will you make me up a pancake mixture in a billy; and put the frying-pan, some dripping, cocoa and sugar into the kit-bag?"

The good chap did this for me, and when I was ready I slung the bag over my shoulder and set out, with the mouth-organ, playing Peppino's litany.

Blue heard me as I passed, with rattling billy, pan, cups and mouth-organ. She was sitting alone in the bush on a log, trying to decide whether she should yield to her faithful lover and get married when she arrived home. He was growing tired of the long wait, and although he had resumed his letters to her, it was with a desperate note that he complained.

I played the mouth-organ outside Redenbach's until Macca came out. Then, in my egotistical fashion, I led him away along the road and lit a fire. Over it, I made the pancakes, which by now were mixed with gum-leaves and hard twigs. Something went wrong with them; they were too heavy to eat. Macca flung them out into the bush and they fell with a dull thud. Some wild creature of the night gave a cry of agony a moment or two afterwards and Macca shook his head at me in condemnation.

On the whole, my festal gathering was not a success. I had hoped to win him with the secrets of my culinary arts, but in that, too, I failed. So with little to say, I packed up my gear and went away home.

"I'll be over to see you tomorrow night, Steve Hart," Macca called out after my defeated form.

The last night! I made ready. I spent the day in prayers to my deities, the wood gods, and kept my heart stainless. But when Macca came, I was speechless. A reckless spirit seized me and I talked, as I had talked to Kelly, of wild journeys and strange meetings; of comical happenings to come and possible romances I might have.

"And you, Macca, where are you going to when you finish up at Redenbach's?"

"To Orbost, perhaps, Steve, for the maize. I might look up that mate of mine, Streak, again. We'll travel together."

I put my arm about him, and drew him to me. He put me away.

"No, Steve. I've been in Bairnsdale lately with a girl I know. I can get that sort of love from her. But from you I want the pure emotion of the mind."

Saddened and broken by this revelation, I said, "I shall give it to you, Macca. Only promise that you will write to me. Swear that you will answer my letters. I shall write poetry to you, and ask only one thing—that you will answer me."

"I will write, and next spring, when you come back to Metung, we shall wander together as we did this year."

"You will truly write?" I mistrusted him; remembering Kelly, I could not believe that he would write. I thought, "The Gippslanders abandon you to your fate, once you have left. And I can't force him to write; I can only implore in the name of flower and leaf, in the name of all beauty, that he write to me."

"I shall write."

"I am content."

Since we had to be up early in the morning, I let him leave early. He led the black mare and I walked by his side, saying to myself:

"Even so, in the old pioneering days, my grandmother walked beside my grandfather in this country of Gippsland. Have I failed them? They walked through life together, facing it gamely. They married early, at eighteen and nineteen. My grandmother had two children when she was my age. She had fifteen before she was finished. And here am I, anxiously, honestly, wanting to walk through the hard days of our country, in just such a fashion, with this Gippslander; but I'm not wanted. It's true. The Gippslanders don't want me. Gippsland doesn't want me. I am despised because I work in her fields, and her sons cannot understand me. I bewilder them, and they weary of me."

I wept as I walked with him across the soil of Gippsland, and through my tears I saw the Southern Cross glittering, and the luminous fire of the Milky Way above seeming to roar aloud in the heavens, to be spuming and foaming over with light. My heart ached. O Time, how vast you are and how pitiless. Well, fly then with me to the end, and from these human eyes blot out the moon and the stars and the human faces I have loved. Surely I shall find escape in the spirit!"

"Macca, will you stand somewhere near the road as I pass tomorrow morning, so that I shall see you?"

"No, Steve, I am going far out into the bush for the day."

"But I shall see you here again next spring?"

"Yes."

"And you will write to me?"

"Yes."

"Then why am I sad? Why do I feel that all is ended? Well . . . kiss me, and go. I shall not see you again, like this."

He kissed me calmly; leapt into the saddle, turning the mare in the harsh gravel.

"Good-bye, Stevie Talaaren!"

"Good-bye, Macca, my one love ever!"

He cantered off into the bush. Gone! I leant over the sliprails, dull with pain.

Suddenly, a reaction set in, mercifully. I felt quite glad, freed from tyrannous bondage that was no fault of Macca's. If only this could have endured! It lasted all night, a calmness, a coldness and a feeling of being sufficient to myself. "So this is how other people feel always," I thought. "They don't appreciate their fortune." In the morning my heart was aching desperately. My chronic complaint had started again.

We passed Redenbach's on our way to Bairnsdale; Macca was not there. I held Blue's small yellow hand all the way. Jim sat beside us, grinning cheerfully, imagining that he would be with us as soon as we got work.

Into the train we clambered. Jim blocked all the light out of the window and could scarcely be extricated from his precarious position, as he lingered saying a long, long good-bye to us.

"Well, Blue, write as soon as you get word about work."

"Right-o, Jim."

"Good-bye, Steve."

"Write to me, won't you, Jim?" I was too ashamed to say, "Tell me all about Macca, won't you?" But I hoped he understood.

"Good-bye, dear little creatures!"

The bell rang out hoarsely. "O, farewell! farewell from the country of Gippsland! You came in mourning to this, the land of your fore-fathers, and you go in mourning, and shall weep forever. O come not again to Gippsland! Return not, lest she give you sorrow that will bear you down even unto the grave! Give her farewell forever if you are wise!"

"I cannot, O Bell, I cannot. I have a tryst to keep in springtime!"

"Give her farewell forever if you are wise!" chanted the bell.

Outward drew the train; the station faded and Jim was lost to view. The new painful life started for me. I sighed and leant back, sick-hearted.

THIRD PART

NO MOON YET

I

I SAT under a shelf of chaotic literature in the dark old room at home, and on stiff linen paper I printed, with a fine pen, long, delicate letters to Macca. One was answered during the weeks we stayed at home, going through our comic mime on the red and white flagged floor, before the streaming eyes of Mia, to whom Karta Singh and Akbarah Khan were now as familiar as brothers.

On the day Macca's first letter arrived, I felt that the heavens had opened and the saints stood before me. I sat day long staring at it, cherishing every remote word:

I sat far round on the bluff near Greenfeast's the other day, Steve, and a poem of Adam Lindsay Gordon's came into my mind.

> "With short, sharp violent lights made vivid,
>   To southward far as the sight can roam,
> Only the swirl of the surges livid,
>   The seas that climb and the surfs that comb.
>
> "Only the crag and the cliff to nor'ward,
>   And the rocks receding, and reefs flung forward,
>   And waifs wreck'd seaward and wasted shoreward.
> On shallows sheeted with flaming foam."

I remembered the old days in the bark hut. Jim tells me that you intend going up to Mildura. I wouldn't advise that, because I hear it is burningly hot in summer. I may go to Orbost with Streak, although, speaking paradoxically, I don't want to go.

These two pages, ending coolly and evasively, fired me to write longingly and passionately, praising not him, but all the beauty I saw through my love of him. But to all my gilt- and deckle-edged scraps of yearning and sorrow and poetry, no other answer came.

We became acquainted with an old drover, whom we called T. O'B., and he took us out one day to a ranch-house (so called) owned by a well-known Australian cattle-king. In the library there,

I found a book of Gordon's poems, among them, "The Swimmer". And learnt to cry with that sad singer,

> I would that with sleepy, soft embraces
> The sea would fold me—would find me rest.

T. O'B. was intensely interested in our wanderings and encouraged the spirit in us by telling tales of his own youth spent on the fields of Coolgardie and Kalgoorlie.

The time neared for our departure, but in the hope that a letter would come from Macca, I asked Blue to defer the day.

"We must go soon," she replied. "The bins are given out on the 28th. It's the 25th now, and I'd like to go up on to the Murray River and see if there's any orange-picking to be done there."

A distrust of the hop-picking had made us decide to take a train up there first, and find out how things stood.

"I am not well," I said. "Wait another day." It was a long warm Australian morning; the tall sapling in the garden bristled with long grey twigs and rattled its harsh leaves in the wind; the garden was dry from lack of rain, and the bricks around the beds had fallen down for lack of binding mud. Through the cool open slit of the window I peered outward. The postman passed, leaving no mail. He passed in the afternoon, again, and again left no mail.

"Well, let us get up and go," I said heavily.

We sat in the dusty railway carriage in the heat of the grey afternoon, and I noticed that we had both grown fatter. Blue wore my double-breasted coat, and I wore her red sweater, so that I might capture from it some of her beauty. Blue was quite stout, and her handsome face shone. Her gold bracelet spun on her wrist whenever she raised her hand.

Out from Dandenong we flew, on electric wheels, past the shriek and the burnt bones of the bacon factory, and into the city where we took the train that was to carry us up to the Murray River. All the afternoon, squeezed between tall, lean, handsome Australian farmers, who wore expensive tweed suits and read good books, we rushed along through the stark country with a "Whooosh" and "Aw" and "Rattle-trapple, whattle-winkle-gapple" as sidings were passed, with uneven shrieks from the timbers of the buildings and the speed of the locomotive.

It was night when we reached the thirsty town of Numurkah. We saw much sand and a few pepper-trees guarded by wire-netting on the platform. Some youths whistled to us, expecting they knew

not what. I promptly brought them to heel and bade them carry
our heavy cases and "blueys" to the nearest hotel. They giggled and
wondered at us, but we were unperturbed and left them standing
on the hotel doorstep.

The Murray River mosquitoes tore us apart all night, but rain
fell softly and dampened the sand for our tired eyes next morning.
We circled around, looking for work, in vain; and then spent one
humiliating hour until the train was due, talking with last night's
cavaliers, trying to make poets and wanderers out of them, to intro-
duce them to their psyche and show them the immortality of man.
But a more dolorous group of gigglers I have never met. I hope
they are all members of the local football team by now, and could
not wish them worse.

Thankfully, we left the flat dry town and the train took us
through country silent and glassy with the heat. Old ladies in
shining black dresses sat in the carriages with us, and children
moaned fretfully with the heat until the mothers arose and brought
them a drink of lukewarm water from the carafe in the corridor.

We changed trains at Seymour, and the police there, remembering
us, intimated that we should move on. The station-master made out
a rolling-stock ticket for us, since there was no passenger train until
the next day, and we were sent on board a cattle train, as a couple
of dark horses, and slept until we reached Benalla. Seymour had
reserved beds for us at a hotel in Benalla. It was early morning
when we got into them. As we undressed, we stared at ourselves in
the long spotted mirror; two wild-looking, stalwart young fellows
with broad chests, black and gold hair and crooked brilliant faces.

We slept until the hotel proprietor knocked us up to eat cold
toast and thick butter in a hot dining-room; then, with bilious
stomachs and fallen hopes, we went to the post-office and sent Mia
a postcard describing our journey.

When the train was due for Wangaratta, we sat on the railway
station talking quietly, while a team of youths stood around, wondering at us, but not daring, because of our suave air, to venture an
opinion on our sex. Our bulging muscles fresh from the pea paddocks
impressed them.

Blue brought out her fiddle when she was in the train and began
to play. An old-timer very politely asked her if he might play it.
She handed it over and, holding it low down on his knee, he played
old bush tunes while he looked absently out on the dry face of his
country. Sorrow was in my heart and my eyes stared dimly and
mournfully at the steppe-like country through which we passed.

At Wangaratta we got out and bought some fruit. The alpine train didn't come for us until evening, so we took the fruit down to the dry river-bed, where the lonely grey bathing sheds stood under silent gums, and there we washed and ate and waited for the hour.

The alpine train was packed with people and, turning off from the main line, travelled into a new land, for us. We went through long grass which we saw as the light flashed over it, and then into a narrow valley between great ranges. The air grew chiller, lighter, making me feel suddenly free of heart.

Under a giant range we stopped in the darkness and got out. A lorry driver collected us and put us on board with about forty others. Blue took out her mouth-organ and played Peppino's waltz among the strangers, and they sang it with her as well as they could. Along the winding road we drove, smelling the dry mountain dust in our nostrils, until the horses turned in at a large white gate, through which we rattled, and stopped. Men and women got down, greeting those who were waiting for them. A clerk holding a paper asked our names.

"Steve and Blue Beesknees? Oh, you two go down to the men's section," said he.

"But we're girls," we protested and the unseen company around us roared with delight.

He took us to a large, empty, lonely building called a "section"; one cubicle of that section was ours. A large straw mattress lay on the boards that formed the wide bed; these were nailed three-quarters of the way across the room, about two feet off the ground, leaving a small space in which to move around a little table nailed to the wall.

It was very clean and brightly lighted. Spreading out our blankets we got into bed. I lay beside Blue and thought of the old bark hut, of the silence there and the smell of the walls, and the stars burning above it in the Gippsland sky. Was Mackinnon keeping vigil there, tonight? Was he lifting to the moon his sad white face and dreaming of me? I lay and made fair images of love to him and burnt them in the fire of my heart.

How glorious the morning was! What a lovely country it brought to our eyes! It is best to come to a strange place in Australia in the dark of night, for the morning has a way of enchanting you with wild and imaginative lights, with flashes of dew on grass and moisture on wood, with gleam on galvanized iron roof and strange footprints on bush tracks.

We were in a narrow valley, rich and moist. On one side towered a high wooded range with red soil visible through the curling green timber, like sylvan hair on a reddened face. On the other side were heavily timbered ranges also, but some distance off. Above them in a white solemnly swirling mist stood a huge mountain of grey and yellow stone, with blue veins visible along its sides. The dry golden splashes of winter waterfalls were to be plainly seen at a distance of about six miles. A brilliant silence lay there, dry, white, steep and invincible.

An old man remarked, as I stood dreaming-eyed and stared at it, "There are wild horses up there. On a clear day you can see them, through glasses, galloping down the ravines." Through my mind their strong hooves thundered, their manes swept the ground and they raced down the white mountains of the imagination, in their neighing glory.

The river running through the valley had a frail swing bridge over its deep bed, and we went towards that, through a paddock filled with tents, where men and women lit fires and cooked their humble meals, while the children played and shouted with joy in the morning.

Beyond the swing bridge, in moist red earth, stood the exotic jungle of the hops, a little faded and old in the morning light, with bamboos and extravagant grass fastening on the rich soil about them. Such a light shone that morning on all that we saw; and it will never shine again. But from all new experiences that blinding light flashes outward, composed of the spirit of the place and the spirit of the one who comes to it.

Ahead of us sped two little dark men, one in dingy white breeches and high black boots. With what an air of proprietorship they examined the hops!

"It is the overseer," we said awedly, and determined to propitiate them.

Avoiding a walk in their revered footsteps, we went down cool, wet paths where the deep, high, beautifully grassed irrigation ditches carried the water to the hop plants. Long wet brown canvas pipes lay soaking in the mud and the sense of much water and great fruitfulness was everywhere in the valley. It stopped exactly at the foot of the ranges, the dry, silent and thinly treed ranges, where the red foxes crept from log to log and the brilliant parrots screamed in the trees.

At a bend in the path we met our overseer and his henchman, and doffed our careless air to him with respectful mien, but when he said, "Goot morning. Dis naice plice. You laike too much?" and showed us the rabbit he had trapped, we knew that we were among the "Good-bye Domenics" again, and rejoiced accordingly.

"*Buon giorno,*" we exclaimed. "*Molti Italiani qui?*" in our rough ignorance of the language.

"What? You spik Italian? O wonder! O joy! Are there many Italians here, you ask? Come with us!"

His name was Vincenzo and the porous skin of his very dark face exuded a constant flow of grease and a wrinkling into smiles, frowns and tears. Thin black hair parted in the middle fell about his sentimental brown eyes that swam in expectant moisture, and he hopped along so quickly that we called him the Little Black Flea. *Pulcinellaniera* was the nearest we could get to it.

He led us to the last, loneliest, loveliest, apart section on the property and said, pointing to it, "Dis where Italy men dey stay!" Sir, we need no telling. Those bright shirts fluttering from the line, those blue, red and green socks, velvet pants, striped under-clothes, and calico berets had signalled the fact to us as we came from the foot of the ranges. Also a heap of spaghetti cartons, with a sprinkling of magpie bones and an occasional fox's leg mingled with the backbone of a dingo, tell us that we are once more among the Italy men.

They peeped shyly out of their bunks as we stood at the door, and said liquidly and lazily to our escort, "*A! belle ragazze, davvero!*" "*Molte grazie!*" we replied politely, and went back to our section.

We idled away the morning among friendly people and were enchanted by the circumstances we found ourselves in. The women in the section battled with smoky fires and pots and pans. We ate bran and honey, which doesn't need cooking. A good few of the hop-pickers were city people, probably descended, like ourselves, from bush stock.

In the opposite cubicle two pretty sisters were living. They had the long golden hair of fairytales and plaited it around their heads. A thin woman with rolling eyes, false teeth and glasses was next door, and farther down in the shadows lived an interesting motley crowd of gipsies. At the very end of the section a beautiful ringing laugh broke out every few minutes. It was like the cry of the wattle-bird that used to come and sing in the garden at Averdrink every morning.

"What a beautiful laugh," we said. "Ah, that wattle-bird, Blue. Do you remember him? What will Macca and Jim be doing now? Blue why can't we write and tell Jim to come up here? Wouldn't he enjoy it all?"

"No, he would have given us a bad name. You'll see . . . we'll have a hard job, as it is, to convince people that we are only adventurous wanderers."

A few hundred more people arrived by the afternoon train, and many old acquaintances seemed to be renewed merrily and with such joyousness that we wondered why we had not come to this enchanting place as soon as we were freed from school.

At noon, in the clear mountain heat, we stood among several hundred pickers, waiting for the numbers of our bins to be called out. We stood on the green grass together, wearing wide khaki trousers, coloured shirts and wide felt hats with snake-skin bands. In fact, I had snake-skin over every bare patch I could find. A skin around each wrist, one about my neck, another about my waist and one around my hat. And they are evil things to wear. The malevolent strength and hurtfulness of the snake lingers in them forever and closes in on the hot flesh with a musky power that feels deathly. One old fellow said to his mate, "They look like a couple of blokes outer Zane Grey."

That made me unhappy. I was always unhappy when the purely physical in me was remarked on. There was no man, I felt, to come out from among the hundreds there and talk of my spirit and my imagination. Why weren't these attributes palpable?

The hop-picking started that very afternoon. It was then that the unkindliness of work showed itself to me. To come here, like a child, and walk around, staring at the strangers, going from fire to fire, laughing and joking, that was the ideal life, although it held a certain deadness of expectancy in it. Sorrow, dullness, quietness and maturity began when the frames of the bins were put up and their bag bottoms shaken out in a paddock down near a broken maize crib where purple castor-oil plants stood around, tall and spiny.

The first thick and beautiful vine fell from the wire with a loud rustle like that of a flying serpent, and it was a pleasure to pick up. But soon, with quick greedy movements, it had to be picked to pieces, and the dark leaves had to be cleaned out of the bin, because if they were too thick there the measurer refused to touch the hops. And that attractive and elfin dampness which we had loved early in the morning became tropically hot and moist at noon, and a sickly inferno, a swampish vat, in the late afternoon. We shifted continually, one at each end of the clumsy heavy bin, trying to hide from the sun in the darkness of the hop shades.

Tired, languid and unhappy, I picked mechanically and tore

down vines to the cries of "Pole-o!" around us. And the grim dark young pole-o shouted with an antic twinkle in his eye, "Pick up yer 'ops!"

"One!" the measurer shouted in the distance. "Two! Three! Four!"

"Pole-o!"

"Pick up yer 'ops!"

I felt the lack of humour and action, and my mind, filled with an *Encyclopædia Britannica* of life, seethed and teemed. Sensations and thoughts fell on my body in a rich rain, so that I overran with romantic desires and poetry; but no one wanted to hear of it.

Ah, the Italians! They came over to us. They pitched their baggy bins-cum-tents right before us, and what joy enters into the heart at the sight of them. The Little Black Flea leapt over to us and performed on his head, with cries of joy, as he introduced a tall, womanish fellow, as handsome as Blue, and as lazy-looking as myself.

"Dis Salvatore Gallechio." The handsome one, golden-faced, blue-shirted, raised his torn cap lazily and said in an Australian Cockney accent, "Ow are yer? Pleased ter meet cher."

"What? Are you Australian? Italian? What are you? Tell us, O golden face from the sun!"

"Oh, I came out from Italy wiv my people from Italy when I wuz young, you see? I lived in Fitzroy ever since. Picked up a bit of Italian from hearing them talking it at home. Of course I can't talk too well. There's a lot of Italians here. This bloke's name's Toni. Ain't he got wonderful eyes? *Dove sei, venga, Toni?*"

"*Dal Nord vicino al Tyrol*," said Toni shyly, his mauve eyes with their fair lashes rolling laughingly as he came towards us. We had never seen eyes like his before. They were a light purple in hue.

"There yar! I knew he come from somewhere near Switzerland. What eyes, eh? *Comme ti chiama tua mamma, Toni?*"

Toni laughed again, modestly. "*O, via, via.*"

"But she must have called you somethink! Well! See this little bloke 'ere," brisky pushing forward a short slender youth, "This is Pep. 'Ow are yer, Pep?"

"Arlright, thenk you," replied the lad, a mere child, with a serious honest face and the look of one destined to grow up in Australia, make money in her, marry in her and, in her bosom, carry forward a new race. He wore a huge hat, a light yellow felt, popular at that time, cocked on his head.

"*Agiusta il cappello, Peppino!*" said the Little Black Flea in a fatherly fashion.

"*Che?*"

" '*Agiusta il cappello,*' 'e said," answered Il Gallechio. "Fix yer 'at!"

Peppino fixed 'is 'at.

"*Andiamo!* Come on 'ome!" cried Gallechio and ran with the boys to the section, for it was now knock-off time. The measurer's hours were fixed, and any hops picked after the last measuring were left lying in the bins all night.

It was a herd-like sight to watch the pickers coming home. They broke out of the thick hop-fields in thin groups, thick groups, animated couples or lonely individuals. The lorries swept past with the fine horses straining and shining in the last glow of the sun. The fires glowed outside the tents; smoke arose from the section chimneys and the hop-pickers dined. We went over to the combined marquee-boarding-house-post-office which was kept by a big handsome man with a frank open face, white teeth and a small brown moustache. His sense of humour was intimidating.

"Well, boys!" said he, strong arms outspread on the counter. "What do you want? More dynamite?"

"No. Do you stock bran? We want a good quantity of bran."

"What's it for? Horses or poultices?"

"Ourselves. We eat it with honey. We shall want honey, too. A large tin of it."

"What?" He shook from head to foot. "Come on, out here, you fellows! Have a look at these human poultices! They live on bran and honey. They *live* on it!"

Drawing a large order pad towards him, he picked up his pencil. "Now, how many hundredweight of bran? How many pounds of honey? You'll need a lot, you know. Hop-picking takes the stuffing out of you."

Discomfited, we mumbled something and walked away angrily. He had drawn an amused crowd around us and through them we walked proudly.

But the tale spread, and in the early morning as we ventured forth in silk pyjamas and great-coats to perform the acts of nature, a large company awaited us in the vicinity of those places indicated for the performance, and from high up in the hop kiln, even, eagerly interested voices cried, "How's the bran going?"

That night, the handsome marquee-keeper had our wants provided for, very amply. He set before us, with a generous hand, a large sack of bran and a kerosene-tin of honey, from which we shrank with writhing bowels.

"We have changed our minds," we said calmly, "and have decided to live on bloater and bread and butter. Therefore, if you will please give us a small tin of bloater paste, one loaf of bread and a pound of honey, we shall be pleased to leave the bran and honey with you for obscure disposal."

The good handsome fellow laughed until he cried and we left him. As we sat in the lighted kitchen of the section, a tall ugly fellow came in and, sitting on a kerosene-case, began to sing a ditty.

> "Of all the little insects, I'd rather be a fly.
> I'd crawl into a dung-heap
> And live there till I'd die.
> For life is a loss, whatever you say.
> And I'd rather drink tea than work any day!"

He was, himself, fly-like in appearance, being over six feet in height, and so very thin that he folded up several times when he sat down on anything low. His faded gaberdine pants were too short for him, and his thin ankles rolled around in his long flat tan boots whenever he turned to look behind him. A long dismally-coloured coat folded wing-like over his arms, a large dusty hat with a coloured band of fly-like stripes running around it hung over an insect-like face, with cunning, crude features merging one into the other and making an indistinguishable and cruel mass at first sight.

When he had sat there, grinning, for a while, he broke out. "Ain't yer goin' to 'ave a cupper tea? No tea? Dontcher drink tea?"

"No."

"'Ow do yer live, then, if yer don't drink tea? Tea's life!"

We had secretly called him, in Italian, Mosca, the Fly, as soon as he came in.

"No Mosca," we answered, "we don't drink tea."

He said morosely, "Well, I'm goin', then. I hate people that don't drink tea. They're not human."

In rushed one of the little fair sisters from her room, crying out, "Oh, I know! I'm the same. Wait on, I'll make you a cup!"

Pulling a villainous face at us, Mosca waited.

Out of the starry night, through the open door, glided a short strong man with a mop of straight red-brown hair brushed in a thick fluffy sweep over the back of his head, and his face, old, plain and brutal, looked like a mask above his young virile body. He swung his hips and swaggered in a tight blue coat and well-pressed white trousers. His red-brown eyes sparkled and, in a light tripping voice, he asked for "Missairs Yearner".

"Oh, Major, is that you?" gushed the little woman with the rolling eyes, the false teeth and the glasses. She rushed out and greeted him effusively.

"Some one play music . . . we dance!" he announced in his squeaky giggling voice.

"Rudolph Valentino not dead when I alive," said Blue, taking the mouth-organ out of her pocket. Rising from the box, he took Mrs Yearner's lean form in his arms, and trod like a cat, with pounce and bounce, across the earthen floor.

Mosca groaned aloud. "But what about me bloody tea? Ain't youse blokes human? How can you live without tea? It's life! I'll die if I don't have a cup in a minute."

In the arms of the Major, the little woman revived and, throwing glances of languorous enjoyment through her glasses and giving ghastly dreamy grins of pleasure from her false teeth, she revolved before us in the dust.

"Orr, yer look awful, missus, yer look terrible. I can't stand it without a cupper tea," moaned Mosca.

Out ran the fair woman, carrying a large steaming cup. "There you are, stranger. Oh, you're just like me! I can't go on without a cup of tea."

Mosca took it without thanks, and sipped it slowly while he watched the prancing couple stirring up the dirt. "Arrh, they look better now! I couldn't stand them before. That woman looked terrible to me. But she just about passes now. Yairs, she'd pass.

> "Of all the little insects, I'd rather be a frog,
> And while the rest were working, I'd be in a holler log."

When the dance was over, Major, the Italian, sat down and talked to us for a while.

Next morning, early, he was at our door with a kerosene-tin full of ripe tomatoes, which he sold us for one shilling. In a reed hut over the river, he lived and cultivated this fruit on a little island there. The garden was well hidden from sight and was very prolific. Major was a malicious looking little fellow, a veteran of the Italian army in the Great War. This entitled him to respect among his fellows; but he was not a favourite, for his light, vindictive voice, his pink-gummed smile, wide and flexible, kept people at a distance. How he carried himself! Yes, with jaunty hips, broad shoulders, alert eyes, grim mouth and red-brown eyes gleaming under a hat of heavy Italian felt, he walked as we said *come un vecchio soldato*. We respected him, too, but we had a feeling that he didn't respect us, or anyone else.

II

OUR cash was getting low and our clothes dirty, so in the week-end we thought we would do some washing down at the river, and at the same time keep a lookout for pumpkins and ripe maize to fill the larder. We lit a fire on a small sandy island in the middle of the river and boiled our shirts, trousers and socks in the tin while the river, full from shore to shore with purple ranges, sang a rusty song over quartz and mica beds down through the willows, the poplars and the wattles. As we fed the fire, retreating back before the cascades of smoke, we noticed that beyond the river frontage lay a fine field of pumpkins and maize.

"How about a nice big dry pumpkin for tea, Bluey?"

And Blue said, "Too right; but wait till it's properly dark."

We did all our washing but the dirtiest things; these we tied up in a bundle and deferred until another day. The boiled clothes were fished out and set on sparse bushes to dry, and we sat by them, drowsing in the mother-song of the river. When the dew began to make the air moist, we folded up our clothes and waited a while longer. The green maize in the paddock had lost its sunny gleam, leaf by leaf, and the little tobacco-seed beds on the slopes of the grey hill had a fine mist of evening around them.

Now was the hour! We left our hiding-place and leapt out on to the largest pumpkin in sight.

"Well, Blue, we'll have to cook it here, because we haven't got a saucepan to our names."

"And wouldn't they talk, if they saw us cooking in a kerosene-tin!"

Wrestling with the cold rough stem, we tore the pumpkin free, then, bringing the kerosene-tin with some water in it up to the bank of the river, we lit a good fire under it, throwing on large logs in our exuberance. Cutting up the pumpkin, we threw it in, with a few tender maize cobs for good measure.

The fire roared, throwing flames and shadows across the grass, so dry and deep. How the pumpkin boiled! We sat laughing around the tin, talking about the good meal we were going to have, and of other nights when we would come into this larder of nature's and eat more and yet more pumpkin. Then the grass rustled underfoot, and a harsh voice said, "What are you two fellows doing with a fire here? This is my property. Did you know that?"

Standing to bushman's attention, with one leg crossed over the other, we drawled that we didn't know it, being strangers here.

"Well, that fire must be put out. It's off the river frontage and on my property, and it's endangering it. Come on. Put it out, now!"

The flames danced around us, and our minds danced with them, performing some quick gymnastics, while the tall old farmer eyed us angrily.

"Well, come on! Put it out!" Suspiciously, "What's in the kerosene-tin?"

"Our clothes. We're boiling them, you know, and soon we're going to hang them out to dry."

"Funny time to wash clothes!"

"What? Funny? Don't you know that clothes are best washed at night? And if you hang them out in the night air they get a wonderful colour; they bleach, they blench, they flinch, they shake. Try hanging out in the night air, yourself, sir, and you'll have a complexion like a lump of snow."

"Well, tip the clothes out now, and throw the water on that fire. It's a positive danger to my property. Come on now, get to work!"

Ah, well, if this was his property, that must be his pumpkin. What a pity! A great pity, indeed! And, the point of contention was this: does boiled pumpkin look like boiled shirt if it is hastily thrown on to a flaming fire?

"But pardon us, sir, if you would be so good, we should like to finish boiling our clothes. You see, we're hop-pickers from down the river, and if we don't get our clothes washed and dried tonight, we shall have to pick in the natural. You understand, as man to man?"

"I see. But hurry up. Are the clothes in yet?"

"Just a few. We want to add a few more . . . these here." I indicated a bundle of dirty socks, shirts and unmentionables which we had felt too languid to wash.

"Well, here you are, lad! Put them in, put them in, boy!" And, stooping, he picked them up and threw them in on top of the pumpkin.

"Ah, thanks!" we said, and the fire blazed up merrily. The odour of cooked pumpkin and dirty clothes was fervent in the air.

"Now just a few minutes more and they'll be ready to turn out. We needn't detain you, sir. We can quite easily put the fire out."

"No trouble, my boys, I'll just stand by in case you scald yourselves," said the farmer thoughtfully.

We thanked him again, and hunted around for our belongings before departing.

"Blue, have you seen the soap and my pocket-knife?"

"No," said Blue.

But the farmer had. He remembered flinging them in with the clothes and said he was sorry, but the light was bad. We agreed with him. We said, further, that everything was bad, and that washing at night was not very successful. He replied that he was glad to hear us agree, and that, from his point of view, there were many occupations far more moral than our present one.

"Now," said he, "come along, and get the clothes out. They must be boiled by now. Turn them out on the grass and throw the water on the fire."

"At your service, sir."

"Blue, bring along a stick." With this, we pulled out our garments, to which a mess of pumpkin clung. We averted our faces while we did this, and took the can as far into the shadows as possible, but the farmer followed us and sniffed around the washing. "Smells more like a dinner than clothing," he said. We lifted out large lumps of glutinous soap and pumpkin and gently agreed with him, saying that we were given to spilling much of our meals down our waistcoats, since on occasion a particular kind of palsy of the limbs attacked us. He was sympathetic, saying that we seemed to be unfortunate in every way.

When we had scooped out every dirty sock, piece of soap, knife, clothing and pumpkin from the water, we let it fall on to the fire, which went out with a savage hiss and many a crackling exclamation. The farmer gave us a civil "Good night" and went off, leaving us to our oats.

All this had taken place in a sort of natural amphitheatre, a dry warm slope, on which, unknown to us, lay many hop-picking lovers, who had been highly entertained by our comedy.

We now began to add to it by trying to explain the matter to each other and blaming ourselves heartily.

"Now look at our clothes! They're ruined! And what about that bar of soap?"

"Yes, but what about my pocket-knife? It's ruined, too. Look at the handle!"

"And you said we'd have pumpkin for tea. Dry golden pumpkin!"

"Well, we've got it. It's imbedded in our clothes and we can have pumpkin whenever we like, and it will always be dry and golden."

Dragging our melancholy load of kerosene-tin and ruined clothing behind us, we crossed the stage and disappeared into the wings of the bush, chanting our sorrows all the way home. And, long afterwards, the lovers left their dress-circle and came down to the hop paddocks to circulate the fame of our comedy, far and near.

The cry for weeks afterwards was, "What about a bit of nice dry golden pumpkin, Blue?"

Every night there were dances in the hall at the hop-fields, but we were too shy to go at first, and just hung around the door with the old men, the children, the dogs and ugly people of our own age. But at last Blue, in her Oxford-bags and red sweater, went in and was soon striding around superbly with a lithe Italian who afterwards danced his way into popular vaudeville at a theatre in Melbourne. I didn't get in at all, being a bit draughty about the feet. It was around the dance hall that we first met Charlie Wallaby, who was to provide us with a home for the long alpine winter.

Charlie Wallaby had the nervousness of a flash of lighting and a body like a blasted oak. Before him, came his hat. It stuck itself, soft and battered, into groups and moved up and down, following their conversation. It was old and green; thin stripes of the original grey band were still sewn on to it, and waved about in the wind. For years he had been flinging it to his dog Spot and saying "Go an' fetch it, Spot", so that it was no longer the hat he fetched back, but a battered and torn remnant. Charl put that remnant on his head at all angles. It was a circular sort of hat and very adaptable. In windy weather he wore it up at the front. In wet weather, the rain decided for him, and smoothed it down heavily over his eyes. When he rode on horseback, he tucked the sides in underneath and, with a point fore and aft, rode like an admiral on the bridge, in the broken saddle of his fine trotter, Capira.

When all else failed and gloom and sorrow filled the room, Charl tucked the brim in all around and stood before us with the small pot on his head and his wall eye flashing merrily, while the few teeth in his large mouth kept up a constant flow of saliva and walnut kernel. Charlie Wallaby was small, squat and immensely strong, and inconceivably hairy. The hair ran up over the top of his shirt in front and his gilt stud glistened from amid a thicket. It met his hair at the back of his neck and, by mutual consent, both disappeared into the collar of his coat.

He was a good looking fellow with a frank, merry mischievous face, and one wall eye that gave him a sly, crooked look. He had very thick black eyebrows and, for lack of front teeth, lisped. In character, he was honest, manly, clean, but fond of wild escapades, laughter and doing nothing. His favourite expressions were "Gee with! Gor blarmie! By joveth!"

He always had a pocketful of walnuts and, on the first day she

met him, Blue wrestled with him in the paddock, in front of a mob
of cheering pickers, and tried to get a nut from him. No man there
had even succeeded in wrestling a walnut from Charl. But, at last,
after a long, subtle struggle, Blue got one; and we thought that that
was a good omen.

We knew that he lived with his widowed mother on a large farm
down the road, and we often asked him to take us there to Sunday
night tea.

"Go on, Charl. Take us home with you," we implored.

"Gee with!" exclaimed Charl. "I got no home. What made yer
think I had, eh?" And he whisked his ragged coat pockets out of
Blue's clinging hands.

"Your good clothes, Charl," we said, tearing pieces out of them
and hanging them on the barbed wire around the sections. "We
know you're rich by the cut, or shall we say, the tear, of your
clothes."

But Charlie Wallaby fought shy of us.

Salvatore Gallechio and the Little Black Flea were our mates
throughout the hop-picking, and we had them well coached in the
duties of our lost James. They raised and lowered us over fences,
robbed orchards that we might eat the fruits thereof, and, panting,
struggled with our rotund forms over miles of rough river-beds. At
night they strolled through the exotic fields with us riding triumphant
on their broad backs, as lordly as Chinese mandarins. The willows
hung over the river, the stars rose. "But where," I cried to my
voluntary rickshaw boy, "is the moon?" "Ah," cried he, bending
under my weight and sweating copiously, "your excellency, *no luna
ancora!*" (No moon yet!)

This cry of his, from the heart of his despair under the burden
of my indifference, became, from that night onward, my cry. Whenever I thought of love, whenever I wondered on the coming of my
life's grand passion, I looked to the east and said, "*No luna ancora!*"
For me, the night was to be dark and moonless over a long period
of years.

The woman who had laughed like the wattle-bird sent us a message,
one morning, asking would we like to come with her and a company
of girls and a sprinkling of Italians for a picnic in the ranges. The
messenger added that a hamper of pastries had been sent up from
Melbourne. We leapt into the air and murmured that we would,
indeed, be glad to come.

The dusty white road sparkled in the hot sunlight and the blue leaves of eucalyptus hung above it like brooding scimitars. We bowed, laughing, to avoid them as we were carried under them on the long narrow lorry which rattled and bounced between the two light draughts that dragged it along. I sat on the very edge of the lorry beside Major and watched the road falling away from under our feet. When the Italian was not looking, I stared at, and admired, his leonine head of red hair which shook in time to the manes swinging back and forth on the shoulders of the light draughts. The sharp tip of a white handkerchief rose from his breast pocket. He sang in a delicate malicious little voice, showing his tongue between his yellow teeth, *"Son tornate a fiorire le rose,"* the song that Tom-catto had mewed at Metung.

"Ur-ur-rur!" groaned the lorry, flinging itself on to a large rock and staggering at the impact. The Italians screamed like women, and Major laughed and gabbled something in a dialect which we all hated, because we couldn't understand. Only the two girls sitting in front didn't care. Lola, who was very dark with Island blood, held her thick dry hair down against her ear, and Primo, who sat with her, stroked it with his long clever Italian hands, letting it fall, and raising it, hour after hour.

Mamie was waiting to drive the draughts as soon as we left the main road and sat intense, in her thin flowered frock, thinking about it. When we left the road she stood up, small and slim, wielding the long whip and dragging at the reins as futilely as a child. The horses ran through the tall dry grass that came up to their soft chins, snapping at it as they went; Mamie screamed with excitement, and the driver, Art, who loved her, stood up beside her, long, lanky, reckless and cynical. We rattled, laughing and singing, past Bosca's green walnut farm and down the hill to the river which was clogged with the rusty red dredges of some old mining plant. It was a little dark river running over slimy round stones speckled with mica. Primo, who was a mining engineer by profession, jumped down to pick up one of the stones and tried to discover whether the spots on them were gold or not.

"If I had a bedder knife, I would tell jolly quick," he explained to me, staring at me with his glorious lazy blue eyes. He looked very handsome, white and tired, in his black suit and wide black hat. He pulled his well cut vest down over his slight, attractive paunch and clambered back into the lorry.

We had climbed the grey stone mountain that rose above the hop-fields and sat down to eat near the dried-up waterfall. The city pastries were consumed in hungry silence, and Blue and I wandered off speechless, afterwards, to lie down languidly.

After a long hour of stupor, we heard feet scrambling over the rocks towards us. The grim black young pole-o, whose name was Digger, stood before us with his tall honest mate, Bill, beside him.

"We'd have been along hours earlier," Digger explained, "but Bill here had no stud for his collar. We had to go along to a shop in the bush and buy one." He laughed harshly and spat.

"What shop in the bush?"

"Oh, just under the ranges over there."

"Show us the stud, Bill."

"Here she is." Bill proudly displayed a stud cut out of a bit of dogwood, and we thought she was wonderful.

Digger laughed again and brushed the thick fringe of jet-black hair out of his eyes. He was a remarkable looking fellow; short, brown, sinewy and fierce, with a Mexican look about him, although he was of pure Australian parentage. He was intensely proud, independent and individual, and spoke and gestured with a rude masterfulness, fascinating to witness. At the mention of anyone fair, he rose to his feet and, spitting contemptuously, drawled vigorously and emphatically: "I *hate* fair people. I like the *black*. I'm *black* myself, and I wish the whole world was the same!" He sat down, then, with a harsh laugh and a proud stare.

There was nothing to do after the picnic but hang around and look at ferns, grey rocks and the yellow-white tracks of the waterfall. Now and then we met members of the picnic party, but they had paired off, leaving us alone, so we just lounged about thinking of more meals, while Digger and Bill treed possums. In the afternoon, the billy was boiled again, and we had what was left over of the hamper. At twilight the lorry was loaded up and we set out for home, with small stars twinkling above us and the sweet-smelling Australian dust rising into our nostrils. The girls lay in their lovers' arms, being kissed and caressed, but we swung our legs over the side of the lorry and meditated on where we were going to after the picking finished.

The following day we set out from our small cubicle to visit a Chinese garden set far away in the bush. The Little Black Flea and handsome Gallechio were to escort us. We had dressed up like lords for this visit, in sharply pressed trousers, tight immaculate coats, spotless shirts, silk ties and brightly gleaming shoes. The two Italians were similarly attired. The Black Flea wore the undress uniform of the Italian Fascisti, and sported on his chest its various orders, little tin frogs, birds, beetles, spiders and red-eyed butterflies. Bearing down on us, black-shirted and breeched, with leggings bearing it all stoutly below, he saluted: "Hé-ah! Hé-ah! Ha-la-la!"

"Cripes!" we exclaimed wonderingly. "The Chinese'll make for the bush when he sees us coming!"

The graceful Gallechio was dressed more sanely, but well up to Fitzroy standards, in a billy-cock hat and a be-buttoned suit.

The sustained labour of dressing, on such a hot day, had wearied us all so excessively that, when only a few yards from the camp, we fell down by the cool river and groaned. But on again we drove our melting legs, through long dry grass and burrs, thistles, docks and barbed wire, until we came to the Chinese garden.

"Hé-ah! Hé-ah! Ha-la-la!" shouted the enthusiastic Fascist.

The Chinese looked out and, on beholding the general of the Italian army before him, with Confucius only knows how many troops behind, he screamed and ran away into the bush. We decorously and honestly picked a few figs, leaving sixpence on the box at the door of the hut, and went home, feeling cheated.

Deserting our escorts at the door, we went to our cubicle to devour in silence. A light fly-like step, full of bounce, and sounding like giant suction pads taking hold of the floor, sounded along the passage. A hand shook the door fiercely and the voice of Mosca cried entreatingly, "Steve an' Blue, are youse there? I know youse are there, lovies? Come on, open the door and let us in. I know youse is sitting in there drinkin' tea. I want a cupper tea. Ain't youse got no tea? Don't youse drink it?"

"No, we don't. Go away, Mosca!"

"What do you want to call me Mosca for?"

"Because Mosca means a blowfly."

"Youse is insulting, lovies!"

"Aren't you always singing, 'Of all the little insects I'd rather be a fly'?"

"It's a lie. I'd rather be a tea-taster than the king of England. Let us in. Give us a cupper tea. Youse are not human if youse don't drink tea. It beats me. I don't know how youse live without it," Mosca said.

We sucked at our figs and stared at the door, beyond which stood Mosca and his eternal thirst.

"I can hear youse sipping something!" he cried with a wild earnestness. "Let us in!" He battered the door madly. "Open it up, or I'll put me leg over the wall and hop in."

"We'll cut your boot-laces if you do," we threatened.

"Youse daren't do that. Youse know me feet would asphyiate you," jeered Mosca. "Oh," he moaned, "won't someone give us a cupper tea?"

"We really have none, Mosca," we assured him.

The voice of the little fair woman rang out. "Come in here, you poor fellow. I've got one ready for you."

"Orr!" breathed Mosca, reeling towards her door, seizing a cup in his hands, and gulping the nectar loudly and gratefully.

We strolled down to the end of the section where the wattle-bird woman was laughing among the Italians. The stone full of mica lay on the table. At the door lounged a short fat Indian hawker with a clean white turban shaking on his head. Delighted to see him, and remembering Gippsland and its romance while conveniently forget-ting its sordidness, we flew to his side.

"Hello, are you an Indian hawker?"

"Yes, miss. Gauda Singh my name."

"Do you go to Gippsland, too?"

"Oh, yes, I know Gippsland too well!"

"Karta Singh! Do you know Karta Singh?"

"My word, I do. Karta Singh! Oh, yes, I know him for years."

What a bond between us! How we delighted in this meeting! He knew Karta Singh; he had looked across to Averdrink; he might have seen Macca and Jim. Eagerly, we questioned him. His white caravan stood outside. I picked up the stone with the mica in it, and held it in my hands as I talked.

"What stone you got there?" asked Gauda.

"We think that it is gold. Or perhaps mica. Do you know anything about it?"

"You show me. I know." Giving it to him, I drew near, and as I did he crushed me to his crackling whiskers and muttered inarticu-lately. "Crackle, crackle," said his whiskers. I wrenched myself free and ran away from him.

After that, we added to our stock phrases the term "Crushed to the crackles". We said it at odd moments, when all else failed; when there wasn't much food and we had to sauce it with a bit of humour; or when an incident took place that had some bearing on what I had suffered from Gauda Singh. Then it was that we looked at each other and murmured absent-mindedly, "Crushed to the crackles!", or "You come for fun?", or "Rudolph Valentino, he not dead while I alive". And, for myself, I had the cry of my soul, *"No luna ancora!"*

After a week of long oblivion in hard work, I found myself walking down a dusty road through thin green reeds. Blue walked ahead of me, between Digger and Bill, and I admired the courtly slimness of her legs in silk stockings and tight brown breeches. Over us hung the dusty gold mist of afternoon; on tall dead grey trees flocks of black and white ibis perched silently. Far down the road, under some green European trees, dust rose thick and pigs and cows wailed.

We were going down to Charlie Wallaby's sale; simply because there might be some food there. Sulkies, gigs and jinkers hung on tired dusty horses beneath the trees. Charl stood with his foot on the sliprails and scraped the bark off them.

"How's she going, Charl?"

"Pretty hot," said he, with an awkward smile, as though there were people around against whom he was conspiring, and he feared we would give the show away.

"Selling anything?"

"Thelling? I don't want to thell anything. I got nothing to thell."

"What's the sale for, then?"

"Oh, I thought I'd like to thee a few people for a change, you know," said Charl languidly, with a grin and a flash of his wall eye.

"Anything to eat around here?"

"Aw, good bit of grath down near the river. Gee with, youthe ith alwayth looking for food!" Charl turned his hat around so that the bow hung over his right eye. As he had said, there was nothing to sell. Rusting machinery lay around, and prospective buyers poked the stock wonderingly.

"Who's the auctioneer, Charl?"

Charl gave his hat a shove that brought the bow around to his left ear. "What do you want auctioneers for? Thereth enough people hanging around, ath it ith. I got nothing to eat, drink or thell!"

We walked home disconsolate.

III

THE hop-picking ended with a grand ball, a free supper, distributed cheques, and the growers' best wishes to the departing pickers. They went in hundreds. The Little Black Flea and handsome Gallechio went with them, after begging us to join them and try the grape-picking at Rutherglen.

"Ah, Aceldama!" we exclaimed airily, remembering the group of laughing vignerons outside the local bank.

"You no come, Steve and Blue?" cried the Black Flea, who really liked us. And the good Gallechio, who loved us with a brotherly heart, said. "Aw, why don't youse come? I don't fink you'll get any work around here wiv winter coming on."

"Rather winter than Rutherglen," said we and wept with them at their going.

The sections were empty now; the voices of the little children rang no more down the earthen passages, and the patient women toiled no more over pots and pans at knock-off time. Major and the rest of the Italians, who, it transpired, were permanent hands, came up from their section near the river and took up quarters down at the other end of our building.

We decided to stay on, for we had begun to love the alpine valley with a passion half sad, half humorous. Tons of free wood were provided by a generous grower and anyone was free to stay as long as he wished. Looking ahead, we saw a romantic and colourful winter, lit with humour and escapades.

The first care was to look for work around the district which, in addition to the hop-growing, specialized in tobacco, nuts, maize and potatoes.

Charlie Wallaby came into the kitchen shouting that he was in a hurry because he had to take in eleven pairs of rabbits to catch the train at Myrtleford.

"Charl, Charl!" we implored, clinging to his coat-tails, "May we go with you? Do let us go! Behold, here about us lies desolation and uncertainty. Gone are the *lares* and *penates* of this year's hop-picking and we are forsaken. Add us, then, to the illustrious eleven pairs and take us with you to the ford of Myrtle. There among cypress with a compress of laurel on our brows, we shall mourn the years!"

"Gee with, you blokes ought to be spruikers," said Charl.

"But . . . may we go?"

"Gor blarmie! I dunno!" said Charl, rushing out of our hands.

A certain weakness, a yielding in his voice, impelled us into the battered gig which stood as thin and shaky as a dragon-fly outside the sections. We were lying back among his tattered rugs when he returned, our feet on the bag that held the eleven pairs of defunct rabbits.

The old white mare between the shafts was called Blossom, which Charl had changed by a lisp into Blothum. Blothum carried us past farmhouses where dogs leapt up with teeth bared trying to snatch the rattling wheels of the gig. Charl cursed them and beat them down. "Gor blarmie, if one of them biteth through the harneth and

givth a good pull, the whole cabooth will break down. Get arp . . .
Bloth-arm!"

"If one of them hits the gig, we're done for, too, Charl, by the
look of it," I said.

Charl reckoned with a gay look that I was right. He whistled out
of tune and sang scraps of monotonous songs, happy and care-free
in the cold alpine air.

Rattling past Duane's pub, we picked up a dead cattle dog and
set it aside respectfully. A passing car had hit it. As we passed the
road that led to Happy Valley, a quiet black-whiskered man passed
us at a quick metallic trot, driving two small black brumbies between
the shafts.

"They run them in from a plathe called the Pinnacleth," explained
Charl, pointing with his whip to two stone steeples away at the end
of Happy Valley.

On we went, past the old mining cuts in the hills, which were of
all hues, fantastic Russian-looking hills of Tartar colouring; purple,
gold and red with an autumnal brown wash and streaks of white and
blue running through them. The wheels played a delicate and
comical music, so it seemed to me, and Blossom's hooves contributed
a stern note of duty. As we rattled along beneath these curious hills,
Charl, Blue and myself appeared to be clowns in an everlasting
comedy.

Crossing the railway line, I looked back across our stage to the
backdrop . . . the snowy height and sharpness of the far alps against
the clear blue sky. I was tortured by love and hatred at the sight of
their aeon-long lives and our short existences, and with that mingled
a feeling of triumph because I, at least, had lived, moved and spoken,
even though I paid for it with the loss of my life.

"Gor blarmie!" exclaimed Charl, drawing up at the railway
station. "It'th shut. Ah well, youthe have had a ride anyway," and
he flung the rabbits back into the gig.

"Now Charl, we want to do a bit of shopping here. We've got
to lay in a stock of groceries for the winter. You keep a look-out for
us as we come out of the shop. You mightn't know us, but we'd
know you anywhere."

"Well, if you didn't know me, you'd know Blothum," said Charlie,
and we left him and went in to order a large stock of food for the
winter.

We took out the cheque, cashed it, and put the silver in our
pockets.

"There's not much of it," I remarked gloomily.

"No, five pounds each to live on through the winter and pay our fares back home in spring."

"And then up to Metung for the pea-picking. Strikes me we won't be getting many groceries, unless we can find a bit of work somewhere."

"I suppose we'd better get some flour and stuff."

"Well," I said, "I think I'll buy a pair of those strong blue drill pants over there. My khaki trousers are worn out." That was twelve and sixpence.

"And a large bottle of oil," I added.

"What's that for?" asked Blue.

"Well, I want it to rub on my arms at night . . . keeps them strong and muscular," I explained.

"For what? Loafing around?"

"We may get work."

"I bet we won't. Anyhow, what are we going to get that will last us all winter? It's only April now. We've got to get something that will last."

"Oatmeal!" I exclaimed. "That's what we want. It lasts for years. Give us a small bag of oatmeal," I said to the assistant, "and a four-pound bag of sugar. There you are. That's enough. We can go through the whole winter on that. What more do we want?"

And stealthily Blue replied, "All the pumpkins and maize we can pinch, every potato we can bandicoot, and every invitation out to tea that we can persuade people to give us."

Laden with our purchases we went out into the street and looked around for Charl. There was no sign. Down the small country town we stared, but found him not. Circling, searching, spying, we sought a familiar figure that lay rolling back in a battered gig, with a green hat cocked over one eye, its bow swinging in the wind, and over the broad form, a torn coat stretched with walnuts.

Ever and anon there passed us slowly a respectable, finely clad gent in a gig; his small immaculate hat and well pressed trousers put us off the scent. But when he had gone past for the third time, Blue said, pointing to the white mare that lumbered between the shafts of the gig, "That's Blothum!"

"But surely the sartorial perfection holding the reins is not Charlie Wallaby?"

We ran after him, shouting and waving our arms. Blothum pulled up with a jerk and we gazed . . . on a new man.

Charl, arrayed in his bush glory, sat idly waving the whip and trying to look unconscious of his sudden metamorphosis. On his head sat a small felt hat of a battle-ship grey colour. It was the type of hat that small boys wear on Sunday. On a black ribbon around it was stamped, "H.M.S. *Bellerophon*" in gold thread. This seemed to suit Charl's wall eye and the long fringe of black hair lying on his brow. He chewed walnuts as he looked at us, and a foam of kernel lay on his lips.

"We didn't know you at first, Charl," we explained shakily.

"By joveth, you couldn't mith me, you thed, and there you are . . . I got you bushed right in the thity." Charl bent down and languidly tore a ticket off the cuff of his new trousers. It fell at our feet.

> Barb-wire twist. Battler Brand.
> Guaranteed for ten minutes.

Or something after that style. As he got down to walk the street and parade himself, we deftly dragged the ticket off his hat.

> Small boy's best English felt, 2/11

and a large placard from his coat.

> Dingo-death. Try our dingo bait.
> It fills to kill.

When he had gone, we leapt up into the gig and found Charl's old togs under the seat, neatly concealing a large bag of mixed biscuits which we rattled under each other's noses. Taking the reins, we manoeuvred Blothum down the street to where the river ran wide and shallow across the road. In the middle of the stream, we ate the biscuits, until Charl ran down to us and, standing on a flat stone, called out, "Come on, Blothum . . . come on!" The miserable animal obeyed his voice and, turning back despite our tugs, she landed at Charlie's side. He got in and grabbed the biscuits.

"Where are we going, Charl?"

"Don't you two want to look for work?"

"Yes, we do."

"Well, the Buffalo River valley growth maithe and I thought we could go down it ath far ath Ding-dong-down-in-the-dale, and thee all the growerth."

"What a name! Say it again!"

"Ding-dong-down-in-the-dale! What'th wrong with it?"

"What does it mean?"

"Oh, I dunno. They reckon back in the early dayth, thome of the old thettlerth lotht thome valuable thtock there and they'd never have found them only they heard the bullockth bellth ringing ding-dong-down-in-the-dale. So when they thettled there, they called it that."

"What sort of place is it, Charl?"

"Orr, bithy thort of town, yer know!" Charl grinned and lashed out at Blossom. "Git arp, Bloth-arm!"

Buffalo River valley was one of the saddest, dreariest, loneliest places I had ever been through. I had heard that the Buckland, which lay in the opposite direction, was almost as bad. In this valley the houses had their backs to the sunset which covered them with a horrid red glow. The few places we saw were of red brick, the large homes of the prosperous growers, and the crimson clay had taken on the last mournful tinge of the sunset, chill with winter. And, ah, the loneliness of the bare hills around, with a few split trees and silver grasses waving on them. One might grow to love it, if he had been reared in comfort there and raised large crops and families and had a voice in the local council chamber. The prosperous looking people who passed us in their cars didn't look at all haunted.

But we were different. We travelled as the old order had travelled, in the slow grief-breathing wood of the gig, drawn by a suffering animal. I, too, could have felt a certain ease, but still tinged with misery, if I had ridden through it in a carriage drawn by something that couldn't feel. And, of course, we were looking for work, and were apt to be regarded lightly and contemptuously, because of our clothes and our manner of life.

Driving through grass and red earth, past big paddocks of dry silver grass with short dark trees in their midst and dry stumps lying everywhere, we searched the valley for work. The country looked blasted; as though great storms had come with axes of lightning and slit and splintered the wood on every hill. The very sky was empty and mournful, and the gums on the far-away ranges above us kept a green stillness, aboriginal and deep.

Following a maize paddock for half a mile or so, we came to the first big property. The busy farmer was loading up carts and a lot of hands ran around and helped him. No work here, by the look of it; too many men already, and no place for wandering women. Charl drew over and asked on our behalf, but the farmer said civilly and indifferently that he had enough men. His brother, farther down the road, might have a vacancy.

On we drove, feeling disappointed, but curiously relieved, too. I began to feel that I didn't care if we never worked in the Buffalo River valley. The houses of the growers looked too bare and for-bidding; their redness and loneliness kept us off, and we sat on in the gig and drifted by, feeling, as each house passed, that we had escaped cold looks and suspicious questions.

A young fellow cutting wood in a paddock was glad to have us stop and yarn with him.

"Woa . . . Bloth-um," said Charl. "Good day!"

"Good day," replied the wood-cutter, a red-faced young fellow with fair hairy arms. Taking out a tin of tobacco and papers, he let the axe fall against his out-thrust knee and rolled a cigarette.

"Nice day."

"Yairs; pretty fair." A long silence. The gig squeaked; poor old Blossom moved her tired feet and shook her head.

"Anything doing around here for the maize-picking?"

"Maize-picking? Ah no, I don't think so. They've got all the old hands on here. Local boys. Things are going to be hard this winter."

"D'ye reckon?" Charl didn't care; he had a good home on his own land.

"Yes. I've been cutting wood here for the past month; I'm waiting for the maize, too. Are you looking for maize-picking?"

"Aw, no; I'm not, but these two here are. They're looking for work now."

"Not much chance here at present. Did you try anyone?"

"Yes, the first place up the road. He said to go down and ask his brother."

"Aw well, I'm working for *him*, and he hasn't got as much maize as the other one's got. Look, that's all there is." He waved towards the maize along the river-bank. "There's six of us going to pick that. Won't take long to cut out."

"No."

Long silence.

"Ah well, better be moving, I suppose."

"Yairs, I got to keep going, too. So long!"

"Hurro!" We moved off, the wretched, ill-fed Blossom dragging her legs heavily.

After some miles of steady going, the road suddenly grew dry and white and the scrub on each side of the road grew thickly above us, so that a weird twilight came about. In this, we drew up to a lonely bush school standing in a deathly still and white playground. A square red tank stood at the corner of the school and we got down to have a drink. One window was open; we climbed in, finding ourselves in a small miserable room, dry and dusty, with the poor vestiges of education struggling through in the shape of ruled exercises that were scattered around, and bits of broken chalk lying in the narrow hollows at the top of each desk. A more mournful place it would be difficult to imagine. Ghosts might have come to be taught there. We got out again and, looking up the hill, saw a small house into which a small boy was running wildly, while he kept his eye on us, to tell father, the pedagogue, of the bad men who had entered the temple of wisdom.

Charl cried impatiently, "Get arp . . . Bloth-arm," and we fled the wicked land, the horrid shore.

As we crossed a large wooden bridge, Charl told us a story, a fairytale.

"See that farm over there? Well, the engineer that was building this bridge used to board over there; he fell in love with the daughter of the house and took her away and married her."

Coming in the middle of this haunted land, the tale seemed miraculous, and I envied the girl while I rejoiced that she had been saved from this desolation.

We drove on; but how far I do not know. Ahead lay a country in which rain fell down on green and golden fields. The Promised Land sprang up in the wilderness. I felt that we went on, into it; and that part of us which turned back died.

I awoke at a beautiful bridge that spanned a rocky river, cool, and bubbling in its mountain dialect over large kindly looking stones. There was almost a sense of the Roman bath about the flat stones that stood on end and formed pools. Ferns and flowers of a rough kind grew there, and the blue sky, which the white and dark timber had made to appear so lowering, came out and danced in the pleasant waters. I thought, "Did the bridge-builder and his lady come and talk by this river? If they did, I bless it in memory of them."

A little house stood among many red apple-trees. Charl got down and went in with us, to see if we could buy some, for we were hungry. An elderly lady came to the door and very courteously asked us to enter into an old bush kitchen, clean, shining, and as alert as though city life lay right at the back door. A red fire beat at the bars of a bright stove, and on the table a waxen cloth lay.

The good angel of Buffalo River valley made us a cup of tea, and set cakes and apple turnovers on the table. She sympathized with us in our wanderings, and told us, as if we had not already known, that she had once had young and defiant daughters who rebelled against their father's rule. With nothing much to say in reply, we sat eating and drinking, feeling unutterable gratitude towards our hostess. We were the captives of our condition and couldn't express to her the wonder of the mind's power which would cause this day to be carried on through the impulses of our children in years to be.

She gave us a bag of apples to take away and into the gig we crawled, heavy with good and gratitude. Blue took the whip from Charl and, snatching the H.M.S. *Bellerophon* from his head, waved it in the air, settled it on her curls, and drove Blossom on through the gathering dusk.

IV

SETTLING down in the sections, we began to starve. It was now autumn; the poplars that grew gigantic along the river let the golden gloves fall from their fingers; the walnuts ripened on a tree down near Greer's farm, and we spent most of the daylight there, eating them. My love for Macca had grown into a pure idealism of all human passion, and I wandered alone, on river and range, lamenting the failure of my desire.

After long weeks of abnegation and worship at the altar of the ideal love, I broke out into letters that implored him to write to me. These were never answered.

Remembering the words of the Little Black Flea on that night when we all stood together on the stony river-bed and heard the solemn hurrying of the water, and saw the black gum-trees moving against the glowing eastern sky, I cried, "*No luna ancora!*" No moon yet! I sang the short stave the Black Flea had chanted as we turned to leave the river, "*Batte . . . batte, batte, sempre batte!*" No moon yet. I walked through the crane-haunted gullies and swamps where the marsh hen waded, in berry sprinkled glades, crying to the sorrow and loneliness within me, "*No luna ancora!*"

Some day, the moon of true love would rise. Yes, you shall rise, O moon, and shine on me, throughout the night of my life. In the knotted boughs of a willow-tree, I lay in the pure trance of the poet, gazing down into the sky- and cloud-filled water, fancying that in their movements lay the whole secret of life. In a moment, while I watch, all will be divulged, I thought. But never, never did the angel descend and ripple the pool.

The mountain of grey, purple-veined stone that stood above the ranges grew to be a dungeon to me, in whose depths, I fancied, lay the One True Love; and I cried to him to come out to me on those holy nights when, poor and hungry, I walked through the bush in old torn trousers and shirt and without a sole to my foot or a hat on my head. The moon shone down on my sad young face, shining there with all the penetration of a moon that is wooing the young to their despair. But I cried, "No . . . for me . . . you do not shine. I walk in shadow . . . *no luna ancora!*"

Yes, the night was dark and I walked alone in it. I found the small tracks of bush animals leading into the ranges; paths of the foxes and wallabies and kangaroos. Behind the hut of old Ming, the Chinese, with its bitter cherry-trees, I climbed and the little red foxes fled before me or slid in under fallen logs and looked out at me with a silver gaze, as I sat printing delicately on dry gum-leaves of all fantastic hues my songs to Macca; my cries to him; my entreaties that he never leave "my one love, ever!"

Up through the sparsely timbered ranges I went, to where the rusty pheasants sat dull and brown on the trees; up and farther up to where the kangaroos fed on the green grass-patch on top of the range. On seeing me, they took to flight, falling like rock with a bouncing, crashing flight down the shale depths.

I carried a home-made note-book and wrote in it my young bewildered thoughts, trying before my time to unravel life. Sitting on the sharp gravel of the ranges I wrote: "I tell you there is no returning. It's all finished, as it finished before, but as it will never finish again. I shall find certain ease of heart in movement, and in the possession of material things; and after, there'll come the eventual happiness that comes to the frail and feeble heart that is too idle to cultivate independence; too foolish, too dull, to explore and open up the unsurveyed brain. Ah, think of all those that have said this before, slowly and painfully, from their numbed hearts. In the sudden visualization of the sorrows of the mass, I find that I, as an individual, don't matter."

And then a bit of verse to make me believe that some day I should be comforted by the praise of minds like my own:

> These are the singing dreams,
> The large soft echoes of the mirrored stars,
> While within the granite goblet, the blue wine of the sea. . . .

Then, in sorrow, I wrote again, trying to open up my brain and look at it:

"Today, even apostasy gladdens me. If false love can be steadfast for six months, there must be a passion that will be steadfast for sixty years. The false is but a faint reflection of the true. Autumn moans and bleeds within the trees. I make friends in order to ascertain the various forms of faithlessness. In love, as in all physical things,

the only loss to be feared is that of balance. Lose that and you have
lost your battle. Poetry, I turn to you:

> "The golden fingered poplars have forgotten
> The arms that held them up; the veins that ran
> From darkness into darkness. Hangs there not about them
>   bitter smells?
> Their upflung hands drip with old wealth. . . .

"I have divided," I continued, from the chair of shale in the
university of the ranges, "the brain into at least two known sections,
one being open to sensual impressions, the other being open to con-
structive, destructive and deductive thought. Into the section open
to impressions are received all the visual, seen, solid objects, such as
landscapes, persons and small but important details, pleasing or
unpleasing. It is this section of the brain that is most active in both
states of waking and sleeping. It is this section, too, that is most
reliable owing to the laziness or lack of co-ordination in the tissues
in which thought is secreted, for, in dreams, it is not only possible
to see the object, but also to feel its proximity. The pressure of
bodies, the physical exertions attendant upon running, jumping,
laughing and crying, are in a dream but minor or soft sensations.
The pain following a crushing blow, a stab, a shot or sudden fall, is
never or scarcely registered. If such a recording does occur it is
only because, at the time of dreaming, the body is suffering some
slight irritation which is magnified by the sensory organs . . . the
exhaustion or satiation of whose powers, I believe, causes the
termination of sleep."

At this point the professor, remembering that there has been
nothing to eat all day, ran down the ranges, across the paddocks and
home to the sections, where Blue lay in bed smoking one of her
cheroots, a vile weed wrapped up in brown paper. Her faithful lover
had, in despair, ceased writing, and she had taken to fuming, from
the nostrils, vast clouds of evil-smelling smoke.

Blue said, "We've got to get food somehow. The money's all gone,
except our fares to Dandenong and Metung. We must eat. Got
nothing left but a bit of bran and honey. Wait on, I'll get us some
dinner!"

She disappeared under the wide wooden space that served as a
bed, and crawled into the adjoining cubicle. "You keep yow," she
said in a muffled voice, "and whistle 'The Prisoner's Song' if anyone
comes along."

The small cubicles in the section were separated from each other by a thin wall of three-ply, which stopped at the boards forming the bed; it was therefore quite easy to crawl along the entire section by getting under the bed.

Blue crawled down the Italian side of the section and Giovanni's was the first room she came to. This gentleman, who had been a member of the Italian *Carabinieri*, prided himself on his keen detective's eye. His table was well spread; the inmates of the section had just been in to have lunch and had hurriedly left, after locking their rooms, to resume work in the paddock.

Blue concentrated on a loaf of bread with a slanting cut in it. She stared at it for five minutes, memorizing that cut, crumb by crumb, then she drew the sharp knife from its sheath and slowly, carefully sliced off the top. Beneath was a replica of Giovanni's cut; Blue compared it with the original model and was satisfied. His butter was the next to receive attention. Eyeing its jagged outlines, she carved slowly and delicately so that its diminished form would not be noticed. Then, his plum jam; certain dark pools form in jam and lie there for weeks, shining and oozing candied sugar. Blue dipped where Giovanni had dipped, and where he had stopped, there did she stop.

Then she hurried on under the bed to Major's room, and found a packet of tea. This was gently disturbed and, with its folds recollected clearly, returned to the original condition. Under again, and down to where José's sugar lay in its basin with a little film of dust to one side, above a sparkling hollow made by a recent spoon. Blue removed the whole surface and artistically dusted the rest, leaving another hollow. Then she wriggled back along the length of the section again and came forth with our dinner.

"Thus," said I to the gods, spilling a libation of tea, "do we keep our few coins, preserve our ancient virginity and live on, but without their knowledge, the gracious bounty of men." And we ate well.

This, however, could not last forever. Fresh fields had to be found, for a daily attack on this section would be open to suspicion. Opposite us was the large section occupied by the Australians, who were also working in the fields, bringing the hop-sets out of the ground, so that the selected sprouts might be pruned and returned to the earth later, to provide another year's crop. But this section was guarded by one of the company who had not bothered to apply for a job. Apparently he had enough money to keep going through the winter without working. This thorn in our side rose late, after the men had departed for the paddocks, and lounged around conspicuously, absolutely frustrating Blue's attempts to get a meal for us.

"We must draw him out," said she. He slept in a cubicle which she called the "Pea-paddock". A peculiar ammoniacal smell permeated it to the exclusion of all others. She had already been in it; for one day, in desperation, she had crawled down under the beds, dragging herself along until she came to a cubicle where a safe full of good food yawned on the wall, and bags of various girths bulged on the table. She crept out from under the bed and stood up in the room, with outstretched hands. There was a snoring sigh. On his bed, sleeping softly, lay the gentleman occupant of the Pea-paddock. As he turned, half awake, Blue was under the bed in a flash, and, almost overcome by the ammoniacal odour, battled against semi-consciousness until she reached the daylight. So we didn't have any tea that night.

"We must bring him out into the open," said Blue again.

She hung around in front of the door, whistling and singing until the gentleman came out. Then she spoke of the glory of the day. He reciprocated with eulogies marked by a strong Oxford accent. Phillip Graham-hyphen-Bishop was a cultured man of good family, and he had been handsome once. He was not ill-looking now, except for a dissipated, leathery face of a pale yellow colour, marked with a leer that came down from his eyes to his mouth corners, and gave him the look of a man whom you could not have trusted with the milk in your tea.

How charmed he was to meet me! Into our kitchen he came, bowing, to talk with me on abstruse things. Blue disappeared and I quite forgot her in the grace of his conversation.

In a low, beautifully modulated voice, he said, "I, for my part, have been somewhat promiscuous in the matter of love. You will be shocked if I tell you that I have had over fifty mistresses. Yes, women are an open book to me. But, age, alas, has almost blinded me, and I do not read any more. Still, I often think," he continued with a leer that almost knocked me down, "that true happiness might be had in a little home with a fine young woman, like yourself, for instance.

"But, mistresses! Ah, what mistresses I have had! The wife of the Chinese consul in Java. . . . Oh well, that was a long time ago. And the daughter of a very high official in Calcutta . . . a name world-wide known; but one mustn't tell tales, eh?" He pulled his dirty trousers up around his shocking shirt and continued to tell them.

"In India, once, I got sunstroke in half a minute. Well, I was crossing the compound, a thing I ordinarily never did in the day-time. I was going to get myself a whisky. One shouldn't have done it, for a boy is at one's beck and call there, and I was bare-headed.

I remember no more. Just falling. The boy found me and pulled me inside and started the punkah going. But it was a near thing. Ah!"

I saw it all in my mind. The blazing glare of the compound (a mixture of bamboo shoots and medicine to my untravelled eyes) and the little figure lying hatless with an intelligent blade of sunlight beating down on it.

"Sex is a glorious thing, my dear young lady," with a hideous snarling leer at me, "and fame is splendid, too. I have known both sex and fame in my life. Ah, what a life! I come of an old family; I have had a fine education, and I know women from tip to toe. What mistresses I have had! Ah, what I know about women!"

Suavely he talked, and sadly I listened, until I saw Blue coming out of his section with two kerosene-cases in her arms. She halted at our door and smiled upon us satisfiedly. "Just found a bit of fire-wood," said she. "I'll go inside and cut it up, and light the fire. Shall I make a cup of tea, Steve? Mr Graham-Bishop might like one. Would you, sir?"

"Delighted, delighted," he exclaimed. Blue withdrew with the cases, in which, I feared, much of Mr Graham-hyphen-Bishop's stores lay. The fire was lit, and we made a fine pot of tea that had been lifted from his own caddy. He liked the flavour very well indeed; better than his own which was also very good, he said. "I know a lot about teas, having owned a tea plantation in Ceylon for some years . . . but not as much as I know about women." He leered fondly at me. When he had gone, Blue asked, "What was he talking about?"

"Got sunstroke once in India, in half a minute . . . awful experience!"

"Wait till he sees his safe," murmured Blue, "he'll get it again and quicker! More awful experience!"

And he did. After that, the foreman strolled around the sections every morning, ostentatiously trying doors and eyeing our quarters very keenly.

Do not think, however, that the eating of the stolen food had lowered the heights of my thoughts. No, still profound, still full of grandeur I lived my mystical days and found transcendental bliss. I strode alone on the ranges all day, coming home to eat of Graham-hyphen-Bishop's food at night. I walked the path of the seer and dreamer at noon, on the red and rugose shoulders of the hills, following the red foxes and the purple and crimson lowries that flew through the tender leaves of the saplings, crying "Quick, quick! Skulk, skulk!"

My thoughts of Macca endured within me, and I wrote letters to him as I sat on logs in the river.

"Who am I, anyway, that I should reproach? You have given to me such elusive and delicate thoughts, old loveliness that will endure forever; groundwork for the coming serenity of the years to be. One night lately I was following the track homeward, returning from a raid on Sullivan's quinces. The moon was climbing high, with one star following. Faintly, beneath me, I heard the dark river's April cryings; and so, I descended the bank, and there, below me, the water was caught under the willows by its black locks and lay deep and still, between log and tree. Then, I remembered you, O night swimmer, and that summer evening when you dived down into deep and unknown waters under the willows. I slipped out of my clothes, and clutching a kindly and ghostly You by the hand, slipped into the chill and strongly pulling water.

"And whenever I do leap to her, the broken voiced water,
The swiftly smooth and breastless one; the inarticulate;
The dark, disturbed, the amber, curbed, and bird rejoiced water,
She clings to me, she cleaves to me, strong, sure and passionate.

"We went laughing all the way home, You and I, for the sheer joy of living, for the warmth of our blood and the gaiety of our companionship. The frightened water-hens skimmed across the wide river that was singing itself into drought."

After writing this, I got up and crawled under the fence to steal a small pumpkin from Sullivan's plot. Along the banks of the river I found a rusty jam tin. I lit a fire and cooked the pumpkin in this, eating it without salt. A horrid meal, but there was little or nothing to eat in the sections. I stayed late under the moon, praying to the breathless waters to send to me, at last, the one true love.

We wrote to Peppino, after a long period of neglect. The letter was full of grace and culture, as any student of Italian will perceive, and we had much pleasure in composing it, while we dined on a fine stew made from meat stolen from the larder of Graham-hyphen-Bishop.

Lunedi, 27,

Maggio.

Mio caro amico Peppino,

Io sono stato lavoro nella montagna. Io non a Metung, ora. Io molto tempo sono senzallavoro. Io sarò eco a Metung in Agosto, in Primavera.

And so on, ending with a plea that he bring his brother Pasquale with him when he, too, returned to Metung in *primavera* . . . springtime.

Often had Peppino told us of the illustrious Pasquale, the intelligent, gentle, handsome one in whose culture, he assured us, we should find gratification.

And enthusiastically in answer to our request wrote this same Pasquale, with that command of the language which we admired living in every fervent phrase.

Dear may frend and of my brother Peppino thank you very muck for that best record you send to me and I send to you one speeely record I see to you when com to Metung we come weel frend I not spik to muck because never see before when I com I geve my write hand very cold ever night frost ever morning well frend remaen remember me to your sester I geve me hand your faithfuly Pasquale rain too muck come water in me hut I what writ this letter good like to you and to me too good night little bird, sing, sing, sing sing song to me.

This letter heartened us. We felt that we had something to return to in springtime in the village by the sea.

Two little Italians, cousins, shifted into the adjoining cubicle; small black-eyed men, their dark-jowled faces half covered by tweed caps. They were very kind to us. The elder could speak a little English and he was teaching the younger man to speak, as well as he could. For long hours in the night the lesson would go on by the light of the candle, while the good Guiseppe taught the merry-faced Michelino the rudiments of his new mother-tongue.

THE TEACHER: *S-s-schellina* . . . s-s-shilling!
THE PUPIL: *S-s-schellina* . . . s-s-shilling!
THE TEACHER: *Ss-scopa* . . . br-r-room!
THE PUPIL: *S-s-scopa* . . . br-r-room!
THE TEACHER: *S-s-sorda* . . . deaf!
THE PUPIL: *S-s-sorda* . . . deaf!
THE TEACHER: *Ss-s-erpe* . . . sneke!
THE PUPIL: *Ss-s-erpe* . . . sneke!
BLUE: *S-s-silencio!* . . . shut-up!

Teacher and pupil both laughed, and half an hour later a soft, insinuating voice called over the low partition, "*Cugin-a-a! Cugi-i-inaa* Blue!" (Cousin Blue), and Guiseppe's pudgy hand passed over a plate of steaming spaghetti. We never touched their safe, first because they were kind and poor, secondly, because we decided that to rob one's immediate neighbours would be *infra dig*. The rest of the Italians must have had their ideas about things, too, for they struggled valiantly to have rooms right up near our door, and be in with us, as it were, and safe. When that failed, they nailed boards under their beds, stopping Blue's progress from room to room, and that was the most cruel blow of all.

The lean days got transparent for lack of food then, and despite the foreman and Phillip Graham-hyphen-Bishop's watchful eye, Blue managed to get into the food of the Australians. Every evening the silence was rent by the howls of those whose food had been lightly, artfully, and sympathetically touched by Blue's fantastic fingers. When the fires had been lit, the safes opened and the bags of groceries brought out, the wail of the "ratted" was loud.

"By cripes," they said, "I wish we could get hold of them! It's someone that's out of work," they exclaimed loudly, in our direction. "Someone that hangs around the camp all day. Let us just catch them at it, and that'll be the finish."

We often paid the lads a neighbourly call at this hour and expressed our sympathy with them, pointing out that they, like us, should keep their safes padlocked. "We never lose anything," we assured them mildly, "and we get a lot of food in every week."

"Arrrh!" they cried bitterly.

These lads lived roughly in the damp dark sections, cooking their food in the communal kitchen at the end and sleeping in the bare cubicles. Tired out, they retired early and lay in their beds, fully clothed, even to hats and leggings, and nursed black spaniel pups to keep themselves warm during the long cold alpine nights.

The Italians and the Australians did not fraternize often. Now and then a visit was paid, during which the Australians talked in loud, aggressive Italian, with quite a good accent, for they were all natural-born mimics.

One of them insulted the Latins so deeply, on a pouring wet day, that he had to leap out of their clutches and take shelter in the rafters of the kitchen; from below they pelted him with flour and, climbing after him, tore him down and flung him out into the rain. By the time he reached home he was only fit to stick down envelopes. But there was no ill-feeling.

V

IT was late autumn; the days were still long and hot. I lay hungry on my bed, listening to the voice of the old Italian Michele, whose voice had haunted me during the last days of the hop-picking. He was now living in the section over the way and working with the rest of the gang in the paddocks. In the morning, at noonday, and at night, his voice poured, harsh and full of light, up to the sun, and as I lay on the rough bags I said to myself, "That is Man, standing in light, on the very summit of the earth, and returning to the sun, through his voice, the light that it has put into him."

Stream upon stream of high unmusical cries he gave, broad blades of unerring light that flowed widely from his dark comical soul. He had heard the Australians singing a melody called "Moonlight and Roses", and as the season deepened into winter, he cried to the tune, with a bold wild haunting note, "Ah! Primavera! Ah! Springtime!"

How he lingered on the notes . . . how he drew out that lovely word, as sweet to the Italian as the name of his country . . . Primavera! In Primavera, what would come to me? Should I return to Metung and find Macca? Would he be unchanged? Ah, he would not even be there. But yet, I shall trust, I said, and hope to find him, as of old, lazy, whimsical and humorous, full of the range-like mystery and poetry of the Gippslander.

Along the now greying river I wandered, among the autumnal trees, and stayed for hours watching the Greek pattern of the waters.

Long afterwards, in another country, I saw them repeated in the flowing winged figures of those that live sculptured on the pediments of the Parthenon. "Tell me," I asked the river as it whirled past, its grey warriors breaking into the virgin shapes of lovely women and the gnarled power of old men, "River, what are you? What is water? It is more than fluid, more than liquid flying. O, I grieve, I grieve to think that the hours pass and I cannot speak your tongue!" Dim with melancholy, slow with the hours of my youth, with the senseless waiting and enduring of human pain, I made for the ache in my mind the answer of the river.

> Does not each river cry its unknown name
> In triumph, in defiance, in despair?
> No throat alike; no water-voice the same
> As its far fellows . . . Still, the word is there!
> Is it not more than shrouds in darkness flowing,
> Than cloakings that a hurried shoulder's flinging,
> Embroidered in the midnight of its swift and spumy going,
> Enchanted into silence by the splendour of its singing?
> O aboriginal voice by shallows broken,
> Clear call around a bend, long undiscovered,
> Heroic moan, unwritten and unspoken . . .
> Dark lip by sedge and starry cresses covered.

Does not each river cry its unknown name?
Weeds, water-shaken, falter it, but still
Its stammer stings man's tongue, he cannot frame
The word cried by the swimmer from the hills.

Blue and I did a lot of wandering around the district in search of deserted orchards, from which we could pick the fruit and bring it home to stew in Major's sugar with a bit of condensed milk from Digger's tin to flavour it.

Good souls, I said, their charity, although unwilling, will surely earn them a seat in the theatre of paradise!

Up the river, near the pumping station, we found some gnarled fig- and quince-trees in a paddock which the rabbits and horses had worn to dust. Here I, hungry and faint for lack of food, ate five large quinces and many sour figs with their skins, and fell almost unconscious after the deed, with a tortured mouth.

There was a deserted house over the river, which we approached with the caution of robbers. "Is it empty? Is it occupied?" we asked with intensity. The dim uncurtained windows were the mystical sounds that the house was trying to put into words, and the pine-trees allied to the house, its timber and its moods, sighed coldly in the autumn sky.

The house stood silent, set back off the road, silent, light, alert, full of itself, absorbed in its own destruction and waiting for a companion to take with it, to accompany it to its end.

"Do not think, old house," I said, "that we are light fools who approach to rob you and go away unremembering. No, to us, what a symbol you are of the past and our future. The very grass that lies flat and dry around you is beloved by us. With reverence and enthusiasm, we approach and pass under the golden quince-trees that keep a silence Hesperidean about you."

Raising the old windows with a kind touch, we got into the empty rooms. One corner was quite full of out-of-date women's magazines, and among them an ancient edition of Goldsmith's poems, in which "The muse found Scroggins, stretched upon a board". In the magazines was a story, an honest bit of unimaginative work, that rolled in the homely vehicle of the writer's style through a grand and glorious country. And the name of the country was Yeats, William Butler. It was illustrated with photographs. Under a grey apple-tree in a Gippsland orchard sat a girl in the refined, modest sort of clothes worn twenty years ago. Her long glistening hair was bunned and knotted intricately, the curves having the lovable effect of an old fashion. She read the spread pages of a book. Startling poetry emerged from the story . . . new to me and ringing out with a mystic challenge.

> To where the water runs its wintry race beneath the stars.

And,

> Tell her I am with the people that I love . . .

> The years like great black oxen tread the world
> And I am broken by their passing feet.

I sat reading for hours; and, often, after that, when the quinces were all gone and there was no further sensible inducement to bring me to this deserted house, I came and sat reading for the twentieth time, above this water into which fell shadow of such amazing beauty. Ah, what a debt of fancy and comfort I owed the old house! What immortality I perceived in the worm-eaten pages of Yeats's poems!

Bemused, I left the house, waded through small streams and strode over sandy and rocky river-beds that the autumn waters had not yet gathered to feast in, crossed the log above the pumping station and walked through the empty hop-paddocks, where on the hop-hills no plants showed yet, and where the fraying Calcutta hemp swung sadly and idly from the wires above.

Far in the distance, the alps shone with a sphinx-red light, and my heart ached as the blue veins of the ranges grew distinct for a moment in the evening light, and then faded among the timber.

At the open fire in the section, Blue sat playing her violin. Outside the door, wreathed around a little plane-tree from top to bottom, as sinuously as a snake, was Art, charmed by her music. His enormous eyes were crossed and gleaming, and his long delicate hands held his battered hat on top of his rumpled hair. He fancied this position when music sounded. Remaining in it for as long as it was humanly possible, he retired, sighing.

Charlie Wallaby was sitting in front of the fire, too, and with him a stranger. A tall stout young fellow, with a pale fleshy face, a white nose with an aristocratic knob on the end of it, a white quivering mouth, thin-lipped, and brown eyes set close together. He stared at the fire with parted lips, the ridges on the upper lip very marked, and his chin jutted forward eagerly and pugnaciously. Blue introduced him to me, as "Pricie-ole-man . . . from Porepunkah". Weaving in and out of the days that followed was this black-coated phantom, with his hands in his pockets, his tweed cap on his head, and a capable, falsely belligerent air of being able to bluff his way out of everything.

That night, when I had retired to bed, I heard Blue trying to inculcate into him some of the beauty of English poetry. "Blow out, ye bugles, over the rich dead!" she cried through the dark. The red fire sent a hungry glow over the wall at the foot of my bed, and I thought with a pang of sorrow of the poet, Rupert Brooke.

Pricie-ole-man said something and laughed. Blue cursed him for a Philistine and a scorner.

"What's wrong with you?" he cried. "I only said that I wouldn't like to get a wiff of the air they blew out over the rich dead. Gee, I bet they were rich, all right!"

He was a disappointment in some ways, but he was poor and out of work like ourselves, so we made a friend of him.

The next afternoon Blue and he came back from a long walk. Her fine face was flushed with joy under the cream tweed Italian cap, and I admired the khaki woollen shirt she wore, the dark red tie, and her waist, bulging a little under the belt of her long wide trousers. What a lovely creature she was! Why couldn't I look like her, always dewy, flushed and sane? What fiend had sent me into the world full of melancholy and frustration?

Blue was jubilant. "What do you think, Steve? I've got into Charlie Wallaby's place, at last. Listen. . . . Oh, what a tale I've got to tell! Steve, we've got a home for the winter, I think. Well, Pricie-ole-man and I were walking down the road, and we called in to an old farmhouse sitting among the trees, and asked if we could have some of the walnuts from the trees. And the old lady that came to the door, a tall stout woman with a white face, looked at Pricie-ole-man and said, 'Aren't you a relation of mine? You belong to the Costs of Porepunkah, don't you? Pricie-ole-man said 'Yes'. So the old lady said, 'Well, I'm your aunt. Come in, both of you, and have a cup of tea. My name is Wallaby.'

" 'Not Charlie's mother!' I cried. Oh, what will Charlie think, Steve, when he sees us turning up to stay for the winter? Oh, what joy!

" 'Yes,' said the old lady, 'do you know him?'

" 'Know him? Why we think there's no one like him anywhere in the alps.'

"She was making puftaloonies all the time we talked and in next to no time had a plate of them in front of us, with a hot cup of tea. Oh, Steve, such a great old place; and she is so kind and hospitable!

You've got to come down. She wants to meet you. I told her all about you. Charlie's mentioned us, she said, and do you know, she's often asked him to bring us down to see her; but the brute wouldn't. What do you think of that?"

"But, Blue, perhaps it wouldn't be well-bred to partake of this fine old lady's hospitality."

"What? Puftaloonies . . . and tea? We shall be like Priestly and the Famous Twenty Trained V-frawgs. Don't talk about it. Come down with us tomorrow. They're killing a pig."

"Yes," I acknowledged, with a watering mouth, "puftaloonies, certainly they make a difference."

"We must get in there for the winter. Aren't you tired of living on Digger's flour and sugar, Major's cheese and Giovanni's jam and Primo's bread? Steve, don't be a fool. Come down and see her; she's fine. They've got plenty. She won't mind."

"No, Blue, we can't go and live on her, unless we have work to do."

"Well, I was talking to Mr Padrone as we went out of the gate, and he said that he had six acres of maize coming on, down by the river. You know that paddock over near Major's tomato garden? He half promised to give us that, if no one else wanted it. So—there you are!"

"That's better!"

It was cold and wet next day. I put on my heavy military coat over my best tailored suit, with stiff white collar rampant and red tie champant, and walked down with Blue and Pricie-ole-man to meet Mrs Wallaby.

Judging from the sounds we heard as we neared the farmhouse, she was having a bad fit of hysterics. Across the cold barren paddocks, shriek after shriek floated eerily to us.

"Ah!" said Blue sagely, as one of the family, "Charlie's killing the pig!"

In a big stable fronting the track, there was grouped the eternal triangle, man, woman and beast. Charlie had the pig bent over a bench and was washing its throat before he cut it. His mother, huge even at that distance, and dressed in an old-fashioned blouse and skirt, helped him to hold its legs. In front of them steamed a large tub of hot water. The pig shrieked wildly.

"Gee with," cried Charlie, "keep thtill, can't you? How do you think I can kill you, if you go on like that?"

"Quick, Charlie, quick!"

"Gor blarmie, mother, I can't find the plathe. Yeth, here it ith!"

He plunged the knife in, and from a high shriek the voice went to an empty, muttering gurgle. The blood ran. Blue felt faint and ran inside, while I, priding myself on my strength and hardness, stayed on, in that pride sinning against the mercy of the world.

Mrs Wallaby was pleased to meet me and curious to discover in me a few qualities that she liked. While Charl scraped the pig and cut it up, she made tea in the old kitchen. It contained an old dresser full of the bound volumes of Sir Walter Scott; there was a table littered with chair legs and crochet work opposite, and a long table drawn up to the fireplace, which was as dusty as a cave; in it burnt a red and yellow fire, coated with ashes. Black pots, pans and kettles hung over it, on hooks. Over the furniture, and the iron bed-posts that bruised our shins, lay a web of crochet work, dirty and spotted with mould, but of fine pattern and done by a good needle-woman.

Breaking through the webs, we entered and sat down at the first hospitable table we had seen since leaving Gippsland. The buttered toast and puftaloonies found a home; and the cups of tea were not neglected.

Mrs Wallaby was a tall fat woman with a beautiful white face and hands as smooth as a girl's. Her hair was grey and when her stomach shook with laughter at Blue's antics she clasped her hands over it, and they shook too. She had a deep nasal voice, sombre and melancholy at times, but rousing and merry when she entered into the spirit of things.

We had faith in her, because she loved a joke and liked to see hearty appetites. We had plenty of both and looked forward to a pleasant winter, when we could tell the tales and sing the songs of other lands while hot puftaloonies were being served up.

We marvelled at the crochet work covering the various furnitures, and exclaimed with admiration at the nicety of its placing. A piece of wide lace, obviously intended for a pair of drawers, hung around the leg of an old bed; while the neck of a nightgown was drooping around an old rusty preserving pan. Insertions for skirts hung every-where, bearing various patterns such as the bell and flower, clover and moss, rooster and bee, the emu and kangaroo.

Charl came in and flung down a large portion of the pig. Mrs Wallaby rolled forward and cut off generous chops which she fried in the pan, and handed out on cold plates to us. We had not tasted pork for almost a year, and fell on it with knives and forks that were twisted, doubled, sprained and fractured into the likeness of anything but table implements. While we ate the fresh pork, dripping with the congealing fat, I felt an awful sickness coming over me. I greened slightly and seemed to be fainting or swimming in waves of glazed air.

With a low but courteous apology I rose and left the room.

During the afternoon, I saw that Mrs Wallaby recognized the strong marriageable readiness in me, which I miscalled "the sorrow of life", and she herded me with vague and tender suggestions towards some unkown destination, the name of which, I felt sure, she would divulge as time went on. She became preoccupied with my strength and silence and wished to have it around her, that she might solve it, and my troubles.

Blue, of course, was the ballad player, the *jongleur*, loved for her music and her laughing beauty; and Pricie-ole-man was a relative and, by the laws of the kindred, always welcome during the cold lean winter months.

So, when we returned to the sections that night, it was with relieved hearts and a big lump of fresh pork which we put in our cupboard. Ten minutes later poetic justice was done, when Digger's big kangaroo-dog, smelling the stranger from afar, rushed in between our legs, and with a snarl of joy dragged the lump of pork out of the cupboard, and like a flash of black lightning was gone.

"Ah well," I said. "We can consider Digger as being paid in full."

"Overpaid," replied Blue and she went to let him know about it.

"What?" exclaimed Digger incredulously. "Youse two with a bit of pork? Why, I haven't seen you buy food since you've been here! *You* never go over to the grocer's van when he comes round. *You* never go over to the butcher's cart. Where did you get the pork from?"

"I just came to tell you that your dog got it from us . . . that's all!"

"But where you two got it from, that's the mystery," said Digger. "I know for a fact that you've had your safe locked on half a bag of bran for the past three months."

Proudly, Blue ignored him.

No change was made in our plans. It was decided that we would shift down to Mrs Wallaby's when we got the maize-picking from Mr Padrone. For we felt that we needed the backing of constant work in order that we might stay with her and have happy consciences.

Pricie-ole-man continued to call and, at night, the group of friends and enemies around our fireplace made the nights heroic with bush yarns, songs and recitations.

Among the men working on the property there had been much surmise regarding us, and the question paramount was, "How do they live? Who keeps them?"

But now that Pricie-ole-man and Charl were to be often seen visiting us, the dark hearts and sensual among them were hopeful, and gave signs that they believed us to be approachable. This was odd to me, since towards all other men I, too, was man, my heart turning womanly towards one only. Those were evil days when a weak moral fibre might easily have been undermined by destructive scepticism. In those days it seemed to me that there was in the world neither man nor woman . . . nothing save a purpose, and that a relentless one, cruel to the very bone.

I lay at night in my room on bags, covered by my father's rug, and thought of Macca and the bark hut. Soon, I said, it will be Primavera, and we shall return. How shall I meet him, then, that one whom I love? In the book in which Blue kept our paddock tallies, I wrote in a fine Italian hand, slowly and with pain:

"As truly and unfalteringly as the compass swings to the north, as inevitably and shamelessly as the light flowers press out on to the dark stems of the walnut-trees, I shall come to you in spring. Is it to the earth or the eager recrudescence of an old dream that I come? When the tenuous and excited blood of youth temporarily blinds me, I believe that you will awaken to me again. I am assured by the lonely and fugitive moments that you will follow me, like one in an enchantment, beyond the bowing trees, beyond those ballerinas of the night, across and through the impalpable lilac swords that guard the fleeing horizon. Ah, faerieland, alas, my lost and fallen dreams, I have murdered them. I am continually haunted by them.

"In the cleared space, in the tree-chequered hollow, there stands the little temple of our imagination, the rough fane of our emotions, desolate and never to be occupied. There is a dark face I must find hidden beyond the bend . . . there is a voice I must listen to."

Then I had to listen to a voice of another sort. . . . A knock at the door.

"Yes? Who is it?"

"Is that you, Steve?"

"It is. Who are you? What do you want?"

"It's Mr Flailer here, Steve. I want to come in."

"What for, Mr Flailer?"

"Oh, just want to come in."

"And I, Mr Flailer, have a fine Martini-Henry rifle here that is longing to meet you. Therefore, come in."

"Oh, I see. Good night!"

I lay on the bed, still. But all my holy thoughts were gone, and another particle of the enchantment of life broke from me, and weakness came into me. I was being shown daily that I was not, after all, a spirit, a holiness of the life force, a splendour of time that had been built up of ancestral cells, each finer than the other in the succeeding generations. I was not part of a coming era of immortal beauty and faith; but a hop-picker before whom a teamster was Mr Flailer, and I was only Steve.

> "The years like great black oxen tread the world,
> And I am broken by their passing feet,"

I said. I was beginning to collect guns of all sorts. The rusty Martini-Henry with which I had threatened Flailer was the first I had picked up. I developed a passion for them, and sought them everywhere. Beyond the river, in a house deserted by the Sullivans, I found two old rifles, together with a quaint broken teapot and old romantic dance programmes. I took home my booty and mentioned to Blue, in passing, that in the old garden stood a large orange-tree well laden with fruit approaching ripeness. We rejoiced and promised to remember.

There was another afternoon when I went down and sat in Sullivan's hop-garden, when the sun was half blinded by dust; when it was limping into the earth like an old man. There was a peculiar mist in the air of the autumn sky. It lay like a salty gold leaf on my face.

I sat under the willow; its little green leaves were drawn in shadow all over my body, and I thought that this was the most miserable noon of my life. I dreamed in torture, trying to find out the reason for Macca's apostasy, why he had not loved me, why he had not answered my lyric letters.

That day I had found, in the sections, a book that postulated a weird philosophy. There were certain laws governing our desires, laws of gratification and withdrawal. It followed that what we desired too strongly was beaten away from us by the stern wave of our own generating. And, when we ceased desiring, the object desired returned to us. How cold I grew, how I shivered as I theorized. In the moist dirt at my bare feet, I traced the symbols of that philosophy. It was a comfortless thing.

I got up and went off home, along the smooth and cool dirt of the river-bank, slipping between trees, now going far down near the water, and then being compelled to go high up into the paddocks. Under some trees at a point where the water had a deep bass voice that broke and faltered into something approaching speech, I saw the tent of the trapper, Blackmore. It was laced up artfully in front, and a round, strong smell of apples, ripe to their very hearts, made the canvas seem too thick. Ah, the apple! The long untasted and satisfying apple! The trapper had cases of them within the tent, for poisoning rabbits.

I rushed home to the section, where Blue sat stirring a decoction of parrot's legs and pumpkins, with black stewed quinces to follow.

"Out upon the parrot and pumpkin stoo, Bluey. Out upon the black quince. *Ich dien!*" I threw out the dessert, and we ate the legs of the songsters. "Yes, I was coming along the river-bank and I passed Blackmoor's tent . . . and, ah, what a smell! Apples, Bluey! We'll go down with a bag tonight, just after dark."

"What a change from quinces," said Blue. "I'm tired of the things."

A warm white twilight came, at length, and I ached with the sorrow of love. As I walked beside Blue, on the main road down towards the paddock where the trapper had the apples stored in his tent, I pretended that Macca was with me. I spoke to him. "Yes, you are with me. That is your pale face I see, and your breast wherein beats your poet's heart.

> My lost love, my lost love, I implore thee, where art thou?
> I wander in dark woods afar from the light.
> Blanched are my lips and my chill brow,
> But I shall return to my true love tonight."

I had translated this from an Italian song, *"Mio Bel' Alpino"*, which I had heard the Italians singing. In a melancholy voice I chanted it,

> *"Dove sei stato mio bel' alpino?"*

or,

> "Where have you been, my beautiful alpine soldier?"

"Here comes Charl," exclaimed Blue. "Hello Charl! Hello, Spot old man!"

"Gee with, Gor blarmie, where yer going with the bag?" asked Charlie. His hat, which was covered with dust, had apparently come before him all the way up the road, in Spot's mouth. Walnuts clicked in his ragged pockets.

"Give us a walnut, Charl!"

"Walnut? Gee with, what do you mean be walnut? I haven't had one for yearth." He chewed away at one and rolled his wall eye at us with an empty, jolly and far-away look.

"Where yer going with the bag?"

"Steve says Blackmoor's got cases of apples in his tent. We thought about going down to have a look."

"Gee with . . . appleth!"

"Come on, Charl. You can carry the bag and we'll give you a few. But we want the biggest share; we've been living on quinces for weeks now. Talk about sick of them! It's inexpressible. Come on!"

Charl hung back in the breeching, cracking walnuts and rolling his eyes. "Gee with, I dunno. What would mother thay?"

"But Charl, you're over thirty! What can she say?"

"All right." Charl fell into step with us, and in the growing darkness we advanced on the river-bank and drew near the tent. We began to whisper, in case Blackmoor was around. The river almost drowned our voices and we got irritated and yelled, "What?" after every remark.

"Are yer thure Blackmoor'th gone?" whispered Charl.

"Yes, goes into Myrtleford every week-end. Smell those apples, Charl?"

"What?" in a loud voice.

"Smell those flaming apples?"

"Can't hear . . . thmell . . . what?"

"Your feet, man, your feet! Anything!"

"Can't be me feet . . . only had a bath. . . ."

"Once in me life," added Blue.

"What? Whose wife?"

"Oh shut up, Charl, get into the tent!"

"Who? Me get in? Gee with! There's nowhere to get into it. I wouldn't untie that knot of hith for anything. He'd know for thure that we'd been here, and I'd get the blame. No one liveth anywhere near Blackmoor but uth."

"Well, get in, and throw out the apples, or bag them for us in the tent." In the soft darkness, the river talked gloomily in its broken bass and across the lonely paddock the wind blew faint sounds.

"Sure no one'th coming?" whispered Charl agonizingly, as he crawled around on his stomach, looking for a bit of space to crawl in under. We felt around, too, and got a place that would admit a rabbit if it wasn't in a hurry.

"Here you are, Charl. In you get!"

"Gor blarmie!" said Charl. "What do you think I am?"

"Too good to be true! Hurry up, dear, and get those large hind-quarters under the flap." With sundry bursting and splitting sounds, Charl got in under the edge of the tent and stumbled over Black-moor's table, knocking down his hurricane lamp and treading on it. In the dark night, his muffled oaths seemed to come out of space. We stood beside the tent and, thrusting our heads forth, sniffed the wind.

"Got any apples, Charl?"

"Gee with, wait on! I can feel thomething . . . wait on! Lithen!" fearfully, "ith that anyone coming? Are youthe two keeping yow?"

"Nothing coming, Charl. Get the apples into the bag. Hurry up!"

The river murmured in the night, gulped, sobbed and hurried on. The hushed trees bent above us, contributing to the dreams of us and our unborn. Ah night, what means all this?

A sudden hard footstep sounded to our right; it was regular and determined. We flapped the tent quickly. "Charl . . . here comes Blackmoor! We're going. Get out of the tent! Hurry up!" And we stood for a moment to wait for Charlie before we ran. He moaned faintly and trod on the hurricane lamp again, and crunched it under his feet.

"Gor blarmie! Gee with! I can't get out. Give uth a hand. Rip open the front of the tent!"

"Can't do it! He'd know. You said he would. Come on, quick! Can't you find the way you got in? Here he is . . . !"

The footsteps were close and determined. We ran, and as we ran we heard Charl ripping the tent from top to bottom as he burst out of it. How we ran! Leaping and zigzagging from side to side, cowering under bushes, tripping over logs and circling around swamps, we dashed off into the wilderness, with a dark figure pursuing us and calling out harshly. Over Sullivan's property we ran, leaping the barbed-wire fence like kangaroos, and fell flat on our faces, to bound up again and rush into the thick scrub at the foot of the ranges. The relentless figure followed us, and we fell down and hid in a patch of bracken fern. Our pursuer, breathing hard, sat down near it and mumbled to himself. For half an hour, we crouched there, and when at last we emerged, he had gone.

We set out towards home. Across the paddocks, we saw a white object moving. "That's Spot," exclaimed Blue. "I bet Charlie's there. Wonder how he got on? Come over and see!"

We ran across the paddocks again in the direction of Spot; but when we got near Charlie he took to his heels and ran back towards the ranges. It was a long time before Blue could catch up with him.

At last, she found him lying in the ferns, panting with exhaustion. She could hardly get near him, because he had rolled himself up like a porcupine and talked in a false voice, saying that he was an old pensioner looking somewhere for a shakedown.

"Don't be a fool, Charlie," said Blue. "Listen to me. It's only us. Me and Steve. You're lucky! Blackmoor chased us into the ranges."

"Gor blarmie, go on!" replied Charl, feebly. "Well, we'll sneak around to his tent and get the apples. I threw the bag out ahead of me. Even if he's there, he mightn't have found them."

"He must be there, because he chased us. Didn't he chase you, Charlie?"

"I don't know. I didn't wait to find out. I just ran, and sang out to you two to wait for me, but I couldn't see you at all. I can't see much at night. I just kept on going till I fell down in a patch of bracken. I had a bit of a rest and then I started out looking for you!"

"Where was the patch of bracken, Charl?"

"Over Thullivan'th barbed-wire fence, just at the foot of the ranges. Why?"

"Oh, nothing." But we thought a lot over what he had told us. "Well, it was a lucky escape for us all."

When we got to Blackmoor's tent, there was only a cow feeding outside it, and there was nothing in the tent except the big hole Charl had torn in it as he leapt out like a frog.

Half-way home, we thought we'd like a nice apple and, opening the bag, we put our hands in, laughing with anticipation.

Charl bit deep. "By joveth! They're quinceth!"

We sat listlessly with one in each hand. "Can't you smell, Charl?"

"Well, can't you?" said Charl irritably. "I thought you thed they were appleth, Thteve? I wish I hadn't jumped out of that tent like that. Do you think Blackmoor will notice that tear much?"

We said we had no doubt but that he might pass over it, and not notice a thing until the rain came. But then again, the tear had such an uncanny likeness to Charl's figure that Blackmoor might be forgiven if he entertained certain suspicions. After which, we took the quinces home and continued to live on them.

VI

ABOUT a week afterwards, Pricie-ole-man brought a stranger down to the sections with him. This was Rheesi, the jockey, a little fair fellow with a soft girlish face, almost handsome with its redness of cheek and golden eyebrows; but the entire face was too small-boned and flat, the skull, in particular, giving a sense of thinness and boxiness.

On the bench along the wall, he put a racing pad and cloth, together with a purple and gold blouse and cap. Stirrups and bits jingled; the blue misted windows of the section looked out on the little plane-tree around which Art writhed and glared when Blue played her violin; and opposite us stood Section No. 1, a long unoccupied galvanized iron shed, divided like ours into cubicles.

I had looked out on this shed so often, with wasted thoughts; and so often had it tempered me with its emptiness, that I longed, through exhaustion of the mind, to have something more than eyes when I looked through the window at that view. The eyes of a furnace would have served me, so that I might have melted down the galvanized iron in an intellectual crucible and discovered what it was that troubled me in the material; or why it was that the red sandstone and gravel mixture on the path outside and the black mud about the doors should be exerting their power in my soul and forcing it to run away and seek the luxury of cleanliness.

The hollows and hills of the dirt floor were neatly swept, but a soft fur of light was picked up by the dust on the surface, and waves of flame advanced and retreated across our faces as we sat about the fire on kerosene-boxes.

Pricie-ole-man and Rheesi had just come back from the races at El Dorado. "Mai word," said Rheesi, "it was cold there, and Ai don't know whai they held the meeting, because there was only a man and a dog attending."

Rheesi had a light sweet voice, petulant and unbushmanlike; and although he had been born and schooled in the backblocks his accent was peculiarly English. The liquid redness of the fire gave a silken look to his face and clothes as he sat staring into the fire, and on the small finger of his shapely little hand he wore a heavy gold signet ring, like poor old Jim's.

Pricie-ole-man sat beside Blue and her hand was tucked into the pocket of his great-coat, which he wore indoors and out. He had a rough, contemptuous way of speaking to Rheesi and the jockey had a languid, important manner of answering him. One could feel that there was a tacit agreement between them to impress us that great affairs were at stake.

Pricie-ole-man said roughly, "What horse do you think you'll be riding at Tawonga, next week, Rheesi?"

Weakly and complainingly, Rheesi answered, "They want me to ride Falselock, but mai word, Ai think All-form ought to go, really."

Observing that I had a lost and lonely look, that Blue, the superb, was already the prize of Pricie-ole-man, Rheesi proposed that he should come down at the next week-end and take me shooting in the ranges, and, for our consumption, should bring a large cut lunch with him.

Blue was at once anxious that he should do so, pointing out that life in the sections had been excessively dull for me, since it had not been my good fortune to discover a mate in whom good taste, natural refinement, humour, looks and spiritual qualities were so well blended as in our new friend, Rheesi, who had proposed to visit us, armed with food. Furthermore, Blue would be delighted if Rheesi would bring down a large loaf of bread, one pound of butter, one pound of ham, and quantities of cheese and a cake . . . which she would skilfully, she said, cut into an enormous and satisfying lunch for Rheesi and myself. "And leave us," she said to me, as we retired for the night, "enough over for the week. I'll skin it out as far as it will go!"

On Sunday morning, Rheesi arrived, shining with the grease of a good breakfast, while we, pale from our pumpkins, greeted him, and tore the case of food from his hands.

"I won't be a minute," cried Blue jovially, and she ran with it into the most secret of the cubicles.

Rheesi and I withdrew to a warm corner and talked with shy delight of our meeting, and of the several poetic qualities that we found in each other. Ah, but he was not Macca; I grieved, knowing that perhaps never more would I ride through the ranges with my love. But I tried to like him, for company's sake; while in the cubicle Blue made us a poverty-stricken parcel of sandwiches around which she wrapped three newspapers, and tied the lot with a length of thick twine.

"Mai word!" exclaimed Rheesi, eyeing the large parcel wonderingly, "that's going to be a good big lunch! Ah!" He laughed and rubbed his stomach in the childish way he had. I felt sympathetic towards him as he took it in his hand and weighed it joyfully, repeating, "Mai word. . . . Mai word, Blue, you can make things spin out all right!" Blue agreed with him and waved us away, up in front of the sections: she was still waving whenever I turned back. The thought of all the food lying on the table in the cubicle made her hands move despite herself.

On this day, out of deference to the kangaroos, I was dressed in wide-legged khaki trousers and brown silk shirt, and strong leather shoes. Rheesi wore heavy breeches and leggings and his nose shone red from under a large felt hat.

Pointing to the large range, three miles distant, I said, "We're going to the top of that." The clouds drifted about it and the veins of space where the timber was sparse showed faintly. "Mai word," complained Rheesi, "that's a long way, isn't it?"

"You will have earned your lunch," said I. "This way if you please!"

I delighted, at that time, in trying out the strength of those who attached themselves to me. Since they could not think as I did, I gave them, not thoughts, but feats of endurance and power. I dragged them through miles of wild hop, ferns, and gum-trees; up steep shale-covered ranges and down kangaroo pads to where the creeks ran crying in the next valley.

My heart cried, "Thalassa. . . . Thalassa!" as I climbed, and my heart was in Metung with my love.

Brown, massive and splendid, my limbs moved under me, thrusting back the savage bushes and the medicine-men stones that cut into the virgin flesh of knees and elbows. We went up a hill covered with stringybark and slight dark saplings that appeared to us, as we climbed, to be standing in a clear sea of the blue heaven. Down, and over the rusty wire fence, turning to the right into a thin bush, where, under craggy branches, ran the track of McDonald's cows. We went farther in to where the creek ran and the ferns stretched for yards, and farther we went to where the foxes sat eating beneath the logs, and came at last to where the ranges stared down into the eyes, giving its hypnos to my hypnos, answer for answer, begging me to cling to it and follow it, none other, pleading that it had a mystical "Yes" which it would one day shout to me, so bringing me to blend with it forever.

At the foot of the range, Rheesi extended the parcel, "Now, mai word, Steve," he pleaded, "we'll have that lunch."

"Rheesi, there is nothing in that parcel. While we have been walking, a fox stole up to you and tore the lunch out. Now it is hidden on the top of Evan's Range. There you must follow me so that your terrible hunger may be assuaged."

Heroic as Cortés, romantic as Quixote, I climbed, and as sad as Sancho was Rheesi toiling from boulder to boulder behind me. In a nightmare of heat, strong thoughts, sweat, and whirling lights from the sun, that escaped under hats, eyelids, into the lips, across the throat, hands and arms . . . in all the wild glory of youth and light, we climbed the range and stood at last on the shady narrow top where the kangaroos fed.

Lying under a tree, Rheesi opened the parcel. I had feared, but my fears had not prepared me for the shock of the small sandwiches and the morsel of cake that Blue had made ready for us.

"Mai word, Steve, that loaf didn't go far. What on earth do you think has happened to it? Only four sandwiches and two pieces of cake! What do you make of that, Steve? Mai word . . . I don't think that's right!"

"You forget, Rheesi, that you have been climbing a steep range with the parcel under your arm. Why this matter is easily explained. Don't you see? Blue has divided the loaf into four and made from it, four thick sandwiches. She has cut the cake in half, and given us half each, also. But you, do you see, have had it under-your arm for hours, and have been climbing high above sea level all the time. That has crushed it down to one-fourth its original size. It is a case of compression by heat and high atmospheric content. We are now some thousands of feet above sea level, and this in itself causes all sorts of compression, such as the bleeding of the nose, fainting, due to a squeezing of the arteries in the brain, and a diminishing of the bilateral cells in bread. Have you never heard of that before?"

Rheesi humbly acknowledged that he had not, and once again wisdom was justified by her children.

Blue was ready for me when we reached the sections and drew me into the cubicle. On the table lay the bilateral cells of the bread, meat, cheese and cake, which had been so grievously affected by the altitude that they had slipped right down into the valley, intact.

Rheesi withdrew to the local boarding-house, bearing in mind Blue's injunction that he should steal all he could from the table, in order that we might have something for supper.

Those were the days of silks and saddles light, of fires burning and no food to cook on them; of nights when the flea-brown violin chanted in bird-like notes under the shadow of Blue's white throat; while her red lips made the peculiar grimaces of bush and gipsy players.

Hearing her, the Italians came down from their kitchen, carrying a red tin lamp that blew a brown light of smoke and flame over us. They stood around her singing, while she played the songs of Italy. With their rough hands on their hips, they smiled at each other, and sang. Their red Southern mouths, curling and moist, bleated out the tremulous songs with their ba-hing "a's", trilling "r's" and trumpeting "u's".

Giovanni, from Tuscany, a brown-faced son of Firenze, hook-nosed, yellow-toothed, with pale pink gums and brown eyes that seemed to have made his whole face tired, had been a policeman (*carabiniero*) and knew, he said, a good deal about ordinances and by-laws. It was he who called the songs.

"José, come arn, José!" cried he. in his nasal, superior voice, lifting a large hand that shone with prominent bones. "*Cantiamo 'La Giovinezza'!*"

Joyfully, they bayed the emphatic lilting hymn of the Fascisti:

> *"Giovinezza, giovinezza!*
> *O primavera, di bellezza!*
> *Nel Fascismo e la salvezza*
> *Della nostra libertà!"*

They mocked the whole world and flung their Duce up on their shoulders, crying, "*Viv' Italia! Viva Mussolini! Eja! Eja! Alala!*"

Maggiore, that little tinkling mouse with the red hair and the burning brown eyes, stood with folded arms and maliciously, clicking his tongue and dirty white teeth, giggled at some satirical remark Primo made. They stared at the violin while they sang, and their figures were as rigid as those who pose in opera. Arms folded over their chests, their eyes flashed seriously and sternly at each other, and then returned to the violin.

They liked our part of the section, those Italians. They made merry there until after midnight, and then departed, with reluctance, to their own quarters.

Next morning, as we lay in bed, we heard odd and untoward clamours: bulky furniture was dragged along the earthern passage to our kitchen, and by the lusty hammering we knew that safes were being put up and crockery was being smartly smacked into place on the shelves.

The Italians had come to take our kitchen.

We had never fraternized with them. We sensed that they despised us; and we thought, rather timidly, that perhaps if they weren't present in such numbers we might have had a chance to work in the paddocks and not be compelled by hunger to steal from them. But they were so generally accepted and worked so willingly for such a low rate of pay that it seemed unnatural to resent them. It was far easier for us, as poet and artist, to idealize them and find the fault in ourselves.

We didn't come out until they had gone and then, with feelings of burning shame and discomfiture, we looked around. Gone was our mild, empty kitchen, with its lack of crockery and food. The morning sun struck through the window and fell on the remains of a hearty breakfast of steak, tomato and spaghetti, cynically left open to us. Feeling that we could not endure it, we fled into the bush for the day, so that we should not be present when they returned triumphant from the paddocks.

But we had to come back at night. What sorrow and bitterness we felt as we walked into the lighted room where they sat eating their substantial tea. Without a word from either side, we retired into our rooms and sat in the dark, filled with shame at the thought of aliens treating us, the natives of the race that sheltered them, in such an unkindly fashion.

They talked about their conquering march into our territory in loud impudent voices and laughed about us.

"Blue," I said, "I know we're not considered to be of much worth here; but, I can't, even as an outcast Australian, let those Italians stay in our part of the section. They have their own kitchen. Why haven't they kept to it? True, we did take a bit of their food . . . but what of that? If they had had any charity, they would have realized that we were in want and, thankful to this country which nourishes them and pays them better wages than they have ever got in their lives, they would have assisted us, as Guiseppe and good Michelino have done. And both those men are married, contributing to the support of families in Europe. These outside, on our room, are single. Of their charity, they might have spared us a crumb from their table. No, they prefer to aggravate our misery by a moral victory over us. They hope to drive us out of this section. I am determined that they will not! Hang the memory of Michelangelo and Raphael . . . I am going to have them turned out . . . tonight!"

When they had finished their tea, we came out, and for all my high words, we sat by our fire, supperless, subduedly, like slaves. Around the table, they sat, playing *Tresette* and laughing with a mocking note of derision, disregarding us completely. "What?" I said to myself. "Are these the genial singers of last night, the poetic Fascisti, black-shirted and brilliant?"

Pricie-ole-man and Rheesi came in and stared in astonishment at our new neighbours. With woeful glances, we explained it all; but after we had said our say, we rose with set teeth, determined to get rid of them.

Their loud laughter was provocative, and defiant were the glances they threw at us as they slapped the cards down on the table. We walked over to the home of Mr Padrone, the grower himself. He was an extraordinary man of the most masterful, cold and intimidating character that I have ever met. His remoteness was palpable, and his decisive, calm, cruel estimation of an employee was devastating. He wandered around the large property with a cigar between his fingers, and any employee he met was figuratively held up, squeezed and put to his ear. When he put him down, he felt that he knew all there was to know. His habitual manner towards his workmen was one of frigid courtesy; but, let a breach come between them, and he would horrify the unfortunate by a slashing, comprehensive summing-up of his weaknesses, delivered in language that burnt with a savage genius.

He was, of course, deeply respected and feared greatly. He never laughed. A high, false cachinnation from a calm, unmoved face was his expression of humorous appreciation, and it had a devastating effect on the listener.

We found it difficult to make him realize that we suffered through the intrusion on our privacy. After all, we were only out-of-work women, staying by his grace in the sections, and the men against whom we complained were regular workers.

In his long, well-furnished room, surrounded by music, books and papers, we felt like dirt. I began by asking him if he would be good enough to give us the six acres of maize to pick, down on the river, and was overjoyed when he appeared to agree. We could scarcely believe it, and thanked him effusively for making honest women of us.

Then, tentatively, I said, "Mr Padrone, we have a peculiar request to make. You know, of course, what we are. Only as you see us, two wanderers, and women at that. We realize that, going about as we do, we can only reap suspicion; yet, unbelievable as it may seem, we are good morally, and have ideals that will some day be more clearly apparent as our generation grows older. That's how it ought to be, and that is how it is with us."

"Well, girls," coolly interested, "I believe all that; but what do you request?"

"You know that we have the kitchen at this end of No. 3 Section. It has been ours all through the summer and autumn. We have been grateful to have lived in it. This morning, without notice, the Italians, Major, Giovanni and Primo, moved up into it with their furniture. And now, as you will see, they sit playing cards by the light of the lamp and making a great noise. Besides, they are triumphant because they imagine that they have marched in on us and deprived us of our shelter. They laugh and talk noisily about it. And apart from the insults, the question is, how are we going to sleep tonight? There will be card-playing until late, and then rough jests among the men all night, and we shall not be able to sleep. Also, they are in the habit of talking lewdly, which offends us."

"What? In English?"

"Oh, no, not in English; but you see, we know enough Italian to understand."

"Perhaps they are not aware of that."

"Yes, they are. When we first came to this valley we talked to them in their language."

"Well, as you know, girls, men are the same the world over. Their tongues, you realize, are always coated because of moral dyspepsia."

"Ah, yes, we know that and understand. We tolerate it in all men, but only ask that we may have our kitchen to ourselves at night. We were there before the Italians, and I could not, would not, move, as they want us to do, and leave them in triumph."

"Ah well," he sighed, "I suppose I must come with you."

His soft black coat was brought to him, and his grey hat. "Now, come on, we shall see. Wait, though! A cigar. . . . There, now we are ready!"

Talking humorously and appreciatively of our life and the maize-picking that he had promised to give us, we went with him to the section.

At the sight of their Mr Padrone, the Italians bowed and said "Good night!" Then, guiltily, they returned to their cards, making a large fuss over them. For one moment, when they first saw him, they had checked themselves, but unfortunately for them a sort of defiance set in, and they laughed and talked loudly in Italian, as though he were not there.

For our part, we were most truly and anxiously subdued. Pricie-ole-man and Rheesi sat respectably on kerosene-cases at the fire, and we invited Mr Padrone to join us. He sat with us, around the fire, and we talked politely of empty things, inwardly wondering if Mr Padrone was going to let us down. A long tense time passed, during which he studied the laughing players carefully. However, at the last minute, the powerful little man arose and went over to the Italians' table. They greeted him again, but the play continued noisily.

Drawing at his cigar, he said courteously, but in a chilly, masterful voice of a metallic timbre, prefacing his remark with a clear cough that was known for miles around:

"A . . . herr! Why have you boys shifted up into this part of the section?"

Primo, who seemed by tacit consent to be the spokesman, said sullenly, in a thick, petulant voice, "Missa Padrone, it wass no goot in dat kitchen at dat end. We come up here."

"What was wrong with the kitchen, Primo?"

"De dorg . . . he fall down!"

"The dorg?"

"Yes, de dorg . . . he fall down all de time!"

"What dorg, Primo?"

"De dorg . . . dorg . . . you know de dorg!"

Mr Padrone regretted that he didn't, adding that the place was over-run with mongrels at present and that it would really have to be looked into. Why hadn't Primo communicated with the Dog Inspector who had called recently, regarding the animal which was falling down in his room all the time?

"Dis dorg different . . . dis dorg what keep out wind."

"I think," I said stealthily, "that Primo may mean not the dorg . . . but the *door*, Mr Padrone."

"Well, *door*!" cried Primo with a look of passion. He should have been grateful. Humiliation can stamp home the true pronunciation of a word more lastingly than a term at Oxford.

"Yes, the door he fall down all the time!"

Mr Padrone held his cigar to his ear and listened to its expensive creak with the air of a connoisseur. "Well, that may be unfortunate, but you are an engineer, my good fellow, and the mending of a door cannot be beyond you. Let me suggest that you remove your goods back into the kitchen and mend the door. It would really be the wisest thing to do, you know."

Coldly, he came back to our fire and, passing it, walked out. We accompanied him home. "A thousand thanks," we muttered. "And may we look forward to picking the maize?"

"Yes. I shall send the foreman over to see you when it is ready."

The maize was ours. We were workers again, and we should be able to stay with Charlie and Mrs Wallaby all the winter, leaving the kitchen we had wrested back from the Italians to be battled over by those to come.

The days passed and the oranges down in Sullivan's orchard grew

riper with the winter sun. We spread the news to Pricie-ole-man.
A night was arranged. He was to come down from Porepunkah on
his mare Seldom-fed, and meet us outside on the road.

On that night a thunderstorm of light and fury boomed and
flashed above the stony fortress of the granite mountain far above.
Ah, how tragic it was to look out on to that ancient moonlight and
see the black rain sweeping over the grey stone, to be followed by
the white grandeur of lightning which threw its twisted limbs over
everything. The granite roared with thunder, and showers as terrible
as the hour of death fled over us.

On the road outside the camp sat Pricie-ole-man on his mare
Seldom-fed. Long and spare was she, as her name indicated, and
a velvet winter coat covered her, but could not soften the sharp
bones that stuck out everywhere from her frame. Whenever the
lightning flashed, Seldom-fed pigrooted with a powerful up-thrust
of her bony legs.

We were dressed in long coats and trousers and carried a sugar-
bag in which to put the oranges. Pricie-ole-man held Seldom-fed
against the fence while Starving Steve and Breadless Blue mounted
to go on a raid again. He flung himself on, in front of us; then
away, pigrooting and puffing, we trod a noble measure down the
white road as the whistling rain fell in the moonlight.

As we passed the railway crossing, we saw a figure leaning against
the cattle-pit, chewing walnuts and tossing a restless hat from side
to side on an unkempt head.

"Who's that?" said Pricie-ole-man, peering through the lightning
and moonlight.

"It's the ghost of the cow that got dragged along by the train
last week," I replied. "Poor beast, it was in full milk, too."

"Gee with," exclaimed Charl. "Gor blarmie! What do you take
me for? Did youthe really think I was the ghost of that cow? I
bet you didn't!"

Charl was a shrewd fellow sometimes.

"You go one better than us, Charl. We give in."

"Where you going this hour er night?" Charl cracked another
walnut on the cattle-pit and laughed. "After more of Blackmoor'th
appleth?"

"No. Sullivan's oranges, this time. Hop on!"

"Bring her over to the potht, then. Way, now! Wee . . . there!
Gee with, just let me get me foot on her boneth and I'll get on.
Come over, yer cow! Hey, wait on!" Charl missed and fell down

on the muddy road. "Come over 'ere. Edge 'er over to the fence, Pricie-ole-man!"

Seldom-fed, poor but proud, drew away and, despite her overload, she pigrooted with vigour and venom.

"Get off for a moment," said Pricie-ole-man, in that bluffing way of his, "and I'll give it to her. I'll take it out of her."

Dismounting, we squatted on the side of the road in the moonlight and lightning, while Pricie-ole-man gave it to her. Seldom-fed solemnly pigrooted up and down the road for ten minutes, and Charlie stood by, his various rags flying in the wind. What a ballet! The thunder drummed in the ranges; the lightning flashed blue and green and gold in the black sky, and on the green grass the bony old mare pirouetted with thin upstretched throat and feet raised to the heavens as though carrying on her hooves a tray of whisky and soda to Olympus.

At last, she stopped, and was drawn over to the fence. In order, we mounted. Blue behind Pricie-ole-man; Steve behind Blue and Charl behind Steve, cracking walnuts on Seldom-fed's thigh bones and handing them around.

" 'Ere you are, Thteve! Gee with, wait a moment, Theldom-fed!" The steed rose in another slow and solemn pigroot, and we rose with it. "Wait till I crack me nut, Theldom." Clonk! " 'Ere you are, Blue, give one to Pricie-ole-man."

Slowly, with a reverend grandeur, we moved along the road under the tragic battle of the night. And often Charl cried frantically and painfully, "Move forward! Move forward! I'm thitting on the bone!" It was the banshee wail that accompanied us on our march.

The rain now fell with a thick hastiness and saturated us all, so that we shrank from it.

"Move forward, I'm thitting on the bone," Charl cried in anguish, and cracked another nut to the tune of thunder and the glint of lightning.

We turned down the road that led to the orange-tree on Sullivan's property, and met tall Sullivan himself, coming out of the storm, homeward-bound, after being out inspecting his fences or bridges. Farmers like a dark wet night for that sort of job. He stopped and stared in horror at the apparition we made, of four heads, arms and hands above, and below, the thin legs of Seldom-fed propelling the unknown through the storm.

"Stone the crows," he said faintly. "What is it?" and held on to the fence in fear.

"Ith me . . . Charl!" said the walnut-cracker, adding in a minor tone of anguish, "can't you move forward a bit? I'm thitting on the bone!" Crack! Another walnut.

"What on earth are you doing out at this time of night and in such weather?" asked Sullivan, as we slowly and carefully passed him, giving one hiccoughing pigroot as a sign that Seldom-fed had noticed him.

"Oh, just going for a ride, yer know," said Charlie casually, and we passed on, leaving Sullivan clinging to the fence and eying us awfully.

Seldom-fed gave another pigroot; Charlie cracked another nut and gave us once more the tune of "thitting on the bone", and we moved from sight into the sweeping fury of the night.

Down another lane we turned, and so thickly timbered was it that a rain-heavy branch of wattle swept us all off. Seldom-fed sighed with gratitude as we fell, and pigrooted heavenward, a prayer on each hoof.

Remounting, we moved along slowly again, over a rough slippery bridge. Its boards were rotten and widely spaced, and under it the river, evil with winter, roared smotheringly, telling of the men it drowned each year and of the little channels in which they lay and rolled until a search brought them to light.

For me, the night seemed to halt here, for apprehension catches fear by the throat. It passed, and we moved on, down a path thick with wattles, to the deserted house.

Through the gate we swung, surging forward to the laden orange-tree. Charl and I got down, and held the bag open, while Blue stood up on Pricie-ole-man's shoulders. He walked Seldom-fed around the tree and, by the light of the storm, Blue twisted the oranges off and flung them down to us. "Don't eat them here," warned Blue, "and leave peel around to be found."

When the bag was full, we started off for home. Charl and I agreed to walk until Seldom-fed got over to the other side of the bridge. The riders departed.

Charl told me that he knew a short-cut through the wattle, to the bridge. So, admiring his quiet bush sagacity,

> Over the mountain's purple brim
> The happy princess followed him

through thick bush, until he fell head over heels in a dam made by the overflow of the river. I followed him. As we dragged ourselves out, I said, "You meant a short dive, through the wattles to the bridge."

We found Blue and Pricie-ole-man waiting for us on the other side of the bridge and, mounting, we were pigrooted by Seldom-fed back to the camp.

The largest share of the oranges was sent down to Mrs Wallaby, so that she might make jam out of them; for, since we were going to spend the winter there, we thought we might as well send the food ahead.

Next morning, Charlie went down and borrowed a preserving-pan from Sullivan's to make the jam in. And afterwards, when Sullivan discovered that the oranges were gone, he remembered the riders of the night, the borrowed preserving-pan and the jar of jam that was blithely presented to him when the utensil was returned, and he looked an embittered man.

The following week, the foreman came to the section early one morning and told us to start picking the maize. It was a crop of Thirty Day Flat Red, or, as we called it, Thirty Years Flat Broke. Dressed in khaki, wearing our snake-skin wristbands, belts and hobbles, we attacked the maize with strong steel hooks riveted to a band of leather through which the hand passed.

Maize-picking is performed by an upward jump, if the picker is small. The cob is grasped, the hook inserted in the husk, and torn down it, twisting the cob out of it at the same time. We threw the cobs into a heap behind us and bagged-up in the afternoon. Then we threw them into a kerosene-tin, and tipped them right into a bag, for a change. As the days passed, we got desperate and did everything in all ways, so bored, melancholy and discouraged were we with the Thirty Years Flat Broke.

The maize paddock stood on the very edge of the cold dark river, whose banks were softly and clearly breaking away through erosion caused by the falling of the willows.

Every morning we rose early and I cooked the porridge and brought it in to Blue, who lay in bed just that favoured little longer which is the privilege of the beautiful. Then off to the paddocks in the frost or rain, our hands and ankles blue with the cold of the alpine country. I, having no socks to wear, stuffed my shoes with the softest maize husks.

Ah, the agony of waiting for the sun to rise and warm you . . . what a useless agony that is! How primitive! You feel, as you wait, that you are a people without a country. You fancy that you are political refugees escaping from a cruel fatherland. It is all discomfort and shivering misery.

As the sun brightened we felt happier and worked with warmer and lighter hands, but I always felt unhappy in that maize paddock. The thought of Macca and Metung in the far-off Primavera was anguished torture. As I worked, I cried out to the dark cold river, "Ah, Primavera!" imitating the harsh cry of old Michele. What feeling, power and hopelessness I put into it.

"Ah, Primavera!"

As a libation I threw a golden cob into the black waters below, crying, "O, for love, true, faithful and happy love, I give you this cob, this golden purse of the earth, wild river!

"Ah, Primavera! Will it never come? Shall we never finish this thick crop?"

VII

WE were soon to shift down to Wallaby's, and on one of the last mornings at the section, as we sat around the fire, a short, slim fellow strolled in, out of the fire and dew of the morning. He was dressed in the olive-grey uniform of the Alpini, the mountain regiment of Northern Italy, and in his hand he swayed a delicate branch of olive . . . "the faint grey olive".

This little fellow could scarcely speak English. We stared at his supernaturally long thin nose, sharp narrow lips, dark eyes, long-lashed, and thin black hair. In his attempts to speak, he made extraordinary mouths, as though he were crying or biting the English language off by the inch, chewing it from side to side and finding it as bitter as gall. It made one lose one's appetite for culture to see how awkwardly he bit his words.

"Ow!" he exclaimed, staring at the fire. "*Buon giorno!*" weakly. He picked up the poker and asked, in English, "Ow you call dissa thing?" His terrible grimaces frightened us; we thought he was about to throw a fit. But he waited, calmly, stroking the olive bough.

"Oh, this? Poker?"

"Ow . . . pokko! Arlraight, tankayou!" A long silence. Then, "Ow you call what you do when sometime one man what come you say 'Ow you do your do do do?'."

This took us at least a week to translate, and we spent hours at it in the paddock, saying to each other, with Abracadabra as a preface: "Ow you call what you do when sometime one man what come you say, 'Ow you do your do do do?' "

At last, I exclaimed, "Why . . . I know what he means!"

"What, Steve?"

"Someone's said, 'How do you do?' to him, and he's never been the same since."

When I saw Salvatore again, I took off my cap to him and said politely, "How do you do?" The troubled, yearning look that he had worn all the week was dissipated in a second. His eyes beamed and his smile came out, lying on two crooked teeth among some very fine ones that he had.

"Ah, owa!" he cried. "Owa dis ow you do your do do do?"

We assured him that it was indeed so.

"O . . . arlraight! What dissa mean. . . . Ow you do your do do do?"

"What does it mean? Ah!" Shaking our heads sadly, we took him aside, and, looking at him with an air of profound pity, we said: "Friend, desist! No further! Stay! Seek not to know what means 'How do you do?' That way madness lies!"

And we restored him to the ways of men by trying to find out what "church" meant in Italian. This took one whole day, and was marked by innocent little errors that have remained in my mind.

"Church?" said he, puzzled.

"Yes, you know!" But he didn't. I drew a rough building on the soil of the maize paddocks, and on its top outlined a crucifix. "See? Church! Cross! *Church!* Big place . . . Sunday . . . many people . . . much money. Sing . . . all time . . . sing!"

"Sting? Ah, yes, mosquito! Yes, I know arlraight! Big mosquito . . . insetto what sting."

"No! No! Big *place* . . . room for God . . . crucifix. Money like this." Blue walked round with her hat in her hand, from maize stalk to maize stalk, looking as much like a vestryman as she could, chilly, calm, benevolent but watchful. Salvatore shrank from her.

"Church!" we repeated patiently. "Cross on top. . . . Cross! . . . *Cross!*"

"*Croce!*" said he faintly. "Oh, I know arlraight!" and with infinite delicacy, he yielded up his hand to a gesture that ended where the tailor's measure begins for a pair of gent's pants, double-width tweed, reinforced seams and strong pockets . . . and he said with a politeness and modesty worthy of better things, "You mean . . . crutch?"

And it took us three days, then, to explain why we had been talking about a crutch.

A wagon drew up to the gate of the camp next afternoon and, with flaps flying, slowly trundled into our midst. It stayed slumbrous and sheet-like on the green grass all day, but towards evening, when the men came home from work, the Indian hawker, Gauda Singh, of "Crushed to the crackles" fame, appeared. From a distance we watched garments being held up against the setting sun, to test their worth; and at night, when Pricie-ole-man came down to see us, we walked over with him to the van. For we bore the worthy Gauda no grudge. Life is long, friend. A red fire burnt in the ashes, and we sat down by it, opposite Gauda Singh, whose harsh white beard rose and fell like a crop of wheat with the wind across it as he gave us . . . "Salaam!"

What memories of Karta Singh, of Averdrink and the bark hut that aroused in me! I almost imagined that Macca would join us soon.

"Well, you fella," said he, and the rude title delighted me with its ring of Gippsland and old days. "What you like for buy? I got fine shirt, trouser and concertina. What more you want?"

Since we had no money to spare, we replied that we had all that man could possibly desire; and, on hearing this, Gauda Singh began to talk of the evil desires of mankind and the punishment which God sent to us. Around that little fire, he raised for us an Indian-Dantesque Inferno, peopling it with white-hot figures that roved through eternal redness in search of peace and cold water.

"In that place, many fire come, and all time full of flame like blood. Big music on roof sing out name of bad man and woman, while fire burn forever. All crawl around, no clothe, and cry to God, but He not hear. No food, no love, no sleep . . . only red hot poker, all time." The voice of Gauda Singh was soft and rich with satisfaction.

From the darkness came the lanky limping figure of Paddy, the boarding-house keeper, crying in a high, sing-song drawl. "Are yer there, Gauda Singh? What er yer got in the way of clothes? And women's dresses? The wife wants a couple."

Gauda Singh regretted, "No, no dress this time. Soon I go India and come back plenty dress for lady."

Paddy moaned. "Would yer bring us back a coloured silk scarf? Good quality. Don't spare ther expense, Gauda. I'll get it from yer when yer come back."

Gauda said, "Yes, I put him down now," and drew out a little book and entered it, although he knew quite well that Paddy would never come to get the scarf, and Paddy knew perfectly well that Gauda would never order it.

They parted with many courteous expressions of gratitude and

Gauda settled down to have a good look at me across the flame. "I like you face, you young girl. If you like, I take you to India with me. You be my second wife."

"Ha," said I, "but if you already have a wife, she would dislike me."

"No. My wife, she love you too much. I take you under my wing like one darling."

"You have too much under your wing already; and then, I see that your pinions are moulting and would provide no shelter for one like me, strong and restless, my good Gauda!"

Unoffended, he continued to talk to us about love and hell until the fire went out, and we went home to bed.

Early next morning, there was a soft tap at the door, and we let in Gauda Singh, carrying a snowy white handkerchief, which he slowly undid. Within lay a beautifully baked johnny cake, puffed up in the middle and lightly browned.

Our courteous thanks pleased the old man, and he shook our hands, saying that by night, when we had returned from work, he would be gone, not to return until next year when he hoped to see us again.

When we opened the johnny cake, a delicate little stew of curried rice and meat lay smoking in it.

That night we left the sections and went down to sleep at Mrs Wallaby's. There were puftaloonies for tea, cooked in a big camp oven over a roaring fire made from the finest railway sleepers. Charl had tons of timber on his property, but was too fatigued to cut it down; and to sneak along the railway line and lift a sleeper from the pile kept by for repairs was the work of a moment. And how well they burnt!

I shall never forget those walks down to Wallaby's at night, after we had knocked off in the maize paddock. We didn't go near the camp, but struck off across the paddocks to the railway line and walked along its harsh stony path until we came to a fence with a bit of bag bound around the barbed wire. We got through and were on the road and walking down towards Sullivan's, whose large families lived in scattered houses all along the road.

The railway crossing lay stark and bare across the road that led to their old homestead, and two great poplars, the poets of the land, shook their bare autumn branches, black and fine, across the stars. Post-and-rail fences, as frail as Chinese writing, lay on each side of the trees against a reddening sky. We lived for things like that.

Over Evan's Range burnt the Dog-star, Sirius, with a scorching red, blue and green fire.

"That is my star," I said to Blue. There, walking slowly, with my eyes raised to it, I prophesied.

"Some day, I shall write fully our life together, with its tragedy and comedy. But better than that, I shall write of Australia and bring lovers to her so that they shall fill the land with visionaries. For 'where there is no vision, the people perish'. But, Bluey, Bluey, I wonder what really does lie ahead in the years? Why does sorrow haunt me.

> ". . . Be thou therefore in the van
> O circumstance; yea, seize the arrow's barb
> Before the tense string murmur.

"But I am lost. I see nothing to seize. I am powerless. Poor and uneducated, we roam our country, fit for no work but that of the paddocks. It is good. It is better than the factories of the city. But, what, my Bluey, lies ahead? I guess . . . and fear."

As we passed little lonely places where the moonlight lay on the soft grass and the wild-looking trees shone like silver, we imagined that we could see the black figures of the aborigines flying through the timber and up into the ranges.

"Australia, Australia," I cried. "Ah, Patria Mia!"

From overhead, like rain that struggled laughing and weeping in the hands of God, came the staccato cry of the plovers, those wanderers from the Russian steppes.

"Ah, what shall I find in Metung in Primavera?"

Old Spot, hearing our voices far off, barked hoarsely. Mrs Wallaby came out and stood on the veranda with a big china lamp in her hand. In a deep, kind, droning voice she cried, "Where are my wandering girls tonight?"

"Here we are!" Forgetting our dreams and visions, we climbed the muddy slope to the house. Charlie sat at the table, eating stewed rabbit and "souping" up the tea from a large cup.

The crochet work was pushed off the table and we sat down to eat. The long, cold, hungry nights in the section were behind us now, and no more would we lie awake at night listening to the ribaldry of the Italians.

When the tea was over, Blue tied a bread-board at the back of her head, like a halo, took the teapot in her hand and pretended to be a saint, disguised as a swagman, who wandered over Australia, rewarding those who were kind to him with drops of the elixir of life. For some reason, Mrs Wallaby loved this little comedy, and made Blue mime it for her every other night. And afterwards, when Blue brought out her violin and played bush-tunes and Italian marches, the victory was complete.

The change from the sections comforted us unutterably and when we looked around the bedroom Mrs Wallaby had given us, we felt that we were truly home, at last. A large black iron bedstead stood in the middle of the room, and a door opened out on to an earthen veranda, on which the dust was dry and red, even in winter. There was a large chest of drawers in the room, and we put our few belongings into it.

Blue took a fine piece of red woollen frieze off the mantel-shelf and wrapped it around her thighs. It looked magnificent against her golden limbs. Enviously eyeing it, I crawled into bed with her. Mrs Wallaby sang out to us from her bedroom:

"Are you all right, Steve and Blue?"

"Oh, yes, and very warm and happy, thank you!"

"Well, good night!"

She sang dolorously,

> "My trials are hard . . . I'll not complain.
> But trust in God, we'll meet again. . . .

"Are you awake, Charl?" she cried when the song was done.

Charl, who was in the room next to ours, said, "Gee with, mother, I only just got into bed. What do you expect?"

"Are you awake, Steve and Blue?"

"Yes," we answered gladly.

"Oh!" And in an Ophelia-like voice she sang about someone who never returned to say that he was sorry, "Or why you stayed away!"

Throughout the night, curfew took place at regular intervals.

"Charlie, are you awake, Charlie?"

"Gee with, what ith it, mother?"

"Steve and Blue, are you awake?"

"Snor-r-h! Yairs . . . yairs . . . what is it, Mrs Wallaby?"

"Oh, nothing! I just wondered."

At twelve o'clock, the alpine train rattled past, with a roar, and Mrs Wallaby awoke to wonder again.

"Soon be time to get up, Charlie, that's the seven o'clock train going down."

"Gee with, mother, ith the midnight train, going up. Oooh," he groaned, "a bloke won't get any sleep tonight!"

R

"Are you awake, Steve and Blue?"
No. We were not.

Each night, across our sleep, the mountain rain fell with a murmur of sensual loneliness, and we clutched at each other in dreams.

Sometimes, as we lay awake, listening to that hissing drip on the roof, to the solitary pattering among the yellow leaves, a fox laughed with a wild silvery note out in the bush, and we caught at each other and cried out at the primitive cry.

"Steve . . . the fox!"

"Ah, Blue! What wildness . . . what mirth and desolation in that laugh of his!"

We thought we saw him leaping the damp, rotten logs and roaming, full of blood-hunger, from tree to tree. The echoes of his cry awoke in us a desire, half animal, half spiritual, to be of the fox and the night.

Against my smooth limbs, the scarlet frieze around Blue's body brushed as she turned, and into my mind leapt the image of the wattle-bird with its harsh cry outside the garden at Averdrink. Macca, Macca, my lost love, where art thou?

Green gum-leaves twisted sharply in my mind, and through them was the blue sky, through which the red and purple lowries flew, screeching. I held all that before me, with the cry of the Gippsland wattle-bird saying, "Go back . . . go back!" And after a long brooding silence, confessing, "Don't go back!"

I brought rhythm to bear on what I saw and heard, and it pressed down, faltering on that keyboard of bush colour. The words came out slowly, note by note, and I listened and remembered them as they came. Arranging them carefully, I turned and said, "Blue, are you asleep?"

"No, Steve."

"Well, in my mind, I have had the green leaves of these ranges, lit by the flying lowries . . . and the cry of the wattle-bird in Metung. And. . . ."

"Steve, I knew while I lay beside you that you were making a poem. I felt it in your brain. What is it?" The scarlet frieze brushed up against me, eagerly.

"It is the road to Redenbach's. Do you remember it, Bluey? After you leave the Cyclone gate at Averdrink, you walk along through a mist of wattles and post-and-rail fences, until you come to where the road divides, and an old one, scattered with twigs and broken boughs, goes down to Redenbach's. What is there that is so pathetic about an old Australian road, lying in all the mystery of neglect beside a new one on which the traffic hurries thoughtlessly? Ah, what richness is in that very neglect! The shadows are different there. They are centuries old and etched so delicately by the trees. The fact that no wheel passes over them gives a virginity which the shadows of the main road have lost. And the little twigs, beloved of the Chinese and Japanese, lie in fine masses over everything; the pale brown skeleton gum-leaf, the most beautiful corpse in the world, is stamped down into the mud and draws its own death-mask there, before it utterly disappears. Chips from old logs bleach on the roadside among wiry grass, and beds of velvety charcoal lie on the fallen logs over pads of dry green moss coloured like wintry sunlight and having those little whiskers with knobs sticking on top of each whisker. And under each chip and leaf lies a little insect, Australian, weird and puzzling. Ah, there are millions of old roads in Australia, Blue, like that road to Redenbach's. Well, here is the poem, at last.

> "Abruptly, the dry road ended clean,
>   At the dry hill's foot . . . at its very beginning,
>   Forsook it entirely, and ran between
>   A mile of scrub, to the river, singing
>   'Follow!' And followed, I would have, but
>   Even before I touched the track,
>   The leaves were stirred and their colours cut
>   By a bird's voice crying, 'Go back! Go back!'
>   So back I went, uncertainly,
>   Thumbing the thought the throat had cried.
>   'Thou art not for this, nor this for thee!'
>   And so, was satisfied."

We fell asleep talking about Metung. Charlie awoke us in the morning, bustling into our room full of energy to get us up and out into the maize paddock. We set out, walking briskly, and as we crawled under the fence and walked along the railway line, I suddenly thought of a woman who had lived long ago. Her name was Maggie Lotton, of Emu Plains, and my mother had known her when she was a girl. For years she had been dead, but I thought I stood beside her on that morning and smelt her clean blue dress brushing against me, and saw the honest strength and beauty of her throat. The earth gleamed with dew and my mind twisted and turned in the wreath of beauty brought by the hours, as I remembered the dead and sorrowed that they should not see this day.

VIII

THE hop paddocks were being turned over by the tractor. The shining slices of mist-breathing soil were trodden down by the Italians and Australians as they worked. Over the many acres glittered the dewy cobweb sheets of the earth spiders, blue, green and gold, holding the mosaics of the sun.

Rustling through our dry crop, we began to pick, looking now into the river and then to the grey granite mountain above, on which the blue veins of boulder knitted to boulder showed clearly. And the waterfalls, strong with winter, glittered in the sunlight. I thought I saw the wild black brumbies gallop across the granite, long-maned and red-saddled by the sunrise.

As we worked, we became aware of a crackling and slicing far behind us and, emerging, saw our friend Salvatore of the Crutch, bending low and gathering to his short hook stalks of the maize we had picked. Behind Salvatore crouched a little dark man with a stubble beard and a bright red handkerchief about his throat, under a soot black hat of gentle depth.

"Owa . . . *buon giorno!* Gooda morning," said Salvatore, with his mouth under his ear and his teeth clawing his chin in an effort to speak faultless English. "I gotta . . . owa . . . dis jarb . . . owa!" He pulled his mouth down like a shark's and rolled his eyes with a sick modesty. "Ai cut . . . owa . . . dis . . . owa . . . mice [maize] while you pick . . . burra . . . owa, you no got for hurry wit mice. Plenty time, owa . . . burra. . . ." The mouth came towards us an inch or so, the eyes rolled heavenward and the head twisted towards the river.

"Oh, very nice indeed. So you have got work at last?"

In his soft tortured voice, and with his wide tortured mouth half in his ears and half in his eyes, Salvatore gave thanks that yes, at last, he "gotta jarb".

"And who's the other fellow?"

Salvatore hit out at him with the hook and curled his mouth towards his nose while his teeth faltered on the edge of his ear. "Dis-a mai friend, Chiverelli."

The bearded one looked up at this and smiled sweetly with white teeth flashing among a black stubble under which the red handkerchief blew like a flame.

"Yes," said he, "me name Chiverelli. Ah," sweetly, bowing to the field, "nice-a mice. Pretty gal," to Blue. "Nice-a da-a-a-y. Nice-a mi-i-ice."

We returned to our maize and picked steadily.

In the afternoon, the amiable Chiverelli paid us a visit for the purpose of culture. Explaining that his thirst for learning was inexhaustible, he pointed to various objects and asked their equivalents in English. Every request was prefaced by *"Come si chiama questo in Inglese?"*

"Long time I am in America," he remarked, smiling sweetly and coldly. Touching the gloves which Blue wore when picking, he said, *"Come si chiama questo in Inglese?"*

"Gloves!"

"Ah, gloves! Gloves! Tanka you . . . gloves!"

Then touching Blue on her broad bosom, he said, *"Come si chiama questo in Inglese?"*

"Ah . . . toe-nail!" I replied brightly.

"Toe-nail? Toe-nail?" with a surprised and delighted smile. "Ah . . . good-a name," he chanted deliriously. "Toe-nail! Ah, good-a name! In America callemzitts!"

And throughout the rest of the day he wailed to himself as he worked his scythe through the tough "mice", "Toe-nail . . . toe-nail! Good-a, good-a name!"

We thrashed our way through the maize, the kangaroo apples, and the castor-oil plants with their mace-like heads, earning our bread in sweat and sorrow.

There was a premonitory crackle in the maize and a little elderly man pushed his way through. Raising his white panama hat and taking his blackened, cracked pipe out of his mouth, he arched both articles and his own frame, in perfect synchronization, bowed, and said, "How do you do?"

"Abracadabra!" cried we, remembering Salvatore.

"How are you getting on?" wistfully from under a weak worn moustache. His battered face, absolutely gnawed by care and failure, was nevertheless lit by the dying fires of what has been an enormous vanity.

He looked fondly at Blue. "It's very hard work, isn't it?" he continued hurriedly and softly. Beginning to help her, he picked and threw cobs everywhere. "I just happen to be your overseer . . . count your bags and so on." The torn black ribbon on his panama hat flapped as he worked and his thin legs shook in tough, gloomily shining leggings.

"What a beautiful young woman you are, if you will pardon my mentioning it." Off and out in a curve came hat and pipe, and he bowed with them.

"Thank you," said Blue formally.

While he worked, he bent above Blue and whispered into her ear, and Blue gave him loud hearty answers, so that he lapsed into an embarrassed silence, which he broke by a loud conceited clearing of his throat, and then fell to singing in a harsh voice full of vibrato,

"My passion unrestrained!"

When he had gone, we stood together, and in stentorian voices, preceded by a harsh cough, we sang in duet,

"My passion unrefined . . . ha ha!"

We raised our hats to each other with a flourish, at the same time taking from our mouths the corn cob pipes we had made for our act.

"*Dove sei stato mio bel' alpino?*" sang Salvatore far in the distance. Oh, what mournfulness in that song! "Where have you been, my beautiful alpine soldier?"

It was raining as we went home to Wallaby's, and along the road we met Pricie-ole-man plugging along, his pale jaw sticking out, and his overcoat bulging with some large jam melons which he had bandicooted from a farm up the road and was taking down to his aunt as an offering.

"The ole man kicked me out; said I did nothing but loaf. That's right; but what else can you do around here? I had a good blacksmith shop, a year ago, but the cars are taking all the trade. There's not enough horses on the road to keep me in tucker. Think I'll get right back in the bush and start up in business again."

He hadn't a penny, but the two big melons sticking out of his coat gave him the look of a man breasting the waters of the world and defying them.

Squelching through the rain, we came to Wallaby's, where the warm fire and hot puftaloonies waited for us. Mrs Wallaby shook her head over Pricie-ole-man's tragedy and made him welcome, for a while at least.

Around the fire we sat, while the thunder and lightning rumbled and flashed over the granite mountain, and the violin was played, until Blue set it down to hear Mrs Wallaby's tales of the early days.

"Down in that old shed on the property over the ralway line, we lived years ago. One day we got word that the bushranger Morgan was riding along the road, sticking up places. We ran into the house and locked all the doors and windows. After about an hour, we saw Morgan and his gang come riding along the road. They called out, but we didn't answer; so, putting a few shots through the house, they rode on. Ah, the early days," mourned Mrs Wallaby, "that was the time! My father was out shooting in the scrub one day; it came right up to the back door then." (It was still there, but we didn't like to dishearten her.) "And he came across half a dozen men skinning a fat bullock down in the timber near the river. They pulled out their guns when they saw him, and said, 'If you don't want to follow these bullocks, keep a still tongue in your head.' Father told us years afterwards."

Pricie-ole-man slept with Charlie that night. They snorted, pushed each other around, and Charl "Gor blarmied" and "Gee with-ed" and "Hey-look out-ed" for half an hour. In the middle of a shower of rain, Pricie-ole-man arose and went into the night. The door closed behind him with a bang.

"Charl," cried Mrs Wallaby dolorously, "who was that went outside?"

"Oh . . . I don't know, mother."

"But I heard someone open the door and go out."

"By joveth, that'th funny. I never heard anything!"

"Is Reg [Mrs Wallaby called her nephew by his proper name] with you, Charl?"

"Yeth, I think tho."

"Reg? Are you there, Reg?"

"Oh gee with, mother, don't wake him up, he'th tired!" said the agitated Charlie.

"Reg! Reg!" persisted mother. "Are you there, Reg?"

"Oh," muttered Charl, "leave uth alone!"

"Reg . . . are you there, Reg?"

"No, mother," desperately. "He mutht have gone outthide."

"You said he didn't, Charl," reproachfully.

"Well, he mutht have when I wath athleep. Gee with, gor blarmie, why don't you leave uth alone?"

"Where's he gone, Charl?" We nudged each other with kindling glee.

"Oh, mother, I don't know. . . ."

"Did he go outside?"

"Yeth, I think he did."

"What did he go for, Charl?"

"Oh, mother, gee with, what thilly thingth you athk!"

Pricie-ole-man came in just then, rubbing his hands genially and shivering. "Go on, move over, Charl," said he. "Gee, it's cold. Snow on top tonight; you can see it through the showers."

"Reg!"

"Yes, aunt," alertly.

"Where did you go, Reg?"

"Er . . . outside, aunt."

"What for, Reg?"

Silence. Silence. Silence. Curfew rang all night, but there was none to heed it.

In the smelly drowsiness of the old farm bedroom, we awoke to a bright morning.

"Charl!" cried Mrs Wallaby in her deep, clanging voice. Charl grunted and awoke to life again.

"Gee with, what day ith it? Where am I?" Charl had a lot of standard jokes to start the day with. "Ah, well, I thpoth I better get up and light the fire for all youthe lathy cowth."

Charl sprang smartly out of bed and rushed outside without any preliminary.

"He didn't dress, did he?" whispered Blue.

"No, what's he got on, I wonder? Pyjamas, I suppose."

"Funny, you wouldn't think that a chap like Charl wore pyjamas."

From the slope in front of our bedroom came the clear hack of the axe, cutting into the sleepers.

"What! He can't be cutting wood in his pyjamas." We crept over to the window to have a look.

Charl was doing better than that. He was cutting frost-covered wood with a frost-covered axe on frost-covered ground . . . in a red and black striped football sweater that just covered his hips, and he had on his battered hat and hobnailed boots. We swooned away from the window, as he grabbed up an armful of kindling and sprinted up the slope to the door, whistling brightly. Soon, in the cold kitchen, we heard him putting the fire together.

"And, ah, what a sight that must be," sighed Blue, as we turned over and went to sleep again.

The sun was well up in the sky when we started out with Pricie-ole-man to work in the maize. Pricie-ole-man wheeled an ancient bike, on which he was going to ride up to Porepunkah and be reconciled with his family. He mounted it, and Blue got on behind, wearing a big blue policeman's cape which Pricie-ole-man had given her and a pair of pants, called the Willie Grays. As she sat behind Pricie-ole-man like a deflated toad, with the wheels whirling under her, the sight was one to affect all physical functions. I could scarcely walk for laughing.

The pants called Willie Grays need a word in passing. A character-istically thorough search of ours, carried out through the drawers in our bedroom, had yielded up these dainties, together with a Francotte rifle and a thousand rounds of ammunition. I was given the lethal weapon and the khaki breeches were handed on to Blue.

Long ago, Willie Gray had gone in on shares with Mrs Wallaby, for the purpose of growing tobacco; but the crop wasn't successful, so he left the partnership, and a pair of military breeches and a rifle. We listened to legends of this wanderer, as we sat by the fire at night; and now, as I looked into the seat of his breeches while Blue whirled up the road with her police force cape swirling out above them, I wondered at the timbre of the wondrous Willie Gray.

As we passed the camp, we had a look in at our section, and shrank away. Our kitchen had been invaded by a new mob of Italians . . . little dark Calabrese, guttural and vivacious, giving flashing side glances and smiles, while their chests heaved agitatedly under their black shirts over such important matters as who would light the fire first. The black shirts, rough trousers and wide flat-topped caps made these unfortunates look repulsive to us and we got down into the maize paddock, glad of the strong beauty of our land, spreading before us.

We had a visitor that afternoon. A lad from Naples. He stole on us from the river-bank, with a wild look in his eyes and a big axe in his hand. He brandished this madly around our heads as he talked, aimlessly, childishly and hopelessly.

"No gotta jarb," he hissed. "Go back Italia! No gotta jarb!"

"What is your name, O axeman wild?"

"Michele Tuberosa!"

"*O bel nome!*" I thought of the heavy-petalled tuberose flowering in some bewitched spot, and its fleshy pink and whiteness held me still in ecstasy.

But Michele Tuberosa hadn't anything fancy about him. He was short, squat and black, with a huge pug nose on which many pustules reached maturity; and behind it, two eternally blinking eyes, large, frightened and frog-like, with the wastefulness of a mad brain wandering through them.

We said, "We shall call you *Il Rospo* . . . the Frog."

"*Si* . . . *si. Il Rospo* no gotta jarb . . . go back Italia!"

"Jump, frog!" we said. "Jump high!"

"Joomp, frawg?" he repeated mechanically.

"*Si . . . saltate, Rospo . . . saltate!*"

Catching hold of a long maize stalk he leapt up and down it, with his frog-like eyes fixed on us unblinkingly. Catching hold of the hatchet, he whirled it around our noses and then buried it deep in the ground.

"Jarmp, frawg! *Saltate, Rospo!* No gotta jarb," he whispered sadly, "no gotta jarb. Go back Italia! Go the priest, no gotta jarb."

Staring away into the dark river, I cried "Ah, Primavera!"

When would it come, this springtime that would take me back to Metung and the calm youth whom I loved?

The days passed, now fair, now foul, bringing to us a procession of visitors through the maize . . . weary Italians, out of work and not too well-fed, carrying home from the river long sodden willow logs; the malicious Major calling to talk with us, and Michele of the voice that poured out to the sun, tramping by with a dead rabbit in his hand, crying out the flowery Italian name for it. "*Coniglio! È buono!*" "*Buon' appetito, Michele!*" we cried mechanically, as we jumped up and down breaking off cobs. A few of these were taken down to Mrs Wallaby at night, to keep her fowls going through the hard winter. On days that were too wet to pick, I worked away doing odd jobs for her; repairing the sewing machine, the veranda, the kitchen, and sharpening axes and saws.

But I was tired of the maize, and my sorrow was increasing, for I felt that Primavera would bring only grief to me when I returned to Gippsland. As I worked, I made a song to sing. It was full of loneliness, but mingled with that feeling was a defiance and ardour that told of many lovers to come, in spite of my vows of faithfulness to the one love ever.

> The loser again! And this time, more
> Was lost than could be spared. I wonder
> What's the perfection I'm struggling for?
> Fifty more blossomings, it'll be under
> Struggle itself . . . eternal war,
> Limitless scratchings and scrapings and rakings . . .
> All in the dark, as here, but for
> Something greater than dry heart's slaking.
> What have I lost that's set me sprouting
> New pinions again? A dream? A haven?
> A refuge from all the old obstinate doubting?
> But . . . what do you want with a refuge, craven?
> What did I lose, you ask? The rare

Evasive young eyes, the chill remote
Line of young lips . . . the shadows where
The lovely chin met lovely throat.
Ah, give me the lips and the throat and the passion!
Give me the eyelids like little white roses
Quivering under the kisses that lash on
Love's articulate gaze as it opens and closes.
Give me a season of greedy love making,
A rummer of passionate blood for the drinking,
Stuff that will set the old obstacles shaking . . .
And, after that, many slow years of thinking.
Of listening hard for the thrush to be crying . . .
"The fiftieth blossoming's dying . . . dying!"

In the walnut-trees, the big black and white jays leapt heavily, as they had among the boughs in the orchard of Nils Desperandum. "For the best . . . for the best . . . for the best! Oho . . . oho . . . oho!" they cried. And gazing on them, I felt, "the slow tears rise". Ah, the past, the past! O, immeasurable and unutterable Time, you are beyond all our conjuring! "For the best . . . for the best . . . for the best! Oho . . . oho . . . oho!"

The buds were filling out a little; when they were purple, it would be early spring and we should be going home. When they had broken into leaf along these alpine hills, I should be in Gippsland.

Tell her I am with the people that I love.

I forgot the black oxen.

IX

MRS WALLABY decided to take a visit to her married daughter who lived at Oxley, and we had to go back to the sections again; for we couldn't have stayed in the house alone with Charlie, because of the kindly, neighbourly interest taken in our movements. Mrs Wallaby was away for a week; when it was up, we took the road again down to their farm.

It was a wet night, and Pricie-ole-man, who had been kicked out again by the paternal boot, came down from Porepunkah and walked with us down to Wallaby's. The grey road shone before us, and I looked at the lamps burning in the windows of Sullivan's house and wondered sadly if ever I would have a home and children with the one I loved. With our scarves up around our mouths, we walked silently through the alpine night, a hand in each of our old mate's pockets . . . and Pricie-old-man, his pale jaw poked out, looked ahead into the darkness with dilated nostrils and bright restless eyes.

Wallaby's was a moody hovel of darkness, veranda jutting forward, frail and faint silver. The rain dripped tiredly from its eaves into the drains it had worn through in the wet weather.

"They're not home!"

"Charl! Are you there, Charl?"

The rain dripped and a leaf fell, but no voice answered.

"Well, let us wait awhile. Charl might be bringing her home from Oxley. Anyhow, we might as well be here as up at the sections." Leaning against the wall, we looked out through the rain at the shining clay path below the house and the walnut-trees beside it.

Along the metal road, the soft rubber-tyred jinker whirled rapidly, and we heard the fast feet of Capira, Charlie's trotter, stamping out the pace of his blood. Spot ran in front. "There they are."

But it was only Charlie. He jumped down and slashed around with his knife in the pitch dark. Capira leapt aside, shied away from the harness, and then trotted humbly across the paddock for a feed. I often felt sad to think that he didn't get a warm feed when he finished his long journey; but it couldn't be done. Charl had enough mouths to feed already.

"We thought your mother would be with you, Charl."

"No, she'th not coming till tomorrow morning."

"Oh."

"Got no food in the houthe. No wood, either." Charl came along carrying the harness, rain dripping from his hat. He opened the door, lit the lamp, and we took command at once. "Haven't had anything to eat all day, Charl." Our Wallaby said that he had suffered from the same complaint.

"Got no wood?" we said incredulously. "What about the railway sleepers?"

"Gee with, I've uthed um all. Wait on . . . what'th around here that we could burn?" We looked around eagerly.

"But what's the use if there's nothing to eat, Charl?"

Blue pulled out the flour bag and shook it. About a pound of flour fell from the sides. "There you are . . . puftaloonies! Now, Charl, what about wood? You don't want that breadboard . . . here, chop it up!"

Charl ran his hands over it, wondering what his mother would say.

"Oh, go on. You never use it. How often do we have bread here? Never. We live on puftaloonies. Just cut it up and that will start her off. Now what about something else to pile on?"

"That safe in the corner ought to burn," pulling it over to the fire and hewing it down.

"And here's a couple of legs off the chairs, and that loose one off the table," said Blue, putting them in front of him.

The fire leapt up in great style; we heated water and washed the dishes, drying them on Mrs Wallaby's nightgowns and her spare crochet work, because we couldn't find any tea-towels.

Charl made a pan of puftaloonies. We ate them with sugar, drank tea and went to bed.

The next morning dawned cold and dark. The rain pelted on the roof; the cat miaowed forlornly in the kitchen, which was damp with runnels of water falling down into the empty fireplace. The jars, dishes and pans looked hundreds of years old. There was nothing to eat and no firewood. We got dressed and wandered around the house, shivering.

Charl got the feeling that a sort of oratorio would liven us up. We were sitting with Pricie-ole-man huddled around a few sparks that we had induced to burn in some damp wood and paper. We heard, as we shivered, a weird caterwauling from Charlie's room, and a nasal whine in a foreign tongue. Stealing over to his door, we looked through and saw our host lying across his bed; the black and red football sweater blazed around his chest, his unshaven face, under the drooping hat, peered down at a small book from which he sang lustily. It was a book of French grammar through which he was going to the tune of "There's No Place Like Home", "Annie Laurie" and "The Prisoner's Song". The first immortal melody was rushed through with these words, made quite erudite by Charl's lisp:

> "Le bath le beeju le bout le brath le cheval,
> Le corpth le cowtu le difference le general.
> La jambe le nez le oil le pied le voicks
> Il na pa de pain toot ma vi la homme est mortel!"

To "The Prisoner's Song", he added a recitative of the wandering of his relatives:

> "Jy voth avec ma famille toeth leth eath.
> Jay deth parenth, a la·campagne,
> Mon grand pear, ma grand mare, duckth ongkles
> Et une tante . . . tante . . . tante."

Refraining from interruption, we watched with interest, as he transferred his attention to a farm catalogue.

To the noble measure of the "Marseillaise", he intoned the merits of various agricultural implements, together with various exclamations of his own that carried the metre along:

> "Manure Distributor . . . hallo!
> In this distributor the feed is the popular Star wheel type!
> Which is the only method of sowing all kinds of manure.
> It is so constructed that even when the mach . . .
> Ine is set to its greatest capacity,
> No manure can escape except . . . tt . . . t
> By being forced out by the stars . . . la, la, la!"

In a wild voice he continued to sing, without tune, a whole page of advertisements:

> "Original Patent Steelbeam Swivel plough, tra, la, la!
> A light two-horse hillside plough, dum, da, de.
> The beam is of highest grade forged steel.
> They are so adjusted, la, la, la, that the plough works
> Perfectly when reversed either way, and all the parts
> Are attached in the simplest but strongest manner.
> Beam, forged steel, two pieces.
> Mouldboard, soft centre steel, highly polished.
> Saddle for mouldboard, malleable iron,
> And shoe, cast iron, chilled on bottom.

"And I feel a bit like that methelf," sang Charl, throwing the book away.

Applauding loudly, we rushed into the dressing-room of our famous tenor.

"Bravo, Signor . . . e bel canto, Signor Wallabio!"

"Orr, go orn," said Charlie sheepishly. "Ah, well," he continued philosophically, "yer gotter do thomething in the bush, yer know. Gee with, yer go mad if yer don't thing on a wet day."

The weather cleared and saved him from this contingency. Mrs Wallaby came home laden with groceries from her daughter's farm, and we ate again; glad to see Mrs Wallaby, and she, overjoyed to see us. She liked to be with young people and coveted daughters-in-law and grandchildren with a sensual longing.

On wet afternoons, when Blue, Pricie-ole-man and Charl sat in the bedroom talking about the bush characters of the district, I stayed by Mrs Wallaby, feeling from her the faint ecstasy of love and marriage that the years bring to women.

She sat heaving and breathing, at one side of the fireplace, the poker twisted in her big white hands and dangling down between her skirt-covered knees; and her hair, piled on top of her head, fell down in silvery-grey globes of looseness.

She droned, while I listened, sleepy-eyed, hypnotized by the rain and the fire, "Charl's a good boy, and a hard worker, too. But he needs someone with him. He ought to get married. He wants cleaning out."

I awoke with a shock of unease and wondered if she meant that I should be his marital chimney-sweeper. Yes, and I was sad, too; for it seemed that she was one of that unending band of men and women, who, for some reason or other, tried to take me from my wandering life and my ideal love, so that I might be mated and tied down to bear and slave, without poetry to fire and console me.

As Mrs Wallaby talked, she was hurrying me away from her, from the alpine district, this farm, good Charl and the Italians . . . yes, from all this that I loved and hated dearly, she was driving me with her words.

I was mentally packing up and saying good-bye while she urged me to think about . . . "settling down. A girl like you can't go around the bush like this forever. It's time you settled down. I don't know what Charlie will do when I'm gone. He wants someone to look after him."

"Oh, stop talking," I was crying inwardly, "because the gold of the poplars is all that's going to remain to me of these years, when I have fled from here. The bitter smell of the walnuts is going to be the tomb in which the thought of all of you will lie, and whenever winter comes in some alien land, I shall smell them, and you will arise to torture me, for you are part of my youth. Don't you understand? Time is flying, and we are going with it . . . into what? Into what, O God? I don't want marriage, or love, or fame, really, in my very soul. I only want to sit and behold beauty forever and know that it will never die."

"If you and Charl settled down on this place, I'd be happy. You can't go wandering around like lost sheep forever, Steve."

"No," I said gloomily; and that negative went on into a complaint in my mind. "No . . . but I don't understand this loose linking up with men and mating and bearing their children. For me, the great love, the ideal . . . the sorrow, and the parting. Perhaps, at last, a little hut in the bush where I can sit eating bran and honey; where I can drink black coffee at evening, when the kookaburras laugh their death-laugh at the sinking sun, and the wallabies come down, shabby and scarred, to graze on the grass in front of the hut. And I shall think of my lost love, forever. I could even make an image

of him out of that buddha-wood my mother used to burn in New
South Wales. And, praying to that image, I would be comforted."

"You'll be going home, soon," said Annie, "and then away up
into that Gippsland. Why don't you stay here and you and Charlie
settle down?"

"I'll come back," I lied to her, morosely and languidly.

The sun sparkled in through the window and lay weakly on the
floor. In rushed Charlie and Blue.

"Come on, Steve, Charl's going to take us out to Happy Valley!"

"Oh . . . good! Ah, that's living, that is, Charl my boy!" To be
going anywhere . . . to be carried along like a babe through lovely
country, that always intoxicated me. Perhaps I had never entirely
forgotten the ease of the days before I was born, and the months
afterwards when I was carried and wheeled about the earth, lying
back for hours and enjoying the earth as it spun slowly past me.

"Gee with, mother, where'th the reinth?" Charl rushed around
the yard and looked everywhere for them. At last, he looked down
the deep well and pulled them up from there, with the full bucket
of water tipping, dangling and spilling musically at the end of them.
"Gor blarmie!" He unknotted the tight wet leather.

Capira was harnessed in front of the shed. This miracle was
performed with the aid of string, wire, screws, bits of wood, and
torn rags. Capira hadn't any harness to speak of, but it was wonderful to see what Charl could do with odds and ends.

The effect was a little chaotic and rattled like a mousetrap, but,
for the first mile, it held together well. After that, Charl had to get
out every few hundreds yards to re-tie the string, push home the
screws, re-wind the wire and tear bits off the fluttering rags. All we
did was laugh and roll about speechless in the jinker. Why we went
to Happy Valley, I have never found out. It lay on the other side
of the range, and was filled with the lonely silence that came up
from empty paddocks, post-and-rail fences and grassy roads. At the
end of the valley stood the Pinnacles, three tall crooked needles of
rock, projecting flinty and blue above the rose-coloured ranges at
twilight. Seen from afar, they made the heart ache with their aloof-
ness, with desire for their ungraspable forms, crumbling in grey,
blue and purple against the sky. The Pinnacles were the home of
the wild horses, the black brumbies that the Happy Valleyians ran
in at a place called Running Creek. There were a few farms and
tobacco-kilns scattered around.

We met a lonely horseman cantering in dark and dignified

shadow against the red and purple mountains, and then turned back and came home. A mob of dogs from a farmhouse howled behind our carriage.

Turning on them, we howled like drovers following a big mob of Herefords, "Head 'em off there! Go round . . . go round! 'Hind, there, 'hind! Come behind! Fore there . . . aft . . . forrard . . . lee . . . astern . . . avast. Oho . . . Oho!" and whistled loud and shrill. Thus, with frantic yells, purpling cheeks, hoarse shouts, mock bellows, moos, boos and moans, we so startled the pups that they fell back in strangling astonishment. We also made Capira bolt, and at a propitious moment the harness broke, and we swung along the road like a broken kite, trailing rags, strings and wires. There was about an hour spent in embroidering the carriage to the horse. It was dark when we got home and Capira stood panting in front of the well.

Out came Charl's knife. A couple of cuts and slashes, and the harness tumbled down around the horse's hooves. Charl picked it up, threw the reins down the well again with the bucket hanging on the end of them, and we went in to eat puftaloonies and drink tea.

"Charl," we said as we sat around the jovial fire, "you look tired. Let us make your bed for you."

Charl usually made it himself. He thanked us for the kindly offer and, turning his hat around so that the bow came over his left eye, he grinned slyly to himself, because he knew that we would make the bed well.

He had no sheets, of course. Gently, then, we smoothed his torn mattress and inserted in it the legs of chairs and bits of broken crockery and tin. Over that, the blanket was neatly spread and a light decoction of thistles, gathered in the dark, with insects attached, was distributed over it. The pillow was set at the head of the bed, and Charl's dirty socks were draped over it, with a thick sprinkling of black pepper to flavour all.

"Come," we cried. "O gentle Jehu, your limpid couch yearns for you!"

Charl yawned, crawled into his unlit room, kicked off his boots, clicked off his garments and flung himself on to the mattress with a deep sigh of content.

Blissful-faced, we listened, listened, and waited. As he set his head on the pillow and drew a peaceful breath, our smiles became more widely wreathed, but nothing was said. No agonized voice cried out in smothered accents. Nothing happened. We waited a

8

long time, and then went to bed ourselves, while from Charl came long, happy snores.

Dashing out next morning, I lit the fire and made tea for him. This I carried to his bedside, tore the bag down from his window and stared at his serene face.

"A fine day, if I may say so. Did we sleep well, sir?"

Charl raised his head from the pepper-sprinkled socks; he moved his frame languidly on the wood, china and tin-stuffed mattress, and said dreamily that he had never slept better in his life, by joveth! After that, we gave him up. The gum-bough bed at Metung, we felt, would have someone worthy of its metal in Charl.

X

THE maize was drawing us slowly through its rows. Salvatore and Chiverelli, as the Good-a Name gentleman was called, were coming close behind us, and the thunderous roar of the tractor as it crawled over the mud filled our ears with an ocean song all day. Ah, Primavera!

In the huts of the Italians, we stood together, balanced on small, crooked, but massive bodies, our dark sensitive faces upraised to theirs. Michele, the sun-singer, stood before us, the beauty of his voice broken up into a mangled chaos of English, with now and then a phrase of Italian dialect of a simian sort flung in. Michele was a small ugly man with a coarse grinning face, thin-lipped, grizzle-haired and grey-skinned. A nose like a soft round button was stuck grotesquely in the middle of his features. He was a sensual little fellow, and he looked repulsively womanly as he moved about the kitchen, washing up, cooking and throwing out dirty water from which he wrung greasy rags. I stared at him, thinking that it must have been his soul which I saw standing on the liquid molten top of the earth, pouring out to the sun the startling cry, "Ah, Primavera!"

He spoke to us in a quick masterful voice. "E-e-e-eh! Ste' and Blue! You soon finish *granoturco?*" (Maize.)

"*In due settimane, Grazie Dio, Michele!*" (In two weeks, thank God!)

"A-a-a-ah! You no like pick *granoturco?*"

"*Ma che . . . no!*"

Dishes of spaghetti lay around; pans black, greasy, full of red vegetables simmered on the open fire; voluble Italian voices gabbled around us; the flames leapt up, and José, with the quiet movements and squeaky mild voice of one who was thinking of himself, little thoughts in a big bulk of flesh, had his neat purple cloth spread over the shoulder of a client and was preparing to cut his hair. He took from their oiled silk coverings the razor, scissors and comb.

> *"Rasoio, pettini, lancette, forbici,*
> *Al mio commando tutto qui sta!"*

sang his little brown brother, Toni, with the large nose that shone under straight, mousy hair. *"Tu sei un barbiere davvero, José?"* said he.

"Sì!" José squeaked mildly, his blade deftly seeking for whiskers, and added, half groaning, half squeaking, that his scissors were blunt. Behind us stood Chiverelli, pointing to our bodies with a big blunt finger and crying in a soft melodious voice to the dwarf who peeped over his shoulder, *"Bella cusa . . . bella cusa!"*

One day, one beautiful day, as we worked, the roar of the tractor seemed to sound louder to us, and as we sped from stalk to stalk, we saw, faintly through them, the Italians working in the paddock next to us. Amazed and excited, we toiled like heroes and, by grey afternoon, were running back and forth among the last thin stalks.

The glory of it! The toil of it! The splendour of tired limbs finishing their cold lonely task at last!

Ah, Primavera! I come to you, Metung, I come. O my lost love, I come!

Through a shower of rain, we ran home to Wallaby's . . . and crouched on the railway line, beneath the police-force cape, watching the mist rising off the river flats, seeing the tall round hop-poles lonely and bare of their green garments.

While I crouched with Blue beneath the cape, I thought of all my lovers, past and to come; I mourned for them, making this threnody as I knelt in the mud:

> Alas, chill earth, within this sombre coming
> Of midnight hours, alas, whom art thou hiding?
> Whose are the hearts perpetually drumming
> Under the flesh? And whose the voices chiding
> The gentle grass and little speckled clover,
> Crying, "Alas, chill earth, whom dost thou cover?"
> Is it Phillip the lost, or Peter the great drinker,
> David the herdsman, John the lithe wine-presser
> That died in youth . . . is it Francis the confessor
> Of many crimes; is it Luis, the false lover,
> Crying, "Alas, chill earth, whom dost thou cover?"

Is it, then, earth, the women thou art masking?
Agnes that loved with man's love; Lila, that could send
Her own heart from her; Catherine, the asking,
And young Olivia, lovely to the end.
And Jule, that would not kiss the lips above her,
Crying, "Alas, chill earth, whom dost thou cover?"

Ah, what a lost, lost loveliness, remember,
Suspires at night. Ah, what great beauty's keeping
Fragrant the marl from April to December . . .
Happy is he that knows where they are sleeping
And grieving their loneliness to all who hover
Crying, "Alas, chill earth, whom dost thou cover?"

With this I hypnotized myself for hours, and sat at the table, radiant, and gnawing a rabbit's leg dragged out of the hot brown stew that Mrs Wallaby had cooked for us.

Charl sat by the fire, strangely quiet, meditative and dolorous. Was he sorry that the maize-picking was finished, that we would soon be going home? Looking up, he caught my intent look, and laughed. Then he broke into one of his three songs.

"I hadn't much to give her,
    So I threw her in the river . . . poor thing!
I didn't like to choke her,
    So I hit her with the poker . . . poor thing!"

Lazily he sang in a tone-deaf way, smiling at the sound of his own voice.

"I'd make a pretty good husband, wouldn't I, Thteve?" said he, and he looked quite handsome in a fantastic way, with his cheeks flushed red above a faint blue-black stubble of whiskers. His wall eye gleamed and rolled beside the fine brown one, and over his white brow the black hair shone. The hair on his chest came up as far as his Adam's apple and gave him a truly manly look.

I wondered whether he would or not . . . and decided to stick to my dreams.

Into the bedroom I went, to get the Willie Gray gun and bring it back to the fire, to run the pull-through down the barrel. That was my chief occupation at night; it soothed me, and I sang my poetry while I worked.

As I clawed around in the dark, looking for the rifle, Charl came in.

"Gee with, Thteve!" Then, in a gentle voice, "What are you looking for? You can't find the rifle without a light, Thteve."

"Yes, I can." I held it up. He stood beside me, at the door, and said quickly, "Do you think you'll be coming back again to thith valley, Thteve?"

"Oh, yes. Of course," I exclaimed with a false heartiness. "Wish I could take this rifle with me. I'd bring it back when I came."

"Well, Thteve, you can have it, if you come back with it . . . to me."

It was mine; my callous young heart rejoiced. At last I had a rifle that would work! I flung my arms around Charl's neck, saying, "I'll be back!" felt a whisker touch my mouth and leapt back like a startled brumby.

"Yes, I'll be back," I repeated unsteadily, and thought that I had paid too much for the loan of the rifle.

In a grave voice, Charl said he knew I would, and made noises and gestures which indicated that our troth was plighted.

I had been bought by a rifle.

Throughout the night I tossed troubled, pursued by my conscience, and wondering what evil would befall me, because I had given my word in exchange for Willie Gray's rifle. Some day, I felt, Nemesis would bring sorrow to me for this paltry throwing away of a word.

Even next day, when the sun shone brilliantly on the metal road along which we spun in the gig, my heart was low. Charl, attentive as never before, treated me in an engaged fashion, where, before, he had tossed me this and that and sworn when I hit him over the head with a rock, just as a joke.

I was no longer considered a man, although I still wore the trousers. I was his love. To comfort me, he went through his repertoire of song, as he lolled back in the gig beside me. His face was pink from a recent shave, and had the look of a baby's anatomy relieved of a mass of black hair; the etiolated flesh shivered in the cold wind. He had trimmed his hair, too. It ran down the back of his neck, so he just continued shaving it as far as he could go, without being able to see the effect. And that was the hair-cut. The jagged horror of it was enough to frighten the horses in the gigs at the back of his; several of them bolted past after ten minutes' steady staring at the back of Charlie's neck.

Rolling back and forth, he sang while I mourned for my lost love.

> "They don't leave you alone till they get you,
> But when they get you, good-bye!
> Wait till you're chasing a bit of fluff.
> Wait, till they get the little birdie in the cage.
> They don't leave you alone till they get you . . .
> But when they get you . . . good-bye."

Broken fragments of this ballad penetrated to my mind. I heard and was embittered. Charl hurriedly altered the words and sang, to the same tune, with rolling body and lazy voice.

> "I'll give you a little nigger-boy
> To water your garden when the sun goes down,
> If you'll marry, marry, marry, marry,
> If you'll marry me."

Alas, thought I, for the songs of the poets, by whom I might have been loved. Surely, in all the world, there waited for me one melodious heart.

Drowning Charl's voice, I sang loudly, to a tune I had composed, Brooke's "Ambarvalia":

> "Swings the way still by hollow and hill
> And all the world's a song;
> 'She's far,' it sings to me, 'But fair,' it rings to me,
> 'Quiet,' it laughs, 'and strong!'
>
> O! spite of the miles and years between us,
> Spite of your chosen part,
> I do remember; and I go
> With laughter in my heart."

And . . .

> "But the years, that take the best away,
> Give something in the end;
> And a better friend than love have they,
> For none to mar or mend,
> That have themselves to friend."

Blue, who had been watching us coming along the road, laughed when we stopped. "I couldn't help thinking," she said, "that you two looked just like an old married couple, rolling along in that gig."

A chill heaviness came into my heart and I walked away without a word. It was a sort of writing over me, and was another one of those chance remarks that had begun to wear me away, touching on my immense vanity and making me turn on myself, destructively. Going into the house I found Mrs Wallaby, bringing from her room piles and piles of crochet work. Even the cat was entangled in it and wailing desolately.

Mrs Wallaby greeted me like a daughter with a sly kind smile.

"What the devil made you do all this crochet work?" I said disgustedly. "Fancy spending hours making this stuff!"

"Ah well, Steve," she droned, in her rich, deep, stuffy voice, "when my husband lay dying, yes, on the very night he died, I just sat in here, minding him, and crocheting. And for twelve months after he died, I did nothing but crochet, crochet, crochet. Night and day. The girls looked after the house. I just sat and did crochet. If I hadn't I'd have gone mad."

For a moment, I took her sorrow to my heart and grieved that she should have had to suffer.

But I was selfish. "Ah, Primavera!" I cried, and thought of nothing but going to find my lost love. The suffering of the world didn't matter to me. I had a sorrow of my own. I was unloved.

Mrs Wallaby continued to sort out crochet, looking worried. That night she and Charl sat talking in her room for hours.

He was up early next morning and brought in our bread and milk with a gay brisk air, but a little while after he had gone into his mother's room, we heard her weeping loudly, and rushed in.

"What is it? What is wrong, Mrs Wallaby?"

"The store's come and taken all our stock, for debt," she cried, and her rough deep wail drowned the cry of the birds and the sound of the spring wind in the trees.

We wandered around worriedly all day, going into the bush and turning over the word "replevin" in our minds, for Charlie had said that they had been replevined.

"Well, we'll have to go home now, we simply can't live on poor Mrs Wallaby like this. I wish we had known they were poor."

"I didn't want to come, you remember, Blue."

"Ah, well, it made the winter brighter, anyhow, and we didn't eat much."

"Oh, if only we had a lot of money!"

But we didn't dream of offering her some of what we had. No, we were the adventurers, *jongleurs*, actors and singers, come to stay for the wet season, to entertain, and laugh and sing, and then depart without paying. In every way, it was understood between us, that we should avoid paying tribute to life.

I forgot the troubles of the Wallabys, and became immersed in the blue gum-covered hillside in front of us. We had crossed the river on a damp log, and sat under a tree, eating buns and staring at the ranges. The earth on them was a glowing sphinx-red, and rooted in it were the sinewy feet of the blue gum-trees. Their curled leaves shone purple-blue like the sea or the Australian sunlight, which has a mauve quality in springtime. They fascinated me, those Greek curls on the ranges. The sense of dry red flesh underneath and the curled, fleecy beard above, sang home like an arrow to my Grecian heart and almost stifled me with ecstasy.

As the wind swept over and through them, they replied in deep-vowelled tones that came to us, muttering harmoniously. To see these fleecy blue-purple curls moving on the red earth . . . ah, that was religion! I was Greek and dreamily pantheistic. This was my Parthenon; these hills bore on their pediments the statues of my heroes and Demeters. From them oozed the ghost of the Greeks, pale Pallas Athene, a mingling of Latin and Pelasgian, for the two races were one in my sight.

I did not speak but, sitting in the shade, I worshipped at the temple of my first gods, the Greeks. I fancied that in me was the universe, and that in one human being, myself, was all mankind, doomed to suffer all the sorrows of existence as well as its joys. Yes. I felt that enormous sorrows lay ahead of me; but that was counterbalanced by an emotion which, for years, I had called "the feeling of the North", which told me that great happiness should be mine also.

"Now, in my adolescence," I thought, "I worship, as is fit, the first aesthetic gods of the world. In my maturity, what shall I, the race, worship?" A madness of being and high purpose burnt in me, and I fancied that I was being prepared for a task of genius.

While I sat dreaming beside Blue in the lonely bush, a shadow of wings, measuring fifty yards from tip to tip, moved back and forward over us; slid to the right, curved over; to the left, swung dizzily and lightly. Confused, delighted, we watched the shadow, wondering if some aboriginal angel hung above, ready to swoop on us. We had delight in the wide arching movements that made swinging earth of us, by crossing and spinning before our vision.

Without rising, we looked up into the sky and saw a large eagle, swinging inward on a closing circle, around and around us. Its shadow advanced and retreated with the lightness and rapidity of mercury in a tube. At last, the bird saw us, and with one great flurry of shadow, gigantic and beautiful, it fled, dwarfed by distance.

When our pleasure and awe had died away, we crossed the bush and went up into the clear grassy glades at the very beginning of the ranges. In a space which had been torn by long struggles, revealing the wet red mud through the green grass, we found a fine mare, lying ill and helpless, her hooves sprawled out from her, as she tried to rise and failed.

Picking up a long-dead branch we put it under her and tried to assist her struggle; but it was useless; ropes were needed. We hurried back and, calling in at Sullivans', told them to go to her as soon as possible. I remembered long afterwards the sentience of the atoms in the dead wood as they met the intimate rounded flesh of the brown mare; though dead in a certain way, they carried feeling when a living being touched them, as the wood of a violin will make a song.

We went home to Mrs Wallaby, stirred by our importance—the finding of the mare, the wings of the eagle—and made her interested and happy by our recital. Charl had gone to Oxley that morning, for help, and would be back at night.

At midnight we heard the powerful, aristocratic pace of Capira on the metal road, up the grass track, and stamping on our hearts, it seemed, as he came to the door. Charl dismounted, talking to him softly and honestly. There was a slash; the saddle fell to the ground; another slash; the bridle fell, and Capira shook himself and wandered off to try to get a feed from the short spring grass in the paddock. In came Charl, squawking like a fowl.

"Hello, Charl," we said. "What's wrong? Got a cold?"

"Cherk . . . ker . . . cherkcherkcherka . . ." squawked Charl.

Looking around the door, he flung a big black hen on our bed. "By joveth," said he, "that'll keep your feet warm."

"What did you get, Charl?" cried his mother.

"Thome grocerieth, a chook, and . . ." he went into her room and they talked for a long time together, while we tried to guess what they were saying, and whether they would get their stock back.

After breakfast I took the hen out to the woodblock and cut off its head. In those days I had no fear of killing things. Death meant nothing to me. While others stood back timorous or respectful of it, it was I who, with an exaggerated courage and callousness, took the axe or rifle and "finished it off".

In a second, the hen's body was fluttering around the yard, and I was calmly taking the thanks and applause of the family. But it appeared to me, even then, that I was putting into brutal acts an intensity and cruelty out of proportion to the simplicity of the moment and, far ahead, I knew my power would rebound hideously on me.

Into the camp oven went the hen, but the long night ride and her agony of fear had toughened her, so that she took hours to cook.

At last the crochet work was pushed to one side of the table, and the brown fowl set out in the middle of a clutter of plates, knives and forks. Just as we were starting to enjoy her, a tall thin old man climbed the slope to the house, and with the shadow of the budding walnut-trees moving over him, came on to the veranda and knocked at the door.

"Willie!" cried Mrs Wallaby amazedly, for Willie Gray had quarrelled with her over their partnership, long ago, and they had not forgiven each other. But a surprised nervous system has no mercy on reflex actions, and one could quite easily greet one's murderer with a smile, if his entry was swift and calm.

When she recovered herself, Mrs Wallaby made it plain that Willie was to be tolerated only, and he was given a second cold greeting. We were introduced.

"Pleased to meet you," responded Willie, giving us a high-handed shake over the table. He sat down and drank tea, keeping his eyes fixed in one place, and he never moved them two inches from that place, which was straight through us and up the wall.

Willie was tall and spare, with a bald head, rainbow eyebrows, popping eyes and a long thin straggling moustache, badly torn, beyond hope of repair. Mrs Wallaby had told us how he fell into a dam while working with her, and had been pulled out by the moustache, which probably accounted for its disreputable state.

When the partnership was dissolved he left, and the only relics of his stay were the military breeches, the rifle and a thousand rounds of ammunition, belonging to a rifle of another calibre. When he came in, Blue was wearing his breeches, and I was cleaning his rifle, in between munching the bones of the hen. Blue didn't know how to leave the room without Willie seeing the breeches, and I didn't know how to get the gun away from the side of the open flour bag in which Willie was sitting, unconscious of the nature of his couch.

At last, Blue, who was eating a large bone, had an idea. Flinging up her arms and with the bone sticking half way out of her throat, she indicated that she was choking. Writhing back and forth in apparent agony, she swept the tablecloth clean off the table and, getting all tangled up in it, rushed from the room. I grabbed the gun and ran after her, pulling the trigger in my hurry and sending a bullet through the walls. Willie shouted and dropped his tea down between his legs into the flour bag, and for a while we kept things moving until we got into our bedroom.

Going over to the door, we looked out and saw Willie's gig standing in decrepit weakness under the walnut-trees. Between the shafts stood a wicked-looking old draught horse whose bulk made the meekness and weakness of the gig pitiably manifest. The horse, tough and insect-like, looked up the hill often, from beneath the dray-winkers around his eyes, seeking Willie Gray, who sat on in the open flour bag with a fresh cup of tea in his hands.

"Yes, I put in some lettuces lately. I don't know how they'll come on. They say it's a bit early for them. But I thought I'd try. And I got a nice bed of peas coming on, and a little patch of turnips, too."

The horse ground its teeth and rolled its eyes, as Willie's voice floated calmly and unhurriedly over the land. Two hours went by and the dissertation on the vegetables continued.

Down below, between the shafts of the weak gig, the draught horse stamped and swallowed and the long whiskers on his trembling chin shook with despair. We were compelled, at last, to avert our eyes from his agony and anger.

Clinging to Willie's pants and his gun, we congratulated ourselves on keeping them in safe hands.

An hour afterwards, two small boys rushed up the hill and cried out:

"Mr Willie . . . you know your horse?"

"Yes, my boys?" Willie indicated that he knew the animal slightly.

"Well, he's run off with the gig and thrown it into the rubbish tip on top of our hill, and he's lying kicking among the old tins and things making an awful noise, and dadda said would you come and take him away?"

We ran into the kitchen gleefully as Willie leapt up from the open flour bag, getting out of it with difficulty, for the hot tea had glued him to it. He leapt away without a word of farewell, his long coat-tails parting as he ran over the ranges, and a great white floury spot blazing between the sights of the gun I levelled at him as he went.

XI

AH, Primavera! Primavera, at last! My heart beat faster and I smiled often, although fear and pain trembled along my veins. "Burn and beat in the walnut-trees, O fires of spring," I said, "and on the gummy and tightly folded buds bloom purple, for I am going to my love. Beyond these ranges, yea, beyond the granite lion mountain and the curled Greek beards of the ranges, stands the axeman of the wind in the blue and white forest of the sea.

"All this year I have suffered; I have been crucified by my loneliness, by the thought of true love, haunted by the pure lips, the eyes drowsy under the golden lashes, and now I am going back to Gippsland, the beloved country that holds the beloved. If it is to his kindliness I return, I shall rejoice in gladness. If it is to Apostasia, then shall I be happy with pain. But, O, if he will be there to say to me, 'Stevie, Stevie Talaaren', while the grallinae call it from the black and white vases of their bodies, Heaven shall have come. And we shall walk again the road by the chanting water, while Blue strides beside us, playing on the violin *'Giovinezza'* and *'Bandiera Rossa'*. Music knows no nationality or creed. I will believe, yes, I will believe that you are there, waiting for me, rejoicing as I rejoice in the return of the wanderer. Look, shall we not be as gods? Who are we but the turners of time? We can enchant it and bring it back again, by the power of our faithful love. We can make this coming Primavera as wild and happy and pure as the last. But, was it truly happy, that last Primavera? And why have you not written? Ah, but I understand! Your faith in my love is so strong that you need not write. And then, again, perhaps you are trying the metal of my love. You wish to test me. Ye gods, have I not been faithful, in my fashion? You have witnessed how, by river, hill and plain, in the roving silver rivers of the moon, I have prayed to my lost love as to a god. In the cells of this earth I have set you; I have made for you a home in the mosaics of the earth, in the temples of the sun that sends down to us the golden domes of light in which we walk and worship. I come to you, cleansed of all evil by my wanderings, by my cold and joyous strugglings in midnight rivers, by my abnegation and my cleanliness of body, heart and soul. Don't ever leave me! O God, if you leave me, I am utterly bereft. I have believed in you with a mortal anguished heart and if you have deceived me and will avoid me I go the way of sorrow. Yes, *la via dolorosa* will claim me. O have pity and save me, I beg you."

Softly and greenly the sun shone on the walnut-trees in the afternoon. We ironed our clothes excessively; we brushed, cleaned and washed, for we were going home. And then, to Metung . . . to what?

The day came in a blur of bush station with the morning wind blowing the grass before it. We sat swinging on the wire fence with Charlie. In the paddocks over the line, the dead trees were thick with black and white ibis. The reeds and the grass were green. It was Primavera. And yet, although I was going home to my mother, and although I hoped to meet love again in Gippsland, fearful melancholy pressed down on me and I mourned as I laughed and sang with Blue and Charl. Pricie-ole-man was not there; he had left Porepunkah and gone to find work in another district.

Into the train we passed, waving to Charl and good Mrs Wallaby.

She was happy, now the replevined stock had been restored to her; but she grieved to see her "wandering sheep" going from her.

"We shall return next year."

Big with work and healthy living, virginal and filled with the bush-genius of our race, we sat staring at them from the window of the train; beyond lay the Greek bearded ranges, and above lay the granite mountain. This was their country. Good-bye, good-bye!

The train moved away from the rusty station; my heart ached as though I were dying . . . it beat slowly . . . the train gathered speed and carried us away. I remembered no more. Like a child, covered by the oblivion of my obsession . . . love, love, love . . . I sat swaying beside Blue through the forever of that day.

The gate of home admitted us to that small untidy garden which was to be our world for a few weeks; and the sudden cramping, after huge ranges, long valleys and wild rivers, was like a physical stricture to us.

"*Come veste la giubba*; gum on the false moustache; cock an old hat over one eye and be a clown," I said to myself.

Mia, small and yellow-brown with the long summer of toiling under the plum-trees, raking up the rotten crimson fruit, wept with joy to see us. Black coffee was brewed, cakes brought out and our muscular bodies filled the small kitchen with movement. Underfoot the red and white flags rocked in their beds, the green ivy still twisted among the tins on the shelf, and above the poet's corner the shadows stayed long and reflectively.

Opening up our packing-case, we brought out our trophies and nailed them to the wall with those from Metung. Beside the six-foot snake-skin, a gift from Jim, was the ticket off the bag into which Macca tipped peas and beans. Above these we set the four guns I had found in the alpine district; the racing bit, a purple and gold jockey's cap, and a beautiful brown hat of Italian felt which Major had given to Blue.

That night we played the new songs we had learnt from the Italians and Australians. Staring at each other as we played in even time, on mouth-organ and violin, we thought back sadly on what was now the remote past. It would never happen, just the same, again.

"Ah, Bluey, remember Salvatore of 'Ow you do your do do do?'" His low mournful voice rings through the maize paddock again, his puttee-clad legs stoutly beside us, as he sweeps the short scythe over the stalks.

"Play on, play on," I thought. "I am as he, that alpine soldier, who was lost in the snow for many days, and the colour has fled from my cheeks, even as it fled from his. But I, like him, shall return to my love again, when the snows melt and the river brings the bodies of the dead down into the valleys."

"Now, José's song, Steve!"

With his olive face tilted proudly and arrogantly, shaking the black curls of his head, he came home from work, his full lips singing, and his feet stamping the damp earthern passage. From far down at the other end of the kitchen, Major's voice resounded. And rapidly José sang, with an affected and romantic thickening of the consonants:

> "*Gira . . . regira . . . piccina l'amore*
> *La vita godere ci fa! . . .*"

"What about Michelino's?"

"What was that one, Steve?"

"You don't remember? That night . . . recall, he stood in front of our fire, among the rest and led them, with his merry eyes laughing from side to side and hands on his hips, he sang the three trumpet notes:

> "*All'armi!*
> *All'armi!*
> *All'armi, i Fascisti!*
> *Abasso, i communisti!*
> *Viva i socialisti!*"

"Yes, yes, wait." Blue hurried into the living enthusiastic notes. We sentimentally forgot how we had been so humiliated by the gentle Fascisti who had marched into our kitchen and taken possession without asking yea or nay.

Again, warmly towards us leans handsome Primo, his blue eyes having soft black smuts of sleepless nights under them. From the darkness of the passage, he leans towards us and sings dolorously:

> "*L'abatjour dolce ninnol accendo*
> *Come facevi anche tu*
> *Nella stanzetta ti cerco in van*
> *Ma non ti ritrova più.*"

Blue dragged from the wall the hat that Major had given her and tilted it on her head. How handsome she looked!

"See, Mia? Maggiore gave this to me!"

"Ah," said Mia fearfully, "those Italians will be the cause of your death yet, you girls. Keep away from them!"

"What? We, Australians, to be afraid of Italians? Never! They enchant us . . . their lunatic English charms us . . . their vivid gestures bewilder us. . . . 'The dorg, he never fall down on us.' And as for causing our death . . . why, look at the guns, Mia!"

The wall was lined with them, all rusty, broken, or bulletless . . . quite useless. "With those guns around us, Mia, no man can touch us."

"Ah, well, be careful. You're young. You don't understand!"

"We are not young. We know everything. We mean no harm, Mia; nothing can touch us." But we felt quieter after that.

The old drover, T. O'B. came up a few mornings afterwards and halted his sulky under the pepper tree and the cattle dogs jumped up and barked at us. Peering from under the hot spicy leaves, he said "Hello" in a creaking, grudging, superior voice. "I heard you were back. I've got to go up to the ranges for a sale today. Might take you with me if you like."

The children flew to the mother, crying out in delight. "Mia, Mia! Going away with T. O'B. in the ranges!"

The whip cracked and was put back in the long metal holder . . . the dogs leapt and barked, the shining body of the horse moved sinuously from the mysteriously given impetus of the crooked, twisting, crossing and recrossing legs below, as we went into the ranges.

It was late August, and the wattle, even at quite a long distance, was so golden and fluffy soft that I felt as though my eyes were hands, that grasped and felt it, pressing it hard and cruelly to crush it into a mass that would end desire.

We drove for a few hours through long hills covered with it, and with stringybark-trees, soft, green and shining, not like the dry red, silver, blue and purple gum-trees of the alpine district we had left. The sale was held in a cattle yard with a small shed attached to it. Over twenty people moved around fingering the goods which were English things, civilized and forlorn-looking in the aboriginal bush. A young married couple, tall, fair and happy, made my heart ache. Ah, Primavera! What have you in your hands, for me, at Metung?

The young couple looked along their straight white-red English noses and out of the corners of their clean blue English eyes at us, and the stiff curves of their fair hair shone in the sun. An old woman, awful in the sunshine, horrified me. She was painted pure white, with black marks for eyebrows and red lines for lips. What a corpse! I shuddered. Age haunted me. I felt unhappy even unto death, and hoped that I should die before I looked like that.

Taking Blue with me I walked away with her, down the hot white road, through the moist green gum-trees that poured out volumes of aromatic oil through the bush.

"Ah Blue, some day we shall be old!"

"Yes, Steve . . . that will be the end! Ah, I don't want to grow old. I want to be like this, forever."

"But how can we stay it? You, at least, are fortunate. You've got a lover who would marry you tomorrow. I . . . well . . . who would want me?"

"Steve, you are a poet; that is enough!"

"Lauré, Lauré! I am young and my plate is empty! When will my two great desires, to be loved and to be famous, be satisfied? It is not enough. Ah, if only I were loved as you are loved! Look, see me . . . there I am in the years to come."

Far down the hot white road ahead of us walked an old woman in her long black silk dress. I shuddered as though a spectre had walked by day.

T. O'B. came along in the sulky and drove us home. On the way, he called in at the ranch house owned by the cattle-king, and we were graciously presented with a silky terrier named Teddy. I viewed him suspiciously, having seen him leading a pack of larger dogs after fleeing sheep in the home paddock. However, we took him home, and he almost ate the walls of the house, so ravenous was he.

For the remainder of the time at home I sat in the poet's corner, writing letters. One to Borrelerworreloil, with whom I kept up a spasmodic and cynical correspondence, mostly about the beauty of the earth and the falsity of man. The other was to the Black Serpent, from whom I hoped to get news of Macca.

I ruined my days at home by introspective sadness. Even while I laughed I remembered that I was unloved, and when I had left Blue and Mia helpless with laughter I went aside to write. . . .

"The thought of the Greek-browed hills still charmingly pursues me. They were old warriors, heroic campaigners, whose swords I could not find. (Which was just as well, for I should have treated them as I did the gun of Willie Gray.) And the blue and faint purple trees that curled about their brows were the thick round shining curls that so long ago moved on the brows of the Grecian men, who with long slow sweeps of their dipped oars drove through the water the legend-laden galleys. When the trees moved and muttered, one to another, in them I heard the vowelled moaning of lost heroes. The dry and sedgy grasses that whisper hoarsely in the swift and pitiless winds of winter are not more desolate in their spasmodic counterfeiting of gaiety than am I. No tree clutches so fiercely the marl with its rough and iron-grey fingers as do I clutch at hope. The very winds can mock at me, for they are not alone, but do, basely, once in every hour, carry away in their raking hands some fair frail bloom that withers as it goes. Nothing is empty nor barren, no one thing walks alone. Why, then, should I not return to you? Do not the tender clouds come to brush against the sky and lip it most gracefully? And if, as it happens often with those same clouds, the sun of your independence smothers and melts me, I shall only slip into some other form, new-eyed and wider-throated, to trail calmly and thoughtfully down newer skies. I think that you are fitting me for some more intricate passion, which I shall be able to transmute into a veritable immolation of self. But what is the hill? What are those trees upon it? They are not trees, but symbols. Ah, Primavera . . . that lone and solitary walker along the foreshore of Metung. I shall have to walk with her, and all desolate, too. But Primavera comes also to the Black Mountains, creeps delicately and greenly into its sombre eyes, and I shall go with her there."

FOURTH PART

AH, PRIMAVERA!

I

Pea-pickers; six; wanted at once. Karta Singh. Metung.—GIPPSLAND WEEKLY.

ONCE more we set out for Gippsland. Blue was calm, I was sick with excitement and sorrow, and Teddy, the sheep-killer, moaned fitfully in the dogbox at the very end of the train.

At Moe, I shuddered as the brazen bell rang out.

"O, who is this come again to seek sorrow in Gippsland? Clang, clang, clang on her heart who seeks for love in me. For, to her, I have none to give. Behold me . . . the door of death! My gates open out on Gippsland and a voice from the soul of the country cries that she shall perish who comes to it, crying for love. The dry land will arise, covered with thorns and burrs, and be a hairshirt to her back; the long hot roads will be flagellants and beat her until she bleeds. O, mourn for her who comes seeking lost love in Gippsland. Before her lie the long desolate days of toil in the lonely paddocks and bitter tears in the night. So do I treat her that she may run from me, thinking me to be death. So do I wear the mask of death, that she may run from me unto his arms. Clang, clang on her heart and mourning within her, forever!"

Behind the wild whiskered men with the squeaky boots and the coats flung over broad shoulders, the red fire buckets flowed into the shape and colour of a bleeding heart, as the train slid backwards and, with a mysterious twist and twirl, set us on the line that led to Gippsland.

Bairnsdale again, and Jim not there, smiling joyously; Macca not there, flushed with thoughts of poetry and love. We are alone.

The tall grey river boat took us up the river again, past reed and kingfisher, white crane and gaping pelican. Yes, into the river we swam with the glassy water washing up in pointed waves against the crumbling banks. My heart beat sick with sorrow. Surely, surely, he would be in Metung.

Ah, Primavera!

Where the river-banks ended, the great blue shuddering body

of the lake began and over it we drifted in a faint brown twilight, with a cold wind blowing the feathers of the white cranes that stood in cameo on the grey trunks of trees brought down by the Tambo and the Mitchell rivers in their floods.

The golden-moustached skipper came and sold us our tickets. And, at last, we rounded the Tambo mouth and saw on the lonely grey foreshore the little shed, Reynolds' hut, in which I had slept with Macca that summer night, long ago. Sorrow almost choked me. I knew then, looking on the hut that had aged and grown away from me in that short time, how utterly I had lost the love of the Gippslander.

The Buccaneer, kindly and handsome, met us at the jetty and carried our cases up to the house. Eb, the eldest son, had grown very tall.

We descended the cliff and lay under the stars on the buffalo grass by a private jetty, waiting for the Black Serpent to come home. She was out picking peas at Greenfeast's. We heard the primitive creak of their buggy approaching, and played our mouth-organs wildly.

The passionate strength of the Black Serpent's good arms closing around me, and her direct kiss, heartened me. I felt that she could save me and return my lover to me. And although I had nothing, not even love, I was strong and rich with the sense of the long years of youth. Time moved slowly and it seemed that life would never end.

About me, the stars, the earth, the speech of humanity, the very eyes that I encountered, strengthened this feeling. Their talk was of mating, of those like us, who held back from mating . . . and the promise of the years to come was clear in my heart. My future, I felt, was in some way presaged by the words of the people whom I sat among and loved.

"Where," we asked as we sat at their table under the fresh light of the lamp, whose globe had been brilliantly polished for the occasion, "where did Jim go after we left?"

"He went away with Grabbems to the city, and something happened to him. Nothing is quite clear, but it appears he met a widow with three children, and married her, and has gone back to the Nicholson, cutting wood for a living."

Oh, how terrible! Jim, our old mate, who lived the free life of a bushman with us in the bark hut, married, borne down with responsibilities . . . like that. We grieved for Jim. We felt guilty also. If we had stuck to Jim he would still have been wandering around with us.

"And . . . Macca?" I asked, scarcely able to get the words out, for fear of a similar answer.

"Oh, yes, he left here some time after you two, and went up to Black Mountain, bridge-building. Don't know where he is, now."

Eb, the eldest son, broke in, "I told you the other day. He's still up in Black Mountain. He got sweet on one of the cattle-owners' daughters up there, and he went far into the ranges with them, taking a mob outback to graze."

Dove sei stato, mio bel' alpino?

Ah, Primavera, Primavera! Where shall I go to hide and weep?

I talked on and jested among them all, praising the alpine district we had come from and telling them my passion for guns. This moved the Buccaneer to go under the house and bring out an old kangaroo gun that he had flung out of sight years ago. Sitting by the fire, I cleaned it up and oiled it.

They gave us their bed that night, and we lay side by side in silence—Blue, because she had just left her lover; and I, because I had lost mine.

Dawn glinted along the barrel of the old kangaroo gun that the Buccaneer had given me and sorrow was tempered with the joy of possession. I thought, "If it becomes unendurable, I can at least shoot myself."

After breakfast, I took the gun out on to the veranda where we had first seen the Buccaneer mending boots; where I had often stood with Macca on summer nights and watched the moon. I tried tremblingly to elicit from Eb the movements of my lover from the day we left up to the present time.

"And you haven't seen Macca since we left, Eb?"

"No. Oh, yes, once. He came down here to go to a dance in the hall, and got drunk. He slept out all night and lost his false teeth. Next morning he was combing the bush everywhere looking for them." Eb roared at the memory.

Here, O Aristotle, was my opportunity to differentiate between the false and the true. The thought of a man raking through the bush and combing the gum-leaves for a set of false teeth, is odious. But, I, loving in the spirit, was undismayed. I went apart and wept for that golden youth, who had got drunk and slept under a gum-tree and lost his false teeth. My tears streamed down across the kangaroo gun and I moistened the pull-through with them, as I dragged it back and forth.

From that day onward, I asked no more. Building up tragic passion from this incident, I saw him, heavy with the sorrows of life, sleeping out and losing teeth in every town he went through, and the thought was not to be supported without bitter tears.

Pale and sickly, I followed Blue out to see the Greenfeasts. Through the shadowy green bush we walked, and down the familiar back roads, moist with spring. Had I not walked here with him in that lost Primavera?

"Look, Steve, there's the bark hut! See the rafters standing high and bone-white above it? It always reminds me of that sad march of Peppino's. I wonder if he, at least, will be back this spring?" Blue played the bars of music that reminded her of him and the bark hut.

In Greenfeast's lonely gully we heard a loud hammering on tin, and came upon Mr Greenfeast, who was putting the finishing touches to a new hut which stood on a little slope in the swampy gully. Behind it rose a rough hill af bracken ferns and dead logs.

"Who is the hut for?" I said.

"It's for you," he answered with a smile.

We said, with due modesty, we didn't think we deserved it. But they assured us we did. It was made of Lysaght's Queen's Head flat iron, with a mixture of their Orb galvanized, a spice of bags and a handful of boards flung in to encourage us.

Assured of a home and work for the coming pea-picking, we returned to Metung and prepared to shift out. We didn't have good old Jim and his fantastic portmanteau with us this time; but Eb told us that he had met Peppino in the township and had told him of our arrival. Peppino was delighted and sent word that he was again picking for Mr Whitebeard and living on his property.

Dragging Teddy away on the end of a rusty chain and carrying a few groceries mingled with greasy bones for the dog, we left our luggage for the Greenfeasts to collect in their buggy, and trod it over the fields to the new hut. We sat down to rest above a small rubbish heap on the dry hill at the back of the local school. Wan with excess of sorrow, I lay by Blue's side, while Teddy looked at us from his bleary eyes.

"Blue," I said, "that dog appears to me to be older than they said he was when they gave him to us."

"It may be so," replied Blue. I again lapsed into a sad and tedious reverie, emerging to behold, in the rubbish heap, a bright blue enamel baking pan. "Blue, that's just what we want in the hut. Have a look and see if it's any good."

"It's got a hole in it, stuffed with rag." Blue brought it back and we examined it closely.

"What poetry there is in such colour. The blue in china and enamel has haunted me all my life," I said. "Shall we take it home to the hut?"

"Heaven knows what's been in it," replied Blue.

"Well, there's only a piece of old rag in it now."

We stayed staring at it for a long time, but finally left it behind, vividly blue in the green grass.

That night, we set out to walk over to Mr Whitebeard's to visit Peppino and his brother, the illustrious Pasquale, who had gently threatened, "I see to you when you come Metung." There was a light shower, and over wet grey shining paths we walked, through lonely paddocks in which dead trees charred into fantastic shapes leant out towards us. Macca and I had wandered through this place last spring. As I walked, the tears went with the rain down my face.

O, the past, the past! I have lost you, my one love ever. And where is Jim, too? Why are we walking alone like this in the rain?

Stumbling over the logs, in the darkness that loomed up when the lights of Mr Whitebeard's home shone in our faces, we saw faint flickering light in the hut of Peppino, which was well removed from the house of his employer. We passed the long shearing shed, where Heggie had gathered his fruitful ticks last summer, and all these things were dear to me, inexpressibly dear. Stealing up to the window, we looked through and saw the Italian boys lounging on their bunks in a hut papered with newsprint. One of them bent over a mandolin, thick with mother-of-pearl, striking harmonies from it, and swaying as he played. The light of the kerosene-lamp glowed over them, and they looked warm and alive with the day's work.

The muscles of Peppino's strong throat moved as he talked; his eyes glittered behind the lashes, and on his ivory face little black moles stood out, giving it the appearance of a mask. On a shelf behind him the china dishes glistened clean. Three other Italians stood around the mandolin player, talking and gesturing calmly.

Enchanted by their contentment, we watched on. At last, moving around to the door, we knocked and went in.

"*Buona notte, Peppino! Come sta?*" we exclaimed.

"Steve . . . Blue . . . I am ver-r-ry glad to see you 'gain. Long time I not see you."

The other lads kept a decorous silence.

"Where is Marc?" asked Peppino, meaning Macca. "And Jeem? He no come dis year? What? He merried? Ah, good, I tink! And Marc, he get merried, too?"

"No, Peppino."

"Where he go then, dis year?"

Ah, where, Peppino? Where? The song that I had written at home a week before was continually in my mind now, and it ran behind my thoughts wherever I walked. While Blue talked merrily to Peppino, the lines whispered behind her words.

> The twilight wind comes wading through the grasses
> And slowly turning silences make moan
> To burdock leaves, her ringing footstep passes,
> And through the dusk the blackbird cries alone.
> Ah, who has robbed the joy of last September,
> Muted the lips and drowned the music low?
> 'Twas I, 'twas I, that in the dark remember
> The singing lads of long and long ago.

Around us, within us, moved time, urging me to my appointed end; and I, helpless and blind, unable to see to what an awfulness it was moving me, to what ultimate joy, past all wrath, it would eventually bring me.

The lamp sent out vibrations of light over the luminous Italians, the mandolin, coloured bronze-red like an autumnal sea, the gleaming dishes, the earthern floor, the aliens' clothes lying about on the bag beds. I was poor and unloved, least of all these.

The door opened and Mr Whitebeard's son put his head, white and fragile, with a heavy crop of golden hair swinging over his temples, around the door into the oily glow of the room. He came in, a privileged guest, the master's son. We sat moodily by, lower than ever, while he was gently and courteously entertained. When he had withdrawn, we rose to go.

Peppino and his friend, Benedetto, rose to accompany us. This was the first time we had seen Benedetto. He was short and dark, with a simian face that looked shrunken and dejected when he sat silent. On being spoken to, he moved the heavy lower part of his face with animal rapidity, while his eyes remained dead. His lower lip moved up and down in the effortless dialect of Calabria. I felt afraid of him; he looked as though he might spring at my throat and not even feel that he was doing it.

However, he was a very respectable animal and moved beside us
in the night, with scarcely anything to say. But I had a fear of him,
and thought, "If, as Mia says, we shall meet our death through
these Italians, a man like Benedetto would be the one to fear. However, we shall guard ourselves. We shall get more guns and I shall
behave with greater austerity when I am with them."

They accompanied us to the hut and we asked them to get us
a large tin of water from the spring, scraping back the moss and scum
while they drew the water.

"*Troppo pesante!*" remarked Benedetto, lowering it and rubbing
his hands. It was his sole remark the whole evening.

Settling into the hut, we went for long walks through the bush,
feeling that this picking season would be dull, for we were now
Greenfeast's pickers, and they had first call on our services. We would
not see Karta Singh often, and there would be no adventurous
comedy like that of last year. Greenfeast had put in more land under
peas, for the fine paddock we had worked in with Macca and old
Snowy had yielded him good profits. As we passed, we saw the
peas waving their little white ears at us from amongst stony soil,
but a fresh immortal spirit of youth came from that ancient soil into
which man had never put a crop before. It had a sad imprinting
power that set itself on my heart and brought a feeling of tears there.

Wandering across the swamps in the gully, we met the Italians,
Peppino, Benedetto and Antonino, and as the sprightly spring wind
blew across the wild flowers, we stood together, bowing and exchanging courtly "*Buon giornos*" and solicitous "*Come stas*". They,
like us, were waiting for the real picking to start and, with time
hanging heavily on their hands, had come out into the wilderness
to startle the snakes and kookaburras with their comely tailorings.
Bowing and smiling, we parted, and Blue and I leapt a log in the
exuberance of youth . . . almost landing on the head of a brilliant
red fox which lay shivering with fear in a trap below.

"*Venite! Venite!*" we cried to our departing courtiers, and they
rushed back to us, shouting, "*Che cosa? Che cosa?*"

"*Una vulpe!*"

"Oh! Oh!" They scampered around, looking for sticks, but they
all proved to be too rotten with swamp damp for any practical purpose. In despair, we stared at each other, until Peppino noticed that
I was carrying a rifle and, tearing it out of my hands, levelled it
at the fox and furiously pulled the trigger.

"Bah!" exclaimed he when nothing happened, and he flung it

at the fox's head. The animal, insulted, expired on top of the trap, gnashing its teeth at the indignity of its death.

It was carried back to the hut in happy triumph and, when the Italians had gone, we took it down to the camp of old Snowy, who was again, this season, occupying the glorified dog kennel down by the foreshore. He had done a lot of trapping and was reckoned to be one of the best skinners in these parts. We crouched beside the good old man while he worked away, patiently rolling back from the blood-purple flesh of the fox, the animal mystery of its warm and rumpled fur, with the map of its life imprinted in blood and veins on the creamy, steaming hide.

As Snowy worked, he mentioned that he had a lot of stale bread lying around "that might be all right for your little dorg". Hungry and almost penniless, we said gratefully that Teddy would leap at it, and our mouths watered as we looked at the big rough hunks of bread which he bundled up for us. Taking them, we departed, with hunks and hide, and we would have taken the fox and roasted it, too, if it hadn't been considered *infra dig* among Australians to do so.

Heartened by the bread and milk, we went out into the swamp again, talking about taking up trapping for a living, instead of picking peas. We reckoned that a good fox-skin ought to bring over ten shillings.

"We'd only have to trap two a week to make our tucker; that's if Greenfeast would allow us to stay on in the hut." We peered under every log in the swamp, expecting to find foxes in traps there, making themselves ready to keep us by dying and throwing off their skins like snakes.

II

THE weeks passed, and from Macca there came no word, no sign. At last I was forced to admit that I was unwanted and unthought of. In my bitterness, I became hard, masculine and truculent in manner, swore and blasphemed, became passionately fond of guns and bullets, killed every living thing I could see around me, and grew to love with a fierce mirthless joy, adventure and extravagant comedy. I was alert for men to offer me insults, so that I might take them as a cue and work them up into a theatrical act, well rounded off, which I would perform before the Buccaneer and the Black Serpent. It was a sad time.

Not slowly did I come into this hardness and vileness, but swiftly,

overnight, because I was unloved. Certainly, very beautiful letters
still came from poor Borrelerworreloil, but, because of his race, I
placed him firmly in the category of eternal friendship. Intensely
Australian, although despised by her sons, I scorned defilement by
another race.

With the narrow vision of youth, I imagined that the Lord had
intended the Australian to rule over my country forever. I sat in
the hut, writing long treatises on its mystery, genius, its loveliness
and the racial splendour of its children. The Italians, I said, lovable
as they were, must first submit, for centuries, to their race being
washed out by toil and intermarriage. And then, not believing
in racial intermarriage, I could see no way out of it for them. I
felt myself to be a true and invincible angel of the Lord, as I sat
in the hut turning these things over.

Peppino, who sat with us, seemed half child, half comedian as
he chanted on the mouth-organ his marches, waltzes and litanies.
That he should ever love an Australian or be loved by her was a
faintly indecent thought to us. We had met him as we came home
from the Buccaneer's, where I had sat all the evening, heavy with
unspoken love and sorrow. He was walking in the deep dust of
the road under trees as sparse and crooked as starved goats. They
looked like thin-legged animals in the night. We filed behind him
up the hill, under the goat-trees, while he played a fast marching
song. We felt true soldiers as we followed him and later he sat in the
hut, playing the march that reminded Blue of the bare rafters
above the bark hut.

Ah, how sad I felt, as he wove his songs. Across the hill stood the
bark hut, beyond lay low ranges that hid Bumberrah with its
lonely railway station, from where, at certain times in the day, the
only train hooted mournfully and passed on.

That night, while Blue lay in bed asleep, I went up again to the
bark hut. As I walked on the track that he and I had shared, I
had for company only fugitive remembered phrases from his letters.
As I passed the corner of the fence where we had hung Jim's
presents, a line flashed through my mind, "I would like to take you
in my arms, as I did last night down by the fence and tell you
again that I love you." Unbearable. I shall go mad. "Stevie, the
best and most lovable Stevie in the whole world." But, why then,
have you left me, Macca? What have I done? Am I so changed?
"Well, Stevie, the day has gone, but it was a good day. A gentle
tattoo of rain on the roof, and all the world's clean; writing to you
seems to harmonize. I wonder if you understand?"

I am at the door of the bark hut now, and I understand nothing; the agony of my grief numbs me and makes me slow and stupid with tears. You are the past; you are time, escaping from me; you are life, the frustrating, flying, flying, flying.

"Please Stevie, excuse the lonely rose, but all the others have gone. You don't know how I'd have loved to have been able to send you a box of exquisite blooms . . . but. . . ." In the corner of the hut stands the small bark table on which you set the roses. Nettles have grown around the door. It swings open and a few rays of moonlight break through the opening and fall on the earthern floor. "Last night, Stevie, you were writing sonnets to me; today, I must answer. . . . Stevie, the only, the one that I love."

I sat in the old kitchen and tried to weep over my lost love, but I had no tears to give. He appeared to me to be standing in that old bark hut, his white face bent over me; I rested on his broad chest and put my arm timidly around his shoulders. "Love is all-powerful, Steve. It is more than millions of money." I vibrated with images of love. I veritably tied him before me, in the spirit; I implored him to be there.

But, at last, exhausted, I had to go home to bed.

Next day, we went with the Buccaneer and the Black Serpent to a sale on a farm along the Tambo River. A car carried us through the yellow-grassed country, soft with falling rain, to the old farm with its tall silo standing like a colonial turret above it.

"Steve, this is the farm where Jim stole the limes and they set the dogs on to him."

"Yes, we return to it, knowing it more familiarly than we did then. It was only a house behind some trees then; limes grew there and dogs barked. Shall we grow to know this house better, I wonder? Who will be coming into it, to toil and think of us, in years to come? Ah, there is a melancholy here as though this house is aware of me. Shall my name be spoken here, I wonder, Blue? Arteries spread out, it seems to me, from a large source, and I wander through them, returning again to the source, and being returned yet again to the outlands of the arteries by small coincidences."

The house was embedded in my being. I sat out in the drizzling rain, waiting for the auctioneers to come. The tall red-gold youth whom we had seen the year before at the Bell's Point sale, stood behind me, examining a pea-rifle. He put it down slowly as we stared at him.

"There's that youth we saw. Yes, I know. Ah, Steve, how like a poet he is!" whispered Blue.

"Yes, Keats must have looked like that; white-faced with rich auburn hair. I wish we could speak to him. Perhaps he, too, can talk in verse, or from a Paterian mind loose streams of prose."

"But what will happen to him in this bush? He'll marry someone with a mediocre mind, who thinks nothing of art and verse, and all the burning flames of the auburn head will lose their fire, and he'll be old."

Blue looked at him, as though she thought it would be the most natural thing in the world for him to fling himself down at her feet and propose a poet's love.

She looked very beautiful that day, with the broken, spicy beauty of a dark red carnation. She was wearing the brown Italian hat that Major had given her, and often to her lips she pressed the silver mouth-organ, which she could play as well as Peppino now. As the rain grew heavier, we retreated to the shelter of the empty silo, and played and sang the songs of Italy. Eb, the Buccaneer's son, sat silently with us.

The rain went. We emerged to pick up the treasured rifle and examine it. A low voice crawled over our shoulders, and said, "Youse can 'ave it if yer like."

We leapt around to face the auburn poet, thinking that after a week or two we would soon change his accent. But he had gone, and in his place stood that sombre and saddest spectacle of the Australian farm—the eldest son of the house. Lightly covered with chicken's fluff from nose to chin, delicately spotted by the early pimple, a little broken-mouthed and more than cross-eyed, he smiled at us, and we really loved the boy. To be able to smile generously and sweetly from such a fiendish mixture of homeliness, won our hearts. And besides . . . the rifle!

"But," I stammered, "we couldn't take it. It's for sale, isn't it? And it's quite good. Might fetch a high price."

"No," said gentle Dave. "It's broke . . . 'ere and 'ere . . . see? Youse can 'ave it."

He wandered off, content, and I, dazzled, took the rifle to my heart. I had got it . . . for nothing.

Ha, the auctioneers arrive! The mud-spattered car was at the gate, and from it, with a lordly haughtiness, strode the apoplectic emperor of Gippsland auctioneers. Years of his trade had carved him with Eastern fidelity into a grand figure for an artist's model. The wind, the weather, the stock and stations he had sold, the whip he had wielded and the buyers and sellers he had looked down on were all bitten into him, as time has gnawed into the Buddha.

Striding through the yard, he spurned the place, he abhorred the vile day that had called him out to sell up the few gimcracks in such a filthy hovel. His red-purple face shone as its muscles with the terrific opening of his mouth. Under his wide hat, his blood-shot eyes glared redly. The many capes of his pale golden cloak, stained with the romance of the weather, opened and shut as he stirred up the mud of the yard with his feet and thundered with immense authority:

"All right, George! Bring 'em in! Now . . . here we have."

Drizzling rain put a fine soft periwig of dew over his hair when he raised his hat for a moment, and his face was blank, unprotected and disliked by the grey sky to which he raised it. Down came the hat . . . up went the short riding crop, and the magical voice, rounded and amplified by years of practice, roared out into the Athens of the old farm.

"Starting at fourpunfour . . . at fourpunfour . . . at."

At his left elbow stood his son, scribbling on a pad hunched up on his arm. A stock-whip hung from the arm of the hand that held the pencil, and the polished plait gleamed, the lash twitched and floated nervously with the energy of his movements. He, too, was the Gippslander, and heir to the magnificent ancient whose purple face was going to be the sail that should puff him into the Isles of Avalon, where, among the heroic shouts of other great Gippsland auctioneers, he should take his rest; and peace be to their immortal souls, for they knew their land and its stock.

The son had the slimness of an intelligent, ambitious but quiet, mother mingled with the stream of his sire, but he was bloating and redding and fattening with his father's living. They were both one flesh and, fatal though it was, it was good to see. These men had a rough aristocratic tradition to carry on, and by right of whisky, stock and cruel marriages they should bring out their kind to sustain that tradition.

We, the lost, gazed at them respectfully, regretting that we had become lopped off the tree of a family as old, in this province, as theirs. Ah, Gippsland, I cried inwardly, we, too, own a share in you, by right of birth and power of desire; but it is denied us. We have nothing to call our own.

The dripping peppermint-gums lashed out, heavy with rain and lively with the wind; the growing downpour streamed steadily over the sloping yard, down the meek twitching hides of the red and white cattle: it made thick tongues of plaited hair on the hide of the cattle dogs and streaked the hindquarters of the waiting hacks.

Disposing of the stock as quickly as possible, the auctioneer took the buyers into the house, where, like a red and white wraith of Celtic dawn, moved the clerk, a son of the old house of McAlister. He moved about, valuing the articles of furniture before his employer came grandiosely to auction them, with that grandiose abruptness of a man who is more accustomed to cattle than to chairs.

"That's Archie McAlister," someone said.

"Ah," we cried, with Chiverelli, "good-a name . . . good-a name!"

"The rumble of the flooded Tambo is in it," I said, "and the white dangerous moonlight of Haunted Stream floods it with glory; and do not the sunsets, dark red with cloud and black with flying swans on the reedy Tambo, seem to have driven their bolts into his gleaming hair? White face of the north and red hair of the unconquered Celt, we watch you, we, the disinherited, and feel the sorrow of those who will never carry on the tradition of their land. It weighs us down."

No, perhaps it is the buns and tea we are eating. Ah, this sale is not like Charlie Wallaby's. In Gippsland, they spread the viands before you. Since the rifle had been given to us, we decided to spend sixpence on buns, and were given a dozen. Lying back luxuriously in the car, with my rifle on my breast and my buns sprawling around me, I thought sadly on love.

Night found us dragging the miserable dog, Teddy, through the rain along the shining back track to the hut. In two large brown paper bags, we had, respectively, buns for ourselves and greasy bones for Teddy. They didn't stay respective very long, for the rain lashed the bags to tatters and bones and buns poured out into the mud. I groped around until I found them, and could even, with my keen sight, pick up fallen currants. Sodden and hopeless, we trailed through the night to the hut.

Tying Teddy to the fish crate, we fell into bed and slept in our dissatisfied perfection of youth, desirous of nothing but the destruction, the breaking down of this simple life into something distorted and hideous. All the foundations were there, in me. I longed, I do not know why, to break away from Blue. In her company, a terrible sorrow descended on me. I made a clown of myself in an effort to escape it, but it recurred again and again. I grew to feel that she must be a menace to me; I fancied that in following her

I should come to terrible things; to unbearable loneliness and wild sin. Once away from Blue, I thought, life will become rich again and I shall flourish. So, I steadily nourished the tempers between us. I encouraged jealousies, envy and pride, so that we might part.

We parted, mentally, on many things daily, but on a matter such as the meeting of Angelo we were fully united in bonds that would hold fast for years.

Rumour of Angelo came before him. The Buccaneer said, "There's an old Italian who follows the local girls around everywhere, frightening them and making them run for their lives."

"Ah," I cried, interlarding every few words with choice blasphemies from a bitter heart. "We shall see this unique one who follows shrinking maidens; we shall pluck a few feathers from this bucolic angel of the back tracks."

Within a day or two, as we wandered along under the goat-trees in the falling afternoon, yarning, as mates do, we smelt an odour like that of garlic and cheese wrapped up in dirty old clothes; we heard a step, saw a shadow and, turning beheld Angelo.

This Lucifer, who had fallen head first, landing on his shattered hat, was an elderly man, with an unshaven face, a silly grin, and dirty garments wanting in buttons at the more precarious points. Walking slowly, we gave him an opportunity to pass us; but he limped behind, grinning from under his broken hat.

I rushed back to him and, grasping him by the greasy lapels, from which my fingers slipped, I cried with joy, I literally wept with ecstasy, saying, "Lo, it is our *cugino*, Angelo! Gossip, how is it with you. What? You don't recall me? Il Steva, the boyhood friend who played La Morra with you in Abandoniente's backyard down in Firenze? Gossip, you are sore changed!"

"*Er . . . scusa mi, io non capisco!*" stammered Angelo, backing in the breeching.

"But you will soon. It will all come back to you. And what is that that I hear? You follow the girls? What? Gossip Angelo, you, the fair, the flyblown, following the girls! In Firenze, remember, it was the girls who followed you. Come, let it be like old times. Ahead, *avanti*, good old garbage, and let us follow you!"

Thus wheedling, with my long stiletto poking at him, I persuaded Angelo ahead, and we walked in his shadow, making loud and admiring remarks about the contours of his figure which rivalled in bulk and bumps the dead logs lying on each side.

At last, embarrassed, he rushed off into the bush. We walked along alone for a while, but turning at a rustle among the red-tipped gums, we saw him emerging from them. "What, old friend, back from your holiday?" Angelo fell over a hollow log. "There, you have a good trip, at least. We are happy that you are with us again. Go ahead, gossip, and give us your shadow!"

Into the track I pushed Angelo, and in his grotesque shadow we walked our way, crying, "Ah . . . good-a name, Angelo . . . good-a name! *Tu sei un angelo davvero!*"

My bright happy ways seemed to have enchanted Angelo. Apparently he longed to see more of me. For on Sunday, as we worked in the hut, washing out, in very little water, our soiled socks, shirts, trousers, handkerchiefs grisly from a recent cold, and the rugs on which Teddy slept . . . we saw a figure approaching through the dead trees.

"Behold . . . Angelo!" said I to Blue. "Here he comes, the indefatigable lover. See the hat?" His new grey hat shone in the wilderness. "It looks as though he had just skinned a rabbit and, after painting a band around it with a bit of swamp mud, jammed it on his head."

His suit of the most ingenious tailoring, all corners and ridges, would have interested a cartographer. Across the front of it he carried the usual collection of Italian orders; butterflies, bees and stars of painted tin.

"Wait!" I shut the door.

Tipping Teddy out of his fish crate, Angelo drew it right in front of the door and sat there eyeing the shut portal of the Queen's Head special flat iron with patient eyes.

"A position I should never have taken up, Angelo," I murmured, eyeing him through a hole in the Queen's Head. "It is Sunday; let us lift up our voices."

Merrily, with our arms thrashing through dirty suds, thick with grease and sweat, we lifted up our voices and sang. A glance now and then through the hole in the door, showed Angelo to be still patient and interested.

Twilight was nearing; the washing was done. "I believe the critical moment has arrived," I said. "Now is the time to act!"

Blue opened the door casually as though there was not a soul within cooee for a hundred miles, and I, raising the bucket of dirty suds, threw it straight out of the door, with the same feeling of remoteness, and . . . how unfortunate . . . knocked Angelo off his crate, drenching da good hat, da fine suit, nice shirt and beautiful boots with the water in which we had washed our unmentionables.

Then, still seeing nothing, we closed the door, and began to sing again. But, through the hole, we saw the silent Angelo rise up, and shake his hat, coat and fist vengefully, before he withdrew into the rapidly approaching twilight.

After a while Blue opened the door and, taking the milk billy, she went up the ferny hill to Greenfeast's for our daily ration. Half way to the top she called out, "Steve, here he is, hiding in the ferns with a big lump of wood in his hand."

Snatching the worst gun from those hanging on the wall, I rushed, mad with enjoyable blood lust, up the hill and found our Angelo crouching under a big log. He dropped the stick, as I rushed at him with foaming mouth, distended whiskers and distended eyes, crying out in Italian, "I shall kill you . . . I shall kill you!"

Shaking and white with fear, he fled down through the ferns. And I to my quarry, palpitating with brutal excitement, my inside dark with the love of killing, my entire being joyous and ecstatic with the hope that he might do something so that I could kill him. He rushed for the barbed-wire fence and crawled under it, and when his hat, pathetically, fell off, my anger broke in me, and I turned on my heel and let him go without another word.

Sick with feelings aeons old and strong, I returned the broken gun to the rack, and we sat down to our tea with a bad sense of having been adulterated by man.

"Hey there's a sale on over at Swanreach," said Eb, next day. "You two ought to go."

We did.

Once more we stood with the Gippsland bun and the cup of tea in the farmhouse, watching the young auctioneer, bloodshot of eye, hooked of nose, arrogant, watchful, Australian, waiting for the stock to come in to be sold.

I was on the lookout for a horse. I had been on the lookout for a long time. Yes, when I bought a horse, I should be my father again, and with horse, dog and rifle, I should ride as he rode, playing his violin and singing at every stopping-place, and living, as he lived, a melancholy, passionate, perverted, failure. The blinding sun of the Western Plain flashed its rays into my brain and resurrected him in an instant. On the dry soil he stood, a small man, with a big deformed hunchback and a very large skull.

But I was on the lookout for a horse. They were all cropping, far out in the paddocks, and a young fellow in blue denims got on a horse and galloped out to round them up and bring them in for the sale.

Standing alone on a green hill, I saw a slender black mare, as wild looking as a brumby. Her long mane and tail floated lightly behind her in the wind. Raising her head, she gave a shrill scream. She was the dark power in that mob. Her serpent neck and head twisted on her shoulders as she looked down. I said to myself, "If that black mare comes into the yard and goes up for sale . . . she's mine."

The young fellow headed the entire mob towards the yards. The black mare who had been farthest out when they started, seemed, as the mob neared the yards, to flash out from nowhere, and led them, galloping like a racer, into the yard . . . stopping there with a snort and flying mane.

A dull enough creature when she stopped, and full of faults. But I said to myself, "Yes, you are like me. When I am in the full impetus of imaginative, passionate flight, I look as you did, winged, fiery, a very god, swifter than all the rest. But when I stop, a plain deformed deadness sets in. My limbs grow cold and sad, my faults are noticeable and I am, physically, a thing to be despised. Therefore, I have to burn all the time if I want to get the things I desire from life. Yes, you are like me."

The young auctioneer flung back his caped cloak and shouted out to the farmer. "This mare to be sold? Good! Well, here we are; aged pony mare . . . look at her teeth, will you, Gilbert? . . . five years; flying R on near shoulder. What? Oh, yes. Used to do quite a bit of racing, before she had a slight accident to the off hind fetlock . . . a mere nothing. Still a fine hack . . . starting at five pound . . . at fi' pun . . . at fi' pun . . . at fi' pun. . . ."

I nodded. The bidding stopped. "Gone . . . at five pounds." I stepped forward and paid out the notes. I was absolutely broke then. He wrote out a receipt in a slanting hand like my own, and as I took it from him I had a thousand things to say, such as: "Yes, I am Gippsland, too. My family have been graziers here for many years. I should be the mother of sons who would be the princes of this province, in thought and action . . . but what am I? Well, you can see. A wandering pea-picker, living in a galvanized iron hut. But my forefathers were the pioneers here. And that is what is really hurting more than anything. I am nothing to Gippsland; I just wander through her, being hurt by her and used by her in menial toil. But you, as you know, are part of her tradition. In the community, you are important. I am the pea-picker."

It was the fate of Macca, too. We were the disinherited children of those who had rebelled against the old order of wooing. My mother had laughed at and left the honourable man her father selected for her. Ah, the old people knew. Theirs was a long bitterness, and they knew that even unto the fourth generation we should suffer.

I had bought the mare. The receipt was in my hand, and I was in a dream. I took the halter around her neck and stood looking at her. She was mine; ugly, indifferent, sleepy after her flash of racing, and dull with a long winter coat.

"You've bought her, Steve, you've bought her," said Blue.

The youth in the denims said, "Haven't you got a saddle? Well, you can have the halter." They had really done well out of the sale.

"I'll get up first, Blue, and you get behind me. We'll ride her home."

Nobly we breasted the hills, halting outside the old house of Averdrink where I lingered to think on my lost love. But we had to move on, for the millions of mosquitoes there nearly drove us mad.

Prancing gracefully with her double load, the mare climbed the steep slope to the Buccaneer's. The Black Serpent came to the door, stared at me and said loudly, "You fool!" Then she disappeared inside to make tea for us, and search for some money to lend me until I had done some work.

Mr Greenfeast let me run the mare in the gully near the hut. On the afternoon of the following day I prepared for my first ride alone. The halter was proudly and tremblingly adjusted, the bag placed on her back, and I bestrode her, moving off at a quick agitated walk and leaving Blue in the hut. I must be alone, alone to feel the nervous silk of her veined hide moving back and forth under my knees; and for me alone must the sawing mouth pull downward to the twin powers of her loose tiny chest, to which the long slender throat fell, fine-haired.

Hatless, in blue shirt and breeches, I bumbled up and down on her amiable body, until we reached the main road with its dry white racecourse-like turns. I touched her smartly with the end of the halter and she answered by breaking into a gallop immediately. A terrifying gallop that swooped upon the rapidly falling curves of the road, that made the fences lurch towards us and retreat with gasping grey rail, that blinded and choked me, as I hung around the black mane of death and wondered with a mixture of agony and glory if this was the end. Down we galloped, and around, and down and around again the sharp and bitterly perilous corners, and like an arrow we rushed at the Buccaneer's gate, pulling up with an angry short snort of venom.

The Buccaneer, who had stood waving his arms in horror at our approach, came over as I jumped off trembling and stood before him on watery legs.

"I'll shoot that thing, if I see you on it again," he said, eying its rapidly rising and falling sides.

But after we had had a cup of tea he came out and admired its various points, discovered its failings, and cut its mane and tail shorter.

Stroking his golden moustache and pulling his black hair, he gave his loud half apologetic, half authoritative cough. "A . . . hem! Now this mare what you think is such a jewel among 'orses . . . pon mai word, ha, ha," (like us, he incorporated the sayings of others in his speech) "as you will see 'as got a broken fetlock. She's been kicked, most probably. See that big swelling on her off left 'ind? That's it."

"Yes, the auctioneer told me about that; but he said it didn't make much difference. She was still good, he said. What's wrong now?"

He waved his hand over her near eye. "Woa now, old girl. Steady, now, steady!" He patted her sympathetically. "Look at that heye!" he ordered me sternly.

I looked at it woefully, far into its opaque blue depths and unwinkingly it stared back at me.

"Blind in it," said the Buccaneer, and he roared laughing. "My word, you got a bargain there, all right. Ho, ho, ho, ho!" His great sea laugh cut me to the heart.

"What else?" I asked feebly.

"A-hurm! Eb . . . come 'ere, Eb!" Whenever the Buccaneer saw a point where he could score off, where he was absolutely positive about a matter, his nostrils dilated tensely, his eyes grew small and keen, and the tenseness and keenness travelled down from his very eyebrows to his quivering forefinger. "I'd say, wouldn't you, Eb, looking at them forelegs, what that this hanimal 'ad at some time or other been ridden until it foundered?"

Eb got down on his haunches and, drawing at his cigarette, said wisely, "I reckon you've struck it, pa."

"Some brute," said the Buccaneer bitterly, "what 'as ridden this hanimal some time or hother 'as galloped it till it foundered."

I leant against the wire-netting fence, wondering why the mare didn't fall down in a mass of decomposition before me.

"What a mare!" the Buccaneer laughed. "What a mare!" He

looked at my haggard face. "Cheer up . . . cheer up. She's all right still. You can ride her, but you'll have to watch her . . . you'll just have to watch her."

I couldn't bear to. Holbein's "Dance of Death" would have been a pleasanter sight. We took the halter off again, and went inside. "Five pounds," he murmured. "Five pounds! Ho, ho, hohoho!" And he and Eb laughed it off together.

III

THE paddocks were lonely that season. I was like a blind person feeling about in the dark for a beloved hand. All day we toiled in the light spring weather and the white flowers of the peas tossed their green-veined petals among us. Over the stones, we crawled, filling the tins and dreaming of love, Blue of her faithful youth who in his weekly letters begged for marriage, and I, forsaken, dreaming of Macca, lost in the Black Mountains.

When evening came with the cold winds, we filled our hats with peas and took them home for the evening meal. Afterwards, we crawled into bed and slept, to rise and work again next day. It was impossible to sit by the fire at night, for the chimney smoked furiously. The only way cooking could be done was by breaking down a big bundle of tea-tree, flinging it on the hearth, lighting it, placing the billy on a hook above it, and rushing outside. From a distance we watched the smoke rising and when no more came out of the chimney, the room was considered safe to enter and eat in.

The working days of a pea-picker depended on the extent of the crop. A first picking in a small paddock took only a few days, for the plants were carefully handled and only the full pods taken off. When the first paddock had been gone over, we were idle for a week or so.

What a morning it was! The sunshine from it promised to penetrate all the coming years of sadness and shine through the mind, carrying with it a remembrance of cool bracken ferns, stiff and dark with dew, and dappled with sunlight.

Peppino stood at the door of the hut.

"Dis morning I go see one my countryman, Leonardo della Vergine. Why you no come wit me? Dis a fonny man. We have tea and cake fill your bell', lik-a Mrs 'Ardy." Peppino jumped with joy at the thought of the virtuous family. "Quick, too quick, you come wit me, Steve and Blue."

U

Dressing with due solemnity, we argued over who was to wear Willie Gray's wrist watch and red flannel rheumatic belt. I said, "No, I will not go unless I can wear them. You will remember, Blue, that you wore them to the Swanreach sale."

I felt that with the surgical appliance worn over my trousers and the large leather watch-case on my small wrist, I should appear more handsome than Adonis. Blue disagreed bitterly. "You wore it last time, Steve, and anyhow, the red belt doesn't suit your colouring."

"It suits me and you know it," I said obstinately. "That's why you want it."

"But it's only for people with rheumatics."

"It is not. It suits me." I buckled it on, tenderly.

Peppino stood outside whistling "*O Sole Mio*" and patting Teddy. "Carm arn. You good dog, eh? Ow . . . doncha bite me. . . . Gerrout!"

Blue gave in; handed me the wrist watch and, with the red flannel belt in place, I stepped out, satisfied, into the glory of the day.

The sun laid its hand on us, and we fell into a dream of beauty, as mystical as religion. On and on, we wandered, over old roads red with spring, trees crimson with it, saplings bloody with it. We took short cuts over rival pea paddocks where the pickers were working among the crops. Such was the harsh light of the day, that the clods looked enormous and golden, cracked fascinatingly, and carrying blue-grey peas, coloured like the Greek hills of the alpine district. Teddy scampered in front of us; the silky rags of his hide flying in the wind.

Walking under flowering trees near the lake, we came to the residence of a retired judge, who had the reputation of being considerate enough to have travellers rowed across the creek that separated them from the rest of the foreshore; otherwise a long walk through harsh bush and a cold wade through shallow waters were indicated.

We looked around for the judge. Seeing a long low shed, we knocked at its door. No one answered; we opened the door and walked into a workshop. An old man dressed in fine black clothes, with petulance and bewilderment written on his little aristocratic face, walked up to us.

"Well?" he asked.

We said politely that we wanted to cross the creek. But he was as deaf as a beetle. So we bellowed courteously the request to be rowed out of his sight. The old man looked around, his little red eyes sparkling irritably.

"My man is not here. You want to cross the creek?"

"Yes," we cried jovially and hopefully. "Can he row us over, please?"

"Troublesome devils," muttered the old man.

Awed and saddened, we crawled away and took to the bush.

It was not so difficult after all. The sand gleamed in the sunlight, and the short stiff grass bounced under our feet. Some sheep grazed in a paddock. Here it was that Teddy revealed his true trade of sheep-killing. After them he coursed in true dingo style, pulling them down by the ears and looked around for a larger dog to come along and finish them off. I aimed my pea-rifle at him, but it had no bullets in it, so with a laughing yelp he coursed after another. Peppino threw oaths and stones and at last, red-mouthed and gay, Teddy romped back to a kick in the ribs.

Rounding a point of land, we were in the backyard of the old farm at Bell's Point where we had bought the blue jug last year.

"Why, we've been here before, Peppino! We know this place! What is your friend like? Is he an old man with a brown shining face, all dwarfed and grotesque?"

"*Si, il grotesco* . . . that's Leonardo!" replied Peppino.

We walked through the unpainted gate under the squat green cedar; the skin of the water-rat was still hanging on its branches. Peppino knocked at the back door.

The short broad man came out, with a boyish sweet smile that was scarcely recognizable. On that wet day we first saw him, he had appeared a ragged, but serenely smiling dwarf, his large grotesque features looming up like a seventh party in a drawing by Dürer, so that we had a sense of him being in the picture at some-one else's pleasure.

A year of proprietorship had changed him into a firm, red-cheeked brown-eyed man, with sensual moist underlip lying loose and laughing beneath watchful benevolent eyes. Whitely shone his teeth as he smiled at us, and his rounded belly made his white shirt and khaki trousers swell out firmly.

"*Buon giorno, Peppino,*" he remarked in the slow lazy voice of an Italian Yorkshireman. "*Come sta-a-a!*" And to us sweetly and slowly. "*Buon giorno, come sta, Lei?*"

"*Bene grazie,*" we answered.

"Come in. Sid down," he said laboriously in English. "*Un minuto!*" he added, disappearing to an inner room.

The old kitchen looked unchanged. The long rough wooden table was there, the form behind it, under the window; a box beside the fireplace, and, the sign of the proprietor, a large guitar on the wall. We sat with our backs to the window that looked out on the misty blue lake; the fine cobwebs across the panes gave this natural canvas an appearance of age and the cracking-up of paints. The form was firm under us. We spread our legs and watched comfortably the preparations for our lunch. Leonardo talked in his lazy easy-going dialect to Peppino. *"Ho preso il crops st' anno; ho venduto il primo sacco al Mr Jonson,"* with English words thrown in easily and nicely.

Moving around the kitchen with a frying-pan full of oil in his hand, he murmured in his luxurious Italian of crops and prices, while his big coarse fingers gesticulated awkwardly, showing the palm all the time. He broke several eggs into the pan, chopped up some parsely and flung it in on top of the oil and the raw yellow globes of the eggs. *"Ma, credo che non posso venire a Melbourne st' anno! Non è sicuro il crops."*

He stopped at the fire, blowing its red flame higher, and the red handkerchief tucked in his belt at the back bobbed as he worked. Through the window the lake gleamed under the misty wind, and we eyed the guitar and wondered if he would play it later. I followed his every movement with delight, through the large shadowy room. *"Un minuto, un minuto!"* He repeated.

A few tomatoes were cut up and added to the eggs and parsley. He waddled from the room and returned with several bottles of wine. Lifting the pan from the fire, he dished up in big old plates the delicately cooked mixture, and poured out wine for us. Fumbling among the glasses he tipped one over.

"Ah, una festa!" he and Peppino cried, and we nodded and smiled. For the spilt glass was a sign that the day should be one of feasting and music. Another glass was filled, *"Un minuto!"* Leonardo went away again, returning with bottles of pickles, glasses of honey, jars of nuts and sweets, and a lump of cake. Stripped kidney beans and fennel roots were added to the *salata*, and cups of weak black coffee were placed, slopping over, at our right hands.

From a shelf he took down round loaves of hard bread.

"Questo pane ho fornato, io stesso!" he cried proudly.

"What? You cook dis yourself?" said Peppino, proud to air his English.

"Per sicuro!" Lazily he took down from a board swinging above the table on wires a large round ball of cheese, of a pink and white colour, streaked like marble. It was so hard that he had to cut the pieces off with a hatchet. "This . . . whatchum callem . . . cheese," he said slowly and delicately, "I make from milk my sheep."

We nibbled the salty slices and found them so much to our liking that Leonardo was soon tearing off slice after slice. The tomatoes and eggs went to find it and, after them, five glasses of wine apiece, followed by beans, fennel, nuts, pickles, lollies and cakes. Talking and eating, we sat fatly around the table, dreaming dazedly of the mistral-covered waters seen through the cobwebs; of the amiable Leonardo whose face now shone like polished furniture, with a dish of apples standing a few feet off from it and indistinctly reflected on the shine. Listening to his slow ruminative accent, we fell into a trance of joy. For the first time, in years, I felt happy, truly happy. Love hurt me no more.

"Ah, Italy," I cried, sipping the wine, "what joys you bring! I give up my dreams of being a great Australian, a pioneer in racial purity and a passionate single-hearted lover of my country. The Australians despise me; they have nothing to give but awkward suspicions. Therefore, I shall forsake them and cling to Italy, to her wine, her slow rich dialects, her foods and her beautiful simian people, faintly savage, faintly over-civilized . . . and old, so old, with Dante, Tasso and Petrarch as marks for their periods of magnificence."

I fell in love with Italy that day, as I sipped the wine. Ah, Italy, you have not loved me well! Perhaps you did not forgive me for holding you lightly when we first met. No matter, your sin against me has bound us together for all eternity.

Their natures made open and free with wine, Peppino and Leonardo laughed loudly as they talked, and we bemusedly stared at the poetry of their faces. Peppino took out his mouth-organ and, leaping to his feet, played a furious dance, "for the old men", as he said. He danced it with Leonardo. They faced each other, Peppino, with his finely cut ivory face sweating out the wine, the black curls hanging over his slanting eyes that glared merrily at Leonardo. This ancient *ballerino* pointed his toes and stepped briskly, clapped his hands and spun around and around, with the red handkerchief bobbing an excited tail in the rear.

While they danced, we kept time with stamping feet. The dust rose from the cracks in the floor, and beyond the cobwebbed windows rose the blue waters and the glassy wind.

Tearing down the guitar from the wall, Leonardo sat on the box by the fire and, plucking the strings clumsily but masterfully, sang in a harsh crow-like voice to the thrum of the music.

Gently we disengaged ourselves from the company and strolled off, with full stomachs, to lie down on the shore. Above in the sky, a large eagle flew glittering against the sun.

At twilight, we were back in the hut with a bottle of wine, a bunch of flowers and the memory of Leonardo della Vergine bursting in our veins. Impetuously, we said to Peppino, "Let us continue the night further, Peppino. We will go with you to your hut and sing there, the old songs of Italy."

"Sorry, Steve and Blue," said Peppino in his soft bass voice, "but Mr Whitebeard son, he tell his fader that he have seen you come dat first night in my plice for see me. And Mr Whitebeard, he tell me, 'Peppino, I no want dis young girl come near my house.'"

"Ah, Gippsland! Gippsland!" I said, and the joy of the day left me; I was a poet no more.

But the thought of Leonardo persisted; the memory of his lonely gaunt farmhouse was sweet. As I toiled in the paddocks I saw through the rainbow showers of the morning, the spilt wine of the *festa* and the glitter of fruits, vegetables and eggs.

Within my heart, Peppino leapt to his feet again, chanting on the mouth-organ, with the deep swift Italian accompaniment; Leonardo's red handkerchief flapped up and down, and above all, the huge eagle flew piercingly in the sky against the escaping cloud and the flying sun. All was evanescent!

"Ah, Macca, you don't come to me!" I cried, and from the torture of my mind, I made poetry. "Macca rides in the Black Mountain, and he sings this song. It was in his heart, really, and I took it from him, and shaped it so that I, too, might know what he thought of the past. Ah, the past. Ah, the past, the past! He knows that I, at night, haunt the bark hut, mourning for him. In dreams he sees me and feels my sorrow. Who can help me? I must suffer alone."

I thought I had made manifest in this song those days when I lay in the old bark hut and listened to the rain drifting across the yellow paddocks from the Tambo River.

> I cropped the true love from her lips
> As we lay close pressed together
> When the stallion rains came in from the sea,
> Treading the ploughlands pitilessly,
> As I caught her closer into me,
> In the wild September weather.
> I cropped the true love from her lips,
> From her eyes that opened never,
> And while I kissed, the stallion, rain,
> Came thundering in from the sea again . . .
> Swiftly I caught him by his mane,
> And we left her alone forever.

IV

At night, by the swinging fence that rose dark against the blue sky on the hill above the bark hut, I stood waiting, imagining that I saw the round plunging body of Macca's mare, reined against the stars and the glowing pyres of evening. I thought I saw my lost love, bending from his saddle; the power of his horse held in one hand, and in the other, the old book of fairytales. His sad voice rang out to me, telling me that he had become lost in the forests of Black Mountain.

One cold windy afternoon I walked alone across that paddock from whose dry grassy breasts I had cried "Patria Mia", as I went to hold a tryst with toil on that summer evening, long ago. Ah, to be able to call back that twilight and see him again!

I had fantastic plans made for the coming years. My object was to find a hut and live therein, alone, with horse, dog and gun, working in the paddocks for the growers who would gradually come to know and respect me. Throughout the seasons I would work, and while I was idle, waiting for the crops to come on again, I should write long letters, rich in poetry, to Macca. I would dedicate my life to him, while he roved the country, learning the bitterness of life and the false hearts of all women, save one. At last, perhaps, when he was very old, he might return to me. Even if he didn't, I should continue to live in such a pure and poetic solitude that the fame of my virtue must spread over all Gippsland; and he, returning there one day, should hear of me . . . must hear of me . . . I couldn't bear that he should not hear. I should be to him the flawless love, the ideal of faithfulness.

Thus I thought as I wandered, gun in hand, over the hill towards Karta Singh's hut. In the corner of his paddock, on the site of the Maorilander's tent, stood another's . . . dilapidated, torn to ribbons by the storms and loosening fluttering strips of canvas to every breeze. A stylish figure stood up in the middle of the wreckage, attired in a perfectly fitting lounge suit, with silk shirt and tie to match. With his eyes on a mirror swinging from the tent-pole, he carefully adjusted an impeccable bowler hat and took a twist at the tie. Our eyes met, spoke volumes and I moved off to enjoy my part of the mystery.

This piece of order emerging from chaos was one of Karta Singh's pickers, dressed up to go into the township. We met him one afternoon when we visited our old friend of the lantern, the staff and the son in Lahore.

The heat of the day was intense as we neared Karta's hut. The long green gum-leaves, with their false look of dampness, hung heavily. The birds were silent; the grit on the road and the three white tents stuck in the bushes beside it were absolutely painful to look at through the glare. Karta Singh was sitting on his tiny stool in front of a big fire.

"Why," thought I, eyeing that little seat and the tall man, "why cannot the things I desire remain untouched, too, like this? Here, there is no change."

"Well, you fella Steve and Blue? How you get on? Where you been? You fella long time stay away." Karta felt around behind him for more wood with which to stoke the fire. His dreary glazed eyes regarded us speculatively; above the metal bangle on his wrist, he now wore one of coloured wools.

"We've been to a place in the alps . . . long way from here. We met a friend of yours, there. An Indian named Gauda Singh. You know him?"

"Gauda Singh? Oh yes, I know little bit."

"What does that woollen bracelet on your arm mean, Karta?"

"This?" He bared the brown stringy wrist and looked down fondly at the twisted flowers of wool. "My liddle granddaughter send this to me from India. This belong my religion."

He pulled open a drawer in his table, and took out a light clean johnny cake. "You fella like this?"

"My word! Gauda Singh cooked one for us, Karta." We moved forward with the usual slowness of Starving Steve and Breadless Blue to take a meal.

"You open billy there . . . you find honey, you fella."

A tall tin of frozen honey, deliciously cool in the hot day, was opened to us. We blessed Karta and broke his bread.

"You fella Steve . . . what wrong your eye?"

"Oh, Karta, something got in it yesterday, and I can't get it out."

"You fella," said he in a low drooling voice, "might be I cure your eye if you like." Opening another drawer, he took out a piece of filthy rag and slowly unwound it until a dirty lozenge like a thick peppermint fell on to the table. "You see this lolly? This very good cure. Might be you rub on your eye and all sore go. You fella, you try if you like. I have this cure for twenty year, and nearly six hundred fella with sore eye rub this on and he get well. You try; might be cure your eye in one minute."

"Might blind me in one second, too, by the look of it, Karta. No, thanks, I'll get along all right without it."

"Well, you fella read one page of Koran; might be make better."
He drew a long book with old yellow leaves out of the same drawer
and opened it at a particularly intricate looking bit.

"I can't read it," I explained.

"No matter; you just look. This very holy language. Might be
cure your eye." I stared at it with my sore eye for over ten minutes,
until I saw a deep twinkle in Karta Singh's eye; then I indignantly
shut the book and said we'd better be getting home.

"You fella," said Karta, "this my last year on this place. Rammi
. . . you 'member Ram Singh, you fella? . . . he go home India last
month. Next year I leave. I go buy bags all over this country, and
sell to pea-grower. Soon I sell out all my things. You want buy good
iron for press your clo'? You like buy good pea-rifle? You remember
pea-rifle you shoot last year? Might be I take twenty-five shillings
for, now, might be I not. God, He willing!"

"Who's going to come here after you, Karta?"

"You know that Italian man, Domenic? He work for Billy Creeker
last year you come? That man lease this place off Billy Creeker for
two year, like me. No good this place now. I finish. Might be
another man he make money." Karta smiled slyly. "This good iron.
I sell for six bob." He went away and got lost in the bags and rags
at the back of his hut, and returned with a rusty old iron.

"What? Six bob for that?"

Karta caressed it. "Yes. Good as new. I use once . . . I never use
again."

"Why?"

"Once I have plenty clo'. I think, 'Tonight might be I iron for go
Melbourne and see my friend.' I have plenty methylated spirit in
bottle. Bottle I put on table. Iron I put in fire. Long time I sit and
drink. Long time iron stay in fire. I take him out. I put him on my
clo'. Long time I drink. Long time iron sit on my clo'. Nexa morning
I wake up. No clo'. Man got no clo', he not want iron. I sell for
six bob."

We haggled it down to one and six.

"Now you buy this pea-rifle. I sell too cheap for twenty-five bob.
If you like, you take home and try. Bring back if you no want."

I agreed on this, and we went off with the pea-rifle, just as the
gentleman of the torn tent and trim tailorings came in and sat
down. He was as torn as the tent, this time, and sat down quickly
in an open bag of bean seed, to hide the loss of the seat in his pants.

"I go Bairnsdale soon in my spring-cart; you like come, you fella?"

Karta called through the trees. "Nice young mare . . . good day,
you like."

Hungry for adventure, I called out in reply, "Yes, Karta."

But Blue dragged me away, saying, "No, Karta, from now on
we've got to work."

The lonely sadness of working in the paddocks used to get too
much for me, for I knew now that Macca would never return to
claim me; no matter how often I lapsed into self-deception I knew
within myself that we were parted forever. Often I ran out of the
paddock and down to the foreshore . . . to the bluff he had spoken
of in his letter. "I sat for an hour," he wrote, "round on that bluff
near Greenfeast's, watching the light on that wild sea, and the lines
of a poem came into my mind . . .

> "With short, sharp, violent lights made vivid,
> To southward far as the sight can roam. . . ."

I, in my turn, sat there until grief and memory broke me down,
and then I lay with my face pressed to the breast of my country,
repeating the song I had made one morning as I lay alone in this
place.

> Lorn is a place, when Love from it withdraws,
> Be it covert or hill. This glade that was so soft
> With grass undying, fluttering wings and haws
> Bowing beneath the white weights of their croft,
> Is chill and dank, the sharp grass short and thin . . .
> From dry snapped stems, the greying brake fern curls;
> The knotted boughs are shadeless, and within
> Their thorny hands, a shining songless merle
> Hops too subduedly from leaf to leaf,
> For those that lie face downward faint with grief.

I went wandering along the shore to where I had hidden the
white stone under the log. The printing was distinct on it, and I
held it in my hands, staring down in sadness, murmuring to myself,
the words, written there, "Don't ever leave me."

I had never thought that this would be the end, really. I had
hoped, in my heart, against hope, that we should both return and
take the stone from under the log, laughing and declaring as his
letter had declared, "Love is all powerful, Stevie; it is more than
millions of money."

Often the beauty of the day was opened before me, and

> "Surprised by joy—impatient as the Winds
> I turned to share the transport—Oh, with whom . . .?"

I cried from the old book of Wordsworth. Then I arose thinking that I would go down to see the Black Serpent, and she would give me peace. So I put down my tin of peas, and walked out of the paddock down to the hut. There I dressed myself in breeches, pressed by Karta's iron, silk shirt and blue tie. I took my gun, and walked with a firm tread and swinging hips out on to the open road which burnt white and deep in the morning sun. It was cool under the shade of the gum-trees whose lower leaves were white with dust. The lake danced in blue and silver dew and flung spears of sunlight into my eyes. A cart rolled heavily behind me and I looked up when it was level. Karta Singh looked down from the heap of bags on which he rode, "You fella like ride? Woa!" to the horse.

I climbed up and sat caressing the twisted length of the horsehair reins until we came to the foot of the cliff on which lived the Black Serpent.

"Hello Stessa!" she called to me, and kissed me with frank lips on the mouth. She flung her large arm around my shoulders, and we walked into the house that I loved. The sun shone hot in the small kitchen; the fire burnt sullenly in the stove, and on the table, over which Macca and I had looked at each other, lay cakes freshly baked.

I sat at the same end, with my back to the window, and watched her busy at her baking. No word was spoken of Macca. There seemed to be a tacit consent between us, and the Buccaneer, that nothing should be said or done about him until the picking was ended, and Blue at home, married.

I knew that the Black Serpent loved me almost with a man's love; and that she wished me to marry Macca and be with her, near her, all her life. It was her wish that I should participate in the wild, glorious, rich life that she had lived with the Buccaneer for over twenty years. I watched her, comforted. The very way she took hold of a jar of jam comforted me. She looked at me, smiling moistly, raising an arch eyebrow and communicating to me her fertility, happiness and power.

"Well, Blue is going home immediately the pea-picking is over," I said.

"To get married, Stessa?"

"Yes."

"Are you going with her?" She leant over me, smiling mischievously.

"I may!"

The rather thin eyebrows were raised with a shrewd meaning,

kind, coy and fond. I clung to her gaze, feeling that if I stayed with her I should, some day, see Macca again. Just to see him . . . even that was enough now.

"So you'll go?"

"No . . . I shan't . . . I can't. I shall wait for the beans. . . ."

"And what else?"

"And follow the trail of the Black Serpent." We laughed. Her little son came in. The rest of the family was at school, except Eb, who was now a fisherman like the Buccaneer. She kissed the little boy and nursed him tenderly, richly. I was jealous. Perhaps she guessed this, for she kept him by her and kissed him many times. At last, I could bear it no longer. I wished to be alone with her, and talk freely of no one but Macca.

I stood up, heavy with love and sorrow. "I am going back to the hut."

She kissed me calmly and walked to the gate with me, her round arms hanging over my shoulders, her fingers holding on to mine, twitching and turning them over, caressingly, with an unbearable feeling of love. I left her, thinking all the way home, "When Blue has gone, I shall tell her everything, and wait around her, until the years bring Macca back to Metung. Some day, perhaps, he will come back."

"Well, Blue," I said, when I got back to the hut, "what sort of a day did you have?"

"Greenfeasts were wild because you left the paddock like that and went away dressed up, while we were all working. Why did you do it?"

"Life is short . . . youth is fleeting, Bluey. I know that some day I shall look back gratefully on stolen hours."

Blue said irrelevantly, "Why do you wear the strap of your rifle under your breasts? It makes them look huge."

I was ashamed. "Does it? I must remember. Well, Blue, I've thought it all out. I shan't go home with you. I couldn't bear to be at your wedding . . . who knows, I might even wear the rifle strap under my breasts there, and confound the clergy. Yes, it's sad to think that we shall be parted, but it's for the best. You'll be happy, married, as I told you long ago. I envy you . . . would God that I, too, could be married . . . where I love."

"If you would only adventure with me, all over the world, and be my mate, I'd never marry, and I'd be as happy as the day's long," said poor Bluey.

"No, Blue. You must go to your lover. It's time you were married."

"But we're only young."

"Ah, but how quickly age comes. And he won't wait forever, that boy. He will marry someone else if you don't agree to be married soon. What day will you go home?"

"Oh, about a week after the peas are finished."

As we lay in bed, Blue talked over the old days in the alps, and tried to persuade me to take her as my mate, forever. But I was anxious to be alone, so that I could win Macca's love back; and I fended her off by telling her that she would be happier married.

In the clear morning, as we strewed our blankets out on the ferns to get rid of the fleas, a young Italian walked up to us carrying an old fashioned muzzle loader.

"*Buon giorno!* Any rabbits here? I look for kill."

"At night, they come, but not at this time of day. Come in."

He entered and loaded his gun, a laborious procedure, admired my armoury, and before departing wrote his name in script on the fireplace: "GUISEPPE TUNCREDI."

As he wandered away through the bush we heard him singing,

> "*Come le rose d'Aprile, le gioie*
> *D'amore son morte per me!*"
> (Like the rose of April, the joy
> Of love is dead for me.)

"Ah," I sighed, "that is exactly how it is with me. Italy strikes the true note always." Just then, it struck another.

"Steve . . . Blue . . . *un minuto* . . . please!"

At the barbed-wire fence stood Leonardo, fresh and smiling in white shirt and brown suit, a hard grey hat cocked on his head, giving him the look of a blackfellow in a silk topper. "Long time you no come for see me. Long time my heart sick for you. Why you no come?"

Oh, hang it all, we thought, why must they become bilious, these good Italians, just because we don't visit them or write?

"Ah . . . hello, Leonardo. No, we haven't had time to come and see you. We are busy picking."

"But today . . . ?"

"Ah, yes . . . today. That's right . . . today. Well, soon, today, we must go and work, you see? Then, in one week, when all the peas are finished, we come and see you *per sicuro!*"

The *un minuto* man looked sad. "How Peppino? You tell him come too. We make one *grande festa* after finish peas the pick."

"Yes, yes," we vociferated. "Yes, too true, we come!" Anything, anything, to get rid of you, dear *Un Minuto*. If Greenfeast saw you talking to us, they would straightway cast us out of the galvanized Queen's Head. Alas for Whitebeards and Greenfeasts, they are solemn and just judges of this Gippsland. If we abided by them, we should have no sorrow; but, then, of course, no joy.

Handing us flowers, bottles of wine, bits of hard cheese, bread and kidney beans, as though he had collected the leavings of the *festa* and sentimentally kept them until we met again, he walked slowly away, kissing his hands and waving the flies off his hat.

The peas ended, and a bad season was predicted for the beans. Blue was not really sorry, therefore, to be going home and escaping the picking.

"Well, Blue, you'll be home soon, telling Mia all about our adventures. And then, you'll marry. Ah well, this year has been dull. Jim is not with us. . . ."

"Nor Macca," added Blue, knowing that the mere mention of his name gave me happiness. "Are you going to wait, to see if he comes back to Metung, Steve?"

"I don't know, Blue. He may never come back. But, in that case, I shan't leave Gippsland, for I have sworn never to go from it until I see him again, for the last time."

"And then, Steve?"

"I don't know, Blue. I only know that I sorrow."

"I know," said Blue. "But he's not worthy of your love and sorrow, Steve. Your love is too pure. He doesn't want that sort of love."

"Blue, we don't know what he wants. Macca is good," I said angrily.

Blue left Metung on a scorching morning. . . . We stood outside the hut, I beside the mare, and Blue beside me, holding out her little yellow hand. The hot sun burnt down on us and stamped that lonely hand on my memory. I looked about and saw the dead trees above us, the lonely gully around with bush and fern up the hill and the grey wire-netting fence dividing us from Lake's property. A gut-hawk flew overhead whistling on an ascending scale. Far away the black crows cried, "Ah . . . ah . . . ! Dead horse . . . dead horse!" From the shaggy trunks of the gum-trees the red sap dripped as dark as bullock's blood. Big hollow logs lay around with the heaviness of the dead, their boughs spread out like arms.

"When I come back tonight, Blue, you'll be gone."

"Steve, Steve, why have I got to leave you? What days we've had together as pea-pickers! I'd rather follow you than marry anyone. Soon we'll be old and we'll look back on the adventures we might have had, and regret that we didn't have more. I do wish you'd let me stay with you. But, you're thinking of Macca all the time. Oh, if you'd only let me follow you! I love your mind, your thoughts and your poetry. I understand it all. And we won't quarrel any more. We'll try not to, anyhow."

"No, Blue," I said calmly and coldly. "You must go home. Some day we'll be together again, perhaps. But you've given your word to marry, and you can't break it now."

Poor Blue. She took my hand tightly in hers when I mounted the mare, and looked up into my face. "No Steve, we'll never go pea-picking again. Good-bye, Steve!"

"Good-bye, Blue!"

I touched the mare with my heel and rode away into the bush, riding aimlessly all day, anywhere, until night.

When I came back to the gully, my heart ached. The owls hooted and the stars shone, and the galvanized iron walls of the hut went "Spink . . . spink" as they contracted after the heat of the day. I opened the door and walked in. I was alone.